"I THINK I SHOULD WARN YOU I'M NOT A MARRYING MAN."

Lorraine whirled about to face him at that. Her blue-gray eyes snapped with indignation. "Indeed you need not tell me that, sir. I'd already guessed! And besides," she added with spirit, "what makes you think I'd have you?"

Raile grinned. "Just so we understand each other, lass," he said easily.

She had scarce heard his words when she felt his arms tighten about her and his body close in on hers, making her tremble with ectasy. And his lips came down hard upon her mouth, and yes, she let his questing lover's hands sweep over her, intoxicating her senses in a way she had never known before. . .

TO LOVE
A ROGUE

TO LOVE A ROGUE

by
Valerie Sherwood

AN ONYX BOOK

NEW AMERICAN LIBRARY

Onyx is a trademark of New American Library.

SIGNET, SIGNET CLASSIC, MENTOR, ONYX, PLUME, MERIDIAN
and NAL BOOKS are published by NAL PENGUIN INC.,
1633 Broadway, New York, New York 10019

First Printing, October, 1987

1 2 3 4 5 6 7 8 9

PRINTED IN THE UNITED STATES OF AMERICA

To valiant Sir Thomas, cat of my teens; big beautiful Sir Thomas, who bounded in on a gust of wind one summer evening when I opened the front door, and dashed on through the living room and up the stairs—and adopted us; Sir Thomas of the thick soft tabby fur who curled up on a blue satin comforter and watched me with his big lamplike green eyes as I taught myself to compose stories directly on the typewriter instead of scrawling them out first in longhand; Sir Thomas, who fell head over heels in love with my neighbor's kitten and—in the time-honored manner of males—promptly stood back to let the strolling kitten and her mother share his dinner; when in spite of his obvious good looks and largess the kitten spurned him anyway, he turned to me with the unhappiest of meows—like any rejected lover; to dear Sir Thomas, friend of my youth, this book is affectionately dedicated.

FOREWORD

It was said by the Cavaliers that the devil rode the Great Storm of 1658 that lashed England, to fetch home the soul of the usurper, Oliver Cromwell. And this tale I now spin you, of love and treachery and revenge, has its roots on a beach in Cornwall the night before that tempest struck—although for my stormy heroine, Lorraine, it begins in Rhode Island on the eve of "King Philip's War" and carries on to Bacon's Rebellion in Virginia and the lush plantations of tropical Barbados.

Indeed it must have seemed to Lorraine that:

The lad she loved on Wednesday, he has proved untrue,
The lad she loved on Thursday, he has vanished too.
Now that it is Friday, she's no place to lay her head—
Or will she find another lad to take her to his bed?

—Valerie Sherwood

I:

ARAMINTA

CHAPTER I

Cornwall, England August 1658

ALONG THE CORNISH coast the sky was darkening. The horizon was cloudless, yet far off to the west above the ocean's glitter there was an odd shimmer, perhaps a trace of vapor trailing. All this breathless summer day the air had been strangely oppressed—the birds felt it. Even now a flight of gannets, their bodies white against the darkening sky, swooped and screamed as they fled back to their nesting places in the cliffs.

From an open casement in a tall plain house almost at the cliff's edge, a young girl leaned out, impatiently scanning the black rocks and white beach below. Her name was Araminta Dunning and she too felt the oppressiveness that dogged the gannets. She tossed back her head with its coil of golden hair and her slim shoulders moved restively in her light blue gown.

He should be here by now, she told herself, studying the sands. *Down on the beach as he had promised, striding about restlessly, waiting for her. Yet she had seen no signal. . . .* Her fingers clenched. *He might have received bad news—as so many others were receiving bad news these days—and perhaps could not keep the tryst.*

Indeed all England was in a ferment. The lord protector's daughter had died some three weeks past, and with her passing the old warrior had lost heart. Word had reached Cornwall this morning that Oliver Cromwell was dying, and Araminta's father—well aware that all he had, he owed to the lord protector—had gone pounding off on a fast horse to see to his own fortunes.

Word had already reached the village of the lord protector's imminent death. When Araminta and her mother had ridden down to the village earlier in the afternoon, their coach had been stoned by the mostly Royalist villagers.

As the first stone thudded against the coach's painted side, Araminta's mother peered out only to be grazed by a second stone. She screamed and with her gloved hands pulled down the coach's leathern curtains, losing her fashionable tall-crowned hat as she did so. Araminta, more self-possessed, stuck out her head and cried to the coachman, "Drive back home—quickly!" Immediately, the driver executed a sharp turnaround, which flung her against her mother's voluminous skirts.

They returned to their clifftop house at a gallop. Araminta's mother alighted from the carriage shuddering. Shaking the broken plumes of her high-crowned hat in the direction of the village, Mistress Dunning wailed that "they" would pay for this infamy!

Araminta had helped her mother into the house, where she retired to her bed chamber. Even now she was lying prone on the feather bed of her comfortable four-poster while a servant bathed her aching forehead with rosewater. From her post by the window Araminta could hear her mother's petulant voice in the next room, complaining that she simply "could not understand it!"

Araminta could understand it. Through the lover she was now so eagerly awaiting, she had gained a glimmering of how the people felt. They had sturdily backed Parliament against the unpopular King Charles, and Oliver Cromwell had led them. But that victory was long won on the battlefield at Naseby and elsewhere. Araminta had been barely seven years old when the headman's ax had hacked Charles's head from his shoulder one January day. "On a scaffold erected before his own palace of Whitehall," she remembered hearing her father murmur, shaking his head. Her father often spoke of the wrongs his own family had suffered at Royalist hands, but he had never wished the king to die.

With the death of their dissolute monarch, easygoing England had been plunged into a Puritanism so strict it chafed. In London the theaters were closed, public dancing was forbidden. One day, when Araminta was ten and strolling through the nearby village of Wyelock beside her father, she had passed a woeful figure with ears nailed fast to the pillory and heard someone mutter that it was "unlawful for a man to laugh anymore!" Her frowning father had promptly pulled his golden-haired daughter away.

After that Araminta had taken more interest in her father's comments at the dinner table about Royalist plots that would "bring this government down about our heads, mark my words!" Young as she was, she had come to understand that an undercurrent of revolt was drifting all across England—even into their remote village.

That undercurrent had flared into open rebellion three years ago in a Royalist assault upon Salisbury led by John Penruddock of Compton Chamberlayne. Oliver Cromwell, now lord protector and uncrowned King of England, had been swift to crush the rebels. Sensing the unrest all about, he had abandoned civil rule altogether and divided England into ten military districts, each governed by a major general with broad powers. Soon even the most submissive villagers had grown tired of living under harsh military law—Cromwell's "sword government," they called it. Not only that, but a hotly resented ten percent tax had been slapped upon Royalists' incomes to pay the cost of all these troops in the wake of Penruddock's ill-fated rising—and the man for whom Araminta waited now so anxiously had been one of those who had galloped into Salisbury with Penruddock, there to seize the judges come down for the assizes. But her beloved had been luckier than some; he had escaped being hanged for it.

To Araminta, impatient of politics, it was all a bad dream.

Only her lover was real—and forbidden.

Still, she reasoned, their own bad luck could well be his good luck. After all, was he not a Royalist, whilst Araminta's parents were loyal to the lord protector?

She could wait no longer! Stealing past her mother's room and down the stairs, she flew outside. Then through the small garden where, on the lee side of a stone wall, the maiden's-blush roses were still blooming—and on along the dangerous path that led down the cliff's rugged face until at last she burst out upon the beach itself.

Araminta had lost half her hairpins on her fast decent. Before her feet touched the sand, the coiled braid at the back of her head had come loose and her great mass of gold hair cascaded down across the back of her tight blue linen bodice and mingled with her blowing side curls (Araminta had fought against wearing a fringe across her forehead like her mother's by insisting fringes were no longer fashionable).

She arrived on the beach in pell-mell fashion, pushing against the sea wind. Around her the sand was deserted, inhabited only by tall wastes of rocks ranged like an army of giants. Still she ran on, hoping to find him. And peering ahead, she failed to see a long trailing strand of seaweed underfoot. She tripped over it and would have fallen full-length upon the sand save for the tall man who stepped suddenly from the shadow of a craggy rock and reached out to break her fall.

"Why didn't you signal?" Araminta gasped. "I was watching from the window, but I didn't see you."

His voice sounded odd. "I was late. I arrived but a moment ago—I was about to signal."

It was not true. He had been there for half an hour, debating with himself, wrestling with his better nature, telling himself that he should abandon his pursuit of this Cromwellian beauty, that loving her could only wreck them both. A moment ago he had decided to depart from the beach and leave her—forever.

But he had waited too long. For even as her soft body plummeted into his arms he could feel his resolve weakening. She was so young, so pliant, so alluring. He caught her in a hard embrace against his strong chest, and for both of them time stood still.

Another flight of seabirds streamed by, homeward-bound in the dusk to the age-old cliffs that rose like a rugged curtain wall behind the beach. The evening air whirred with their wings, the dying sun turned their flying bodies a rosy hue. They were like airborne jewels, long necklaces of rose quartz flung high above the white lace of the surf.

Araminta's lips were parted softly. She looked up at her lover with her heart in her eyes. He could feel her heartbeat.

It was a magic moment.

He opened his mouth to tell her good-bye, but could not bring himself to say the words.

The waves crashed against the rocks, sending up showers of spray like trailing white veils. Soon the tide would be coming in, the beach would be awash. But not for a while yet, not for a while. . . . For now, they had the beach to themselves. There might not have been another living soul upon the earth. . . .

"Araminta," he murmured hoarsely. "Araminta. . . ." And his lips brushed the gold of her hair.

There was everything to keep them apart—and they both knew it.

Only one thing bound them—the tenuous threads of a love forbidden. First love for her. Perhaps for him the last.

He knew he should let her go, but still held on to her. The blood rushed through his veins—he had no desire to let her go. Instead his grip tightened.

As if in blazing answer to the sweet sharp inward call of both their straining bodies, the light from the red ball of the setting sun seemed in that instant to detach itself and change. The sky abruptly exploded into a fierce and wonderful radiance, a sudden burst of green. A strange, compelling sight.

Araminta looked up, startled.

"That must be the famous Green Flash," he said with a quick smile to reassure her. "I have heard of it, of course, but this is the first time I have ever seen it."

Her lips were parted, as she drank in the radiant green world that had erupted around them even as their bodies touched. Her blue eyes had been turned to emerald by that marvelous flash of burning copper green that suffused the sky and sea and turned the cliffs and whitecaps an unreal—magical—color.

"Don't look so startled, Araminta," he murmured, cradling her in his arms and letting his hands rove along her slim upper arms caressingly as he spoke. "The Green Flash does not linger. It will soon be gone."

It will be gone, yes, but it will leave its mark. Araminta looked up at the sky, awed, for the moment meant so much more to her than it did to him. *She knew the Green Flash was a glimpse into the future, and the face you were looking into when the sunset sky turned emerald would be the face you would hold in your heart all your life long. . . .* She remembered her grandmother telling her long ago that to the women in her family the Green Flash meant coming face-to-face with Fate. It was as if a great celestial fist had slammed down upon the sheer wall of cliff behind her and the whole world echoed with its force, intoning: *You are his now, you will be his forever. . . .*

"You have been shy with me," he murmured, for he could feel the heat rising within him at the touch of her soft pale flesh. Just her light breath on his cheek seared his senses.

Araminta clung to him in sudden wild abandon. "Yes, I have been shy," she admitted. "But I will be shy no longer!" she promised in her soft hurried voice.

A thrill went through him. Her meaning was clear. After all these weeks, she would resist him no longer. All her virginal refusals were behind her now. . . .

But one more thing needed to be said.

"Araminta, if Shirlock dies—"

He was reminding her of the duel he had fought over her. One day a week ago, Araminta had made an excuse to walk down to the village—hoping to see him. He had been riding at a leisurely pace toward the cliffs—hoping to see her. They had both feigned surprise at their meeting and she had announced that she had come to look for wildflowers in the woods. His offer to accompany her had been instantly accepted and they had spent a pleasant half-hour strolling through

a sheltered little copse. While she breathlessly warded
him off, they had gathered a handful of wildflowers.
Then just as they were sauntering out from beneath
the trees, holding hands as lovers are wont to do,
Robert Shirlock, an ardent Royalist, had chanced to
ride by on his horse.

Shirlock brought his mount to a halt at sight of them
and considered them down his long nose. He was in a
bad mood for he had gambled the night away and had
lost a packet. The glowering look he gave her reminded Araminta that her father had once testified
against him in a court of law.

"Are you no longer one of us?" Shirlock demanded
of the man beside her. "What are you doing with this
Cromwellian slut?"

With a curse, her lover had sprung forward and
seized Shirlock's bridle. "You will take back that foul-
ness, Shirlock! And apologize to the lady!" He spat
the words between his teeth. "*Now,* if you please!"

Shirlock gave him a mocking look and tried to wrench
the bridle away. It was held fast in an iron hand.

"Lady?" Shirlock sneered. "Take the wench if you
want her. But bed her down in some cow pasture as
she deserves—do not strut her about among your
friends on public roads!"

At that point Shirlock found himself dragged from
his saddle and tossed to the ground. He jumped up
immediately—white-faced and with a naked blade in
his hand.

And just as quickly faced another blade as long and
as bright as his own—and better wielded.

Their duel was fought on the spot. A sudden clash
of raging tempers and steel on steel—fought out venge-
fully while Araminta shrank back against a tree trunk.
Her hands came up to cover her white face (though
she could not resist watching them through her fingers), and she prayed with all her heart that *he* would
survive.

It was quickly begun and as quickly ended. Thrust
and parry, thrust and parry, leaping from hummock to
tree root to hummock. And then of a sudden her lover
slipped. As he dropped down upon one knee, his arm

was fully extended and his sword was thrust directly into Shirlock's body.

Araminta would never forget the surge of relief that coursed through her that *he* was unhurt. It took her a while to realize how badly the other man had been wounded.

From that moment, they had been obliged to meet in secret, for Robert Shirlock had lain in a coma ever since. A duel not properly witnessed in which a man was killed was accounted murder, and Araminta's lover had made no secret about who had done the deed. Indeed he had ridden into the village leading Shirlock's horse with Shirlock lying prone across his saddle, found the local barber-surgeon, and told him crisply to "Tend this man, for he offended me and I think that I have given him some hurt."

"Hurt" was an understatement. It was muttered all about the village that Robert Shirlock would not recover.

Araminta sturdily refused to believe that.

Now she touched her fingers to her lover's lips to shush him. "He will not die," she insisted. "The sword cut you gave him was not that grievous! He will not die."

"But if he does—"

"Then it will make no difference between us!"

He smiled down at her wistfully, but she could see she had not convinced him. Perhaps part of his pensiveness was do to the fact that his fingers had been deftly working the hooks that fastened her light blue bodice down the back. The bodice, stiffly boned, began to fall forward, sliding away to leave her firm young breasts—shielded only by a sheer chemise—exposed to his absorbed view. But Araminta seemed hardly to notice, so intent was she on convincing him.

"Other men have fought duels and been wounded and recovered," she protested. "Why should Shirlock die?"

But he remembered the sword thrust—so much deeper than he had intended. He had meant only to teach the fool a lesson, not to run him through. But his foot had slipped at the wrong moment and he had delivered perhaps a lethal thrust. Shirlock was well-born and had friends in high places. There would be hell to pay if he died.

"Oh, my darling, do not think of him!" Araminta entreated passionately. Even as she spoke, he was unfastening the last of the hooks that held her skirt in place. Though her entire dress was sliding down toward the sand, she had not chided him or demanded that he stop.

Still some last vestiges of honor held him off.

"If Shirlock dies, I must away, and quickly," he warned her even as his fingers toyed with the riband that held her chemise.

"We will go away together!"

"We can't. I have no money."

Her dress had fallen away entirely now, beneath his urging. Araminta, caring not, pressed toward him, her arms around his neck, her eyes looking up into his, swearing silent allegiance. "I have a little money. And I can sell my pearls and the locket I was given my last birthday. They will fetch a bit."

"Not enough." It would not carry them out of reach of the vengeance of Shirlock's wealthy family and friends. He spoke with decision—but still pulled the chemise riband, and the light cambric chemise floated down to join the dress upon the sand at her feet.

Only then did she seem to realize that she was standing naked before him, pale and slim in the dusk, and she gasped. He caught her by the shoulders and held her away from him, unmindful of her blushes, to drink in her beauty.

Araminta was not quite prepared for that, but she stood her ground while the flush that tinged her cheeks gradually spread down her entire young body, turning her milk-white flesh a rosy tint. She had no doubt what the next step would be and she was not quite prepared for that either, but she wanted so desperately for him to know she would stand staunch at his side whatever befell them that her voice was almost a wail.

"Then . . . then you must go away and come back for me!" she cried.

He scarce heard her words, so intoxicated was he by the sheer feminine loveliness of the sight before him. Araminta had held him off in the woods even though his importunings had made her blush, she had held him off at numerous gatherings, whenever they had met. But now in this lonely place with only the clean salt smell of the sea and the music of the waves breaking on the rocks, she was on the verge of giving herself to him.

He sensed her hesitation. And even though she was so warm and lustrous and desirable that he could scarce resist taking her without preamble, he made a last manful effort to withstand her charms.

"Araminta," he said sternly—and his voice was husky, for it was himself he was fighting. "Are you *sure?* You have but to pick up that gown"—he nudged the fallen blue material with the toe of his boot—"and put it on again and walk back up the cliff walk. You can forget me." He said it almost with a groan, for it was the hardest speech he had ever made, but he loved this reckless will-o'-the-wisp of a girl and he would make no move unless she was truly certain.

Araminta went into his arms like a child, trusting him completely.

His better nature—always faltering—abandoned him completely at her swift capitulation, at the sudden collision of her soft bare young breasts with his own hard chest.

"Araminta," he murmured, deeply moved. "Araminta. . . ."

"I intend to follow my heart," she whispered. She was trying to look very brave, trying to feel brave, although at the moment she did not. "I love you," she murmured. "And I promise you that I will never, never change."

His arms tightened about her. At once, he flung down his cloak, lowered her young body to rest upon it, and began tearing off his clothes. She watched him with blue eyes big and dark in her pale face, feeling a little frightened.

"The world will separate us," he warned her somberly. And it was one of the few chivalrous gestures he had ever made, this man who had known and thrust aside so many women.

"No." She shook her head and the slight motion disturbed her breasts, making them ripple deliciously, overpowering his senses. She moved her hips too, sliding them about to a more comfortable position on the folds of his cloak, and he swooped down toward her. Their bodies closed with a thrill that amounted to mutual shock. Her voice shook when she said tremulously, "I will never be separated from you in my heart. Never."

Then his lips cut off further conversation and his questing lover's hands brought to Araminta a sweeping intoxication of the senses as he caressed her hair, her shoulders, her pulsing breasts, let his hands trail down delightfully over the smooth cool skin of her stomach and sleek young hips, toyed with the curly golden hair at their base. He was in no hurry and, as she moved beneath him, gasping, half-laughing and half-protesting at his playful impudence, a kind of magic stole over her. He led her on and on until she was gasping with new and fiery feelings, her ardent body pressing upward to close with his. She was hardly aware that his knee had stolen between her own, her thighs were pressed tightly against his, until his strong masculinity had found her secret place. His grip on her tightened, and Araminta drew in her breath in a swift sharp gasp at the sudden stab of pain within her. Her body was trembling but she clung to him still, trusting him, determined not to cry out. Another, deeper thrust and she wilted against him, shaken.

"There," he murmured caressingly. "It is done, Araminta—the rest will be pure pleasure."

And pleasure it was. When the pain subsided, Araminta felt herself caught up in a strange wild rhythm unlike anything she had ever known. It lifted her, buoyed her up, brought her back to earth only to carry her upward again in reckless abandon. All her senses marched with that rhythm, every nerve end alive and tingling. Fantastically she felt herself to have become part of him, and a fierce joy rushed through her as his breathing harshened and the tension mounted. The inner drumbeats quickened and they hurtled along faster, ever faster, until at last the clamor in her own ears drowned out the sound of the booming surf. Sea and sky and the wheeling stars were one in beauty along with their straining bodies—and for those few brief wonderful moments they owned the world and nothing could touch them, nothing. . . .

She came drifting back to reality feeling somehow victorious, as if she had won a great battle. She looked over at her lover brightly to see if he felt the same.

He was lying beside her, staring up at the stars. She thought breathlessly: *What a wonderful place to have made love—the first time!* And knew that she would never regret missing that virginal marriage bed she had dreamt of—for her bridal bed this night had been the clean white sand, her wedding march the timeless roll of the surf, her cathedral the great blue vault of heaven.

"Should I pack?" she asked suddenly, and his hand that had been lightly stroking her stomach was suddenly stilled. "Have you decided where we should go?"

"No, do not pack." His voice was moody. "If Shirlock lives, I will find a place for us here—somehow."

Araminta shrugged and her soft breasts bounced with the slight motion—this time he paid no attention. "Anyway, why talk of fleeing?" she said lightly. "Who knows, my own parents may be fleeing before long! They say the lord protector is dying, and if he does die, we may have the king back again!"

"If so, God be praised!" he muttered.

Those were not quite the words Araminta would have used.

"Our coach was stoned in the village today," she informed him. "Last week, no one would have dared!"

"Stoned?" He turned sharply toward her. "I had not heard about it."

"My mother was terrified. She near ruined her hat trying to get the curtains pulled down!"

"I do not wonder, if stones were being hurled at her!"

"Oh, I do not think they meant to injure us," said

Araminta thoughtfully. "I think they just wanted us to know how they felt."

"Would that I had been there!" he growled. "I'd have been glad to show them how *I* felt!"

Araminta sat up. She her her palms against his chest and pressed him back upon the sand. With both hands she then flung back her long hair, well aware that his eyes were watching her, looking up heatedly at the pale pink tips of her breasts agleam in the starlight. She leaned over him temptingly, the soft tips of her breasts lightly grazing his chest. "You cannot fight all the world for me, you know." Her gentle fingers traced lovingly around his strong mouth, still taut with anger.

It was too much for him. He drew her back to him. "No, but I wish that I could, Araminta."

Sincerity rang in his voice and Araminta knew that he had spoken the truth. She felt that their love was predestined, that from the first moment, she had known this would happen between them. That he would pursue her, that he would not lightly give up the chase, that he would not be denied.

All her instincts had warned her that he was dangerous. But the warnings had counted for naught against the reckless ecstasy of his kisses.

And now at last on this magical night when the Green Flash had illuminated the evening sky and shown her her destiny, she had surrendered herself to him.

She would be his.

Forever.

She clung to him wordlessly and he took her once more, took her with a fierce loving abandon. Again she rose in splendor, leaving earth behind. Again floated back, trailing stars through shimmering unreality, to find herself once more upon the sands of Cornwall.

With her lover.

"Promise you will come back to me," she said in sudden anxiety. "Whatever happens. Say it! Say, 'I will come back to you, Araminta . . .' "

"Though hell should bar the way," he finished for her in a thick voice. "But you know that my family will never accept you—nor will your family ever accept me! Oh God, Araminta, to what kind of future am I condemning you?"

She flung her arms around him as if to ward off the thought.

"To the only future I want or shall ever want!" Her voice held a ghost of a tremor, and perhaps that tremor was for that young foolish Araminta who had planned to be married in her father's house amid great celebration but who must now look forward only to a hole-in-corner wedding somewhere far away. "We will run away together! We will go to some new land where nobody knows—or cares—that our people were on opposite sides!" Her head lifted, on inspiration. "We will go away to America!"

"It's late," he said abruptly. "You must get back." He got to his feet, pulling on his clothes. "If I keep you out too long, they will miss you, there will be an alarm raised."

Araminta scrambled to her feet, gasping from that strange new feeling within her. She felt dizzy, but he caught her at once, supporting her as tenderly as if she had been a child. Silently he cursed himself for not having held back, since God alone knew what the future might hold for them.

He helped her into her clothes and she was grateful for his assistance, for her fingers had suddenly turned all thumbs and she felt shy with him again, despite their new intimacy.

"Tomorrow," Araminta whispered, flinging her arms around his neck.

"Tomorrow," he echoed firmly, pushing her away.

Loath to go, turning often to wave back to him, Araminta walked slowly up the path and lingered in the dark garden sniffing maiden's-blush roses.

No longer a maiden she. . . . Araminta blushed to think of how brazen she must have seemed in his arms. And yet . . . he had not minded, indeed had welcomed her fresh young ardor.

After a while she went inside through the garden door, and tiptoed up the stairs. As she passed her mother's room, she could hear a light snoring.

All was well then. She had not been discovered.

And tomorrow? Araminta shivered deliciously. Tomorrow she would meet her lover on the beach again, and they would make their plans to run away together.

But the morrow was the thirtieth of August—a day that would be remembered forever as the day the Great Storm of 1658 struck England. It roared across the country, leaving destruction in its wake. It blew the chimneys down, tore off shutters, broke casements, burst asunder woven thatch roofs and sent them like so much blowing straw into the sky. It knocked down barns and killed livestock and sent frowning church steeples crashing down among the oaken pews. It uprooted trees and tore great sections from the hedges. It took off half the roof of the Dunnings' house, sent sheets of water cascading over the furniture, drenched the valuable feather beds, made a shambles of their garden, and tore the maiden's-blush rosebush almost to pieces.

When Araminta tried to look out the window toward the beach, her mother screamed at her to come back lest the casements suddenly crash inward and the glass cut her face. She couldn't see the beach anyway—the beach was gone. In its place great rolling breakers dashed white-crested against the cliffs, exploding green against the gnarled jagged rocks, sending up plumes of spray some ten or twenty feet into the air.

When the storm was over, barns and cottages lay in ruins and the village had something more than politics to think about.

Araminta had received no word from her lover.

In midmorning, the day after the storm, she slipped away from the vast cleanup job that was going on at home, with servants scurrying about hanging everything out to dry and pulling furniture here and there. She donned high-patten boots, tucked up her skirts, and ventured down the muddy road to the village. All the way down, under a still gray sky, she shuddered at the devastation the storm had wrought: old trees lay supine, torn out by the roots, ruin everywhere.

The storm had altered the village skyline, too. Half the church steeple had been plunged into the churchyard, wreaking havoc among the moss-covered grave-stones. Two cottages had been stove in by falling trees, and many others were unroofed. But the place was a beehive of activity. All up and down the single street, torn-off shutters were being nailed back, men were clambering over roofs trying to repair them, women were distractedly hanging out quilts and bedding to dry. Ordinarily Araminta might have been the recipient of frowning looks—but not today. Today she passed unnoticed through the village, picking her way over debris and broken tree limbs that littered the cobbles.

At the end of the street, Araminta could see that at least one village business was still operating—the local tavern. Although the swinging painted sign that read "Stag and Boar" had been entirely blown away and the tavern roof was mostly gone, the jovial owner, looking none the worse for wear, was smiling broadly in the doorway. He moved his rotund form aside to let a barmaid scuttle by with a tray of pewter tankards toward a little knot of men who had gathered outside. Araminta hurried forward, for she could see that the men were surrounding a mud-caked rider in a still-damp plumed hat. He had obviously come a distance, and by the rakish cut of his expensive though spattered coat she judged him rightly to be a Royalist.

Intent upon the stranger, no one noticed Araminta's approach. She edged closer.

The man on horseback eagerly drank the ale the barmaid had handed up to him. As Araminta watched, he drained the tankard.

"I've a thirst," he admitted, handing it back to be refilled. "For I've come a long way and must go farther. 'Tis true, the rumor—Cromwell, the usurper, is dying. Lord, I had to fight my way here through the storm to tell you that!"

"The devil rode the storm across England so he could fetch back old Oliver's soul!" observed someone in a dry voice, and there was general laughter.

"The devil got more than one soul," remarked another wryly. "Robert Shirlock passed away at the height of the storm! And the man who fought him, another good Royalist, had to flee the country lest he hang for the deed!"

There was a general unhappy growl, but Araminta fell back as if she had been struck. *Her lover had fled without telling her?*

She turned and ran away, unobserved, panting back up the road that would lead her at last to the tall house on the cliff. And face-to-face with reality at last.

On the third of September—the anniversary of his triumphs at Dunbar and Worcester—the lord protector, Oliver Cromwell, died. Araminta's father came home back from London with a strained face. She could hear him pacing at night in the library and she knew that even though he spoke cheerfully at dinner, saying that Cromwell's son Richard would now succeed him and there was naught to worry about, the vacant look in his eyes said that there was everything to worry about. She guessed that Cavalier boots might soon be marching through the village.

Wistfully she wondered if *his* boots would be among them—for she still had had no word from her lover, and his family did not deign to speak to her.

By October Araminta knew for certain that she was pregnant. She sat for long hours looking down at the beach that had been her undoing, but the white sands and twisted forms of the gnarled old rocks stared back, giving her no comfort. Though she stared bitterly at rosy sunsets and asked herself if the Green Flash had betrayed her, every morning she awoke hopeful that she would hear from him.

Still he did not return. Or write.

By mid-October Araminta had made up her mind. Cook—who secretly sympathized with the unhappy daughter of the house and was the only one in whom Araminta confided—had heard that her Cavalier had been seen in Falmouth only the week before. Araminta entrusted all her jewelry to Cook to sell—there was little enough. She counted up her coins, packed enough for her immediate needs in a basket, and with Cook's connivance and a helpful farm cart, set out in secret for Falmouth.

That first night on the road, Araminta settled herself uncomfortably in the cart and looked up at the moon shining down over Cornwall. *He is in Falmouth,* she told herself sturdily. *I will go there and I will find him! He would never send me back to suffer shame and humiliation and perhaps worse—perhaps to be turned out of the house by my father and whipped through the streets for giving birth to a bastard child! No, we will be married in Falmouth and he will take me away with him—to America!*

Araminta was young, but she was determined. Two weeks later she and tall, dark Jonas London took passage on the merchantman *Northern Star* bound for the colonies. They were married on shipboard by the captain, once England had disappeared in the distance.

The winter crossing of the Atlantic was terrible for the pregnant Araminta, who was feeling queasy anyway. Wild winter winds and snow and sleet lashed the deck. When she and Jonas arrived in Rhode Island there was snow on the ground. Araminta stumbled ashore, heavy with child, to learn that she was to shiver the rest of the winter in a rude log cabin in a lonely valley.

They reached the cabin late at night, having journeyed up a rude trail by wagon with only the constellation of Orion lighting up the southern sky above the black silhouettes of hickories. Somehow she had not imagined America like this, austere and lonely, and Araminta—suddenly certain that her child would be a girl—asked herself bleakly what future there was for a girl-child in this rude land.

As if in answer, just as the horses reached the cabin, the whole valley was bathed in a sudden vivid display of northern lights. A glow emanated above the dark tree line, eerily shimmering, the ethereal folds of some vast heavenly curtain swirling across the northern sky from east to west, as if blown by the Winds of Fate.

Araminta drew in her breath sharply and her baby stirred within her. If the Green Flash had illuminated her destiny on a beach in distant Cornwall, then this display of northern lights that welcomed her to Rhode

Island seemed to draw a curtain of mystery across that destiny, as if to say: *You are not to know, you are never to know.* . . .

In the full glory of a late New England spring, Araminta London gave birth to a daughter—and named the beautiful child Lorraine for her grandmother.

What follows is the story of that daughter.

II:

THE TAVERN WENCH

CHAPTER 2

The Light Horse Tavern
Rhode Island
June 1675

A THIN SLICE of early moon bathed the hilly Rhode
Island countryside in its pale light and silvered the
rude but sturdy log walls of the Light Horse Tavern—a
relatively new alehouse that had been completed only
four years before in 1671. Inside the low-beamed common room, enjoying the cool night air coming in through
the open casement beside them, four young men
lounged. All four intently watched the dainty sixteen-
year-old tavern maid, whose name was Lorraine
London—and for whom each privately lusted in his
heart—as she moved between tables performing her
duties.

"Mistress London-who's-never-been-to-town looks
rather better than usual tonight," muttered one of
them.

The youngest of the four, whose name was Bob,
fiddled with his tankard and sighed. "Think you that
any of us will manage to bed her, Philip?" he asked
plaintively. "She frowns and turns aside with her head
in the air if I but speak to her!"

"Aye, I think one of us will," answered Philip
Dedwinton softly. He leaned back, swinging a neat leg
as he watched the tavern maid from beneath russet
eyebrows. His clothes marked him as the dandy, from

his gleaming tan satin coat with brass buttons to his full breeches of good brown cloth, gartered at the knee and decorated at the sides with great loops of yellow ribands. Only his shoes struck an unfashionable note for, like everyone else in the room, he wore the comfortable and readily available Indian moccasins. His full lips curved in a slight smile. "*I* will bed her, Bob. And I will do it this very night!"

The third member of the party, whose name was Bradford and who had his brown head bandaged from a recent brawl, gave the speaker a ribald look. But the fourth, who had arrived earliest and was already much the worse for drink, burst into derisive laughter and banged down his tankard upon the wooden table.

"What a fighting cock!" he gibed. "All of us have tried, and she'll have none of us. What makes you think you're the better man, Philip?"

"The fact that I've a head on my shoulders," declared Philip. His brown eyes narrowed. "Keep your voice down, Clamp, or you'll alert the wench. "I won't have you giving my hand away."

Clamperton, past caution, continued to laugh uproariously. "I'll make you a wager on that, Philip—for I've need of easy coin!"

Philip favored his friend with a cool look. He was very sure of himself. Indeed he looked exceedingly handsome with the candlelight gleaming on his russet hair and regular features, his body shown to advantage in the tan satin coat newly purchased in Providence and in which he was now sweltering for fashionable effect. "Three golden guineas says the wench is mine before cockcrow,' Philip murmured in a hard voice.

"You're on." Clamperton agreed instantly. All four of the young gentlemen were prosperous farmers' sons and Clamperton and Philip both had ready coin. "But I'm told she refused you in better days," he added slyly.

"I never offered for her," insisted Philip. "She'd have accepted me if I had! The wench fancies me," he added, downing his ale.

"Aye, Mistress Lorraine fancies you," growled brooding brown-haired Bradford, least fashionable of the four. "Mayhap she'll even have you, Philip. But you'll have her in a marriage bed and no other way. You will not bed her lightly!"

"You forget," said Philip in a cold voice, "that I know her better than any of you. Her family were our neighbors before her father set out for the West—God knows what became of him! Indians got him, like as not."

"Yes, Indians got him, like as not," echoed Bob, who admired Philip past all common sense, and especially envied him his new tan satin coat. "She'd a haughty way with her when her mother was alive.'

"Mistress Lorraine's mother was gentry," Clamperton pointed out. "For all they'd no money, she had delusions about how the girl would marry—above all of us. But then the mother died and the father bound the girl as a dairymaid to their neighbors the Mayfields and took off for the West. She tries to put a good face on it, does Mistress Lorraine, but anyone can see she pines for better times."

Philip snorted. "Life has its ups and downs and Lorraine is on the downs." He shrugged. "She's in need of protection . . . and I think she knows it," he added softly, studying the girl across the rim of his tankard.

"And *your* strong arm is offered to protect her?" jeered Clamperton. "Faith, ye'd best not let Lavinia find out you spend so much time in this tavern ogling Lorraine. Not if you want to marry Lavinia, as I don't doubt ye do!"

Clamperton had brought up the name of the richest young woman thereabouts—Lavinia Todd—on whose fortune Philip had already fixed an acquisitive eye. Philip frowned at him.

"We'll not be bandying Mistress Lavinia's name about in a tavern!" he growled.

"Aye, send her to Providence where she belongs!" chuckled Bob.

Philip gave Bob an impatient look, then peered down into his tankard. "Seems I'm out of ale."

Clamperton shrugged. If Philip wanted to play both ends against the middle, it was no affair of his. He banged his pewter tankard down energetically upon the rude wooden board. "More ale here," he called. "Mistress Lorraine, if you please."

Lorraine, who had been too far away to hear their conversation, came over quickly at his call, her full russet skirt swinging from her shapely young hips. The four young men admired the graceful sway of her walk that carried her between the tables. They took note of her light step, of the smoothness of her skin, of the way her color seemed to come and go, of the tantalizing roundness that pushed softly against the much-mended material of her worn russet bodice. It was not an unfashionable dress, for it showed to advantage her white neck and shoulders and had full sleeves puffed to the elbow, with a daintily ruffled thin white linen chemise showing beneath. The chemise too was much mended, but none of the absorbed four pairs of eyes noticed that, so distracted were they by the daunting beauty of her countenance. The fresh young face that turned toward them had large eyes of a soft blue-gray— that same dusky heart-stopping blue-gray of distant hills at dusk. And those blue-gray eyes were fringed with sooty lashes and winglike brows that contrasted dramatically with her hair. Her thick shining hair, sun-streaked till it was in the main as pale as hemp, was worn young-girl-fashion down her back in a shining cascade that swung as she walked.

Her youth, her freshness, her clean-scrubbed beauty— and of course her unfortunate circumstances—presented a temptation to them all. She who had been serenely above unsavory propositions not so long ago was now forced to serve them ale in the Light Horse Tavern for her very bread.

Still none would have known it from the fearless blue-gray eyes that met their gaze levelly.

"Ale for all of you?" she asked, reaching for the heavy tankards.

Bradford put a hand over his tankard's rim. "Enough for me for now," he declared. "I'm off to Providence tomorrow with my father to buy horses and I'll need a clear head."

"Three tankards then," said Philip, adding softly,

"Mistress Lorraine, you do light up the room tonight with your presence."

Lorraine flushed, giving Philip a wary look, but when she saw the obvious sincerity in his admiring brown eyes, her white teeth flashed at him in a smile of amazing sweetness.

"When the wench smiles, she looks like her mother," muttered an older man nearby, studying Lorraine over his long clay pipe.

Hearing his remark, Lorraine hestitated for an instant. Then her dainty hands swept up the three tankards and she whirled away to refill them with ale.

But that overheard reference to her mother had made her wistful, remembering. How she had loved the stories of Araminta's early life in England, of her elopement, and especially of her romantic shipboard wedding after she and Jonas London had sailed from Falmouth on the *Northern Star.* . . .

"Why weren't you married on land before you left?" she had asked, fascinated.

"Because we didn't want the banns read," her mother had replied wearily. "They would have found us."

"Who? Who would have found you?" persisted Lorraine.

"My father. Richard Cromwell was still in power—which meant my father still had influence. I don't know what he would have done to me."

That silenced Lorraine.

"But if you really wanted to marry Father so much that you'd run away to do it, if you'd told him that, wouldn't they have relented?" she asked after a while.

Her mother gave her a jaded look. "No," she said briefly.

"You mean—"

"That like as not I'd have found myself . . . Oh, it doesn't matter, Lorraine. It was all so long ago."

Yes, it *was* long ago. England had slipped through Richard Cromwell's fingers—fingers more used to holding a book than holding a sword. The Cavaliers had predicted he could not hold the country—and they were right. England had a king again—handsome and dissolute Charles II.

"But haven't you tried to write to them? To tell them where you are?"

Fearing her father's vengeance, Araminta had sent a letter to Cook. But the news Cook had written back had been shocking.

Araminta laid down her sewing and considered her small daughter gravely.

"My father shot himself the night he learned the king was coming back to power. When my mother reached him he was still alive. She had him carried out to the family coach and rode with him toward the village, urging the driver to hurry. It was a rainy night, the horses slipped on the road, the coach went over the cliff. It was a long drop. Neither of them survived it." Strange how calmly she could say those words now. When first she had learned of it she had been inconsolable.

Lorraine digested that.

"Then weren't you . . . ." Lorraine had tried to choose her words carefully. "I mean, you said they were wealthy. Didn't their dying make you some kind of heiress?"

Some kind of heiress. . . . Heiress to the evening stars, to the Green Flash, to seductive magic on a lonely beach. . . .

"Everything they had was confiscated by the Crown," Araminta told Lorraine calmly. "There was nothing left—no one, nothing to go back to. I'm only sorry that they didn't forgive me—before the end. It would have been nice to have felt they believed I had done the right thing in marrying Jonas. . . ."

"Did they hate him so very much?" marveled her daughter.

Her mother shrugged. "Things were different then. England was divided, tempers were high. You could lose your head for doing, saying the wrong thing. And Cornwall was always a Royalist stronghold."

"But Father—why didn't *he* go back afterward? I mean, *he* was a Royalist, wasn't he?"

Araminta met her daughter's eyes squarely. "I knew your father's family would never accept me, Lorraine. *That* at least would never change!" She opened her mouth to say more, changed her mind. "As for our going back"—she gave a short laugh—"there's never been any question of our going back. We've never had the money!" She leaned toward her daughter. "And I'd rather Jonas didn't know we had this conversation, Lorraine. The past saddens him. He has enough burdens without thinking on the past."

Her mother's voice was so bitter that Lorraine asked no more questions. But sometimes she dreamed about what it would have been like had things been different— had the king not returned to his throne, had her father's family forgiven him, had her mother's people not been dispossessed and had welcomed them back. She supposed she would be riding about in a coach with plumes waving from her hat, paying calls on the local gentry.

Not serving tankards of ale in a rude country tavern to men who stripped her with their eyes and made coarse jokes about her behind their hands.

Her mother had liked to talk about Cornwall, about the rugged beauty of the countryside, about the gnarled sea cliffs where the seabirds nested, about the tall house on the cliff where she had been a carefree young girl, about everyday life there—but not about her escape, or Falmouth, or what came after. It was as if Araminta's life had ended when she left the shelter of her home.

I suppose she was disappointed in my father never really being able to support her, Lorraine told herself honestly. But her mother never complained about Jonas. Indeed she was unfailingly kind to him. *She married him for better or for worse and she kept her bargain,* thought Lorraine. She had to admire her mother for that. Still, it was a commentary on love—that things didn't always turn out the way you planned.

Jonas London was a tall silent man, except when something stimulated his interest. He had grayed noticeably with the years. Though Lorraine had been told her father was a Royalist, he never talked about it. Indeed he never discussed politics at all. He had left English politics behind him when he adopted this new land. He was more interested in "ventures," coming home excitedly with wild tales to which her mother listened quietly, seldom making any comment.

But sometimes, later, when she was alone, Lorraine would hear her mother crying.

"What was it Father said that upset you?" Lorraine once asked her mother anxiously.

Her mother had looked up at her with tear-wet lashes. "Jonas is a dreamer." She stated it without bitterness as a fact that must be faced. "He will never, never change. He believes that in some miraculous way the past can be mended and we will be rich and we can return to England if we like." She sighed and dashed a hand across her eyes. "It isn't going to happen. Make sure you aren't like that, Lorraine."

"I will," promised Lorraine in a small voice. She looked on her delicate mother with compassion. She herself was so much sturdier. *She's cambric and I'm muslin,* she had thought dispassionately. *I'm tougher and will wear better.*

And in a way that had proved true. Lorraine's health was robust, as was Jonas'—but Araminta flagged sadly in the harsh New England winters. She grew paler and thinner every spring. Until at last she was so ethereal that it seemed that any light breeze would blow her away.

So it was no wonder that she succumbed to one of the fevers that were ever visiting the colony—not even a very bad fever, just something that had been transported aboard one of the many ships that cast anchor in Narragansett Bay.

Lorraine had loved her mother passionately and, when Araminta died, felt that her own life was over. Certainly everything changed for her from that moment. Lorraine London, whose elegant and beautiful mother had once promised her a genteel English education, was now a bound girl. After her fragile mother had died, Jonas, who knew his creditors were closing in, had sold what little he owned and had taken off to try his luck in the western reaches. No one had heard from him since; he was presumed dead.

Lorraine, then thirteen, was left behind, bound as a dairymaid. Because Jonas "could no longer take care of her," he had petitioned the court before he left to bind the girl to the Mayfields, an elderly couple who lived on the adjoining farm.

Lorraine had not minded the work on the farm. She liked the Mayfields and she found it pleasant to drive the sleek lazy cows, with bells jangling softly, through meadows bright with daisies. And the Mayfields had found a cubbyhole room for her in their cottage and treated her as if she were their own daughter. True, carrying the big crocks of milk was hard work, but Lorraine enjoyed skimming the cream with a big spoon in the cool recesses of the springhouse in summer, and making butter with the round wooden churn. The open-air work and good food gave her radiant health that glowed in her pink cheeks and sparkled from her wide blue-gray eyes.

Then, two years later another blow had fallen. Both the elderly Mayfields had been carried away by a fever; their only living relative, who lived in Sussex, had chosen not to occupy the farm, and all of the Mayfields' possesions, including their land and goods—to Lorraine's dismay, her own articles of indenture—had been sold at public auction.

Lorraine would never forget standing up there in the sunlight, surrounded by the farm wagon, pigs, a couple of lowing dairy cows, their bells jangling, old Mistress Mayfield's favorite battered rocker, the milk crocks and pots and pans, the blankets and comforters and cutlery and beds and tables—and being sold just as if she herself were a chair or a table!

Oddsbud, proprietor of the Light Horse Tavern, had bid her in. She remembered staring at him fascinated, feeling as if she were standing on the outskirts of hell. He stood, legs spread apart in his stained trousers, rocking back on his heels, looking her up and down as if she were a mare or a ewe he was buying.

But she had since learned she had nothing to fear from Oddsbud— it was Oddsbud's wife who was the enemy. Oddsbud had turned out to be an easygoing fellow, but his shrewish wife had been irritated by the sight of Lorraine, insisting at the top of her voice that Oddsbud was a fool, that they needed a bigger and stronger wench who could help with the heavier chores instead of a slender girl of fifteen summers. Nevertheless, over the woman's shrill protests, Lorraine's papers had changed hands. So, carrying her few possessions in a linen square, Lorraine had followed the arguing couple to their tavern.

Oddsbud's' wife had housed young Lorraine in a loft under the eaves, which had the advantage of a ladder that the girl could pull up so that late roisterers could not get at her. That was more for Mistress Oddsbud's comfort than Lorraine's, for the tavernkeeper's wife objected to having her sleep broken by what she dourly characterized as "trouble" but which others might have described as mayhem. For the young bucks who frequented the Light Horse Tavern were a restive lot and given to roistering that often ended in bloodshed.

It was a hard life for the young girl who had been brought up to have such hopes for the future. And there were nights after Oddsbud's termagant wife had been particularly scalding in her scorn, or indeed had taken the broom to her to emphasize a point, when Lorraine had stared hopelessly into the darkness through the chinks in the eaves and remembered the warmth at home and her mother's love—all gone now, vanished like the smoke from a winter fire. . . .

At times like those, she asked herself how her father could have left her and gone off to seek his fortune. But sadly she reminded herself that men—especially new widowers—did that all the time, believing their paths in the western lands would be too hard and dangerous for their tender offspring. Lorraine had heard nothing from her father since he had left and now she felt that she never would. His bones might even now be bleaching upon some lonely plain or in some deserted valley, shattered by Indian arrows or tomahawks. Yet there were nights when she could only cling to the hope that he was well and would return soon to free her from this travesty of a job where men could strip her boldly with their eyes—and slyly reach out to pinch her as she walked by carrying brimming tankards of ale.

Perhaps the worst thing of all was that Philip should

see her brought so low. Lorraine had loved Philip Dedwinton ever since she could remember, admiring the handsome lad from afar, watching him ride out with his sisters, looking disdainfully about him as if he owned the earth!

Though the Dedwinton sisters had always snubbed Lorraine, believing rightly that she would present competition to the marriage hopes of any one of them if she chose to, Lorraine had been taken from the first by handsome young Philip. She had admired him across a groaning board in the churchyard on holidays and amidst the attentive congregation at Sunday services.

Nor had Philip Dedwinton failed to notice the bright-eyed young girl who watched him covertly—and blushed if he turned to look at her. Later, when Lorraine was a milkmaid out chasing the Mayfields' brindle cow across their small meadow, Philip had had his chance to become a hero in the girl's eyes. The Dedwintons' red bull had broken through the split-rail fence and gone charging into the meadow. Philip, who was riding by, saw the bull and seized his opportunity. He galloped into the meadow and swept Lorraine up on his saddle—exactly as knights of old must have swept maidens up on their big war-horses. No matter that Philip knew the red bull to be tame as any milch cow. Lorraine looked up at him adoringly, sure her masterful young neighbor had saved her life . . . and won her heart forever.

Russet-haired Philip was well aware of how Lorraine felt about him. The summer she was fourteen he had come calling and had made his intentions plain to Lorraine—and even plainer to tight-lipped "Mother Mayfield," as Lorraine called her. In the months following, Lorraine had managed to hold him off, but it hadn't been easy.

Especially one night beneath the gnarled apple tree when there had been dancing, Philip had seized her by her slim young waist and bent her back in the shadow of its branches. Her lips had responded to his wildly and it had been a shock to her to realize that he was actually *undressing* her there on the summer grass!

She had scrambled up, flushed and indignant, and

had given Philip's excited face a ringing slap. He had caught her wrist in punishing fingers and for a moment anger had blazed in his brown eyes. Then he had let her go and she had rushed back to where the older women were grouped, preparing food at the outdoor fire. They had noticed that her color was remarkably high and her blonde hair was rumpled, but then, she was young and overheated by the dancing. No one had thought much about it except Lorraine herself, who couldn't sleep that night for remembering the fiery feel of Philip's questing hands sliding down beneath the thin material of her bodice.

She loved Philip with all her heart, but she was determined not to be had cheaply. Hadn't her mother told her that which was cheaply got was held in low regard? Lorraine didn't want Philip to hold her in low regard! She wanted to marry him and to love him always . . . and be loved by him. The very thought of being loved by him held her in thrall. Ah, Philip, Philip . . . with eyes closed she dreamed about him. with eyes open she watched him tremulously—but through lowered sooty lashes.

Philip, who was several years older, had responded elegantly to those stolen looks. He had strutted and paraded and preened and had even toyed briefly with the idea of marrying her. Indeed he might have impulsively offered for her had he been there when the Mayfields' estate had been settled. But—fortunately, he realized now—he had been away visiting realitives in Providence at the time and so was out of touch with things at home while these changes took place in Lorraine's life. Philip had come back to find Lorraine already two months into her new duties as tavern maid at the Light Horse Tavern.

Philip's attentions did not cease, but they changed character subtly. For a tavern wench was fair game, was she not? He pursued Lorraine openly with hot attentions, catching her in corners when he could, finding occasion to brush against her pliant young body as she moved about the room, enjoying the shock of the contact which it was plain she felt, whis-

pering to her in husky accents words and suggestions
that made her blush.

Lorraine was all too uncomfortably aware of him.

As she filled the tankards, Oddsbud, the tavernkeeper, smiled genially upon her. She had proved a
good investment for him. Hot young bucks came from
miles around to view and woo this wonder with the
dazzling smile and moonlit hair. Three sturdy well-
to-do widowers in the neighborhood had already offered to wed her, each promising eagerly to pay
Oddsbud's price if she would but have him. But the
girl with the blue-gray eyes had turned them all down.
A number of others—including Philip—would have
bought her articles of indenture, but without promise
of wedlock. Although his harpy of a wife had sneered
at him as a fool for not taking a profit when he could,
Oddsbud hesitated to turn the little wench over to any
man with a hot light in his eyes.

"What are ye waiting for, Oddsbud?" his wife yowled.
"A preacher to come and take her way to pray with
him?"

In truth, Oddsbud was not. But he felt abashed at
times before Lorraine's level look, and some vestiges
of gallantry—mostly lost like his youth—kept him from
playing this last shabby trick on the young girl who
had known so much misfortune. And, he told himself,
although her beauty sparked fights—especially by that
wild young crowd led by Philip Dedwinton—the in-
creased trade she'd brought to the Light Horse Tavern was worth a bit of trouble.

The tavern was filled with smoke from long-stemmed
clay pipes and noisy with coarse voices. Up until the
time Philip had delivered his compliment, Lorraine
had wished herself anywhere else. Now, coming back
to the table with three brimming tankards of ale held
high, there was more spring in her step. Carefully she
made her way between the revelers—husky farmers
for the most part, but with a drover or tradesman here
and there among the company. Walking in Philip's
direction, she studied him openly as he lounged back
against the wall, his muscular right leg drawn up so
that one moccasined foot reposed upon the wooden

bench on which he sat. There was an arrogant quality of ownership in the smile that he bestowed upon her—a smile that made her blush and miss a step, almost spilling the ale upon a buckskinned fellow as she passed his table.

"Ho, there!" cried Tate Corbin, the man in buckskins, ducking. Then, "Missed me!" with a loud guffaw as Lorraine hastily righted herself.

Carefully, as if they had been the china cups her mother had so briefly owned before Jonas London had gambled them away, Lorraine set the tankards down upon the table. As she did so, her young breasts were tantalizingly near Philip Dedwinton and he moved forward quickly to take the tankard, brushing them with his arm.

Lorraine jumped as if she had been scorched and retreated before his mocking glance, every nerve aquiver. He would not have dared to do that when she had a father and a mother to protect her! In silent shame she fled across the room, found work to do among the barrels and kegs piled up in one corner.

"Aye, I'll have her this night," vowed Philip lazily, and rose. He beckoned to Tate Corbin, who got up and followed him out to confer unobserved.

CHAPTER 3

THE CONVERSATION BETWEEN Philip Dedwinton and Tate Corbin was held around a corner of the tavern where the horses of the guests were tethered. It was a low-voiced discussion, but not so low as to go unremarked by a new arrival who was bent down out of sight. The stranger was fumbling in his saddlebag for something which he found and put into his pocket as he listened. The conversation was of sufficient interest that the stranger stayed immobile in the shadows until, chuckling, the two locals swaggered back into the inn. Whereupon the stranger stood upright again and stared after them, a thoughtful frown upon his dark face.

He was a man whose frowns would be marked uneasily by most men. Tall and extremely light of foot, with lithe sinewy muscles and robust good health, his was a figure to reckon with. His powerful shoulders bulged the fine cloth of his blue coat, and his lean hard hands were gentle and sure as he gave his horse's head a pat.

"I won't be long here, laddie," he muttered in a soft Scots burr. "Once my business is conducted, there'll be hay and grain and a stable for you this night."

And he set forth toward the tavern's green-painted door.

In the doorway he paused, stood at his ease, and looked cautiously about him as was his custom, his keen gray-eyed glance only seeming to be casual—for he was a man who saw much that others missed. These were country rustics who peopled this tavern, he decided. No man among them was wearing a wig, nor had a coat cut properly to fashion—except possibly the young brown-haired dandy seated at a board by the window with three cloddish friends.

Not that he himself wore a wig. For he hated the things, much preferring to let the sun shine on the good thick head of hair God had given him, and having a fine contempt for powdering and preening.

His brief survey of the room had told him much about these people—and about the way they lived.

As he stood, slowly pulling off his gloves, the company in the low-ceilinged common room turned curiously to survey *him* through the smoke.

They saw a weathered face atop a tall muscular body. His dark thick hair was drawn neatly to a small queue at the back of his neck. Straight dark brows and beneath them gray eyes of a disturbing lightness that raked the room completely without warmth. Beneath those cold eyes, surprisingly, was a mouth that turned up naturally at the corners, giving its owner a most genial look, indeed a deceptively gentle appearance. Many men had mistaken that look for weakness until a hard hand or a bruising shoulder had taught them better. He wore a blue coat with silver buttons, fitted to the waist and skirted, that boasted city tailoring, a pair of dark blue breeches encasing his lean thighs, and a pair of dusty boots beneath which the discerning eye could perceive the gleam of fine leather.

The tall stranger was a sight to make any tavern wench stand straighter and pat her hair and pluck nervously at her skirts. A sight to make the men's gaze turn thoughtful, wondering who he might be and what his business was in this backwoods part of Rhode Island.

Just as the stranger moved into the room, Lorraine stood up from where she had been kneeling among the kegs and turned about. For a startled moment they faced each other full on, and the lean gentleman in the blue coat lost stride for just a fraction of a second.

So forcefully did that fresh piquant face strike him that it was a moment before he could tear himself away to answer the tavernkeeper, who had hurried forward to usher this fine gentleman to a chair by the hearth.

"I prefer this one." His guest demurred and nodded toward the window where the four young gentleman sat.

The stranger's voice was brusque, accustomed to command—and to being obeyed. The landlord, taking note of it, gave him a respectful nod, although it was with a sigh that he led his guest to a table beside the boisterous foursome. The traveler settled his long legs upon a rude wooden chair and leaned back against the wall to watch as Lorraine approached.

His gaze raked her up and down in silent appraisal, pausing longest on her lovely torso and then critically evaluating the beauty of her face. Lorraine's cheeks were hot under that punishing stare as she came forward to inquire in a soft voice what he would have.

"Some ale and a bit of conversation," said he. "And then whatever you have by way of supper."

"The ale and the supper we have," she said carefully. "But the conversation, sir?"

An alert silence prevailed at the next table. Every eye there was upon her, every ear straining to hear.

"Yes," said the newcomer. "Who are you? And to whom do you belong?"

At that brusque question, the young girl drew herself up haughtily. "My name is Lorraine London, sir. And I belong to myself. Although I am bound for another year to the keeper of this tavern."

"Hmm," he said, seeming to lose interest. "You may bring my ale, Mistress Lorraine."

As he waited, he glanced about him, studying the patrons more closely. A likely lot of clods, he thought dispassionately. He was late and he hoped the man he was to meet had not given him up and left the tavern. It could be that he had missed him. His horse had thrown a shoe a short way out of Providence and the blacksmith had taken near half a day to reshoe it. If he missed his man here, it meant he would have to search for him, and there was danger in that—for them both. He was tempted to quiz the tavernkeeper, but years of experience in these matters had taught him to stifle such impulses.

Raile Cameron was the stranger's name and he was at heart as much a fighting Scot as ever were those ancestors of his who had lost their lives at Flodden Field. Raile cared nothing for the law—for it was English law that governed these colonies, and what had a hardy Scot to do with that? But he cared very much for well-laid plans and hated to see them go astray over a small accident like a horse throwing a shoe!

His ale had not been brought before his question was answered.

A fellow in worn leathern clothes, wearing the Indian moccasins that most men in these parts affected, came jauntily into the inn. "Have ye heard the news?" his great voice boomed out. "Harley Moffatt's horse threw him and Harley hit his head on a stone not ten miles from here. They say he's dead."

"I knew Harley well," said Oddsbud soberly. "And a great shame it is. 'Twas his bad leg made him lose his seat on the nag, no doubt."

Harley Moffatt was the name of the man Raile Cameron had come so far to see. And there could be only one Harley Moffatt with a bad leg in these parts. So now he'd have to take the arms elsewhere. For Moffatt—scoffed at by many as an alarmist—was expecting imminent war with the Wampanoags. Their chief sachem, Metacomet, whom the colonists called half-scornfully "King Philip," using the Christian name that had been given him, had been very active. Moffatt claimed that while Rhode Islanders were mired in endless lawsuits over land ownership, quarreling with Connecticut and charging plots and counterplots by powerful Boston interests, "King Philip" Metacomet had been quietly gathering his forces. A wily and dangerous leader, the Indian had been fined back in 1671—which had done nothing to improve his temper.

Last year one John Sausamon, a "praying Indian," had reported trouble brewing—and been murdered for it. Three Indians had been executed at Plymouth for the crime, which had only deepened the unrest. Colonists like Moffatt, who believed the Wampanoag chieftain had already made an alliance with the powerful Narragansetts and could put ten thousand men in the field, were alarmed and taking their own measures. Moffatt's "measures" had led him, a wealthy man, to arrange for a shipment of contraband arms to be delivered up the Providence River for the defense of Rhode Island. Cameron had that shipment waiting on his sloop in Narragansett Bay and was to have received his instructions from Moffatt tonight on where to land it.

At first Raile, by nature suspicious of elaborate plans—which too often smacked of treachery and nonpayment—had resisted the idea of journeying so far inland across the low hills of the Rhode Island countryside. Why couldn't his man meet him at a "safe" tavern in Providence? Why this out-of-the-way hole? But when he had learned that Moffatt had a bad leg which made travel difficult for him, Cameron had acquiesced. And here he sat, his only contact a dead man, and a valuable arms shipment subject to search and seizure lying in the bay.

He was about to rise and take his leave when his departure was stayed by the sight of the girl. A bonny sight she was, and the slimy plot he'd heard hatched outside was about the taking of her virginity.

Raile sat back down thoughtfully. It was not late. He could still spend the night at that inn he had seen along the road. As the girl brought his ale, the buckskinned fellow who had been plotting outside with the dandy by the window, reached out and grabbed roguishly at her bodice. She jumped away, sloshing the ale over his coat. With a happy roar, he rose and would have thrown his arms about her, but the dandy, right on cue, roared, "Sit down, you dunderhead! Let Mistress Lorraine alone!"

Casting a grateful look at Philip, Lorraine set the tankard of ale carefully down before Raile Cameron and turned to flee.

Philip called her over. "I'll not have you mauled and pinched by such ruffians as that," he growled.

And Lorraine, remembering all too well how many times Philip's jealousy had errupted into tavern brawls over her, said uneasily, "Let be, Philip. The man is drinking heavily and meant no harm."

"No harm, is it?" cried Philip angrily. He half-rose in his chair. "By God, I'll teach him to manhandle you!"

Anxiously Lorraine pressed her hands against his chest, urging him to sit down. "Please, Philip, do not fight him on my behalf."

Philip seemed pleased to have her dainty hands pressing urgently against his chest and sat back docilely enough.

With a sigh of relief, believing the brawl averted, Lorraine moved back to the stranger's table. "Your supper will be ready soon," she promised him. "Though 'twill be only cold meat and bread, I'm afraid, for the fire is out."

Raile nodded. "That will suit me well enough," he said indifferently. And then, "How do you come to be so well-spoken, Mistress Lorraine? Your accent bespeaks of town."

" 'Twas my mother's influence," she confessed. "She was a lady and did school me well."

"To serve ale at this tavern?"

Her blue-gray eyes clouded. "To marry," she said bitterly. "But when she died, all things changed."

"Aye, they have a way of changing," he agreed, remembering his own childhood on Scottish shores where the world had been green and young and full of promise. He roused himself. "But you are very young, Mistress Lorraine. Your circumstances may alter for the better."

" 'Tis to be hoped," she sighed. "I'll bring your supper now."

Raile ate slowly. As he consumed his cold venison and thick slab of brown bread and washed it down with tankards of ale, the small crowd in the tavern thinned out—farmers who must be home, for they'd be up before cockcrow, a tradesman or two who must open up shop early. Finally only the buckskinned fellow who had reached for Lorraine and the foursome of young bucks at the next table were left—and one of those had already passed out from drink and slid down from his bench, his head lolling as he snored loudly.

Lorraine liked the tall stranger. She liked the way he looked at her—as if she were a lady. The way he spoke to her—with respect. Respect was something that was sadly lacking in her life these days. Philip could take her out of all this—and she hoped he'd get around to it eventually—but meantime he was content to be free, not saddled with a wife, and where did that leave her? Working long hours in a tavern, the prey of rough and careless men.

She began to polish a tankard with a piece of coarse linen. Unmindful that Philip was watching her keenly with a truculent expression on his handsome face, Lorraine strolled back to Raile's table.

"Was your supper good enough?" she asked him.

" 'Twas the best cut I could get."

Raile smiled at her, keeping an eye meanwhile on Buckskins, who was easing around in his seat as if to reach out again for the girl. It was Raile's intention to foil the nasty plot he had heard concocted outside. Tavern wench she might be, but her virginity was probably the only valuable thing she owned outside of her very considerable beauty, and Raile did not like to see it stolen under false pretenses. "The meat was very good," he said, loud enough for the young dandy, Dedwinton, to hear. "But the view was even better, Mistress Lorraine. I've been beguiled by watching your sweet face."

She flushed prettily. "You must not say such things," she murmured. "I do but work here for my bread."

"And does that work become tedious?" he asked bluntly.

She gave him a swift honest look from those steady blue-gray eyes. "It becomes hard," she said gravely. "Especially when I must pay for the breakage others have caused and it is tallied up against me so that I may have to work more than my years of indenture to pay for it all."

"Breakage?"

She nodded gravely. "Aye—if the landlord's wife

decides the men have fought and broken things because of me."

"And do you then set suitor against suitor and ignite these disputes?"

Vehemently she shook her head. "Never. For I like not brawling nor"—she turned and threw this recklessly in Philip's direction—"nor brawlers." She heard Philip's tankard come down hard on the table, but ignored it.

"What is not your fault should not be charged against you, Mistress Lorraine."

"In life," said Lorraine bitterly, "even an accident of birth may be charged against one."

Raile looked at her in surprise—for it was just such an accident of birth that had sent him off on the wrong road in Scotland. Illegitimate and plagued by his father's legitimate sons, who seemed to nourish some spite against him, young Raile had had a stony life indeed. But now all that was behind him. Still, he could understand—and sympathize. " 'Tis sad you must learn this hard truth so young, Mistress Lorraine," he said softly.

Lorraine gave him a very sweet smile that showed off the matchless perfection of her white teeth and the soft curve of her ripe young mouth. At the next table the threesome who were still upright watched alertly—especially Philip. Rage was kindling in his eyes as he bent his head for some whispered conversation with his friends Brad and Bob, and signaled Tate Corbin, seated nearby.

Lorraine turned to take the now shining pewter tankard back where she had got it, but she did not walk past Corbin as the trio expected. Instead, seeing a bench that was set awry where its last occupant had left it, she turned and moved toward it. Raile's attention, diverted for the moment from the young men, followed her delicious figure and her lushly outlined young hips and buttocks as she bent to move the bench back into position.

It was a moment of inattention that was to cost him.

A hard fist slammed into his slightly turned jaw and sent him spinning from his bench. At the same time, a

TO LOVE A ROGUE 55

moccasined foot kicked over the table holding his trencher and near-empty tankard.

Lorraine screamed.

Raile rolled as he fell and, quick as a cat, was back
on his feet, instantly sending his assailant—the grinning one called Brad—backward across a table. But a
second man, Dedwinton, came flying forward, and
from the velocity of the assault both contestants went
staggering toward the door and through it, locked in
each other's arms.

Out into the summer night they went, with Corbin
and Philip's two friends plunging after. It was dark
under the trees but it seemed plain to Lorraine, standing in the tavern doorway, that the tall stranger was
equal to taking all four of them, from the agile way he
leapt about, striking a blow here, parrying a blow
there, sending his jostling opponents into disarray.

Oddsbud's wife, who had been muttering as she
counted knives and spoons in the corner, now came
running forward to grasp Lorraine's arm and pull her
roughly back into the room. "I saw you!" she cried in
a fury. "You flaunted yourself before that stranger
and you caused this to happen! Look at this trencher—
all dented . . . and that knife—bent! You'll pay for
this, never fear!"

Too upset to speak in her own defense, for she *did*
feel that she had flirted with the stranger—perversely,
to irritate Philip—and if anyone *was* hurt in the fray
out there, it would be her fault, Lorraine kept silent
under the woman's assault, but struggled to break free
of the clutching bony hands.

"Now, now!" cried Oddsbud, huffing up in an attempt to restrain his wife, who was fairly dragging
Lorraine across the floor in her rage.

Outside, Raile, who had just knocked Brad spinning
against a tree bole and was now grappling with the
heavily muscled man in buckskins, heard Philip's voice
ring out loudly: "I'll teach you to take liberties with
Mistress Lorraine!" And a pistol ball sang through the
air.

Raile, who had handful of fringed buckskin shirt
clutched firmly in his left hand while his right was busy

delivering a punishing blow to his assailant's jaw, instinctively ducked as the ball whizzed harmlessly over hie head into the trees. Letting go of Corbin, he made a grab for his own pistol stuck in his leather belt. But even as his hand darted toward it, a stick of wood, held firmly in young Bob's eager hands, came down solidly on the back of the Scot's dark head and his world exploded into a bright flash of colored lights. He fell heavily to the dew-wet ground.

Inside the tavern's common room, Lorraine heard Philip's roar and then the sound of the shot, and paled. Oddsbud's wife released her with a suddeness that made her stagger back.

When they heard Brad's anguished drunken cry of, "My God, Philip, you've killed him!" both Lorraine and the tavernkeeper's wife would have rushed outside but that Oddsbud grabbed both women and pulled them away from the door.

" 'Tis the devil's work tonight," he growled. "But the lads, right or wrong, are from around here and the stranger's not! 'Tis best we see nothing and hear nothing—do you understand me?"

For a few moments, amid a flurry of shouts from outside, Oddsbud's wife grappled with him in silence. But finally she wrenched herself free. "You keep your hands to yourself, Oddsbud," she panted. "See nothing and hear nothing indeed! I want to know what's going on in my own woodlot!" Lifting her skirts so that her scrawny calves came into full and unattractive view, she sprinted with surprising speed out the door. Oddsbud followed in full pursuit.

Left alone in the common room, Lorraine leaned upon a table and put a hand over her eyes. *Oh God, that* she *should have been the cause!*

Suddenly she was grasped by a pair of hands and, turning with a start, found herself staring into Philip's face. He had a cut on his cheekbone and his eyes looked wild.

"My God, Lorraine, I've killed a man," he muttered. They'll have me up for murder—of that I'm sure! And all for jealousy because you showed him such preference!"

"Preference? Oh, Philip, how could I prefer a man I've seen but for an hour or two?" She was so upset she hardly knew what she was saying. Though Philip had changed toward her since her station in life had worsened, he was still the man she loved. "Surely you have not killed him?" she cried. "Perhaps he still lives!"

Philip's voice sounded distracted. "He came at me, Lorraine, and he was pulling a wicked-looking pistol from his belt. I lost my head and shot him." He cast a hunted look around him. "If only there was someplace to hide till I can get away later. Oddsbud will stop me if I try to reach my horse through yonder doorway, but he did not see me slip in here—they all think I've run away into the woods, and some have gone there to look for me. Ah, Lorraine, 'twas all because I love you so!"

CHAPTER 4

LORRAINE STARED UP at Philip. Around her the world seemed to have spun to a halt. Even the shouts outside were muted, dimmed.

Because he loved her so! Those words she had hungered for—and to come at such a time!

"Quick, I'll hide you in my room," she said. "There!" She pushed the ladder toward him and he took it. "Up the ladder with you, and I'll say you did not come this way. Then when all is quiet you can slip away and ride to safety."

"Wouldst do that for me, Lorraine?" Philip's breath was warm on her ear.

"Yes, yes! But hurry!" She gave him a push and returned to the doorway to stand in it, living proof that none could come or go by this door without passing her. Behind her she heard Philip's soft moccasined footsteps quickly receding.

Looking out, she could see the tavernkeeper and his wife standing by the woodpile. Behind them the dark trees formed a barrier and there was no one else in sight. Lorraine looked about for a body but saw none.

Suddenly a figure darted around the corner of the building. It was the buckskinned man, Corbin. He ran to Lorraine's side.

"Did Philip come by this way!" he gasped. "He killed that fellow! Brad and Bob are carrying his body away now to hide it for a while, but Oddsbud's wife has a tongue that will soon be clacking and they'll find the body and there'll be the devil to pay!"

Hiding his body . . . that pleasant stranger with the genial smile? Lorraine swallowed and a quiver went through her. Still, she reminded herself that she owed her first loyalty to Philip, whom she had ruined this night with her indiscretion.

"No, Philip didn't come by here," she told Corbin, for she neither liked nor trusted the fellow.

He gave her a ribald wink. "And *you* wouldn't tell me if he had, would you, Mistress Lorraine?"

She flushed angrily, but was spared a retort by the Oddsbuds' return. The tavernkeeper was forcibly dragging his wife with him.

Lorraine moved aside to let them pass. Corbin gave her another knowing look and went off to untie his horse. From the trees Brad's voice called, "Ho there, wait for me. I'll ride along with you."

"You'll pay for this tomorrow, Lorraine, you brazen hussy," screamed Oddsbud's wife as he dragged her through the doorway of her bedroom at the far side of the common room. "I'll take a whip to you, I will!"

"Shut up!" Oddsbud kicked the door shut with his foot and their shouts became muffled behind the thick door.

With her heart still beating triphammer beats, Lorraine climbed up to her room and carefully pulled the ladder up behind her. She groped about in the loft, where only a little moonlight glimmered in from under the eaves.

In that warm darkness, scented by the fresh straw that filled her mattress, a pair of arms came around her waist and a quick kiss smothered her gasp.

"Alone at last with you," murmured Philip's fond voice.

Lorraine struggled weakly in his arms. How she wanted him! And tonight—tonight he had killed someone because of her. Wrong though it was, he had been driven by a lover's jealousy—of that she was certain.

"No," she murmured. "Please, Philip, no. Philip, you've killed a man tonight. You can't stay here, you must think . . . plan." Her voice broke off for he had begun to pull her dress down off her shoulders. The worn material tore and the rip was one with her sob of worry for him as he pushed her down firmly into the straw beneath him. "No, Philip," she whispered urgently. "It isn't right, and at such a time, how can you think of—"

"Hush," he chided, "or they'll hear. Do you want them to hang me, Lorraine?"

Oh God, no, she didn't want that! But . . . but Philip was taking liberties with her she'd never meant to allow any but her someday bridegroom to take. She tried to pull up her bodice, gasped as she felt her chemise, suddenly unloosed, come slithering down over her firm young breasts, felt Philip's hands seize them eagerly. She felt a hot pair of lips and a warm wet tongue nuzzle one pink-tipped trembling breast.

Hot anger swept over her, and something else, something she could not identify, a worldly magic as old as Eve—but the anger was uppermost because Philip *knew* how she felt about letting a man take her lightly.

She began to fight him in earnest, silent and gasping. Writhing in his arms, she kicked at his shins, her small fists pounding against his chest.

Philip was hard pressed to keep her wriggling from beneath him and he dropped upon her suddenly, pressing her down by sheer weight and buried his face in the silky softness of her hair. His voice came to her muffled.

"Oh, Lorraine, I want you so," he whispered yearningly. A very real passion throbbed in his voice. "And think . . . think, Lorraine! I'll have to flee. They'll be searching at my house tomorrow—here too." His voice was a goad. *"And who knows when I'll see you again?"*

That gave her pause, and in that pause she ceased to fight him. Suddenly she found her skirts whisked up to her waist to meet her bodice. Now her hips as well as her breasts were naked beneath him on the straw mattress.

"No," she whispered wrenchingly. *"No!"* But his

hard mouth came down on hers and she was fighting for her breath as well as for her virtue.

As Philip held her down and moved lustily atop her, Lorraine discovered to her horror that he had already undressed and had been waiting for her, trouserless. She recoiled as his manliness brushed her, and renewed her battle, turning this way and that in her panic as she tried to escape.

A shriek rose in her throat as there was a sudden painful thrust within her—but the shriek was lost when his mouth gripped hers. The sob that shook her body seemed not to move him at all as he thrust again, draining her of strength. She lay back weakly, her consciousness fading partly from pain and partly from lack of air, for his gasping mouth had nearly cut off her breathing.

Philip, holding her quivering body so firmly in his grasp, having her welded to him as it were, ran a hand lightly down her spine and she felt it tingle the length of her. A pulsing rhythm thudded against her senses as he thrust hard and thrust again. To her amazement, out of the near-swooning and the pain, something new was happening. A kind of awakening, a keening of the senses. That magic she had only glimpsed before was winking at her now, beckoning her onward. The brushing of his muscular body against her own was a kind of gentle fire, and the hard wild motion within was arousing strange passions she had not known she possessed.

With a strangled gasp, she surged upward toward him and his long body jerked in surprise at the suddenness of her onslaught. Then low laughter rippled deep inside him and he held her not quite so tightly, no longer fearing she would pull away. He let her slender body move sensuously and sway beneath him, enjoying her as she herself was transported to heights of joy, wild pleasures she had only half-imagined.

At last he was spent and lay panting beside her.

"By God, you're wonderful, Lorraine," he murmured, reaching over to fondle her breasts, feeling the sensitive nipples harden to passion under his touch.

"Take me with you," she entreated, turning toward

him and flinging herself half over his body so that her young breasts were crushed against his chest and her face was only a breath away from his own. "Oh, Philip, take me with you! I'll not complain, I'll share whatever hardships you must endure, I'll *help* you escape—only take me with you."

Her entreaty seemed to stir something in him, for he was silent for a while and then without answering he took her again—took her fiercely, as if to make up for something he'd missed. She moved beneath him, pliant and willing, her heart burgeoning with joy, for she thought that by his body he was giving his consent— he was going to take her with him! He was so strong, so masculine—and she would manage to mend that wild unreasoning jealousy that drove him.

"I've always loved you, Philip," she murmured. "I always will."

A kind of muscular spasm went through him—she guessed it to be triumph that she had admitted her love at last. But why should she not admit it? She had given him everything else!

Her sudden soft-voiced confession seemed to madden him, to spur him on. His hands upon her roughened, his grip was so tight she felt her ribs would break beneath it, his breath rasped in his throat as he strained to possess her the more fully, bruising her tender flesh. Finally he left her with a strangled snarl that was almost a sob.

Bewildered by his lack of tenderness, Lorraine reached out tentative fingers and touched his body, was amazed that he jerked away from her. "Philip—" she began.

"You're a witch," he mumbled. "You'd take my strength—like Delilah!"

She understood then, and a soft laugh rippled through her. His strength—of course, he would need his strength tonight to make his escape. She lay back with a little sigh of contentment and began to imagine her new status. She and Philip would make their escape down- river to Providence—he would have to stop by his home perhaps for money but they would be gone in the morning mist—they would take ship to some place far away and on board the vessel that was carrying them to all her heart desired, they would be married.

A lovely daydream with her naked hip now pressed against the man she loved, beside her.

But escape was something that must be more than thought on—it must be carried out. Tentatively, she said, " 'Tis quiet downstairs now. Oddsbud and his wife must have gone to sleep. Should we let the ladder down quietly and make our escape now?"

Philip mumbled something and pressed a kiss on a trembling nipple before he rose and began to dress. She could hardly see him in the darkness but she began to dress as well—in her other dress. There was not much difference between them, to be sure—both were russet, both were worn, but at least this one, while much mended, did not have a bad rip in it. She wished she had something better to wear, for both these homespun gowns represented her status as a bound girl and they were part of all the unhappiness she was leaving behind her.

"Wait here until I've cleared the door," he murmured. "Then after a moment you can come down."

She waited quietly for several minutes, then crept over and peered down into the dim empty room below. It was almost daylight, and as she moved to lower herself, she realized that the ladder was gone. Philip must have thoughtlessly removed it.

Then it struck her with shock: Philip meant to leave without her! He was not going to subject her to the dangers of his escape—he was going to run for it alone! Oh, no, he must not!

She lowered herself through the hole in the low ceiling, and dropped catlike to the hard-packed earthen floor below.

Before her the inn door stood open, and to her surprise, Oddsbud came through it carrying an armload of wood for the fire. She had not known he was up and wondered fearfully if he had seen Philip. But his words were for her.

"Lorraine!" he exclaimed. "Up already?" He gave her a surprised look, for Lorraine usually had to be roused by much calling and pounding on the ceiling.

"I . . ." she choked, no good explanation coming to her.

At a noise behind him, Oddsbud's attention was diverted. But Lorraine's eyes dilated as, through the doorway behind him, young Bob swaggered in wearing the stranger's blue coat. The tavernkeeper, standing stock-still with the load of firewood clutched in his beefy arms, stared at those silver buttons, those dark blue velvet cuffs. "Where did you get that coat?" he whispered hoarsely. "Don't tell me there was murder done here last night?"

Bob shrugged and laughed. "Of course not," he scoffed. "I diced the fellow for it and won. Like the fit?"

"It hangs on you. That fellow's shoulders were inches wider," said Oddsbud, eyeing the sky-blue coat in alarm. He added slowly, " 'Tis folly for you to wear it, Bob, for many saw him wearing it last night."

Bob laughed again. He had a pleased and reckless air about him, and he went over and sat down. "Bring me a tankard of ale, old fuss-box, and stop your whining. No harm's been done that will overset you!"

Shaking his head, Oddsbud turned to Lorraine. "Bring the lad his ale."

Lorraine hesitated. She wanted to run after Philip, but wouldn't that give away the fact that he'd been here? she asked herself guiltily. She'd done enough to him already! As she stood uncertainly, through the door erupted a frightening sight.

A man with a bloodied dark head and a torn cambric shirt stained with mud, his gray eyes bloodshot and blazing like seven devils in his white face, burst through the door and was upon Bob before he could even rise from his seat. The man's hard fist smashed into Bob's surprised and frightened mouth, bloodying his nose and sending him back hard against the wall. A blow from the left and one from the right rocked Bob's head from side to side.

"And now," the man said in a low deadly voice, "I'll relieve you of that coat, you thieving swine. And if you so much as crease it when you take it off, you'll get a ball between your ribs!"

Terrified, Bob saw that he was looking down the barrel of a large pistol held in a very steady hand. "I only borrowed the coat," he choked, his dazed eyes staring in fascination at the pistol. "You'd not yet come to and I thought you'd not miss it for a while. I meant to bring it back!"

There was a growl of disbelief from the man before him. Lorraine and Oddsbud stood transfixed.

Bob was sweating now, and terror shone in his eyes. "I didn't mean to hit you so hard with that stick of wood last night!"

"Came at me from behind, you did, while your friend took a shot at me!"

Bob swallowed. "Philip never even pointed his gun at you—he fired up into the trees!" He struggled out of the coat as he spoke. " 'Twas but a game. We were only funning—"

"Fun!" Cameron roared as he reached over with a rough hand, and seizing young Bob by his shirt, shook him so hard his teeth rattled in his head. "I heard your fancy friend and that clod in buckskins planning outside how they would start a fight and lure the girl out—and make her think Buckskins was dead to gain her sympathy—and then into the woods with her so Satin Coat could bed her! And now I've no doubt I was the 'corpse' that was used to hoodwink her!"

Lorraine's eyes grew wide with comprehension and horror. She felt the strength leave her limbs and almost crumpled to the floor.

"Does a wager mean so much to you rustics that you would jump a man from behind?" Cameron snatched his coat and stuck his gun back in his belt. "By God, I'll teach you manners!" Raile roared. In fury, he drew back his arm and delivered such a blow as sent the quaking young man across the room to end up stretched senseless over a table.

"A good job, that," said the tavernkeeper in a pleased voice. He studied Bob's fallen form admiringly. "And something I've often yearned to do myself."

"A . . . wager? Did you say a wager?" asked Lorraine in a voice that shook.

"Aye, the satin-coated dandy planned to bed you by

a ruse." Raile swung around to see her swaying, white-faced, against the doorjamb, her hemp-pale hair a tumbled mass, her face such a picture of woe that it wrenched his heart. "And from the look of you, I see he managed it."

Lorraine nodded in misery. Her slight form seemed to shrink as she leaned against the doorway staring out into the morning mist where Philip had gone—without her. She was fighting for control but her body felt spent and used. Her lips moved tremulously as she fought back tears.

"If you'll but point out where the tall laddie is, I'll punish him for you, lass," Raile added grimly.

Lorraine opened her mouth to answer him but no sound came out. The weight of the world seemed suddenly to have fallen onto her slender shoulders, and had the very ground dropped away from beneath her feet at that moment, she would have taken no notice. Swallowing, she moistened her lips and tried again to answer the stranger.

"He is gone," she mumbled. She peered outside, feeling numb. "I suppose he must have gone home. He told me he must fly for he had killed you. That as you fought you had pulled out a pistol and he had whipped out his own and shot you, unthinking. I felt . . . I felt it was my fault—that he had killed you out of jealousy over me and would most likely die for it." She covered her white face with her hands and rocked in silent misery.

"So he played on your tender sympathies," muttered Raile in disgust.

"Fool of a wench!" Oddsbud turned from admiring Bob's fallen form and spat. "Ye must have known young Philip's been courting Lavinia Todd down Providence way?"

Lorraine hadn't known, and a spasmodic shudder went through her body.

Raile swung a bloodshot gaze toward Oddsbud, who fell silent—till he thought of business. "You're forgetting!" he cried indignantly. "You can't leave! You owe me for last night's ale and supper!"

The tavernkeeper's sharp voice brought Raile's lowering attention onto him again. " 'Tis pay you want, is it, landlord? For letting your patrons be set upon in your establishment and half-killed and left out in the trees by your woodpile to die? Well, here's for the ale and the supper!" He threw a coin on the table so hard it bounced off and rolled across the hard-packed earthen floor, turned contemptuously, and went out, brushing by Lorraine, who sagged in the doorway.

He untied his horse and mounted, a stern figure in his sky-blue coat and muddied boots and trousers.

As he wheeled about, prepared to make off into the morning mist, he caught sight again of the girl, trembling with wordless grief in the doorway.

"Ride with me and I'll take you out of here, Lorraine," he said evenly. "You've only to climb up, and we're off."

Lorraine dropped her hands and looked up, caught a wavering vision through her tears of a tall grim man astride a big brown horse.

Ride with me!

He offered her escape! And how could she stay here and face them, all those men, Oddsbud's patrons, with their sly grins, their catcalls, their covert pinches, their guffaws, and see the knowledge writ plain across their smirking faces that Philip—Philip, whom she'd loved with all her heart and had believed loved her too—had bedded her, not for love, *but on a wager!*

Oh God, she could not face Philip!

Lorraine gave no thought to the future. At that moment she cared not if the tall man on the big brown horse was the devil himself. He had offered her escape and she would take it! Without a word she ran toward him and he swung her up before him on the saddle.

"Ho there!" roared the landlord, erupting wrathfully after them out of the tavern. "You can't take the wench with you! Lorraine's indentured to me for another year!"

The Scot, who cared not overmuch for the law, had nevertheless a fine feeling for liberty—his own and others'. His sinewy arm was locked about the girl's slender waist and he felt the swift thud of her heart, felt her young breasts bounce as she started fearfully at the tavernkeeper's wrathful cry.

"I've just loosed her bonds!" Raile wheeled his big horse about, sending Oddsbud scurrying back. "She'll have a taste of freedom with me!"

"I'll have the law on you!" shouted Oddsbud, shaking his fat fist but staying well back from the armed stranger.

"Be damned to your laws!" Raile called back over his shoulder. "I'm taking the girl with me—for shame that you'd hold a woman's body in bondage!" He nudged his horse with his knee and they were off in the morning mist.

"After them, Oddsbud!" cried his wife, who had come out in time to hear this last exchange of words.

Irresolutely Oddsbud turned to go inside for his musket. Then he paused to look after the wild pair, flying down the road on a fast horse. The last he saw of them was the girl's pale hair streaming back in the wind and Raile's broad shoulders as they disappeared from view.

"Hurry!" bawled his wife, shaking him frantically by the shoulder. "Can't you see they're getting away, you fool?"

Oddsbud shook her off. Some tattered shreds of gallantry were still left in him. In his heart he felt reluctant admiration for the durable stranger who had after all been struck down at Oddsbud's establishment and left for dead.

As for Lorraine, he'd miss the sight of her pretty face and figure flying about, bringing sunshine into the dim smoky recesses of his tavern. His wife would miss her hard work too, for all she'd complained about the little wench! But it was true the girl's beauty had brought out the devil in the wild bunch hereabouts. There'd be less breakage with her gone, fewer dented tankards and broken heads! And hadn't she as much as admitted that young Philip—a lad whose people had influence in these parts—had had his way with her?

Suppose she claimed it was rape? What would the community say about that? Could be he'd be brought up for keeping a bawdy house if the girl pressed charges! Anyway, he wished the little wench well—damned if he'd publish her as an escaped bondservant, whatever his shrewish wife demanded.

"Get inside," he growled. "You've food to prepare this day."

"You've been witched by Lorraine's pretty face same as the others!" scolded his wife, giving him a clout as she flounced away. "It was an evil day we took her into the tavern!"

"Well, the evil day's over," Oddsbud muttered. "For she's gone, and from the look of her as she went, she'll not be back."

He followed his wife in and began moving barrels. Still thinking about Lorraine, he paused and leaned upon one of them. It was true he'd been bilked of the wench's services. That in itself was enough to put an angry gleam in his eye.

But suddenly his face cleared and he struck his thigh and rent the tavern's musty air with a loud peal of laughter.

There was a way out of this situation that would leave him with both a chuckle and a profit. Ever since young Philip Dedwinton had returned from that long visit in Providence, the impudent young buck had been after Oddsbud to sell the girl to him. Oddsbud had hung back, knowing too well Philip's plans for her. Well, Philip had no way of knowing she'd run off. This very day he'd journey over to the Dedwinton farm and sell the girl's articles of indenture to Master Philip, giving as his reason that she was a bad influence at the inn, always causing fights and ruckuses of every kind!

And when Philip came over to claim her, he'd clap the lad commiseratingly on the back and tell him Lorraine had learned about the wager and had run way in a huff. He'd not be out of pocket—Phillip would! A good day's work indeed!

Oddsbud leaned against the barrel and shook with laughter.

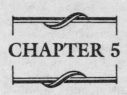

CHAPTER 5

THEY HAD NOT gone far when Raile brought the horse to a halt. Lorraine realized that the Scot was turning the horse around and heading back toward the Light Horse Tavern.

Until that moment Lorraine had been content to slump against him in her misery. But now she sat up abruptly.

"Why have we changed direction?" she demanded in alarm. And more wildly, before he could answer, "Oh, you haven't changed your mind? You're not . . . oh, you're not *taking me back?*"

The tall Scot gazed down on her in some wonder.

"Faith," he opined ruefully, "if you but knew me better, you'd know that I rarely change my mind. I'm not the kind of man who goes back. Once gone, I stay gone."

She felt bewildered. "Then why—"

"So your late employer will be seeking us in the wrong direction," he cut in. "Lass, d'you know the roads hereabout?"

"As well as any, I suppose."

"Then lead me past the tavern we just quitted by some back road or cowpath, for I'm thinking I hear the sound of a waterfall over yonder and I've no mind to be trapped between white water and the law."

The law! Yes, of course the law would pursue them

both—she the escaped bondservant, he the man who had helped her escape!

Lorraine peered ahead through the mist. "I think . . . yes, turn hard right at that big tree. There's a little brook. Your horse can walk along its bottom for a while and we can lose any pursuers, even if they follow us with dogs!"

Raile looked down into her clear upturned eyes, so luminous in the wavering light, with approval. "I doubt me they'll pursue us with dogs," he murmured. "I heard none barking about the inn."

"No, Oddsbud's wife hates them. She told Oddsbud she'd have no dog about, for a dog would gobble up the scraps she throws to the chickens and *they* at least can be stewed and served at table!"

"Such a woman must have been hard to live with," he muttered, wheeling his horse.

"*Awful*," agreed Lorraine with feeling. She felt the warmth of his body as she swayed against him when they made the sharp-angled turn. Swiftly she righted herself, turning her head to hide a blush.

Raile appeared not to have noticed.

Moments later they found the stream—a bare trickle beneath the aspens. And after a mile or so he said, "We're well past the tavern by now, lass. Bring me back to the main road by the shortest route."

She did so, taking him by barely discernible trails, gold-washed in the early-morning light, and shadowed by trees that loomed up and disappeared like vanishing giants.

"This road," she warned him, "will take us to Providence."

"I'm aware of that, lass. 'Tis the same road I used yesterday."

So he had come by way of Providence then. . . . She waited for him to say more, but he did not.

On through the morning mist thundered the big brown horse, the sound of his hooves muffled on the soft dirt of the roadside. The stallion's riders were silent too: the man because he had a mighty ache in his head from the heavy blow he had sustained last night, the girl from a mixture of indignation and grief, for all the dreams she had cherished these last three years had blown away into the mist.

She was thinking, remembering, reliving . . . that wonderful night at harvest time under a full orange moon when Philip Dedwinton had drawn her away from the other young people who were laughing and dancing around a bonfire. Pulling her behind a mountain of corn husks, he had brushed his lips against her cheek, and when she would have run away, he had seized her hand and told her huskily that she was the loveliest thing in Rhode Island. She had been so young and full of blushes. Her mother was still alive then, and her father had not yet gone away. Her future had seemed bright.

And then Lavinia Todd had blown in like a gale from the Atlantic.

Lorraine shivered.

"Are you cold?" asked Raile sharply, feeling the quiver of her slight young body against his arm.

"No," said Lorraine in a choked voice. "I'm not cold."

Not her body. Just her heart.

Lavinia had arrived, with her wonderful gleaming dark brown hair, her haughty smile and scathing bronze eyes, with her gorgeous London clothes and her flirtatious walk, just after Lorraine's bright doomed world had crashed. It was the week after Lorraine's father had bound her to the Mayfields. So Lavinia had always referred to Lorraine—with a supercilious sniff—as "Who? Lorraine? Oh, you mean that bound girl?" And then her laughter would trill. Lorraine had heard her say it more than once and had smoldered.

For in a way, Lavinia had moved into the spot Lorraine was just beginning to occupy before her mother died.

Reigning belle.

Country Rhode Island society was not so class-conscious that a bound girl who came of good family could not attend picnics and outings—as the indulgent Mayfields had always let Lorraine do. But it was hard on Lorraine, appearing in worn dresses, the patched and mended remnants of better days, and seeing Lavinia in her rich and fashionable creations lording it over everyone.

She remembered the sparkling snows of that first winter after Lavinia's arrival. Lorraine, still saddened by her mother's death, had been trudging down the road carrying a crock of butter to one of Mother Mayfield's neighbors. Philip, dashing by in a one-horse sleigh, had reined in his nag and swept Lorraine up, wrapping both her and the butter crock up in a blanket.

"We'll deliver the crock of butter later," he had declared. "You need cheering up!"

He had driven her triumphantly all the way to Providence, where merrymakers had spilled out of one of the stone-end houses. One of those merrymakers had been Lavinia Todd, languishing on the arm of a young Providence rake as she picked her way daintily through the snow in a pair of tall pattens.

How sharply Lavinia had looked up at Philip, ruddy-faced from the blowing wind and so handsome in his new red cloak! And then her gaze had strayed to Lorraine, and her bronze eyes had gleamed with a predatory light.

Somehow from that moment Lorraine had found herself pitted against Lavinia in everything: In quilting—Lavinia deft with a needle, had won easily. In dancing—Lorraine was perhaps more graceful but Lavinia knew all the new steps and was quickly the rage. In conversation—Lavinia knew the latest quips from London and dazzled everyone with her wit and knowledge.

And yet through it all, Philip had remained true.

Or so Lorraine had thought.

But then had come the Light Horse Tavern. Lorraine, cleaning the pewter tankards, had seen Philip Dedwinton riding by openly with Lavinia and Lavinia tossing her bronze curls as she glanced at the tavern windows. Lorraine's heart had ached over that, but every time Philip strode into the tavern's common room he had had some fully reasonable explanation for squiring wealthy Lavinia: Mistress Lavinia's horse had gone lame, and he had carried her back home. Mistress Lavinia's mother was ailing and he had volunteered to escort Lavinia to the doctor's house.

Oh, he had been very convincing. . . .

And the little tavern maid had believed him, every word.

Lorraine shuddered as she thought about it, and the shudder caused her breasts to bounce again along the stranger's hard muscular arm that circled her lightly. Lost in her bitter thoughts, she leaned back against his chest, entirely unaware of the contact.

But if Lorraine was unaware of the touch, the arm that held her so securely was not. Even as he frowned from his headache, Raile Cameron was all too aware of the soft brushing of the girl's sweet young breasts. The light strands of fair hair that blew back against his sun-bronzed face seemed to have their own delicate perfume.

A luscious wench this—and brokenhearted. His own heart went out to her.

"Are you tired?" he asked abruptly.

"What? Oh . . . no, I'm not," said Lorraine in confusion, coming back from her memories.

"The horse needs resting. D'you know where there's water?"

Lorraine peered about her. She had been barely aware of where she was, but now the mist had lifted she could see that she was in familiar territory. The Mayfields had lived not far from here.

"Up ahead there is another stream and a beaver pond. 'Tis not far—I know the spot."

He gave her an approving look. "We'll stop there, lass, and linger through the day till dusk, for I've no desire to be passing some lumbering farm cart whose driver will have naught better to do than to describe us to all comers—and reveal the way we are going."

"Of course." There was a catch in her voice, for it had come to her suddenly that she was a girl on the run. If she was caught it could mean a whipping—or worse yet, the pillory! And of a certainty it would mean a long stretch tacked onto her time of indenture.

From that moment until she told Raile where to turn off through the sun-washed trees, Lorraine kept an anxious lookout for farm carts.

With Lorraine's sure directions guiding Raile's expert hands on the reins, the horse picked its way carefully over the fallen leaves and twisting vines while his riders bent their heads to avoid the low-hanging branches that sometimes threatened to sweep them from the saddle. The patch of woods was thick and brushy, and had been left in its natural state because the land was swampy in spring and hard to drain. Around them a woodland that as they approached seemed alive with singing fell into a hush as they passed. Even the horse's hooves were muffled as he trod across a forest floor carpeted by violets.

"Here we are," she told him at last.

Raile reined in, dismounted, and lifted Lorraine down, setting her feet on the sponge-soft mosses and feathery green fronds that bordered the clear waters of a spring.

They both drank thirstily from their cupped hands. The water was cold and clear.

While the horse drank, Raile looked around him appreciatively. He stretched his arms and sniffed the air. "Wintergreen," he said, and reached out and touched with his finger the sap that oozed from the broken limb of a small black birch tree. He tasted it.

Lorraine shook out her skirts and took a deep breath. She tossed back her head and ran her fingers—wet from the cold spring water—through the pale tangles of her hair. The result was more fetching than she knew, and the man's eyes lingered.

"These are the Chipmunk Woods," she told him with a sigh. And to his questioning look: "In summer the chipmunks are everywhere here—chattering, scurrying about. . . ."

"One would gather you know this place well," he murmured.

"I used to live right over there." She pointed. "It's out of sight through the trees. This place belonged to the Mayfields once and I was bound to them after my father left. They were good to me. . . ."

As if to justify the name she had given these woods, a fluffy little chipmunk suddenly appeared over the top of a fallen log and sat and jabbered at them. Raile, who had been lounging against a hickory trunk admiring Lorraine, straightened up and the chipmunk took off hysterically, making a wild leap for the next fallen branch and disappearing precipitately through the long grass. "We'd better not linger here," he suggested. "Not if there's a house that close. Someone might come to the spring to find water—and find us."

Lorraine shrugged. "The Mervises live there now. In fine weather like this, the men will be out working in the fields on the other side of the house and the women will bring them lunch. They have a well close by the house—they won't bother to come all this way to the spring."

He was looking at her steadily. "Perhaps you're right, but let's move on."

Leading the horse across the soft spongy earth, they left the little spring with its scents of wintergreen and hickory and followed the meanderings of the narrow spring-fed stream until it broadened out into a wide pond surrounded by aspens.

Raile's restless gaze searched the edge of the beaver pond, found a little hillock covered with grass and violets where the tree branches dipped low and they would be hidden from the view of any casual passerby.

"I think you might like a chance to bathe and rest," he said gently, indicating the hillock. "Meantime I'll prowl about and see if I can't find a bit of hay for Old Ezra here." He patted the horse's long neck. "For I doubt me they took such good care of him at the tavern."

"I'm sure they didn't," said Lorraine with feeling—but her voice had steadied. "Oddsbud's wife insists they short the food of all the animals in their care. But there should be plenty of grass around the split-rail fence just beyond the trees there, for the Mervises lost their horse last year. They think the Indians must have butchered the horse, as they've done so many others, because they never found the poor beast. So now the Mervises are afraid to pasture their cow near these woods lest they lose her too."

"Let's hope they're still cloistering the cow!" He grinned. "Where is this split-rail fence?"

"Just head in that direction." She nodded. "You'll

find it." She was kicking off her shoes as she spoke. And as Raile moved off through the trees leading the obedient horse, she sat down and impatiently pulled off her garters and stockings, for the one thing she wanted most at this moment was to slip into the water and wash the very feel of Philip Dedwinton from her body.

To be free of him at last.

Yet even as the thought crossed her mind, she knew it would not work. There had been too many years of loving Philip to throw off his memory with a single contemptuous gesture.

She stripped off her dress and petticoat and chemise—carefully, because the fabric of all three was old and worn and they were all she had in the world. Then, with her fair hair bound up, she stepped gingerly into the beaver pond, shivering as her foot sank into the cold water.

Lorraine washed quickly and sprang out to seek a patch of sunlight. She dried herself with her petticoat, and hung it up at a sunny spot in the branches of a nearby aspen.

As she tugged on her shoes and stockings, eased into her chemise and russet dress, she became aware of a gnawing feeling in her stomach and realized she was hungry. Usually, at the tavern she tried to find an apple or a piece of bread to take to her room, but last night she had missed that, and this morning's breakfast as well.

Her gaze roved speculatively about. There was certainly no food in sight, but she remembered a patch of wild strawberries not too far from there. Of course, they were across the road, which Raile had wanted to avoid in the daylight hours, but she would be careful, and if she hurried she could be back with a kerchief full of strawberries before Raile returned.

Eager to be doing something that would take her mind off Philip and the hurtful events of the night before, she ran through the woods. Minutes later she had crossed the road—looking up and down it first to make sure it was empty. From the road it was but a short walk to the strawberries—and there they were, on a sunny bank, nestled red and ripe among the dewy green leaves. Quickly she picked enough berries to fill her kerchief and hurried back through the woods to where she had crossed the road.

No sooner had she reached the road's edge than she was stopped by a sudden sound from around the blind turn—a masculine voice, pleading:

"Ah, do have me, Lavinia. I promise you I'd make a much better husband than Philip Dedwinton, for all know that he pursues Lorraine London when he's not off courting you!"

And Lavinia's voice, answering frostily, "You mean that blonde tavern wench? Oh, that's all over. Philip cares nothing for Lorraine—he told me so!"

"Then he lied!" On a despairing note. "I passed him on his way to the Light Horse Tavern only last evening. Lavinia, I can't live without you—"

The muffled ending to his words was punctuated by a sudden sharp sound like a slap and Lavinia's angry, "How *dare* you, Walter?" As if Walter had seized Lavinia in his arms and been abruptly thrust away.

There was a snort from a horse and the sudden pound of hooves coming straight toward Lorraine from around the blind turn.

At the sound of those hooves, Lorraine, who had been frozen into immobility by the shock of hearing familiar voices from out of nowhere discussing *her,* was galvanized into action. She plunged across the road, hoping to reach the other side and disappear into the trees before the quarreling pair could reach her.

She judged wrong.

For as she leapt forward, a trailing vine tripped her and sent her sprawling, along with the kerchief of strawberries, into the road.

Lorraine had barely reached all fours before there on a sleek gray horse pounding around the turn was Lavinia Todd, followed by a young man astride a big rangy roan. Lorraine recognized him as Walter Grimes, one of Lavinia's more persistent admirers.

Lorraine scrambled up from the dirt, dusting herself off from her fall. She was humiliated that her rival should see her without her petticoat and with her damp hair uncombed. It would have hurt her even worse if Lavinia had known what had happened last night, but the pair of them were thundering toward her from the direction of Providence and couldn't know yet what had happened at the Light Horse Tavern.

Though Lorraine might still have had time to dart across the road and disappear into the trees, the thought never once occurred to her.

Something taut and angry in Lorraine had snapped at the sight of elegant Lavinia bearing down on her looking so fashionable in her smart plum riding habit, her purple petticoats fetchingly displayed from her sidesaddle.

Lorraine staggered to her feet and planted herself squarely in the middle of the road.

Lavinia looked as if she would have liked to run Lorraine down, but she pulled up impatiently, her mare sidestepping and dancing at being halted so suddenly. Walter, who had come up beside Lavinia, brought his horse to a rearing halt and reached out to steady her mount.

Lorraine ignored Walter, who was staring in amazement to see her so far from the Light Horse Tavern. Her blue-gray eyes focused on Lavinia.

"I am surprised to find you out riding so far from home, Lavinia," volunteered Lorraine. "I should think your mother would keep you close to home in times like these." For it was no secret that there had been Indian attacks on several outlying cabins recently and there were some who felt the roads weren't safe.

Lavinia shook her head and her bronze curls blazed red in the sunlight. The implication that she was afraid to ride out because of recent mutterings about Indian uprisings brought a flush to her high cheekbones. Lavinia had often boasted that she was afraid of nothing. As she stared down coldly at Lorraine, her voice dripped contempt.

"I am surprised to find *you* taking off from your duties at the tavern," she said. "I would think you could ill be spared. After all, *someone* must scrub the floors and carry out the slops! Yet here you are bumbling about, strewing strawberries. . . ." Lavinia cast a significant look at the kerchief of strawberries, some of which had spilled out upon the road.

"The tavern?" Lorraine's winglike brows shot up. "Oh, that's all over," she said, measuring Lavinia with her steady blue gaze.

Lavinia peered down at her, puzzled. "What do you mean, it's 'all over'?" she demanded rudely. "You're indentured there for another year, aren't you?"

Lorraine smiled almost fondly at her erstwhile tormentor. *No one knew better than she that when a man chose to marry a bound girl he must first buy up her articles of indenture! And Lavinia would know it too!* "Not anymore, Lavinia. Hadn't you heard? Philip is going to buy my articles of indenture from Oddsbud. It's all arranged. We're to be married three weeks hence. I'm surprised Philip didn't tell you, for he's always told me he feels toward you like a brother."

The thunderstruck look on Lavinia's face was ample reward for Lorraine's outrageous lie.

"I don't believe you!" Lavinia gasped.

"Oh, but it's true." The mocking blue-gray eyes turned upward were insolent. "Philip's building us a stone-ender on his father's acreage. Until then of course I'll live with his family. But for today I couldn't resist roaming about—it's so good to be free again!" Her laughter rippled.

"That's a lie!" Lavinia snatched her hat from Walter's hand. "I'm going straight to Philip!"

"You do that," Lorraine told her tranquilly. "And while you're asking Philip questions, ask him where he slept last night—and with whom!"

Lavinia's face turned white. She bent forward in the saddle and struck at Lorraine with her whip. "Out of my way, wench!" she screamed.

Luckily Lavinia's aim was not very good. Lorraine sidestepped neatly to let Lavinia's gray mare thunder by her. Walter turned his head to give Lorraine a shocked look as he galloped on after Lavinia.

Lorraine stood with her back very straight and watched them go. But once they were gone the smile faded from her face and she was surprised to find she was trembling. She closed her eyes and leaned against a tree for a moment to steady herself. Then she lifted her head and hurried back, carrying the strawberries that were left in the kerchief to the beaver pond.

She had scarcely had time to open the kerchief and spread out the meager lot of bright red berries before Raile arrived. She did not ask him how he had got the bucket of grain or the armload of hay he carried—nor the still-warm pie wrapped in a linen napkin that rested on the grain-filled bucket, but he chose to answer her curious look.

"I met a likely lass." He grinned. "One who thought it a lark to find a bit of hay and grain and some food for a stranger."

Lorraine decided that Raile was the kind of man who would always find "a likely lass." And wondered briefly who the girl was, for she knew, at least by sight, most of the girls who lived on these outlying farms. Probably Jenny Mervis, with her wide hips and her boisterous laugh, Jenny, who boasted she "could get any man in Rhode Island!"

"Was she a brunette?" she asked, reaching for the piece of pigeon pie Raile had sliced off for her with the knife he carried in his boot.

Lounging comfortably with his back against a tree bole, Raile asked, "Brunette?" His dark brows lifted. "No, more hazel-haired, with a fine full figure padded in all the right spots and a roguish way about her."

Lorraine flushed at his teasing voice. That would be Tillie Mervis, Jenny's younger sister, whom her mother called "a handful."

"Why?" he asked curiously. "Do you know her?"

"Yes. Tillie Mervis."

"She'll be a terror loosed upon the countryside by next year, I'd say," he mused. "There's a man-eating look in her eyes." Raile studied Lorraine over the piece of pie he was lifting to his mouth. There was a droll look in his gray eyes.

As Raile finished his repast, he commented on how tasty the strawberries were. Then he glanced at Lorraine's petticoat, hung up on a tree branch to dry.

"I take it you've already had a dip in the pond, Mistress Lorraine? I've a mind to try it myself."

Lorraine remembered thinking to wash the touch of Philip from her body—from her wounded heart.

And how it had not worked.

"Yes, I've already bathed," she said unevenly.

Was that pity she read in the tall stranger's eyes? She turned her head resolutely away. "I'll nap while you take your dip."

It gave Lorraine a strange feeling to lie there listening to a naked man splashing in the water a few feet from her, a man she had known but a few hours, a man she had broken bread with but once. . . .

She began to think about Raile—it helped take her mind off Philip and the grinding ache that seemed to fill her breast and penetrate into her head. What was he doing here, this Scot? And what would happen to him if he were caught, now that he had chosen to carry off a bondservant?

She heard him come out of the water, heard him shake himself like a big dog in a way that spattered the leaves with shining droplets. It was quiet for a few moments then, and she assumed he had finished dressing.

She turned to speak to him and realized with a gasp that he was standing at the edge of the pond—alertly, as if arrested by some sound—stark naked, with his back to her.

In that moment she took in the vibrant masculinity of the man, the darkly tanned arms, broad bronzed back, and sinewy shoulders. Where did he live and what did he do, she wondered, that he went about stripped to the waist? And although his well muscled thighs and narrow buttocks were pale, his feet and ankles and lower legs were bronzed too.

She was staring at him, fascinated.

As if alerted that she was looking at him, he swung about and smiled at her. Engulfed by embarrassment, Lorraine quickly turned away and said in a smothered voice, "I . . . I was just going to ask you what you did for a living."

"As little as possible," he answered in a bored voice.

Out of the corner of her eye she saw him begin to dry himself with his shirt.

"I mean"—her voice quivered slightly—"that your feet are tanned as if you go barefoot."

Raile tossed away his shirt and grinned in her direction. He'd have wagered it was not his feet that had occupied here rapt attention!

"I do go barefoot. On deck," he explained.

"Oh, so you are a sailor, then?"

"In a manner of speaking," he said crisply, and began to tug on his breeches.

"Are you . . . dressed?" she ventured, not daring to turn around again and meet the ribald glee on his face.

"Dressed enough," he told her carelessly.

She turned and saw that he was clad in his trousers, toweling his lightly furred chest dry with his white cambric shirt. "I'll hang up your shirt to dry on this branch," she offered hastily. "The sun will make short work of it."

Raile watched her appreciatively as she reached up to pull down a leafy green branch. The slight movement made her young breasts ripple most attractively beneath the worn homespun and showed to advantage the glorious head of fair hair that cascaded down to a narrow, supple waist.

Having finished her task, Lorraine sat down again on the soft grass facing him.

"I have been thinking only of myself," she said soberly. "But it has come to me that I have put you into some danger. The law would give you at least a flogging for having helped me. Perhaps . . ." She gave him a troubled look. "Perhaps worse."

"Ah, but that would be the least of my crimes," he told her mockingly, although he was pleased that the little wench should evince concern for him. "The law would be delighted to hang me—but for other reasons. You may set your mind at rest, Mistress London. This escapade with you puts me in no worse case."

Escapade. . . . So that was how he viewed it?

She frowned. "You are a highwayman, then?"

"On these roads?" His dark brows shot up. "Faith, 'twould be a devil's hard ride for poor pickings!"

"For a Scot," she meditated, "you are a long way from home."

"We Scots develop wandering feet," he agreed easily, studying the depth of her blue-gray eyes and marveling how dark were the long lashes that fringed them—in sharp contrast to her pale hair.

"You have traveled much, then?"

He nodded. "Here and there." Best for her not to know too much about those travels. If they should be caught, any show of knowledge on her part could tangle her into the plot about the guns and perhaps cost her her life.

Something in his look made Lorraine feel conscience-stricken, for she had not told Raile that she had been seen and recognized.

"When I crossed the road with the strawberries, I ran into two people I knew," she confessed.

"What?" He looked angry. "But they could spread the word where you are, lass!"

"I don't think so," she said in a penitent voice. And told him briefly what had happened, ending with, "So now Lavinia's out to find Philip and will drag Walter all the way to Philip's house to get the straight of it. And Philip will try to hush it all up of course and his sisters will probably insist they both stay the night, for the older one is half daft about Walter and near swoons when he comes about. So it will probably be tomorrow before anyone runs to Oddsbud with a tale about where I was seen."

Raile grinned at the little wench's spirit in taking on her adversary, but he rose with decision.

"We'll away, lass—just in case."

Tossing their wet things over their arms, they walked on through the woods. Lorraine was crestfallen that she should have caused them to trudge along until dark, for Raile would not use the roads until then.

They passed a mud hut, unroofed, its chimney stones scattered. It had been damaged by a hurricane that had stormed in from the sea before Lorraine's time. The sight of it made her remember something.

"There is a place not far from here where we could rest," she told Raile eagerly. "A safe place. 'Tis an old ruined mud-walled house. Its roof blew off in a storm long ago and its chimney fell down and the people who lived there said they were tired of the raw life of the colonies and went back to England."

"Does no one live there now?" She shook her head, and he said, "Lead the way, lass."

They had not far to go. Nestled in the trees, almost concealed by the rapidly growing underbrush, they found the house—walls crumbling, thatch roof gone. Together they gathered up armloads of rushes and carried them inside. As Lorraine sank down cross-legged upon them, her back against the broken stones of the fireplace, she remembered her mother remarking that she had never slept on anything less than goose feathers in her childhood. Lorraine's glance flickered over the Scot's smartly tailored blue coat with its shining silver buttons. He was gentry too. . . .

"You'll not have slept on rushes before," she commented, settling her russet skirts around her.

Raile gave her an astonished look. "I've slept on rushes, deck planking, bouncing farm carts, soggy earth, tree crotches—and once atop a thatched roof with a hornet's nest nearby and men with guns prowling below looking for me. Name it, lass—I've slept on it!"

"And feather beds?" she murmured, watching him.

"Well, that was mainly with women," he drawled, and was amused to see her blush.

"You're . . . married?"

He shook his head. "And usually," he added humorously, "I spent only part of the night in those delightful feather beds. My leave-taking was often by way of a window just as the rightful owner of the house and the lady came cantering up!"

Lorraine considered this conversation about beds dangerous. Around them the air was heady with the scent of hickory and wildflowers and the perfume of spicebush leaves that they had crushed beneath their feet. She took a deep breath. The air was so soft— more dangerous still! She hitched up her knees beneath her wide skirts and thought to change the subject.

Raile must have divined her fears, for he suddenly began to make an effort to entertain her. He told her about an encounter with an irate husband on the grounds of a country house outside Paris when the ivy beneath the lady's second-floor bedroom broke and sent him sprawling into the garden below—and how on another occasion he had been stuffed into a closet in Venice by a frantic lady whose husband was even then bursting through the door. He had ended up diving out the window into a canal, and been fortunate enough to be picked up by a passing gondola that contained a lady even more beautiful than the one he had just left!

He had had so many affairs, she thought uneasily, surely it would be dangerous to fall asleep in his company! Remembering how Philip had pressed his advantage the moment he had her alone in the loft, she moved away uncomfortably.

Raile took her sudden movement to mean that she was trying to get out of the sun, which was now knifing down through the branches, hot across the skin.

"I'll move your pallet over to a shadier place," he offered, rising lithely to his feet.

"No, no, I can do it!" Lorraine was eager to keep him at a distance, but he insisted, dragging the pile of rushes into deeper shade.

And nearer his own pallet, Lorraine noted in alarm. She sat down as primly as she could, tucking her skirts carefully around her. A fool she might be, but not a harlot, she told herself fiercely. She had let Philip make a fool of her last night, but that was no reason to fall into bed with the first attractive man she met!

Nervously she began to talk. The afternoon dragged on. She talked about everything: about the newly arrived parson who'd been discovered seducing the Meadows' dairy maid; about the local plans for a new inn; about the fear of Indian unrest. Soon Lorraine's lids grew heavy as she talked, and her voice slowed down.

"You look tired," said Raile when she paused. "Go to sleep, for there'll be little sleep for either of us this night."

"Oh, I'm not tired!" Lorraine protested, jerking her slumping body upright.

"Then at least keep quiet and close your eyes," he recommended. "And perhaps sleep will come." And when she looked rebellious, "Remember," he added, "if our voices should be heard by someone prowling nearby, they'll investigate and discover us."

"I could keep watch while you sleep," she offered.

"A good suggestion. I'll make sure the horse is where he can find enough grass, and take you up on it, lass."

He was gone for a while and when he came back he saw that she was staring at her hands with a woeful expression on her young face. *She is remembering last night,* he thought. And yearned to lay his hands on the lad who had done this to her. He was careful then to make ample noise to herald his approach. She looked up hastily and passed a hand over her face, dashing something bright from her eyes.

"He's not worth crying over, lass," he told her sternly.

"I . . . I know. I wasn't crying." Her expression was defiant, but her voice held a hint of a quaver.

"Keep watch, lass," he said cheerfully, for he guessed she did not want him to belabor the point or to pry into her feelings about Philip. "An hour will be enough for me. When the shadows lengthen, wake me up. Then I'll let you sleep till dark and we'll be off."

She nodded. Her own eyelids ware heavy, but she kept her gaze on him, even as he drifted immediately into slumber.

What manner of man was he? she wondered, studying him. He lay relaxed with one hand on the hilt of his sword, the leather scabbard of which had seen better days. His bearing, his manner, his every gesture bespoke gentle birth, yet her inmost heart told her he was an adventurer, one of those men who live off the land, taking their fun—and their women—where they found them.

And leaving them there.

Indeed, had not his entertaining stories about French

countesses of doubtful virture and hot-blooded Venetian ladies told her that?

Oddsbud's cynical wife would have pointed out that since she had already lost her virtue, she had nothing more to lose. But Lorraine would not have agreed. Shamed she had been, and brought low, but being knocked into the gutter did not force one to remain in it. She would go on as before—no, better than before, for she had shaken off her articles of indenture!

On that rising note her heavy eyelids closed at last and she drifted off to sleep.

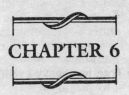

CHAPTER 6

WHEN PHILIP DEDWINTON left the White Horse Tavern, he set out for home at a good speed. Halfway there he slowed his pace and finally stopped altogether, wrestling furiously with himself in the dawn.

Lord, what a revelation last night had been! How different from that hard-faced whore on the Providence waterfront whose favors his swaggering older brother had bought for him as a "gift" on his fourteenth birthday—how different from the giggling unwashed scullery maid he'd got drunk on hard cider last summer and lain with in a dark hallway! Lorraine had fire and freshness and—shame flooded him at the memory—she had said she loved him.

And to his way of thinking, proved it.

His face grew hot at the memory of her soft yielding lips, her pliant body that had trembled beneath him, her fresh young ardor that had returned him passion for passion.

He reined in his horse abruptly. He could not afford to lose all that! And some inner voice warned him that he *would* lose her, lose her forever, no matter how she felt about him now, when she learned the truth of the shabby lie he had told her.

And she was the woman he wanted. He knew that now, knew it like a knife turning in his heart.

He wheeled his horse about, dug his heels into the

animal's flanks. Lorraine must not find out she had been won on a wager; he would make amends, he would fabricate some likely lie before it was too late!

In panic he sped back the way he had come.

And found Oddsbud alone, standing in the door of the White Horse Tavern, smoking his clay pipe. Lorraine would be out back, no doubt, probably pressed into duty feeding and watering the horses. And wondering why he had not returned. . . .

Philip leapt off his horse and came right to the point. "I've come to ask you what you'll take for Lorraine's articles."

Oddsbud considered him benignly. What timing, what perfect timing! He'd been wondering how to let Philip know that Lorraine was for sale before word got around that she was missing, and here was the lad himself!

"I've been thinking on ye, Philip," he sighed. "And 'tis plain the wench fancies you. Make me a reasonable offer."

"I have not enough ready cash." Philip exhibited his few coins. "But I can give you a note of hand?"

Oddsbud frowned. Take a note of hand and he'd end up in court trying to get his money! And Philip's father would step in and claim his son had been defrauded.

"I'm not interested in pieces of paper," he told Philip impatiently, "but in yellow gold. What've ye got?"

Philip bethought him of the betrothal ring he carried in his pocket. *It* was of yellow gold and set with a garnet—a stone Lavinia Todd fancied. Philip's father had planked down good money for the ring and Philip was supposed to present it on bended knee to Lavinia on Thursday next to bind the match.

He could tell his father he'd lost it! And arrange to have Lorraine keep on working for Oddsbud for a while with the world not knowing it was Philip who owned her. That way Oddsbud would still be responsible for her keep, but Philip could visit her every night at his pleasure.

He drew out the ring. "I can give you this," he said. "But it must be a secret between us."

"Why?" demanded Oddsbud suspiciously. "Are you telling me the ring's stolen?"

"Certainly not, but 'tis a betrothal ring and 'twas destined for"—Philip looked uncomfortable—"other hands."

A betrothal ring no less! The sly young devil!

"I'll take it," said Oddsbud instantly. "And the coins too, or course. I'll get you Lorraine's papers now. Wait outside here, for my wife would not like it if she knew what a pittance I was letting the girl go for. But under the circumstances . . ." He winked conspiratorially at Philip and disappeared into the empty tavern.

As he searched for the papers, which, along with his other valuables, he kept under his mattress, his wife entered carrying a broom. "What're you doing there, Oddsbud?" she demanded suspiciously.

"I'm selling Lorraine's papers!" Oddsbud grinned, tossing her the coins. No need for his wife to know about the ring!

"But she's run away!"

"Quiet," growled Oddsbud. "The lad outside doesn't know that!"

Mistress Oddsbud pocketed the coins and held her peace. Oddsbud went outside and shoved the papers into Philip's eager hands.

Flushed and triumphant now that the deed was done, Philip swaggered rather grandly to a table in the empty common room. "Pour me a tankard on account, Oddsbud." He wanted to be sitting there waiting when Lorraine came into the room. Then he'd fabricate an explanation for having run off, and cap it by showing her the articles he'd bought. She would be overwhelmed with delight, of course. He sat there meditating on what to tell her.

In silence, Oddsbud brought the ale. He was hoping another customer would come into the tavern before this hot young buck thought to inquire as to Lorraine's whereabouts. Before witnesses, Philip was less apt to demand the return of his betrothal ring.

At that moment, Lavinia Todd, stung by Lorraine's taunts, was galloping up the road in fury with her purple skirts flying. Walter, on a lesser nag, was hard put to keep up with her.

"Wait, Lavinia!" he kept calling. "The horses can't keep up this pace!"

If Lavinia heard, she paid no attention. She was in full cry as she approached the Light Horse Tavern.

Philip heard the thunder of approaching hooves and went out to see what was afoot. He still had not formulated what to say to Lorraine when Lavinia reined up before him.

"Oh, how could you, Philip, *how could you?*" she choked. Her trembling mount seemed to echo her own distraught manner.

So Lavinia had heard about the wager! Well, he must brazen it out. "How could I do what?" he demanded, trying to look innocent.

"How could you buy Lorraine London's articles of indenture and promise to marry her?"

Philip looked dazed. How could Lavinia possibly know what had only just transpired? He rallied. "I never promised to marry her!"

By now Walter had reached them.

"Oh, yes, you did! She told me so!" Lavinia was leaning forward in the saddle, shouting down into Philip's confused face.

"No, I swear—"

"Can you look me in the eye and tell me you did *not* buy her articles?" she challenged.

"Lavinia, 'twas only a wager!" He managed to look aggrieved.

"A wager! What do you mean, wager?"

Their bickering had brought Oddsbud out. He had heard most of the conversation and now he saw a way to profit from it.

"I've not sold Lorraine's articles to anyone," he declared mildly. "The wench ran away this morning with a stranger who came to the inn last night."

Philip spun about. He was staring at Oddsbud glassy-eyed. "She . . . ran way?" he gasped.

"Aye." Oddsbud regarded him guilelessly. "As all know. There was no use in pursuing them—the stranger had a fast horse. They'll be far away by now."

"I do not believe you!" screamed Lavinia. She jerked her horse's head around and thundered back the way she had come, with an unhappy Walter pursuing her.

"You tricked me!" Philip accused Oddsbud. He was panting, his face pale. "You knew Lorraine had run away—yet you sold me her articles!"

"Now, now, you young bucks never recognize a favor when you see one," chided Oddsbud. "The girl's conspicuous, and where can she hide? And the man's a stranger who'll be on his way soon without her. Ye can claim her at your leisure and"—he winked slyly at Philip—"for her running away, ye can tack another year or so onto her term of indenture. Besides, the wench is angry with ye now—ye'd be taking a spitting cat to your bed. And do you want her around whilst you're wedding that angry hieress who just yowled at you? Get you married, lad, bed your bride and make sure of her dowry—and *then* go after the bound girl. Ye can have *both!*"

Philip fell back. There was sense to the tavernkeeper's words. With Lorraine gone, making up with Lavinia should not prove too difficult. Even if Lavinia learned about the wager, he could pass it off that he was drunk, and beg forgiveness—women liked that. His older brother was always getting away with things by gracefully begging forgiveness afterward.

Still he glared at Oddsbud. The fellow had tricked him. And now he could not even exhibit those articles of indenture—he must hide them.

He growled that he was in need of a metal box. Once he received it, he bade Oddsbud a surly good-bye and mounted up. As soon as he was out of sight of the tavern, he left the road, walking his horse over the spongy ground. He knew a place by a small tinkling waterfall where he could bury the papers safe and dry and return for them when he needed them.

Gleefully the tavernkeeper watched him go. The lad was off to secrete the papers somewhere. Meantime Oddsbud planned to turn the ring over to a sea captain he knew, in whose ventures he sometimes bought shares—pity, the fellow had been here night before last, he might have sailed away by now. Ah, well, the evidence would be gone and the chickens would never come home to roost—he'd even be considered a kindly soul for not advertising for his runaway bound girl!

Chuckling, he went back inside his tavern. As he did so, a blazing arrow struck the tavern's thatched roof and set it alight. Oddsbud never had time to reach his musket. A dozen Indians converged upon him.

Philip of course knew nothing about it, though if he had bothered to look back he would have seen the smoke. He rode for some time through the forest, and at last, the way having become too narrow and himself about to be swept from the saddle by low-lying branches, he left his horse tethered to a tree and walked on moccasined feet through the brush toward his destination. He could hear the rippling sound of rushing water and smell the scent of wintergreen as he knelt and with a wedge of rock scooped out a small hole. He put the metal box containing Lorraine's articles into it, and had just covered it up with the soft mossy earth when he heard a twig snap and a low-voiced Indian command.

Hidden by the concealing underbrush, Philip froze. There were rumblings of Indian troubles all about these days, and now and again an outlying cabin had been burned, some distant settler's family murdered. And here he was, caught out alone and on foot in deep woods without so much as a knife, let alone a musket! He began to sweat as through a narrow gap in the leaves he saw a war party of some twenty dark-skinned men file swiftly past on silent moccasins. It seemed to him that all the Indians in the world were out there—pray God they would not find his horse, for then they would come hunting for *him!*

At last they were gone and Philip could breathe again. Grown stiff from his rigid position, he still stayed where he was for the better part of an hour before he found his horse and made his way home by a prudently circuitous route.

Lavinia, careening wildly down the road to Providence with Walter pounding behind her trying vainly to keep up, did not fare quite so well.

She had not ridden half a mile before she heard from Walter in the rear a sudden shout that ended in a gasping cough. She turned in the saddle to see Walter's head loll forward. He was gazing down fixedly at an arrow that had pierced his chest. He pitched from his saddle in a kind of horrible slow motion and as he did so Lavinia could see that the arrow had gone clear through his body and come out on the other side.

Lavinia never faltered. She flung herself forward, lying along her horse's neck, and dug her heels into his sides. Behind her two dark-skinned warriors had leapt into the road and one loosed a silent arrow.

It was dead on target, and had Lavinia's mount not stumbled over a rock just then, she must surely have died as swiftly as Walter had, but that slight stumble—though the recovery was swift—saved her. The arrow went through her hair, only grazing her scalp so that a little trickle of blood ran down her forehead and into her terrified eyes.

Her horse dashed around a tree-sheltered bend of the road and Lavinia rode on, screaming all the way to Providence with Walter's riderless horse galloping after.

Ten minutes later Oddsbud and his wife were dead and the Light Horse Tavern was burning to the ground.

The chief sachem of the Wampanoags had made his move at last. Ten thousand Indians would soon be on the march.

And all New England was about to go up in flames.

CHAPTER 7

EXHAUSTED AND ASLEEP in the ruined cottage, Lorraine and Raile were ignorant of these fast-moving events. They were so far back from the road that the sound of hooves did not penetrate the underbrush as Lavinia went pounding by, nor the hooves of those men who came up the road later to retrieve Walter's body and to stare solemnly at the still-glowing embers of what had once been the Light Horse Tavern.

Finally Raile started awake at the sound of an owl and stared up at a bright moon shining down through a cloud-splashed sky. He glanced alertly at the girl, for a moment angered that she had not awakened him. Lord, it was late! But a quick look at Lorraine revealed her lying in crumpled fashion, like a tossed-aside rag doll, sleeping an exhausted sleep.

She did not even stir as he rose, snapping a twig. She lay curled up like a child, her long fair hair cascading over one slender arm, shimmering pale in the moonlight, and he thought: *How young she looks, how untried.* . . . And once again wished he could give young Philip Dedwinton a thrashing.

Well, they'd better be on their way. Still, after all she'd been through, he was loath to wake Lorraine. Let her catch a few winks more while he watered the horse. He padded off to find his horse and lead him down to the riverbank beneath the trees.

The horse drank thirstily, then shook his head so that big drops splattered Raile. Raile chuckled and patted that long neck. A good horse was Old Ezra, as the man he'd hired the beast from had promised.

Suddenly he pulled on the horse's bridle, urged him back into a shadow of the trees.

Out on the black shining river was a long canoe with three Indians in it. They were paddling purposefully toward shore. It was plain they hadn't seen him.

While Raile stood silent, holding the horse in check, the Indians beached their canoe, hid it beneath some overhanging branches, and stole along the bank, disappearing into the trees. They carried tomahawks in their hands.

A scouting party, if he was any judge. . . . And that might mean more canoes coming along at any time now, drifting downriver from the interior. At least these three had not been heading in the direction of the ruined cottage where the girl lay sleeping.

Raile frowned. The Indians had gone directly inland from the river; they might head toward Providence—or away from it. He could take the girl and ride down a road to Providence that was barely a trail, but who knew where the Indians were going? He might run into them. And while he would not have hesitated to take on the three of them, there was Lorraine to consider. She had been through enough without having to dodge Indian arrows!

He felt he had remained motionless long enough. The Indians—whatever their intentions—were out of earshot by now. Swiftly he guided the horse back to the road that led to Providence, gave that big sleek rump a light slap and sent it on its way. "Old Ezra knows his way around here. If ye get lost, Old Ezra will bring ye back to me," the man from whom Raile had hired the horse had boasted. Old Ezra was going to have a chance to make good that boast this night! Ah well, he had paid almost what the horse would cost for the hire of him, so the farmer would be out little if the horse never returned.

In any event, they would not be riding Old Ezra. Raile had found other transportation down on the riverbank.

Back at the ruined cottage, Raile stood looking down at the sleeping girl with compassion. Even when he bent down over her, she still did not awaken, so deep was her exhaustion. Then suddenly her eyes snapped open, filled with fear at sight of him hovering over her.

Before she could make a sound, he had clapped his big hand over her mouth.

"Quiet," he warned. "There are Indians about and it may be they're up to no good."

"Are the Wampanoags attacking?" Lorraine whispered fearfully. "We've been expecting it ever since Sausamon was murdered last year!"

"Sausamon?" He frowned.

"John Sausamon was an Indian convert who always kept us posted on what the Indians were doing," she explained. "Three Wampanoags were executed at Plymouth for his murder. And after that . . ." Her voice trailed off. After that, unease had spread throughout New England, and there had been occasional murderous outbreaks. All Rhode Island was on edge. Lorraine reflected on what it must be like to find an Indian with a tomahawk come bounding through your window, or to be cut down by a silent arrow whilst you were clearing your land.

"What I saw might have been a scouting party."

"Oddsbud said if only the Wampanoags attacked, the danger would be here in Rhode Island—but if the Narragansetts joined them, all New England would be finished!" she added. She shared the belief hereabouts that the Wampanoags' chief sachem had already formed a tribal confederation amounting to some ten thousand warriors. "Were the Indians you saw Wampanoags?"

"I do not know one Indian from another," he muttered brusquely. "But get up and follow me as quietly as you can. We are going downriver."

She looked startled, but scrambled up with alacrity and followed him like a shadow as he made his way quietly to the riverbank.

"What of the horse?" she whispered.

"Old Ezra would prefer not to travel by canoe," his voice wafted back to her.

She clutched his arm. "But shouldn't we warn somebody? About the Indians?"

"There were but three of them," Raile said, pulling the Indians' canoe out from under the concealing branches as he spoke. "Best to outrun trouble this night, for we'll have plenty of our own if we stay in this vicinity."

Oddsbud, she thought uneasily, *and the law.* She realized that she was now a hunted thing and could be hauled back to face her tormentors.

Impatiently Raile urged her toward the canoe and she climbed gingerly into it, hoping it would not tip over.

Moments later they were paddling downriver, speeding along with the current, heading toward Narragansett Bay and the fast ketch that waited at anchor there.

The wild shore sped by, dark trees and occasional settlers' cottages seen fitfully through the scudding clouds that kept blowing across the moon's bright face. Around them the surface of the river was smooth and dark and shining. Tense, both hands gripping the sides of the canoe, Lorraine sat silent, for Raile had warned her that voices carried far across the water.

"Keep a sharp lookout for war canoes," Raile muttered. "Don't say anything if you see one—just point."

Seated before him, Lorraine shivered. *Every man's hand is against us now,* she told herself, and felt her heart thump at the thought. *The Indians would kill us where we are, and those I once thought were my friends would drag me back to humiliation and servitude—and worse.*

Still they pushed forward over the smooth dark water, and still her thoughts pursued her. Not a light showed on the dark shore. They might have been alone in the world, gliding over the face of a continent.

Behind Lorraine, upriver, lay her past and the man she had loved for most of her short lifetime—a man who had proved false. Shatteringly, hurtfully. Ahead lay an uncertain future. With her now in the canoe, paddling swiftly, expertly, was a lawless man who had known many women—far too well! He had proved trustworthy thus far—still, she had known him but a matter of hours. What did she know of him really?

Lorraine set her delicate jaw and stared fiercely ahead of her at the moon's path in the shining water.

She would take her chances! Anything was better than returning to the Light Horse Tavern.

And yet how strange it seemed to be leaving Rhode Island like a thief in the night, floating downriver in a savage war canoe!

III:

THE *LIKELY LASS*

CHAPTER 8

Narragansett Bay

TO LORRAINE, SITTING tensely in the forepart of the canoe, the night seemed very long. She had offered to help with the paddling but her offer had been met with a curt refusal from a man whose arms must surely be made of steel bands, so tirelessly did they move them along.

Mists covered the water now, dampening the tendrils of fair hair that curled on her forehead and making her chemise stick uncomfortably to her body. And the dark shoreline—whenever the mists parted to reveal it—seemed distant, unreal. Perhaps it was the mist, the near-soundless drifting, that gave Lorraine that strange feeling that they were alone in the world and would never meet anyone they knew ever again.

So caught up was she in that feeling that it was a shock when behind her she heard Raile's soft triumphant, "There she is, there's the *Likely Lass!*" And looking up, Lorraine saw, still barely discernible in the mist, the topmost and furled sails of a small ship.

Had Lorraine known her ships—and she did not— she would instantly have recognized this fleet, impatient-looking little ship, with its sweeping rakish lines from stem to stern, as a smart ketch in the new Restoration style, with a round-tuck stern that would identify it at a glance to the practiced eye as being of British origin. The ketch's bowsprit was set over the stem, and she

103

sported reef points as well as bonnets. Somehow, even in the darkness and the fog, the ketch seemed a lean greyhound eager to be off.

Lorraine would never forget the stirring excitement of those first moments when, in drifting fog and the soft diffused light of a waning moon, she was handed aboard the dark ketch.

"Cap'n's back and he's brought a wench with him," she heard a disembodied voice above her mutter. Raile boosted her up a short rope ladder and a pair of huge muscular arms with shirtsleeves ripped off at the shoulder lifted her lightly over the side onto the deck.

"Welcome aboard the *Likely Lass!*" A laughing Irish brogue filled her ears and Lorraine looked up into the face of a blond giant, his wild Celtic countenance lit by a broad grin.

"Mistress London, this great ox is Derry Cork, the best gunner afloat," came Raile's easy voice behind her.

"And with hardly a gun to me name on this wee vessel," added Cork with a chuckle.

"And this is Malcolm MacTavish, my first mate— none better," Raile said, as he began to introduce the men surrounding them.

Lorraine saw a frown cross the face of the gray-haired Scotsman who loomed up before her, but he made her a grave bow.

Raile continued. "And this is André L'Estraille, our ship's doctor." She met the merry amber eyes of a handsome Frenchman, whose bow swept the deck.

There were other names, but Lorraine in her excitement hardly caught them. There were common seamen hovering about too, and they looked to be a cutthroat lot, but Raile did not introduce them.

"What of Moffatt?" Derry Cork was asking.

"Dead," Raile told him briskly.

"Ah-h-h . . ." Cork sucked in his breath.

And what now? The question was being silently asked by everyone in the little knot of officers who surrounded them. But it was to MacTavish's practical question of "Where will ye be stowing the young lass?" that Raile addressed himself.

"In my cabin," he said briefly, and Lorraine felt a sense of shock.

She opened her mouth to protest, but closed it again at the steely look Raile gave her, a look that told her as plainly as words: *Say nothing.*

She would have plenty to say, she told herself hotly, *the moment they were alone together!*

Lorraine was ushered by the impassive MacTavish into the small stern cabin that served the captain. And left there.

She stared around her. Fitful moonlight streamed in through the stern windows and now revealed, now concealed the cabin's sparse furnishings: an oaken table spread with charts, a bottle, and silver goblets; some wooden chairs; a couple of sea chests. And a single narrow bunk.

It was that last that worried Lorraine.

She had a sudden rash impulse to dash out upon the deck and demand that she be put ashore at once. She had even turned toward the door before she stopped, wincing at the thought that her demand might be greeted with hard masculine laughter. And a cool question: *Why should I let you go?*

Suppose he did put her ashore? Where would that leave her? Somewhere on a wild coast with probably dozens of warlike Indians between her and civilization! And if she did manage to make her way back to Providence, what could she expect? To be taken back to the Light Horse Tavern by an angry Oddsbud, to be cuffed and snarled at and probably beaten by Oddsbud's wife—and then to settle down to perhaps years more of humiliating servitude as punishment for running away.

And all the while having to face the knowing grins of those who knew that Philip Dedwinton had had her on a wager. And watching Lavinia, in "royal" purple, ride by with him triumphantly, tossing her bronze head. Worst of all, having to face Philip himself!

Lorraine swallowed. It came to her eerily that life was set to trap you, that Fate was a hard-hearted jade. And that made her even angrier at the cool Scotsman, Raile Cameron, whom she now considered her captor.

She wondered what story he would tell her presently to justify installing her in his cabin? That he must "protect" her from his men? From that decent-looking gray-haired Scot? That pleasant Irishman? That gallant Frenchman? Indeed, she might be safer in one of their beds than in his!

Of course there was the off chance that he was giving her the use of his cabin for herself alone and would find some other place to sleep. She studied the sturdy door and her eyes gleamed. She could latch it!

And have it kicked down, her common sense told her, if she had read her man aright.

No, she could not have him come bursting in, enraged—and humiliated before his men. It would shorten her chances of persuading him to take her—unharmed—to some safe sane place and to leave her there to make her own way.

Men were impressed by resolute women, she told herself, wearily. *Weren't they?* Indeed she had not been resolute enough with Philip—she had succumbed to his ready lies and her own treacherous emotions. *This* time she would not succumb, *this* time she would fight! And if the wild fellow who had brought her here thought he would find her meekly undressed and waiting for him in his bed, he would learn his mistake soon enough. She was grateful to him for helping her escape, but not *that* grateful!

It occurred to her suddenly that he was exceedingly strong. She had just had a demonstration of that strength. He had paddled all night and then boosted her up effortlessly on that shaky rope ladder she had clung to with such desperation.

She frowned and her gaze searched the room. The moonlight obligingly showed her that there were two pistols in evidence, also several swords hanging on belts from long nails in the walls.

On impulse she picked up one of the large pistols. She was not sure she could manage it, but she told herself it was worth a try.

Then she took up a position behind the wooden

table, facing the cabin door, and sat down—heavily, as the ship lurched when its anchor came aboard. She concealed the pistol in the folds of her skirt, and sat tensely waiting.

They were moving now, timbers creaking, sails unfurled taking the wind, and running fast and silent down the dark waters of Narragansett Bay toward the open ocean.

In a huddled conference on deck the question of where they were bound caused a tug-of-war within Raile Cameron. It would be easy to drop down to New Amsterdam, which was now New York, where guns were always in demand against the warlike Iroquois and the mighty Mohawks. Or over to Philadelphia, where the new settlers pushing ever westward could certainly find use for guns against the Indians. Or father south to Virginia. . . .

But there was the girl to think of now and Raile had no doubt that there would be notices of her escape posted, which could reach to Virginia and beyond.

So to Derry Cork's question, "Do we go upriver now and find the settlers Moffatt represented?" Raile shook his head.

"I saw an Indian scouting party tonight," he told Derry soberly. "And men desperate for guns will take them by force. No, I think we'll away from Rhode Island."

"He's saying he'd like to be paid for the guns, Derry," explained MacTavish dryly. "And Moffatt's friends might not pay—not if they're under fire and can't lay their hands on ready cash!"

"Where then?" wondered Derry.

Later, in the moonlit cabin, Raile gave the same answer to Lorraine that he had given to Derry on deck.

"We're for the Indies," he said lightly. To Derry he had added, "There's always trouble there—with the Spanish, with the Maroons, with the pirates. Always a ready market for guns." To Lorraine, he now substituted, "There'll be ports there, lass, where you'll never be missed."

He had meant "missed from Rhode Island" but

Lorraine's fingers tightened on the pistol. "What do you mean 'never be missed'?" she asked in a tight voice.

Raile's gray gaze had been sweeping the room—and noted something missing.

"You can lay the pistol on the table, Mistress Lorraine," he said evenly. "I'm not about to assault your virtue!"

Lorraine drew in her breath and, reluctantly, taking the pistol from the folds of her russet skirt, she laid it with a slight clatter upon the wooden table.

Raile took the pistol, toyed with it idly. He seemed to tower over her. "I'm tired," he said scathingly. "So I'll say this but once. You'll sleep in that bunk." He jerked his head toward it. "But not with me. *Not unless asked.*"

Lorraine was glad the cabin was dark. It hid her furious blushes. "I only thought—" she began hastily.

"I know what you thought," he cut in. "But if I'd intended to ravish you, I could have done that in Rhode Island—no need to bring you here to the *Lass!*"

That was true. She could feel her cheeks burning.

"I'm sorry," she managed.

"Good. I'm glad to hear that you are." He put the pistol back where it belonged, said over his shoulder, "Go to bed. And have no fear, I'll keep you safe from my crew."

Lorraine stumbled to the bunk. It was not his crew she had been afraid of, but Raile himself!

Kicking off her shoes, she lay down cautiously, and watched him yank off his boots and shirt. She stared in surprise as he spread a blanket on the floor before the door and—still clad in his trousers and with a pistol beside him—lay down upon it.

As it came to her what he was doing, hot shame spread through her. Raile had saved her from servitude at the risk of his own skin. He had brought her here and offered her his cabin. And now she was comfortably lying in his bed while he himself lay stretched out on the floor where any motion of the door as it pushed against him would wake him.

He was guarding her with his body!

"Good night," she whispered. "I'm sorry."

There was no reply. The tall Scot had fallen instantly asleep.

At first wakeful amid the strange surroundings, Lorraine lay there studying the man whose long body blocked the door. She watched him with a kind of fascination, still half-expecting him to rise and ravish her. But he continued to sleep soundly, and gradually, lulled by the slight creaking of the ship as it breasted the dark waves, some of the tension went out of Lorraine and she slipped back into contemplation of the heartbreaking events of her last hours in Rhode Island.

Bitterly she thought of Philip and his treachery. Of Lavinia and her scorn. Of what all the local rustics would be saying about her, how the stories would mount and change and grow worse with time. Her hands clenched. All this had been visited on her and yet she had done nothing to deserve it, nothing!

But tension and anxiety had woven a silent web, casing her in. Exhausted by all that had happened, at last she drifted into sleep, oblivious of the rhythmic roll of the ship, unaware even when morning came.

In the morning, the tall man whose body had last night blocked the cabin doorway moved and stretched. In a lithe gesture he gained his feet and walked over and gazed down silently at the sleeping girl.

She looked heartrendingly young and defenseless lying there, he thought—and it was a long time since he had harbored such thoughts about a woman, for life had hardened him. He saw that she was lying as she had first lain when she had watched him with worried eyes from the bunk. Her fair hair was a shimmering tangle upon the pillow, and her tattered skirts had ridden up to reveal a pair of shapely legs. After a moment's hesitation Raile reached out and gently pulled the coverlet down. He would be going out the cabin door in a minute or two, he told himself. No need for any passing member of the crew to look in and view such a delectable sight.

That he wished to reserve the delectable sight of those dainty bare legs for his eyes alone was a thought he brushed aside in true masculine style.

Lorraine did not even stir as the coverlet was gently tugged down. She was deep in sleep. She did not stir as the tall man dressed, leaving off his boots, for he preferred—like most of the crew—the feel of the bare deck planks under his naked feet in weather like this.

Silently he went out and closed the door behind him.

Lorraine slept soundly through the day and Raile ordered the cabin boy not to disturb her. His lass would eat at her leisure, he informed the lad.

The trim ship moved steadily forward, aided by a brisk wind, hours passed, the shadows lenghtened, and evening came. Raile supped, glanced at the tired girl, who never roused, wondered if he should not wake her for the evening meal, decided against it, and then stretched out as he had the night before at his place by the door.

And still Lorraine slept, although now it had become an uneasy broken sleep lit by fitful nightmares. She was flailing about in the bed and Raile, hearing her cry out, got up and padded across the floor planking barefoot.

Looking down at her, he caught his breath. In starlight Lorraine's misty form was endlessly enticing, her parted lips were a challenge, her sweet young body held the promise of endless delights.

"There now," he murmured, gently touching Lorraine's wet cheek. "There's no need to be frightened, lass."

"Philip," she whispered in her sleep. "*Philip* . . ."

If she had poured a bucket of cold water over Captain Cameron's head, she could not have cooled him quicker. His fingers left her cheek as if scorched.

Lorraine awoke with a start, saw a tall dark form hovering above her, gasped, and clutched convulsively at the coverlet.

"You were dreaming, lass. You cried out."

"What . . . what did I say when I cried out?" she asked, confused.

"You said, 'Captain Cameron, please wake me, I am having a nightmare,' " said Raile caustically, and she blushed.

"I'm sorry," she said contritely. "I'm afraid I woke you." For Lorraine had no idea that she had slept all day; she imagined it to be but a short hour or so since she had come on board.

"That's all right, lass. Feel free to wake me if anything frightens you again."

"I will," she promised in a sleepy voice. And rolled over with her back to him, sliding back into dreams again.

The tall captain considered her soberly. His own heart was racing and he was filled with thoughts that worried him. How ready his body was to respond to her!

He walked to the stern window and stood staring out of it, imagining what it would be like to have this slender lass always beside him, sharing his ventures. He saw her suddenly in an older, more confident version, bravely gowned, with his children around her knee.

It was a tempting vision.

Captain Cameron found himself gripping the sill of the stern window, mesmerized by it.

At last he shook his head to clear it. He was almost in a cold sweat.

It had been a long time since he had cherished such feelings—and then it had ended in disaster. No doubt *this* affair would end in disaster as well—if he let it go that far.

He had no intention of letting it go that far. He would go on taking his women as he found them—and moving on. Always moving on.

Still he cast an uneasy look back at Lorraine, asleep again and tossing restlessly upon the bunk—and with every toss, in his mind he tossed with her. That slender outflung arm he imagined now upon his breast—a gossamer touch. The skin of her cheek had been so smooth, the swelling of her upthrust young breasts would be so silken . . . This girl was magically constructed to tempt men, and he recognized it well.

But recognizing it did no good—it was what to do about it.

Captain Cameron's strong jaw tightened. He would

do nothing about it. He would carry the little lass to a safe place as he had promised, and there he would leave her.

Again in sleep she murmured, "Philip," and Raile, listening, told himself sternly that he was being warned. No matter how badly that young whelp Philip had used her, Lorraine still loved him.

Raile's lip curled in derision at himself.

Abruptly he left to take a turn upon the deck—but that did not help either. Tonight the ship had wings, it was flying over a silver sea, and anything was possible—even to him. He passed an angry hand over his eyes as if to clear his vision, then strode purposefully back to his cabin. The deck watch gave him a curious look as he passed.

Lorraine was still restlessly asleep in the bunk, still tossing. It rent his heart that she should be lying there only a few feet away calling out for that bastard Philip!

Cursing himself for a fool, the Scottish captain fell at last to sleep.

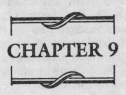

CHAPTER 9

A Week Later

THE WIND BLEW fresh, and like the silken mane of a nervous white Arabian mare who takes the bit in her teeth and charges forward gallantly, the *Likely Lass*'s white sails billowed and she skimmed across the glittering blue-green water.

Sailor's weather!

Lorraine leaned against the ship's rail in the sunshine and watched a pair of herring gulls swoop and dive over the ship, then gracefully rise to swoop again. It seemed to her that her life had changed the instant she had come aboard, for life on the *Likely Lass* was like nothing she had ever known before: carefree, exhilarating.

Lorraine had learned much since the fleet ketch had flown down Narragansett Bay toward the open ocean. She had learned that while the crew was French ("Picked up from the gutters of Bordeaux," was MacTavish's grunted comment), the ship's officers were an international lot. Aside from the dignified Scot, MacTavish, who was first mate and navigator, there was a dangerous-looking Dutchman with very blue eyes and bright yellow hair and wiry muscles named Jakob Helst, who was the sailing master. The ship's gunner was that huge carefree laughing Irishman Derry Cork. The rest were English save for the ship's doctor, a handsome Frenchman, André L'Estraille, who wore

113

outrageously fashionable clothes and fawn-colored curls that Lorraine suspected of being a wig. His eyes were a remarkable amber that in sunlight approached an unusual brassy gold. L'Estraille had been quick to tell her that his middle name was Champion—as, he explained volubly with lighthearted Gallic gestures, indeed he was, *mademoiselle*, in all things, especially *l'amour!* His delighted amber gaze had wandered caressingly over Lorraine's dainty figure as he spoke. Then Raile had cut in with a chuckle to warn her, "Pay no attention to this fighting cock, Mistress Lorraine. He's our ship's doctor, here to bind up our wounds if we have any, and to leech us and bleed us at his pleasure!"

"You forgot to mention I'm the best blade aboard!" boasted the handsome Frenchman, flashing a grin at Lorraine.

"The best blade?" Lorraine was impressed.

In response to Raile's level look, L'Estraille coughed. "After the captain, of course," he corrected blithely. "But his expertise, I understand, is in naval warfare, whilst I prefer single combat. My prowess in duels is unmatched in all of France, *mademoiselle*. I have fought the best beneath the most famous dueling oaks of my native land for the honor of—"

"Various ladies," supplied Raile. "Of whom Mistress Lorraine will not be added to your list, André."

The Frenchman sighed and shrugged. Lorraine liked him at once, and spent considerable time talking to him, for he sought her out at every opportunity when she came on deck.

After only a few days on board, she felt she had poked into every cranny of the vessel. She was bewildered by the amount of gear needed, the spars and anchors and canvas and ropes and tools, and by the number of craftsmen that seemed to be necessary to keep a small ship afloat—there were coopers who made barrels, and carpenters and sailmakers, and caulkers whose responsibility it was to keep the ship watertight, as well as the ordinary seamen who swarmed over the rigging.

The food left something to be desired. The fresh

fruit was beginning to run out, the fresh milk acquired in Rhode Island had long since turned to clabber, and although the water in the casks was still good, Lorraine was already tired of the salt fish and onions and dried beans and cheese and hard ship's biscuit which were the sailor's standby.

But life had certainly changed for Lorraine.

She had waked that first morning after her long sleep, to find Raile gone and the cabin boy knocking on her door asking her if she would not like some breakfast. Since she had fallen asleep fully dressed—and waked to an enormous hunger—Lorraine struggled up on one elbow to call: "Yes, please. Do come in."

A towheaded lad, ruddy-faced and eager, entered. He told her his name was Johnny Sears and he didn't stop talking as he set her food on the table, explaining volubly and at length that his parents had died on a trip to Marseilles and that rather than return to the guardianship of an uncle who hated him, he had—he put it rather grandly—"taken ship" to reach Barbados. Eventually. He was rather vague about that.

"Well, you're in luck," laughed Lorraine, biting into one of the hard biscuits. "For 'tis to the Indies we're bound, according to the captain."

A momentary frown shadowed Johnny Sears's young face. "Well, that's not to be helped," he muttered. Obviously he had hoped to sail around a bit and see other shores before reaching his destination.

Lorraine gave him a shrewd look. He was young and cocky and he had a winning smile, but somehow she doubted his story. Perhaps because she was a waif herself. She sighed. It took one to know one. . . .

She put down her biscuit and gazed upon him sympathetically. The sun was pouring through the stern windows and in the harsh light he looked very, very young.

"What do you want to be, Johnny, when you're a man full grown?" she asked.

He grinned at her and his boyish chest expanded. "I want to be a gunrunner like the cap'n!"

Raile was a gunrunner? Lorraine felt her back stiffen

with shock. And yet she supposed she might have guessed him to be doing something like that . . . unlawful.

Johnny Sears was alarmed at her surprised expression. "I thought sure you knew," he mumbled, casting a surreptitious look at the bunk from which she had emerged.

Lorraine caught that look. It said: *A woman usually knows the profession of the man she's sleeping with!* Her chin lifted. She was not accountable to Johnny Sears, nor would she discuss her sleeping arrangements with him!

"You won't let on I told you?" prodded Johnny in a worried voice.

"No, of course I won't." Crisply.

"Because the crew thinks we're carrying cheese and woolens. I'm the only one that knows what's underneath—outside of the ship's officers. I heard them talking about it one day when I was bringing them a bottle, and the cap'n told me if ever I breathed a word of what I'd overheard he'd drop me over the side to feed the fishes!"

Lorraine doubted Raile would do that, but obviously his threat had intimidated Johnny, for the lad seemed truly upset. So the crew didn't know either. . . . They had looked to be a cutthroat pack when she boarded. Lorraine wondered what they would do if they found out, and suddenly felt less hungry. She pushed her food away from her.

"Cap'n wants you to eat," urged Johnny, distressed. "He told me so."

Lorraine favored him with a smile. It occurred to her that she might have tumbled from the frying pan directly into the fire.

She said no more because at that moment Raile swung into the cabin. He was still dressed in the same dark trousers he had worn before, and below the knee his muscular legs were bare. He seemed to bring the brilliance of the day in with him, along with the sea air and the freedom one feels on a ship in the trackless ocean. He bade Lorraine good morning and reached for his shirt.

"Bring another trencher, Johnny," he told the cabin boy as he slipped into the shirt. "I'll breakfast again with my lady."

Johnny Sears fled.

Raile drew up a chair and sat down at the table. His gaze passed over Lorraine appreciatively. "Faith, 'tis the brightest this cabin has been," he murmured. "I trust you slept well?"

In truth Lorraine had waked with her mind swarming with confused dreams of Philip and Lavinia and purple bridal gowns and things going wrong—and mixed up in all of it a disoriented memory of a pair of arms and Raile's voice soothing her. She peered at him suspicously but his face was expressionless. Then she remembered how frightened she had been and how he had lain across the door protecting her from God knows what, and her tension disappeared.

"I'm sorry," she said shyly. "About the pistol last night."

"Night before last, lass," he corrected her easily. "Ye've slept the clock around."

She blinked. "I must have been more tired than I thought! Anyway, I am truly sorry I didn't trust you."

His grin was reassuring. "I'm not surprised you'd think you needed protection against a cutthroat crew like mine," he said dryly. "We left Marseilles in a hurry and André—the ship's doctor, whom we'd picked up in Marseilles—rounded them up for us." He had started to add: *since he speaks French and would attract less attention*. Then he realized she'd wonder about that, and added quickly: " 'Tis André's first voyage with us."

"And the rest of your officers?"

"Have been with me for a long time. MacTavish the longest." His voice was laced with affection when he spoke of the gray-haired Scot. "We're from the same part of the world, MacTavish and I." Returning to the subject uppermost in his mind, he looked at her keenly across the table. "For your safety, lass," he said bluntly, " 'tis best those on board consider you my mistress."

"But—" she began to demur.

He held up a hand. "Hear me out. I've a reputation with the sword that tends to keep men in line, but if the lads thought you were not spoken for, they'd compete for your favors. 'Twould make for dissension and we've a long voyage ahead of us. I'd prefer to make it without threat of mutiny." To her troubled expression he added gently, "MacTavish will know the truth. Should aught happen to me, lass, MacTavish will see you safe ashore."

"I like MacTavish," she volunteered, not quite ready yet to agree to the charade.

His smile flashed. "Aye, everyone does. He's a good man, is MacTavish."

Still uncertain, she looked at him through shadowed lashes and veered off on another tack.

"What cargo do we carry, Captain Cameron?" she asked innocently.

"Cheese and woolen cloth," he replied instantly. "And I'd prefer you to call me Raile. It makes better sense"—his lips quirked—"under the circumstances."

"Is that why we ran without lights last night? To protect a cargo of cheese and woolen cloth?"

An almost melancholy smile settled over his strong features. "I see Johnny's been talking to you," he sighed.

"No, he hasn't!" she protested, but a telltale flush was spreading over her expressive features.

"And guns," he added lightly. "Beneath the cheeses and the woolens, we carry guns. But I'd thought 'twas best for you not to know that. A smuggler's life can be short."

And the tenure of a smuggler's lady even shorter. . . .

"Is that why you came to Rhode Island?" she asked curiously. "To sell the guns?"

He nodded. "But Moffatt was dead when I got there."

She remembered now hearing in the tavern that Harley Moffatt's horse had thrown him and he was dead.

"You look startled," he commented.

"It was just that . . . I had met Harley Moffatt," she blurted.

"And thought him above dealing in smuggled guns,"

he said thoughtfully. "We're none of us above trying to save our lives, Mistress Lorraine," sighed Raile. "Moffatt and some others expected an Indian uprising."

"Oh, yes," she agreed quickly. "Everybody does."

"They were hoping to be able to meet it—with my guns."

"But when you learned that Moffatt was dead, why didn't you try to find the others?"

At his sardonic expression, she said, "Oh," in a contrite voice. And looked down in embarrassment, picking at her skirt. "I've caused you no end of trouble," she muttered.

"There's no need to feel that way about it, lass," he told her softly. "What I choose to do is my own concern—and I felt like taking you with me."

"But you should be able to sell your guns along the coast somewhere without making the long voyage to the Indies, shouldn't you? Perhaps New York? That isn't so far."

He shook his head. "I'm too well known in Hudson waters, lass."

"Virginia then!" she hazarded. "Perhaps you could drop me off in some likely town? For I'll have to make my own way somewhere."

He listened to her suggestions, drumming his nails. "I realize that," he said gravely. "But we cannot go to Virginia, lass—I've my reasons. No, I'll take you to the Indies. One of the islands—you will be much safer there, where the law cannot catch up with you. Perhaps a Dutch island where English law does not hold."

"But . . . but I don't speak Dutch!" cried Lorraine, bewildered.

"No matter," was his ruthless rejoinder. "You can learn."

She sat back, silenced by his sharp tone. Then she set her jaw. "Perhaps I do not want to learn, Captain Cameron!"

He sighed. "If you would break the law, lass, then you must be ready to run. Now that the war is over between England and Holland, I can deliver you to Curaçao. After I have finished my business in Barbados."

He was deciding her future very high-handedly! she thought, but she turned away and fell silent. She would much prefer to be left in Barbados, where English was spoken. Somehow she would have to find a way to stay there. She would not let him take her on to Curaçao!

Having made that decision, she brightened.

"As to the voyage being long, let me be the judge of that—you'll brighten the way for all of us, lass."

She had liked him before, but now she had begun to like him very much indeed. There was something reassuring in his confident manner, in the very way he spoke. And despite the caressing way he looked at her, she had begun to realize that he would not force his attentions upon her.

Johnny Sears brought Raile's breakfast just then and set it upon the table before him. At Raile's reproving look he scuttled away again. Lorraine, glad of the interruption, said no more, but watched Raile attack his food. Her mind was clamoring. First she had let Philip seduce her and now she had run away with a smuggler and must face the knowing looks of all those men outside this cabin who believed her to be his mistress.

Raile's voice cut into her scurrying thoughts. He had finished his meal and was rising. "We'll take a turn around the deck if you've finished," he suggested politely, pushing back his chair.

Lorraine recoiled. "Oh, no, I couldn't! I mean . . ." She looked quickly away. "All those men will think I am—"

"Sleeping with the captain?" he finished softly.

"Yes," she choked.

"Indeed I hope so," was his cool rejoinder. "For 'twill protect you after a fashion. But of course," he drawled, "if you insist upon sticking to the truth, lass, we can always make it so!"

He was mocking her! Her face flushed and she gave him an indignant look.

"I am sorry," he sighed. "I realize that you are very young and that all this is a new experience for you. But I promise you that no one will give you offense—

you have my word on it. Indeed they will all envy me!"

"I cannot go out," she said, pouncing upon the first excuse offered. "For, as you can see, I have torn my dress and I do not have another." She fingered the tear in her bodice, a tear through which her worn chemise showed.

"Faith, that's easy mended," he said humorously. "I'll even find you a needle and thread."

Lorraine looked dismayed. Somehow she had not imagined that this tall fellow would have such commonplace equipment about.

He did not realize, she told herself, that her sudden shyness came not from expectation of insult, but from an unwillingness to meet the eyes of his men, knowing they *thought* her to be his mistress.

It would have to be faced eventually, of course, she realized—but she would postpone it as long as possible.

Her smile as she accepted the needle and thread from his strong hands was a trifle wan.

"I have a comb for you," he added. "And Johnny will bring you a bath."

"You couldn't find me some hairpins, could you, Raile?" she asked wistfully. "For I have lost all mine riding about the countryside!"

"I doubt it," he said. "But I'll ask about. Meanwhile you can tie your hair back with a scarf." He produced one of palest blue silk. "And when you've done, you can come out on deck and view my ship."

"Thank you, but I want to wash my hair and I'll just dry it in the sun here at the open windows."

"The deck is better, lass."

"Perhaps later."

"As you like. I'll leave you now. And later on, we'll fashion a hanging for your bunk so you can have more privacy." For it was not in Raile's mind to let odd rumors concerning their separate sleeping arrangements circulate about the ship. If hangings were put up, word would be spread that the captain's lady was modest. Whereas now, if through some emergency the door were to be flung open, it would be very plain that the bunk was occupied only by Lorraine, and that might lead to trouble.

"You are very good to me," she said gratefully, touching the comb he had given her.

Raile turned away, frowning. He was not sure whether "good" was exactly the way he wanted her to view him. He thought, as he made his way to the deck, dogs and children, parsons and kindly schoolmasters were "good"; plainly he did not cut a very dashing figure in her eyes!

Lorraine bathed slowly. Then she mended her dress and washed her long fair hair. She had hoped to be forgotten for a while, but Raile came back while she was drying her hair. He found her standing on a chair so that she might lean far out one of the stern windows and comb her wet tresses in the whipping sea breeze.

"Come away before you fall overboard!" he laughed, and when she shook her head at him, he strode over and scooped her up so swiftly that she almost lost the comb.

"Put me down!" she sputtered.

He gave her a look of derision, and with her still in his arms, moved toward the door.

"Oh, no, I don't want to—" she began, but they were already out on the deck before she could finish her protest.

And so in full sunlight Lorraine London made her appearance on the deck of the *Likely Lass*.

Raile put her down with some ceremony and waved an arm to MacTavish, who came over and joined them.

"Mistress Lorraine." The impassive Scot bowed slightly. "I trust you slept well?"

Remembering Raile's words, *MacTavish will know*, Lorraine gave the old Scotsman a clear, direct look from her dusky blue eyes. "I did, sir—I was not disturbed."

Raile's grin flashed. "Did I not tell you she'd look even better by daylight, Tav?"

"As pretty a sight as these eyes have gazed upon," agreed MacTavish soberly, taking in the flushed young girl with golden skeins of light tangled hair flying in the sun. But he looked worried when he glanced back at Raile.

At once, as if they had been waiting on cue for this moment, the ship's officers appeared, led by André L'Estraille, the ship's doctor, who executed a dazzlingly low bow despite the sudden roll of the ship.

"Your servant, *mademoiselle. Mon Dieu,* you shine like sunlight!" he exclaimed. "A veritable *princesse!*"

But Lorraine was not to be fooled by such jollity, *Rather I am the one who looks like a servant, and you the master of the house!* she thought wryly, for the splendor of his full-bottomed fawn-colored wig and scarlet satin coat heavily laced with gold braid almost overwhelmed her.

She returned him a low curtsy.

"Thank you," she said in as cool a voice as she could muster.

She nodded to the others and would have beat a hasty retreat had not Derry Cork's booming voice stayed her.

"Ah, 'tis the beauty!" he roared. "We've been watching for ye, colleen. Ye stayed long abed, Mistress Lorraine!" This was accompanied by a sly wink that brought color flooding into Lorraine's cheeks.

She had been about to make some excuse and flee to her cabin, but now she stood her ground and returned the big Irishman a haughty look.

"I was tired," she stated.

"Sure and I thought you were afraid of us," he suggested mischievously.

"I am afraid of nothing!" cried Lorraine, stung.

"Is that so, indeed?" Derry Cork grinned and cast a merry look at Raile. "Sure, we're eager to learn more about the brave colleen who could shoot the cap'n down in such a short engagement," he said shyly. "Perhaps ye'll favor us with your life story when we sup?"

Lorraine was furious at Raile who had catapulted her into this embarrassing situation. Well, she would just pay him back for all this humiliation—one lie was as good as another!

"I'm afraid dinner will have to wait," she said airily.

"For me at least. I expect to be taking my meals in our cabin, for I must look fresh and rested for our wedding."

"Wedding?" echoed Derry Cork, amazed, and the Frenchman leaned forward in fascination. Even Mac-Tavish's iron jaw dropped, while Jakob Helst stood bemused.

Lorraine gave them all a winsome smile. "Why, yes," she said. "We'd not time to be wed in Providence, with all my tall cousins in hot pursuit. We're going to have the words spoken over us on some likely island—aren't we, my sweet?" She turned to Raile, looking up at him with her lips parted in what seemed to the ship's officers tender anticipation.

Raile's expression was impenetrable. Shutters seemed to have slipped over his gray eyes, leaving them murky.

"We'll discuss it," he muttered.

"Yes, of course we will." Honey fairly dripped from Lorraine's voice. "I shall be in the cabin if you want me, my sweet. Gentlemen." Her curtsy included them all and she strolled away from them down the deck with an ever-so-slight swagger.

There, let him think about that, this fellow who was so anxious to make her appear to be his mistress! Let *him* assume the role of prospective bridegroom!

CHAPTER 10

RAILE FOLLOWED LORRAINE into the cabin and closed the door behind him with his foot. Lorraine was aware of his presence but she did not turn. Instead she crossed to the stern windows and stood before one of them, tossing back her still-damp hair to dry it.

"Mistress Lorraine." The captain's voice was stern, formal.

"Yes?" she threw the word indifferently over her shoulder.

"I think I should warn you, I'm not a marrying man."

Lorraine whirled about to face him at that. Her blue-gray eyes snapped with indignation. "Indeed you need not tell me that, sir. I'd already guessed! And besides," she added with spirit, "what makes you think I would have you?"

"What you said on deck just now," he answered reasonably enough.

"Oh, that!" Lorraine shrugged. "I have decided that I would prefer to be considered an overimpetuous betrothed rather than some chance strumpet you chose to bring back with you to while away the voyage!"

Raile grinned at that characterization. "Just so we understand each other, lass," he said easily. "I've managed to avoid the banns thus far. 'Tis my intention to go on avoiding them a little longer."

Lorraine sniffed and gave her long hair another toss. "You may avoid them all your life for all I care. I am but trying to arrange it so I can look these men in the face! After all, 'tis bad enough to come aboard looking like a serving wench!" She glanced down bitterly at her worn and shabby clothing. "But then to have them know that we're sharing a cabin—do you want them to consider me some lightskirt scullery maid on holiday?"

" 'Tis not my way to bring scullery maids aboard the *Lass*," Raile murmured, and from his inscrutable expression Lorraine could not know that he was thinking how very pretty she looked with that fiery expression lighting up her eyes. "Only beauties," he added with a chuckle and a narrow look.

"No doubt!" she scoffed. "There must have been dozens!" But she felt her face flame nonetheless.

"Oh, not so many as that, lass," he disclaimed lazily. "But what made you blush as you said that?"

What had made her blush had been the way he was looking at her. It was the same way Philip had looked at her, of course, only from Raile it seemed different, more compelling. For this tall fellow was more of a man than Philip would ever be.

"Well, now we can both act a part—I the blushing bride, you the eager bridegroom!"

"As you wish." He nodded. "I'll even play along with you and dine alone with you here in my cabin."

He had given in too easily, she thought. What deviltry was he planning?

"No need to change your habits," she said hastily. "You will no doubt want to continue dining with your officers. Johnny can bring me a bite and I don't mind eating alone."

His broad grin undermined her confidence. He stood squarely before her, a splendid fellow, broad-chested, calm. And with a wicked twinkle in his eye. "But such behavior would hardly become an—how did you put it?—an eager bridegroom, now, would it?"

Before Lorraine could form a proper answer, he walked to the cabin door and went out, leaving her to gaze after him apprehensively. She had thought to sting him with her words, for it had nettled her to be dragged summarily on deck for the inspection of his ship's officers, but he had been altogether too agreeable.

She flung herself down at the table, ignoring her still-damp hair, and sat leaning her elbows on the table's wooden top. Why had she done this? Why had she pretended to be Raile's affianced bride? What madness had come over her?

Lorraine was not the only one pondering her motives. Outside on deck, as he calmly accepted the congratulations of his ship's officers, Raile was wondering the same thing.

Only to MacTavish did he tell the truth, and that was when they were for a moment alone near the whipstaff, by which the ship was steered.

"You're not to believe the little lass, Tav," said Raile in a low voice. "There's no marriage intended."

"But you've already accepted my congratulations on it," answered the brawny Scot. "Faith, that's a singular thing to do if no wedding is intended!"

" 'Twas Lorraine's idea, for she does not want the men to consider her a light woman. 'Tis to achieve standing that she spun the yarn, Tav."

MacTavish shook his gray head with the wonderment of a man who would never understand women. "Has she no fondness for ye then, laddie?"

Raile was looking out to sea at that moment, watching the whitecaps of the waves foam and glisten in the sunlight. "No, I think she has none, Tav," he said softly. "But we'll keep her secret, for if aught should happen to me, I'd want you to see her set safe ashore."

"Aye, ye can count on me for that," said MacTavish. He looked curiously at the younger man. Raile's jaw was set, but for all that, his gray eyes revealed no expression at all as they swung around to encounter MacTavish. Still, the stern Scotsman who knew him of old thought there had been something wistful in the tall young captain's voice. Perhaps he was only remembering another woman and thinking on her, MacTavish told himself, for he was all too familiar with Raile Cameron's checkered past.

By evening Raile seemed to have forgotten Lorraine's outburst of the morning. Still his attitude had changed subtly. It was a debonair Scotsman, correctly dressed and wearing his boots, who presented himself at table.

Lorraine noted his festive garb and that he was wearing lace at his throat and cuffs and felt vaguely resentful that in her worn gown she could not match him.

"I would have changed my gown for dinner had I not left all that I own in Rhode Island," she said rather stiffly (ignoring the fact that the gown she had left behind was no better). "Indeed I have managed to tear this flimsy fabric again." She indicated her sleeve, which had caught on a nail in the cabin wall not five minutes before. "I doubt I can mend it so that it will not show."

"Stand up," commanded Raile.

"What?"

"I said stand up so I can look at you." He sounded impatient.

Lorraine came to her feet and he looked her up and down coolly.

"You're a wee bit on the thin side, lass," he observed. "Didn't they feed you well at that tavern?"

"Not very," admitted Lorraine.

"Then you should eat more," he announced. "You only picked at your breakfast. Here, try this Indian porridge. We got the corn in Rhode Island so you should be familiar with it." He scooped out a large helping and piled it on her trencher.

"Not so much," protested Lorraine, sinking back to her seat.

He was still watching her narrowly from across the table as he broke apart a piece of rock-hard biscuit and demolished it with his strong teeth. Lorraine felt uneasy under that calm inspection but forced herself to eat—even the second helpings he insisted she have.

When they had finished their dinner and the table had been cleared, Raile, leaning back sipping his Madeira, said what was on his mind.

"Lass, if you had your choice of material for a new

gown," he asked her suddenly, "what would you choose?"

"Purple silk," said Lorraine instantly, for she had always envied Lavinia her "royal purple."

Raile laughed with a flash of white teeth. "I've something much better," he assured her. "Something that will bring out the blue of your eyes."

Going to the smaller of the two chests, he rummaged about until he dragged out an enormous piece of sky-blue silk with a handsome *fleur-de-lis* embroidered in gold thread in the center. Edged in gold and sporting gold tassels, the whole thing was lined with dusky blue-gray satin that had a rippling silvery shimmer as he picked it up and carried it over to her.

"Could you not make do with this?" he asked.

Lorraine stared at the beautiful undulating material resting in his arms but she did not reach out to touch it.

"It looks like . . ." she began, and stopped.

"You're right," Raile told her amiably. " 'Tis a funeral pall, meant to be draped over a coffin. Handsome piece of goods, isn't it?"

Lorraine was familiar with such palls. She had seen them draped over the tops of peaked coffins and spreading down over the shoulders and waists of the black-clad men who struggled along carrying those coffins. But the palls she had seen in Rhode Island had been of plain gray or brown stuff edged in black braid— meager and dull compared to this. She remembered her mother telling her that in England every parish had two or three palls that they rented out for such occasions, but that aristocratic county families, such as her mother's, had their own—in their case a gorgeous red velvet one edged with black Italian silk.

"But wouldn't it be wrong?" she asked, troubled, for they must have this pall on shipboard for *some* reason—she shuddered to think what.

"Oh, this pall has never been used over a coffin, nor ever will be," Raile assured her coolly. He pushed aside his glass and draped the material over the table where Lorraine could view it better. "Jacques Le Loup, who sailed with me—we called him Jocko the Wolf— had this cloth made up for himself in Jamaica. 'Tis

Italian silk and French satin. Jocko bought the fabric from the buccaneer market on the waterfront and had it embroidered with the lilies of France by an English wench in Port Royal."

So the pall had a romantic past. Lorraine continued to stare at it, feeling both attracted and repelled.

"Whenever he got drunk—which was often—Jocko would laugh and toss this cloth into the air and catch it and roar that even if he couldn't live a Frenchman he'd die a Frenchman—he'd been run out of Paris for debt, you see. Anyway, he'd carry the thing ashore with him for his drinking parties and fight anyone who touched it—and I'd have to have both him and his pall carried back aboard when he got too drunk to walk."

"But won't he mind, this Jacques?" she wondered, looking longingly at the beautiful material.

"Not Jocko."

At the finality of his tone, Lorraine looked up sharply. "What happened to him?"

Raile's face had sobered. "He got drunk one last time and fell overboard in Bordeaux harbor. Drowned in deep water before anyone could save him."

"But how could that happen?" cried Lorraine. "He was a sailor, he must have been able to swim!"

Raile grimaced. "He could not, unfortunately." Then Raile went on to explain the circumstances.

"Our ship's doctor had left us at Plymouth, you see. The other doctors roundabout had declined to join us, but Jocko boasted that he would find us another. He ran across André L'Estraille in Bordeaux the very day he died. They were old friends and Jocko got me to sign André on. Then Jocko was so exuberant about sailing with his old friend that he took André on a tour of the waterfront taverns. They were still on their feet when they came aboard, but just barely. Cook was making some coffee, hoping to sober them up, when Jocko suddenly gave a whoop and cried. 'Look at that! 'Tis her face! I've found her at last!' He leaned far out over the rail and with a howl he fell over. Three of us leapt in to save him but the harbor water was dark and foul and we couldn't find him. He never surfaced. We had to give it up."

"What do you think he saw in the water?" asked Lorraine, awed.

"Visions," said Raile, frowning. "He'd been in love with a girl in Alsace. She was frail and had died long ago, coughing her life away while Jocko watched and agonized. He never forgot her. And when he was drunk he always thought he saw her face—in tree branches, in the patterns of the clouds, in the depths of the sea, in the murky light of waterfront taverns."

"He was always faithful to her?" Lorraine asked, charmed.

Raile's eyebrows elevated. "Oh, I didn't say that," he corrected her in a cool voice. "Jocko chased every skirt in sight—and when he was hot on the scent he could see them around corners! But when he was very drunk," he added softly, "he remembered only one."

Lorraine gave the captain an uncertain look. She had imagined Jocko's frail but lasting love gathering him into her arms at last—albeit a cold and watery embrace—but Raile's comment had blasted that romantic illusion.

"And so you kept this square of cloth," she mused. "In memory of your friend?"

"Yes." He nodded. "I was of a mind to carry the pall out to sea and send it floating away upon the waves in memory of Jocko, but it slipped my mind and now I'm glad I didn't. Even more than he loved the bottle, Jocko loved the ladies—he'd be honored to have you wear it. Indeed, were Jocko alive, he'd have offered it to you himself. So if you think you could manage to make a new gown out of it . . . ?" He was watching her keenly.

"Oh, I think I can manage," Lorraine assured him hastily. With great care she gathered the shimmering material to her. How soft and silky it was to the touch! Oh, how often she had dreamed of having a dress made of fabric as fine as this!

She rose and held it up to her body, looking down and considering critically how she would fashion her new gown. She stood awhile studying it, absorbed. When she looked up at Raile at last her eyes were shining.

"Thank you," she said shyly.

Raile shrugged. "Thank Jocko," he said.

"I thank you both."

From that moment on, making her new dress became an all-consuming passion with Lorraine. She had inherited her mother's sense of style, but though clever with a needle, she was out of practice, for Oddsbud's wife had given her no time to sew. Carefully she cut the cloth, praying she would not make a mistake and ruin it all. Johnny Sears came around to admire her handiwork and stared at it round-eyed. She might consider herself out of practice and awkward, but to him Lorraine seemed astonishingly deft.

"You're to tell no one what I'm doing, Johnny," she cautioned the lad, waving her needle to emphasize her words. "I want it to be a surprise when I come out of the cabin wearing this dress."

Johnny promised. He had formed a childlike attachment for Lorraine and would have done anything she asked of him without a murmur.

After her second day of straining her eyes in the cabin over her fine stitches, Raile ordered her summarily out on deck. "You need sun, lass," he said bluntly. "And air. If we run into a squall, you'll find yourself cooped up inside long enough!"

"But I want to finish this!" she protested.

But her captain was unyielding.

"After you've spent a while on deck, you can go back to it," he told her, and held open the cabin door. "Unless you wish me to carry you out again?"

Lorraine rose to her feet with alacrity. She had no desire to repeat *that* performance!

Out on deck she realized it felt good to be standing in the sun flexing her cramped shoulders. It felt good to have the wind tangling her hair and cooling her cheeks and blowing her skirts about. It was a beautiful day. The *Lass* was sailing along beneath a sky of cloudless blue. There were men scrambling about aloft, a barefoot sailor was whistling off key as he swabbed the deck, and the wind sang its wild song through the rigging.

Raile left her looking out to larboard and went to

consult with MacTavish over some matter. Leaning lazily on the rail, dazzled by the sea's glitter, she decided that she was glad Raile had come to get her, for it was indeed a glorious day.

After a while she felt eyes watching her. They seemed to bore through her back.

She swung around, but there was nobody there. Just Raile and MacTavish, and the men scrambling in the rigging. In the distance, near the prow, Helst and the ship's doctor argued over some small matter. Still the uneasy feeling persisted. She felt it as she walked restlessly about the deck, a kind of prickly feeling that told her all was not well.

She forced herself to stay on deck, hoping to spot her watcher and covertly studying the ship's officers as they came and went. Derry Cork might be a giant, but there was a steadiness in his green gaze. And the Dutchman, Jakob Helst, might look like a blond, blue-eyed cutthroat, but his smile on her was friendly and open. MacTavish she would have trusted with her life. And André L'Estraille—well, perhaps with her life, but not with her virtue! Not a man among them that she would have been afraid to meet alone.

And yet she could feel it rippling along her spine. *She was being watched.*

At last she gave up her fruitless search for the watcher and strolled back to her cabin.

Although she said nothing about it, the incident had clouded her day and she was still troubled by it when Raile joined her for supper. It made her more silent than usual.

She took a small bite of the fish one of the men had caught to vary their monotonous ship's diet, and sighed.

"Are you not feeling well?" asked Raile with a sudden frown, for to him Lorraine looked a little wan.

"Oh, no, I'm very well," she assured him.

"But your needlework goes slowly?" he guessed on a note of sympathy.

Lorraine laughed and shook her head. After working on her new gown for several hours yesterday, she had found herself getting back her skill.

"Perhaps you are tired? . . . No? Then we will stroll

about the deck after supper. Soon we will be in waters to see flying fish. Who knows, we may see one tonight!''

The stars were out when they walked, and the ship scarcely rolled, seeming to glide mysteriously over a glassy phosphorescent sea. The night seemed to close them in and the breeze was scarce a sigh through the rigging.

"A windless night," he commented. "Soon we will be in more southern waters."

Southern waters . . . it had a lovely sound. And it was lovely standing there beside her tall captain in the starlight, feeling the broadcloth of his coat brush her arm—for, hot or not, he had worn it to please her. Lovely to look down at his fine hand resting lightly on the rail and see the white lace spilling over it—in her honor. And yet his clothes, she realized, did not really matter so much, for it was the man who made the clothes—his sinewy body overwhelmed them, shaped them. Indeed she felt he would cut a dashing figure in whatever he wore!

And yet it was far more than Raile's strong masculinity that appealed to her. She cherished his kindness, his unfailing gallantry toward her, that warm, protected feeling that swept over her whenever he came near.

I think I'm falling in love with him, she thought dreamily—and jerked herself up short.

She had fallen in love with Philip, who had never had any intention of marrying her, who had only wanted her virginity—on a wager! And now she was falling in love with this smuggler who had told her brusquely he was "not the marrying kind."

She must guard herself well for she knew this tooattractive captain wanted her—and he was not going to have her on his terms! She did not want another affair that would be gone like smoke.

Still, the night was treacherous—and soft.

She knew she should go in, away from him. But she could not bring herself to do it. The lure of the night, of the man, was too strong.

"Lorraine . . ." His voice was caressing and he bent his dark head down toward her own fair one.

Sternly she warned herself that he would take her, love her—and one day he would leave her to mourn. She knew that! She with her hard-won recent knowledge about men!

But he was so close and the soft night air was filled with tender magic. It lulled her. As he bent down, involuntarily she swayed toward him. In the stillness of the night their lips would meet . . . and meld . . . He would whisper words he did not mean and she would respond with senses swirling. For long exultant moments she would tremble against his breast, all her defenses flown away into the night.

And after that he would bear her away to his cabin and they would share—really share—that bunk of his for the very first time. Passionately.

She knew it, *she knew it!*

The world seemed to wheel about slowly, she was almost in his arms, nothing could stop it now.

But something did.

Abruptly a sultry flash of green lightning rent the sky. Sea and sky became momentarily a vivid fleeting green. Thunder rolled ominously and Lorraine jumped back as if the lightning had flashed a warning to her personally.

"What is it, lass?" Raile asked huskily. His hand had been about to slip behind her, to fit against the small of her back. His lips had been so near, so close to her own softly parted ones. And yet . . . He saw how pale she had suddenly become, and . . . Did he imagine it? Was that real terror—no, perhaps it was just anxiety—in her eyes?

"That . . . the flash of green . . ." she muttered, confused, and leaned away from him.

Raile tried to reassure her. His hand crept behind her head, cradling it. " 'Tis but a lightning flash, and I'll wager the storm will go around us. Anyway, the *Lass* is a stout craft, as I've good reason to know."

But the moment was broken, the magic departed. Lorraine pulled away from him.

"It . . . it wasn't that," she murmured, and memories were flooding back to her as she spoke.

"What, then?" he demanded.

"It was the color—green," she admitted diffidently.

"So?" He shrugged. "I've seen pink lightning, lavender, yellow—all shades."

"No, it was something my mother told me once." Lorraine's mother had spoken of it but once, and perhaps later regretted it—but her comments had made an indelible impression on Lorraine.

Back in Rhode Island on a winter's night, her father, Jonas London, was out chopping dry kindling in the moonlight, for the fire had gone out and fires once extinguished were hard to relight. Young Lorraine and her mother were huddled near the cold hearth. Lorraine was stirring the ashes disconsolately with a poker, trying to revive a spark. Her mother was attempting to sew with fingers gone stiff from the cold, straining her eyes to see her mending by the light of a single candle.

"Do you think I'll ever live in a fine house like the one you grew up in?" Lorraine had asked of her mother wistfully. "One where servants make the fires and mind them and never let them go out?"

Carefully the older woman had pushed her sewing aside and gone to stare out of the rude cabin's single window. Outside in a panorama of moon-drenched white, the Rhode Island countryside lay covered with a blanket of fresh-fallen snow, bridal white, and the icy trees were glistening against a night-blue sky.

"Lorraine," she said softly, "there is something I want to tell you, while Jonas is outside. Something I have been meaning to tell you for a very long time."

Caught by something portentous in her mother's tone, Lorraine had stood the poker against the hearth and sat down on a small three-legged stool, hugging her flannel skirts tight around her to keep warm. How frail her mother looked tonight, how thin. . . .

It was then her mother told her about the Green Flash.

"It is something that happens—oh, so rarely! But sometimes just as the sun is setting, all the light seems to break apart and there is this wondrous flash of green that turns the sky to emerald. It foretells the future, Lorraine, for if the Green Flash should chance to light the sky when you are with an admirer, it is that man and no other whom you will love for the rest of your days."

"Why did you tell me about it now?" wondered Lorraine.

Her mother had been looking out the window as she spoke, watching Jonas chop wood in the snow. Now she turned and faced her daughter. Her voice was stern.

"Because I saw how you looked at young Philip Dedwinton today, Lorraine."

Lorraine had flushed bright red and had looked down at the floor in confusion. She had loved Philip forever, but she hadn't known it *showed!*

"He will offer for you, Lorraine, I am sure of it. When you are a little older. But don't marry him. Wait."

"Why?" The words were wrenched from Lorraine.

"Because he's not good enough for you." She sighed at Lorraine's discomfiture. "Wait for the Green Flash." She turned back toward the window and the falling snow. "I . . . I tell you this now, Lorraine, because I may not be there when it happens."

It was the first warning Lorraine was to have that her mother felt her life might be drawing to a close—and in the tumult of her thoughts about Philip, she missed that warning.

But her mother's voice had caught on her last words, and Lorraine, uneasy in the presence of such great emotion—and wanting desperately to change the subject—asked in a small voice, "Did you . . . did you see the Green Flash with Father?"

"Yes." Her mother nodded and dabbed at her eyes. "I had run down to the beach to meet him. I was peering about among the rocks as I ran, wondering where he could be—for I could not see him. I was looking for him and not at the sand beneath my feet. I tripped over a length of seaweed and would have fallen full-length on the sand had he not appeared suddenly and leapt forward to catch me. He lifted me up and there was a light in his eyes I shall never forget. . . ." She paused, reliving those magic moments when the air had whirred with the sound of wings and the waves beating against the age-old rocks had thrummed a throaty distant love song. When she spoke again, her voice was husky. "And just at that moment—while he was holding me in his arms—the sky seemed to burst apart into a flash of vivid green that took my very breath away. It was then I knew." She turned and looked at her daughter very steadily. "It was then I knew that your father was the man for me and that I would always love him."

Lorraine thought of her father, who had let the fire go out, and of all the difficult times, the hard life this man of her mother's choice had given her, and for a treacherous moment she wondered if her mother might not have been better off with someone else.

As if she had caught her thought, her mother said slowly, "Perhaps you will see the Green Flash one day, Lorraine. Then you will know what I mean."

Then, with the coming of spring, her mother was gone.

And now the snows of Rhode Island were far away and melted, and moss was growing on her mother's headstone. The man her mother had loved too well was gone too, lost in some uncharted wilderness. All their fortunes scattered to the winds. . . .

But just now there had been all that vivid green in the sky—and the Green Flash at sunset, her mother had insisted, was the harbinger of a great and lasting love.

It wasn't sunset, of course. It was already quite dark, the moon was out. And the flash had been a flash of green lightning on the water. Or was it? Was this perhaps another form of the fabled Green Flash her mother had told her about?

"You see," Raile told her patiently. "There's no more lightning. The storm is going around."

But the storm I feel in my heart isn't. . . . Perhaps I have been swept here by design, perhaps I was meant to belong to you and you to me. . . .

It was a troubling thought.

She stared at him, distraught. She had been about to make a terrible mistake! A casual affair wasn't what she wanted. That wasn't good enough. With her it was going to be all or nothing. No matter how damnably attractive the man was.

"It's very late," she muttered, and turned softly away from him, heading for the cabin and safety.

Raile watched her go. Fleetingly a sad expression crossed his strong features.

He thought she did not care for him.

CHAPTER 11

The Lady of the Lilies

RAILE DID NOT come back to the cabin until after Lorraine was asleep. The next morning he was gone before she waked, and to her surprise, did not come back to share her breakfast.

"Where is the captain?" she asked Johnny Sears as she sat down at the table.

But the cabin boy only shrugged. He seemed anxious to get away. Lorraine did not deter him.

She ate her breakfast feeling perplexed, for Raile had made it a point to breakfast with her, bounding into the cabin exuding masculine vitality. Without him breakfast was a lonely meal. Ah, well. . . . She told herself he must be occupied with ship matters, and after breakfast sat down determinedly to her sewing, for this was to be the gown of her life!

She sewed all day, making good progress, and was looking forward to showing the results to Raile when he arrived at dinner. So it was really upsetting when Johnny Sears brought her dinner along with a message that the captain would be dining with his officers and sent her his compliments.

"He sends me his compliments!" she repeated, amazed. "Is something important happening, then, Johnny?"

"Not as I know," mumbled the lad.

"Oh, come now, Johnny, you always know everything!"

140

But he was not to be cajoled. He served her and fled, leaving her to poke at her food.

She went out on deck for a few moments after she had finished her dinner and heard sounds of roistering coming from the room where the ship's officers ate. Ah, that was it! Some celebration, no doubt—perhaps of somebody's birthday. Satisfied, she turned her heel and went back inside.

But when Raile did not show up for breakfast next day and later sent her "his compliments" again instead of his presence at dinner, there could be no doubt.

He was avoiding her!

Bent over her needlework, Lorraine considered that. She frowned down at the lovely, slippery cloth. Surely there could be no reason— She gave an irritated gasp as she stuck her finger with the needle and drew blood, put the finger in her mouth, and continued to puzzle.

Had she mistaken the hot look in his eyes? Was he really not much interested after all? Was it only compassion that had driven him to help her to escape in Rhode Island? When he did not show up the next day, she was forced to take action.

"Johnny," she told the cabin boy when he again brought her her dinner and the "captain's compliments," "will you please tell the captain that I will be joining the gentlemen for dinner tomorrow night? I will be wearing my new gown and I would like him to escort me."

If the cabin boy looked a little surprised, at least he made no comment. When he came back to clear the dishes, he told her that the captain would be delighted to escort her.

Will he indeed? thought Lorraine tartly. *Then why did he not come to tell me himself? One would think this was some towering galleon instead of a small craft where he could be at best but a short walk away!*

She set about her sewing again with a vengeance, for she must be ready when he came—indeed she had hardly stirred from her task these last three days!

When she had quite finished, when the last stitch

was taken and the thread bitten off, she shook out the dress and tried it on at last.

The dress *felt* right. The full sleeves seemed to be puffed out the same amount on each side, the bodice smooth, the hem even, the neckline . . . Well, it was a bit low, but she had designed it that way. Still, how could she be sure the gown was right from every angle? She wished again for a mirror, but that was something the ship did not possess. Raile scraped his face clean with a razor with the skill that came of long practice; he did not use—or need—a mirror.

Still, when she heard his long step approaching the cabin door, she knew a moment of panic.

Oh, for a mirror!

He knocked once, then swung open the door and stood transfixed.

Lorraine needed no mirror once she saw the look of approval in his eyes.

"You are bravely gowned indeed," he murmured, his keen gaze passing over her from head to foot.

Lorraine stood queenly and proud for him to observe her handiwork. She was flushed with pleasure that all her hard work should have turned out so well.

What Raile saw was heartbreakingly lovely—an aristocratic girl dressed for a ball in some manor house, not for dinner on a smuggler's ship. But if he sighed in his heart for her, he did not show it.

Lorraine knew that the taut blue silk of the bodice emphasized her tantalizingly tiny waist, but she could not realize how dramatically or how elegantly the wide rippling blue silk skirt moved with her slim hips as she swung about to display not only her silvery satin petticoat but the sweeping back of her gown.

Raile took down his coat, and as he dressed, she kept up a running flow of conversation.

"Do you think the dress really becomes me?" she worried.

Raile sighed. It became her far too well.

"It is not too short? The hem is not uneven, the seams skewed?"

"Perfect, I would say."

"Do you like the way I used the *fleur-de-lis* on the

bodice? I could have used it on the back of the skirt, you know."

She stood before him, graceful as a swaying flower in her sky-blue gown. Soberly Raile considered her back as he was tucking in his shirt.

"Such a beautiful back needs no decoration," he said slowly, observing the long shimmering hair which she had let cascade down.

Lorraine felt a little thrill go through her.

"I made these satin rosettes for my shoes out of scraps of material that were left, and decorated them with gold tassels from the pall." She turned around and lifted her skirts so that he might view her transformed workaday shoes, giving him a glimpse of her slim ankles as well. As he inspected the shoes, she wished fervently that her legs were not encased in much-mended cotton stockings but in elegant silk stockings like Lavinia Todd's!

"Excellent," he said, and shrugging into his coat, he proffered her his arm. "You will astonish all comers!"

Lorraine took his arm. "Do you really think so?" She looked up at him anxiously. "I *do* want your ship's officers to approve of me."

Raile hid his amusement as he escorted this wonder from the cabin onto the deck. "There is little fear that they will not," he murmured. "Indeed they will be overjoyed that you have at last decided to honor them with your presence."

"Oh . . . you mean they have *expected* me to dine with them?" she said, a little unnerved.

"Rather let us say they hoped you would," he amended gravely, swinging open the door of the officers' mess and escorting her inside.

Lorraine had steeled herself for this moment, for they were standing about talking—and to a man they turned and gaped at the sight of her. Their combined gaze seemed to focus on the gold embroidered *fleur-de-lis* on her bodice.

"Begorra, if it isn't Jocko's coffin cloth!" cried Derry Cork, his green eyes bulging.

Lorraine winced. It had been too much to hope that

the cloth would not be recognized, but she *had* hoped that no one would say anything! It was a tricky moment and she drew in her breath, afraid they would laugh at her. Or perhaps disapprove. And she found herself suddenly very much desiring to win the approval of these men.

She need not have worried. Raile carried the day with aplomb.

"Aye, Jocko's," he agreed. "But ye'll agree with me, gentleman, that Jocko would never have looked half so good in it!"

A roar of laughter greeted his remark and a general flurry of friendly comment. Before it had ended, their glasses were filled and André L'Estraille had lifted his in the air.

"To the gorgeous *demoiselle* in her *fleur-de-lis* gown!" he cried, his sparkling amber eyes devouring the sight of her. "To the Lady of the Lilies—French in gown and French at heart!"

"To the English flower," corrected one of the English officers with a reproving look at this impudent Frenchman.

"To the lassie with eyes as blue as heather," intoned MacTavish surprisingly in his deep bass voice.

"To a brave colleen!" boomed Derry Cork, striking his fist upon the table for emphasis.

"To the *jufvrouw* with hair paler than the Rheingold!" joined in Jakob Helst, waving his glass.

"To the American beauty," said Raile softly, his gray eyes glinting across the rim of his glass. "Found on Rhode Island's shores. . . ."

"To *la belle* Lorraine! May her skies always be as blue as her gown!" the doctor insisted.

Amid a masculine chorus of "Aye!" Lorraine found herself blushing.

Finally Raile stopped them with, "Enough of toasting! A man must eat and we'll all be too drunk to do it if we don't take our eyes off the lass!"

Lorraine gave him a relieved smile of thanks for ending the toasts. He met her gaze squarely, lifting his glass to her in a mock salute.

Lorraine felt her color rising and quickly addressed

herself to her food, scarcely looking up until the meal was half over.

She paid little attention to Derry Cork, who had managed to wedge himself in beside her when she sat down; she only edged slightly away from him when he got too close.

Across the table she saw Raile observing Derry with a stern eye. The Irishman seemed not to notice. She turned away to respond to a rather stiff compliment from the Englishman on her right.

Derry Cork was making some sly comment about her being so brave a colleen, would she not care to go and help him fire off one of his guns? Ah, she could shoot the waves to pieces, she could! And it was not so difficult to fire a piece—indeed she could watch him and then have a go at it herself.

Lorraine was saved from responding to the idea of her personally firing one of the ship's brass cannon when Raile's voice cut in from across the table. "We'll not be firing the guns for Mistress Lorraine's edification, Derry. There's no need to announce our presence on these seas to those who haven't yet seen us."

"Is there no way to test your bravery then, colleen?" Derry Cork teased her. He sighed and, draining his blackjack tankard, set it down too near the edge of the table, where his arm promptly knocked it off onto the floor.

Lorraine saw the tankard falling and pulled away, hoping her lovely new skirts would not be stained. Derry had dived to the floor, scurrying to regain his tankard. As he rose and banged the tankard back upon the table with his left hand, Lorraine had the errie feeling of a tug at her garter and having her skirts dragged up a little. Something touched her bare skin and she jumped. She was about to turn and give Derry Cork an indignant look for reaching under her dress, when she realized that what she felt was not a man's fingers giving her leg a surreptitious caress, but something furry, little claws—and then abruptly as her skirts shifted, sharp little teeth brushing her bare thigh.

Lord, a rat must have run up her skirts! With a

scream, she staggered backward and, throwing her skirts up into the air, tried to rid herself of the thing. She screamed again as the little creature's furry body thumped against her leg.

Hardly had Lorraine opened her mouth to shriek than Raile had knocked over his chair in his haste to come around the table. Every member of the company had surged to his feet by now and Derry Cork was leaning on the table laughing uproariously.

Peering down below her raised skirts as she pivoted, Lorraine saw to her horror that the rat's tail had been forced under her garter—no wonder she could not rid herself of the creature, it was attached to her!

She whirled about, kicking her leg outward to rid herself of the small beast while the company watched appreciatively as her pretty legs seemed to appear and disappear beneath her skirts, but Raile, after one look at the dead rat, reached down in exasperation and tore it free.

"Damn you, Derry, any more of your tricks and I'll—"

"I but wanted to test the courage of your brave colleen!" gasped Derry between guffaws.

"Let's test yours instead!" Raile's hard fist collided with Derry Cork's jaw with a force that sent the big Irishman sprawling into the corner with a surprised look on his face.

"Ah, now, Cap'n!" cried Cork, aggrieved. He scrambled nimbly to his feet as his wrathful captain bore down upon him. "I meant the little colleen no harm—ye know that!"

Raile came to a stop and his teeth came together with an audible snap. "You try me sorely," he muttered, and turned abruptly to Lorraine, whose skirts were decently lowered now. "Are you hurt?"

"No." But she was shaking all the same.

"Allow me to escort you to your cabin," he said, and formally offered her his arm.

Lorraine took the arm thankfully and let him bear her away.

She was still trembling when they reached the cabin, and she turned upon him defiantly. "I'm not going to be set upon and made sport of!" Her voice shook. "I had enough of that at the Light Horse Tavern!"

Raile gave her a look of sympathy. He reached out an arm to give her a commiserating pat but she flinched away from it. He sighed and ran a hand through his dark hair. "Derry meant you no harm, lass. He's a rough fellow, a prankster by nature, but now that I've stretched him across the floor for it, he'll mend his ways where you're concerned."

"I should hope so!" Lorraine shuddered, for she could still feel the touch of the rat's fur and the sudden contact with his sharp little teeth.

"I knew it would be difficult having a woman aboard," muttered Raile.

"Yes!" She was almost in tears. "For you've no control of your men!" she flung at him. "In a proper ship, this would never have happened!"

A baffled look crossed his strong countenance. "I swear to you, lass, that the next man who gives you offense will cross blades with me!" He patted his sword's basket hilt meaningfully.

That was not what she wanted—more fighting. She wanted to be treated as a lady.

"I will never sit down at table with Derry Cork again!" she declared bitterly.

"Ah, but you must," Raile's voice was steely. "For you must not let him think you're afraid of him. He takes a small boy's pleasure in practical jokes and you must not become the butt of them, for I've no wish to kill him."

She looked up. "Kill him?" she faltered.

"Just so. I'll seat you between myself and our ship's doctor next time. L'Estraille knows how to behave toward a lady. I promise you, you won't find any more dead rats up your skirts."

Lorraine tried not to show how shocked she was. The easy violence of this way of life appalled her, and yet Raile was only defending her, as he saw it. She told herself she must be very careful not to precipitate trouble; she did not want anyone's death on her conscience!

"They're rough men, lass, but most of them have

the sense to recognize a lady when they see one. Derry's a bit slow, but by now he'll have learned—the others will be having a word with him."

She looked up uneasily. "Fighting?"

He shrugged. "Discussing it," he said shortly. He gave her a wry look. "Perhaps they are teaching him manners—and saving me the trouble."

Lorraine sniffed.

The next morning found Derry Cork still fingering his jaw and casting sidewise glances at his captain. Raile ignored him, escorting his lady about the deck with much ceremony. Lorraine went along docilely enough. She understood that Raile was—by example—explaining her status on this vessel and demonstrating how a lady should be treated.

She resisted the idea of dining with the officers the next night but Raile was firm. "My officers have planned something for you," he explained. And in answer to her wary look, "Something you'll like."

Still, even leaning on Raile's arm and trying to look as if nothing could disturb her, it took some courage to go in to dinner and face them all again.

The faces ranged about her were grave and courteous. Anxious to please. Raile made a point of seating Lorraine between himself and the ship's doctor. Derry Cork was subdued and conversation was strained.

MacTavish finally broke the ice.

"D'you dance, lassie?" he asked bluntly.

Lorraine gave him an astonished look. If he had asked her if she used warpaint to color her cheeks blue, she could not have been more surprised.

"Yes . . . I dance," she answered tentatively.

"I have only my pipes," sighed the Scotsman. "And whether you and the laddie here"—he nodded at Raile—"can tread a measure to them on a swaying deck, I'll not be knowing. But I've a mind to play my pipes for a while this evening."

"That . . . would be wonderful," said Lorraine, round-eyed.

Raile was smiling at her. "I'm a bit rusty, but I'll lead you out upon the floor," he told her gallantly.

"I claim the honor of the second dance!" cried the Frenchman exuberantly. "I'll teach you all the latest steps they're dancing in Paris!"

She guessed that in their way they were trying to make amends for the fright she had been given at the table the night before.

Around her the company relaxed and talk became general. Cook had outdone himself. One of the crew had caught several enormous fish today and one was brought in roasted whole on a pewter charger of such size that Johnny Sears, who served it, grinning, seemed to sag under his burden.

There was a round of applause at sight of the fish and they all fell to, drinking and laughing and eating the catch of the day along with flavourful Indian porridge and the more usual onions and beans and mellow golden cheese. Lorraine relaxed too, laughing at the French doctor's witticisms. To her surprise, she found herself enjoying the company of these men, listening to wild tales (told with some exaggeration for her benefit) of their exploits in exotic places. Before the meal was over, she too was chiming in, repeating stories she had heard in Rhode Island of wild escapes from Indian encampments and other frontier adventures.

Raile, she observed, was smiling at her.

Lorraine had never thought to play hostess to men like these, dangerous men culled from the corners of the earth. But if rough men were to be her portion, she would learn to master them too!

"Mistress Lorraine," Raile said. "It is time for dancing."

"Oh," she said. "Oh . . . yes, of course."

Out upon the deck they went and MacTavish tuned up his bagpipes. Lorraine thought the noise quite hideous, wheezing and howling. But as the ship's company, who had gathered silently about in the background, began to stamp their feet in time, she came alive to the spirit of the music, which had echoed off the crags and down the glens of Scotland, calling the Scots to frolic and to war.

Raile took Lorraine's hand and led her out "upon

the floor" while his lounging officers watched. He taught her a spirited highland fling and she was quite breathless when André L'Estraille stepped forward, gave her a wondrously deep bow, and called out to MacTavish to "Pipe us something with a French sound to it!"

MacTavish tried his best. His wailing efforts on the wheezing pipes sounded distinctly strange and would have made Paris shudder, but it was French steps nonetheless that the ship's French doctor taught her to dance to the wailing music of the bagpipes. Lorraine found herself moving with natural grace beneath the Frenchman's expert tutelage. They danced twice more so that she could "conquer the steps," as he airily put it, and then she was claimed by the agile ruddy-faced Dutchman, Jakob Helst, who whirled her about, and in turn by the other officers.

When she finally waved them away, breathless, and Raile murmured in her ear, "You'll not need my protection now, lass—you've won them for yourself," Lorraine felt ridiculously proud of her accomplishment.

That night, after they had retired to his cabin, Raile rummaged in his sea chest, tossing things out upon the floor until he found a small gold locket on a delicate gold chain.

"A medal for valor," he said with a grin, handing it to her. "It took some courage to cavort about the deck to MacTavish's pipes, but you took it all in good part and made friends tonight, lass."

She felt close to him suddenly, as if she had known him always, and her hand shook a little as she took the locket.

"Thank you," she said softly.

He was smiling at her in an intimate way and when he moved to clasp the locket around her neck she jumped at his touch.

"Oh, did I catch your hair in the clasp?" he asked, noting her sudden start.

"No," she replied in a smothered voice. She was sure his next move would be to kiss her, for she could feel his breath against her neck—and she did not want him to. Searching for a way to divert him, her gaze fell

upon an object that had rolled out from the tumble of
things Raile had left on the floor as he searched the
contents of the chest for the locket.

"What are you doing with that?" she asked, pulling
quickly away from him.

"With what? Oh, this?" He followed her gaze,
reached down, and picked up the object. It appeared
to be some sort of root, hard and translucent. "This is
ginseng." He proffered it for her inspection but she
shook her head and refused to take it from his hand.
"Have you never seen ginseng before?"

"I have indeed," she said in a tight voice.

He looked down at the piece of root in his hand,
held it up, and sniffed. "Very aromatic. This ginseng
belonged to Jocko. He'd given it to me for safekeeping and I've never known what to do with it."

"I'd get rid of it," she said with a sudden vehe-
mence. "I'd throw it overboard!"

Raile's dark brows lifted. "Expensive food for fishes,"
he murmured. "And why would you do that, lass?"
He was looking at her curiously.

It was all tied in with her mother's dying—but Lorraine didn't intend to tell Raile that. She might break
into tears! Still, the unbidden memories flooded
back. . . .

Somehow her mother had got hold of some money.
From England, she had said vaguely, a small bequest
from a distant relative who had died. It was in the
spring after a snowy winter—and it was to prove to be
the last winter of Araminta London's life.

Lorraine had been there when Araminta had offered the money to Jonas. "There," she had told him
with a sigh. "Now we can pay our debts."

Jonas had made a strangled sound in his throat, and
Lorraine guessed that his pride was hurt that he could
not pay his own debts. But he took the money without
a word and stalked out. He had come back excitedly
some hours later, and Araminta, who was darning
stockings, looked up and at his expression dropped
her thimble.

"What is it?" she whispered. "What have you done,
Jonas?"

"You must have made our creditors happy, at least," said Lorraine cheerfully. She was hoping there'd be enough money left over for a new dress.

"Well . . . not just yet," he admitted. "They'll have to wait awhile longer. You see, there was this wonderful opportunity—"

"What do you mean, Jonas?" Araminta's voice cut in, grown suddenly shrill with apprehension.

His chest expanded. "I've invested the money in a venture," he told them grandly, and now Araminta, aghast, could see that he had been drinking as well. "I've packed off enough ginseng to China in the care of Benjamin Nicholls to make us rich. It will pay back a hundredfold on the investment, Nicholls is sure of it!"

"Oh God!" moaned her mother, and her face dropped into her hands as if she could bear no more.

After that Araminta's heath went downhill fast; her gallant heart was failing at last. Jonas was seldom home. He spent most of his time at taverns, drinking. And so Lorraine found herself alone the night her mother died. She would never forget Araminta's last disjointed words.

"Tell him, do tell him"—Araminta's weak voice had risen wildly—"that I still love him . . . as I did . . . the night of the Green Flash."

"I'll tell him," Lorraine promised huskily. She was still sitting there weeping when Jonas staggered in. Lorraine told him Araminta's dying words but they seemed not to move him. He stumbled out and she did not see him for three whole days, not even at the funeral, which was of the plainest sort, with a cheap peaked pine coffin. Lorraine was joined by a handful of neighbors, the only mourners for the brief ceremony performed in the drenching rain.

When Jonas finally came back, he was sober—and had news.

"I'm going west," he told Lorraine. "And since there's no one to take care of you, I've bound you over to the Mayfields."

Two blows falling at once! Lorraine had felt her

world cut out from under her feet. Even her freedom was gone!

And in her mind it had somehow got all mixed up with ginseng.

"Why would you do that, lass?" Raile repeated. "Why would you throw the root overboard?"

Lorraine stopped glaring down at the root and looked up.

"My father spent the last of our money buying up all he could of this root and shipping it off to China on a 'venture' in the care of someone named Nicholls." Her lip curled. "We never heard from either the 'venture' or Nicholls again!"

"Ah, but you might have," was his thoughtful comment. "This root is highly valued by the Chinese— they'll pay a fortune for it. Your father might have become rich from his 'venture.' "

"So he said." Lorraine's voice was resentful. Thinking back, it seemed to her that all the money her father had ever got his hands on he had squandered away on "ventures," as they called these efforts to send something overseas to be traded or sold. This strange-looking root reposing in Raile's hand was a symbol to her of all that was wrong with her life.

No doubt Raile "ventured" as well as smuggled! Somehow that made everything worse.

"My father," she said dully, "did not fare well in life. But if he has survived—as nobody believes—he will still be 'venturing' somewhere."

"Is that so terrible, lass?" he asked her softly.

"Yes! Yes, it *is* terrible—for it cost my mother her youth and her looks and her health." Lorraine's voice broke and she flung away from him. "Oh, do not talk to me about the past," she said. "And get that root out of my sight. I am grateful to you for the locket, but it . . . it must mean something to you, since you carry it about. I cannot accept it!" She began to struggle to unclasp it from around her neck.

"Wait, lass." There was sympathy in Raile's voice, for he was remembering his own unhappy boyhood.

His hands clasped over her own trembling ones. "Keep the locket. I assure you it means nothing to me. I won it in a game of cards in Bordeaux. The young fool who wagered it flung it down as a stake and stalked off when he lost."

"Then this"—Lorraine had given up trying to unclasp it and now her hands slipped from his and she opened the locket, peered down at it—"this woman whose picture is in it means nothing to you?"

The young face painted into the locket seemed to stare up at her accusingly. It was a challenging face; it belonged to a girl in a yellow dress with heather in her red-gold hair.

"Nothing at all," said Raile. His voice was wooden.

She held on to the locket uncertainly, staring up at him, trying to discern if he was telling the truth, but his gray eyes revealed nothing.

"I ask you to keep it," he said gently. "As a souvenir of this voyage. Surely even *your* thorny pride can have no quarrel with that, for it is a trinket only, and not very valuable."

As a souvenir of this voyage. . . . The words bit into Lorraine. They had a good-bye sound to them.

"I will keep it," she said tonelessly. "And wear it in the spirit in which it was given."

A trace of bitterness appeared around his mouth then. "By all means," he agreed. "Wear it in the spirit in which it was given." He looked away and then asked abruptly, "How do you like our ship's doctor?"

"André?" On that subject, at least, Lorraine could wax enthusiastic. "I think he's charming—and such a wonderful dancer! Did you notice how cleverly he moves his feet?"

"Yes," muttered Raile. "He is nimble as a monkey. I noted that you danced more than one dance with him."

"Oh, *yes!*" Lorraine's face had brightened, for she loved dancing. "But I fear I have not yet mastered the new steps he taught me. Do you think we can persuade MacTavish to play for us again tomorrow night?"

Raile looked away. "Yes, I think Tav might do it—if you ask him," he said, then went to the door and paused. "I'll away while you prepare for bed, Mistress Lorraine, and I'll knock to warn you when I return."

"I think you might call me Lorraine, since we're sharing a bedchamber," observed Lorraine, fingering her locket.

He gave her a long slow look. "Sharing it . . . Are we?"

And he left, leaving her to ponder over why he had said that.

CHAPTER 12

MORNING FOUND LORRAINE leaning against the fleet ketch's starboard rail, basking in the sun in her beautiful new gown. She had been standing there but a short time when once again she had the prickly sensation of being watched. She swung about to see the ship's doctor striding down the deck to join her, looking debonair as usual in the morning light.

"Ah, the beautiful *demoiselle!*" He greeted her with an elaborate bow, making a fine leg as he did so. " 'Tis hard to believe that you made that dress yourself. Faith, you've a talent with a needle! That gown puts all the Paris fashion dolls I've seen to shame!" He stood back and studied her critically.

"You give me too much credit, André," Lorraine demurred—for after last night's dancing they were on first-name terms. " 'Tis the fabric that makes the gown." But she could not help dimpling at such open admiration. She herself had never even seen one of the small French fashion dolls he spoke of, but she knew that they were shipped out of Paris in their finery so that their gowns could be copied full-size for the lucky women who could afford them.

"A fine dress indeed—'tis too bad ye've not a new chemise to match it!" The Frenchman smiled roguishly.

Lorraine gave him a reproving look, lifted her brows, and lightly flicked the worn ruffles of her chemise sleeves that spilled out from her elbows. She had no intention of discussing her intimate apparel with him, even if he *was* a superb dancer!

André L'Estraille seemed not to notice.

"Ah, would that we were in Paris!" He sighed. "Where we could replace these threadbare ruffles with Alençon lace—or *point de France!* I'd buy you a chemise so thin you could slip it through a keyhole!" That roguish smile again lit his handsome face and he cast a meaningful glance toward her cabin door as if to say: *That* keyhole!

"But we are not in Paris now, L'Estraille," came Raile's cool voice from over their heads. He swung down a ratline, landing lightly beside them on strong bare feet. He looked very fit, clad only in his trousers, with the muscles of his deep chest and sinewy shoulders rippling and gleaming bronze in the sunshine. Lorraine wondered suddenly if it could have been Raile's gaze she had felt upon her just now. No, it had not been the cool contemplation of those light gray eyes she had felt—it had been a more malevolent stare.

"I wish you would not drop from the skies into my conversations with Mademoiselle Lorraine," complained the Frenchman, looking aggrieved.

Raile laughed. "I'll thank you not to be bothering my lass with your keyhole chemises!"

André regarded his captain warily. "Ye'd cross swords over it?"

"I might." But the smile that went with the words was good-natured. "If I thought you'd gone too far with my lass here."

André's shoulders shrugged in a completely Gallic gesture. "The English have no *savoir faire.*" He sighed. "No *éclat.*"

"But they do have good eyesight and good hearing where their women are concerned," countered Raile in a warning voice.

Lorraine felt that this exchange had gone far enough. "I would speak to you in your . . . in our cabin, Raile," she said, touching his arm lightly.

With a grin at the discomfited Frenchman, Raile

strolled off after his hurrying lady to their cabin and closed the door.

"If you flirt with our ship's doctor," he warned, "you may come out the loser, for flirtation is his game."

"I wasn't flirting with him," said Lorraine frankly. "I felt someone watching me—I've had that feeling several times on deck—and I turned around to see if I could catch whoever it was. And there was André, striding down the deck toward me."

"L'Estraille watches all the pretty ladies," murmured Raile. "He was following one jauntily down the cobbles in Bordeaux when Jocko first introduced us."

"I . . . It wasn't like that," Lorraine admitted a trifle sheepishly. "I felt . . . well, *evil eyes upon me.* A menacing stare."

"Then it definitely wouldn't be L'Estraille," laughed Raile. "For he has naught in his heart but seduction!" For a moment he looked at her more keenly, this slip of a girl alone on a ship full of men. "I'll watch over you, lass," he murmured, and she lowered her eyes, all too aware of the sudden heat in his.

When she looked up, she found him studying the ruffles of her chemise. Although they spilled out fashionably from the elbows of her big slashed sleeves, they were so threadbare they looked about to disintegrate.

He thought a moment, then went over and opened the smaller of his two sea chests, bent over it. When he rose and turned, she saw that he had something white in his hand.

"See if you can make do with this, lass," he suggested crisply. "The fabric may not be quite thin enough to go through a keyhole, but perchance it will serve—it was given to me by a lady."

Make do with it! Lorraine stared down at the delicate snowflakelike white lace that was deeply set into the fine cambric handkerchief he had tossed to her. But this was Venetian rosepoint—she knew because her mother had had a scrap of it still when she was a child. She looked up at him, dazzled.

"Won't you . . . miss it?" she asked reluctantly, for she did not wish to rob him of a treasured keepsake.

"No—nor the lady either," he said with a rueful shake of his head. "For the last time I was in her home port, I learned she'd had the bad taste to marry somebody else."

"Oh, well," Lorraine said hastily. "In that case!" She took the delicate swatch of cambric and lace with delight—and spent the rest of the afternoon happily sewing pieces of the kerchief to her chemise sleeves so that when she appeared that night at dinner, the lace that dripped from her elbows caused André L'Estraille's brows to lift in amazement.

"Why, what miracle is this?" he cried, reaching out to touch the delicate lace gingerly, as if to assure himself it was indeed real.

"A miracle by a man who makes miracles happen!" laughed Lorraine, glancing merrily toward Raile.

For a moment the eyes of the two men met. Steel bit into copper.

André looked away and subsided. But during the meal he often cast a narrow look at Raile, as if measuring him.

The next morning a gusty wind was blowing as Lorraine stepped out on deck, and she had a hard time keeping her skirts down. From the stern she saw the ship's doctor strolling toward her. Suddenly after a wild blast of wind that took her skirts riding high, he stopped abruptly and focused, fascinated, on her legs. Lorraine reddened and bent almost double, clutching her skirts. When she looked up, he had gone.

The wind had died down when he came back, beaming.

"Ah, *mademoiselle!*" he hailed her blithely. "I have for you the one thing your costume requires!"

"You have hairpins, André?" she cried hopefully, for it was difficult to keep her hair tied back.

"To hold back that wondrous cloud of gold? *Mon Dieu,* no! Let it fly about! I have—these!" He held up the sheerest stockings she had ever beheld.

Lorraine had never owned a pair of silk stockings.

In Rhode Island, silk stockings were worn by the Lavinia Todds—not the Lorraine Londons!

"Oh, André, I couldn't accept them!" she demurred in confusion.

"Why not? You have accepted a gown and a petticoat from Jacques Le Loup!"

"Yes, but he was—"

"Dead?" he mocked. "*Mais* if you can accept from a dead Frenchman a petticoat to encase those swaying hips, can you not accept a pair of stockings from a live one? I've been waiting for a pair of legs that would do them justice!"

His manner was so rollicking, his logic so comical, that Lorraine began to laugh.

"Wait, there is more!" He produced a pair of blue satin garters trimmed with silver lace rosettes and placed them calmly in her palm.

"What else do you keep in your cabin, André?" she gasped.

"Come and see," he suggested wickedly.

Raile, who was standing in the prow, had turned and was observing them. His hawklike face darkened and he turned abruptly away.

Lorraine saw that from the corner of her eye. So it *was* possible to make the inscrutable captain jealous! Her heart sang and laughter seemed to bubble up in her voice as she thanked André warmly.

"Thank me by wearing them, *mademoiselle!*" he countered.

Lorraine went toward the cabin with a slight swagger for the benefit of Captain Cameron. He did not turn. Perhaps, she thought, irritated, he did not care!

Lorraine had eased the sheer stockings up over her legs, marveling at their wonderful silky feel, and had pulled on one blue silk garter, when the door burst open and the captain stood there clenching and unclenching his fists.

"Come in," she said calmly.

"Thank you, I am in." He shut the door behind him so hard that she jumped.

"André has given me a pair of silk stockings," she volunteered.

"And a pair of blue garters," he added grimly.

"With silver lace rosettes," she amplified.

"I have observed those too," he said heavily.

She bent to fasten the other garter, then deliberately lifted her skirts and whirled around so that he might view her pretty legs.

"Don't they look nice?" she challenged.

He made a strangled sound in his throat. "*Nice?*" he echoed. "Is that the word you use for it? Don't you know that damned Frenchman believes he has *bought* you for the price of those stockings and garters?"

Lorraine's skirts dropped and her color rose. "That is not true!"

Raile strode over to her and caught her by the wrist. For a moment she thought that he might toss her onto the bunk and strip the stockings and garters from her legs, but that was not what he had in mind. He dragged her over to the smaller of his sea chests, tore it open, and stuffed some coins into her hand.

"Give those to L'Estraille," he grated. "Thank him, *but pay him!*"

"I will not!" gasped Lorraine, struggling to his grip. "He'd be insulted!"

"Then *I* will do it!" he cried. Dragging her along beside him, he burst out onto the deck, came to a halt an arm's length from the Frenchman.

"In plain English, L'Estraille, I owe you for those stockings and garters which have taken my lass's fancy. Here." He thrust the coins at the other man.

"But no, *mon ami!*" L'Estraille took a step backward, laughing. "They are a wedding gift! Did *mademoiselle* not tell you?"

Raile opened his mouth and closed it again. He turned to consider Lorraine narrowly. "No, she did not."

"You did not give me the chance!" protested Lorraine, taking her cue from André.

"I realize the gift is a little early, but why should I not give it to her now?" continued L'Estraille guilelessly.

Raile continued to study Lorraine. She was growning restive under that penetrating gaze. "Why not indeed?" he murmured—and turned on his heel and left them.

Lorraine sighed and turned her attention to the doctor.

"Do you know what the men call you, my fair Lorraine?" André asked.

In truth Lorraine had not given much thought to the men, who were all French and spoke in a tongue strange to her—it was the ship's English-speaking officers she had cared about. But now, at something sardonic and amused in his tone, she looked up questioningly.

"They call you the captain's bride," he said softly. "But I doubt me we will ever see you wed to him. . . ."

Lorraine's chin went up.

"And why not?" she challenged.

"Because I think you well may wed another man." He smiled. "Me, for instance."

Lorraine sniffed and turned about, intending to leave him, but with lightning speed he was there to block her path.

"I think in the end it will be me or nothing, my lovely *demoiselle*," he murmured, and there was a hint of warning in his voice.

"Thank you, I shall take my chances," said Lorraine stiffly.

"Ah, that you are already doing," he countered, but he moved aside to let her pass. Then he changed his mind and seized her hand.

"André!" she said warningly.

"Ah," he said. "When you lie restless and alone in your bunk tonight, think of me! I will remind you that although yon tall fellow who is now scowling at us may lay claim to the rest of you, in those stockings"—he nodded significantly downward—"the legs"—he chuckled wickedly—"the legs are mine."

"André, hush!" she said, breaking free and feeling mortification flood her face with color. "You will shame me before the crew!"

He shrugged. "The crew is French, *mademoiselle*, they will understand. It is the English who will not, and perhaps"—he turned his narrow gaze toward Raile—"perhaps a Scot here and there will not either."

She felt very sure a certain Scot would not!

CHAPTER 13

RAILE HAD LITTLE to say to her for a while after the stocking incident. He was usually out on deck attending to his captain's duties. When he was in the cabin, he was either sleeping or bending over his charts. Lorraine was certain it was because of the stockings, but she was afraid to bring up the subject. Silently she cursed herself for her folly.

The ship's doctor of course had no such qualms—and would have made light of Lorraine's if she had voiced them.

She had become very self-conscious about the stockings. Every time her knees brushed together and she felt the slight rasp of silk, she was reminded of what André L'Estraille had said about the legs they encased being his. The words had been spoken in jest, of course—still, they tallied too well with Raile's angry "Don't you know that damned Frenchman believes he has *bought* you?"

Certainly from that moment, André's all-too-obvious courtship had stepped up its tempo. She had but to look around to find the gaudily dressed ship's doctor at her elbow. His impressive fawn periwig seemed always to be brushing her shoulder as he danced along at her side. She told herself all this attention was because she was the only woman on board the vessel, and such men as André L'Estraille must always needs be pursuing a woman.

She was more preoccupied with keeping clear of Derry Cork, whose practical-joker nature she mistrusted. But Derry was on his best behavior these days and although sometimes his eyes lit up roguishly when she passed, he had not made her the butt of any more of his pranks.

The days passed sunnily—save for one thing: she still had the feeling of being watched. Not in her cabin—never there, but on deck often. Too often.

Not even André's merry raillery completely freed Lorraine from that feeling of having somewhere a watcher in the shadows. . . .

Came a day when her invisible pursuer seemed closer than ever. *Closing in,* was the thought that came to mind—chillingly. It was a steamy hot day with little wind. Even André, that paragon of fashion, had shed his coat in deference to the sticky heat, which was making him irritable. On deck beside her now, he mopped his brow.

"Devilish hot, isn't it, *mademoiselle?* I always think we must be getting close to hell on such a day." He launched into one of his many stories, this one about a hot night on the Left Bank of the Seine.

Lorraine was scarcely listening. The men were clambering about the rigging, orders were being shouted, for the sails had been drooping from lack of wind and at last a little breeze had come up—they must take advantage of it.

André talked on unheard. The skin on the back of Lorraine's neck prickled. Even before André had come up to her, she had had that feeling, now stronger than ever, of being *watched.*

Certainly André was not the watcher. André was beside her.

She cast a quick furtive look up into the shrouds, searching for that mysterious unseen face that always seemed to be there, probing eyes that seemed to seek her out and follow her about whenever she came on deck. But although her wandering gaze raked the sails back and forth, she saw only the sailors intent on their work. She did not see . . . *him.*

Still she knew he was there.

Watching her.

She dropped her gaze, frowning down at the deck. He was hereabouts *somewhere,* she knew that—even if she couldn't see him.

"Mademoiselle Lorraine, you are not attending!" André's voice, sounding vexed.

Lorraine started.

"What . . . what was it you said, André?" She was apologetic. "I must have missed it. Something about Paris, wasn't it?"

"*Mon Dieu!*" he exploded, wiping his perspiring brow with a kerchief. "That was fully five minutes ago. I have taken you to Naples and back again and you have not heard a word I said!" He looked affronted.

"Do tell me your story again, André," she said penitently. "I will promise to listen this time."

The Frenchman snorted. "That I will not, *mademoiselle!* I never repeat myself. *Mon Dieu,* I could have been proposing marriage, and you were not even listening!"

"But I could not accept you, André, for I have no intention of . . ." she began, then stopped in confusion.

"Of marrying anyone," he finished for her softly. "It is true, is it not? This is a platonic relationship you have with our tall captain, not a hot love affair?"

"No, no, I—"

"He sleeps across the door, does he not? Not in your bed?"

Lorraine opened her mouth in horror. How could André know *that?* Then she remembered that one night a fight had broken out among the crew, someone had come running for the captain, knocked, and promptly pushed open the door—only to find Raile's long body lying against it.

He had scrambled up at once, commenting that he must not drink so much or he'd fall overboard next time instead of to the cabin floor, and Lorraine had thought that was the end of it. But the story must have got around and André must have heard it and drawn his own conclusions.

"Come, *mademoiselle,* the truth!" André's intent attractive face was bending very close. "You are a virgin, are you not?"

Lorraine's face was flooded with color, but on that point at least she could speak the truth. "No, I am not a virgin, André! But it is none of your affair!"

He gave her a mocking look and his amber eyes flashed brassy gold in the sunlight. "I was only going to say that if you are, then our captain is a fool!" was his parting comment. He made her a stiff bow. "Your servant, *mademoiselle*." And left.

Lorraine, thoroughly upset, wandered down the deck after he left. She came upon Derry Cork leaning against the port rail and talking with the Dutchman, Jakob Helst, who was fond of card playing and had a deck of cards in his hand. Neither of them saw her and Lorraine would have gone on by save for the shocking content of Derry's last remark, which she caught.

". . . strangled with her own hair," he was saying.

"Aye, terrible," muttered the Dutchman, shuffling the deck of cards idly on his knee. He shook his head. "Who would do such a thing to a woman?"

"La Garrotte would do it," Derry Cork assured him. " 'Tis said he had strangled many women with their own long hair. Do you not remember, Helst? The town was alive with searchers our last day there—you had but to sneeze and you would trip over one!"

"I was cosseted with Cook playing cards," admitted Helst. "And losing as well. So I didn't know what was afoot until you all scrambled aboard shouting that we were sailing immediately!"

"Aye, I had forgot you were not out in the town to see," agreed Derry Cork.

"The things that happen in Bordeaux," sighed the Dutchman, as if to say: *Nothing like that would ever happen in Zeeland!*

At that point, out of the corner of his eye, Derry Cork saw Lorraine standing there and noticed her horrified expression. The demons of humor that drove him caused him to embroider his story still further.

"I can tell you what you missed, Helst," he said, raising his voice slightly so Lorraine would get its full import. "Two dead women, both found in separate alleys. Horrible sight they were—eyes bulging, tongues hanging out, dead as doornails—with their long hair wrapped around their necks!"

Lorraine turned and fled. She did not hear Derry's chuckle, but the Dutchman did. He turned and looked after Lorraine, then turned back to Derry. "You've frightened the captain's wench," he said reprovingly.

"Ah, now." Derry grinned. "She only overheard what we all know about La Garrotte's methods and how he had half the women of Bordeaux scared out of their wits!"

"Nevertheless." The Dutchman looked after Lorraine's rapidly retreating back with some indecision. For a moment he appeared about to go after her to soften Derry's frightening words, but then he thought better of it. The captain was a jealous man—Helst had seen his expression harden when the saucy Frenchman paid too much attention to Jufvrouw Lorraine. So he shrugged and instead suggested a game of cards.

Lorraine, hurrying along the deck, felt a shudder go through her. La Garrotte, the Strangler of Bordeaux, strangling women with their own long hair. . . . And all the crew were Frenchmen, picked up, according to MacTavish's contemptuous words, "from the gutters of Bordeaux" by André L'Estraille. It gave the Watcher in the Shadows new meaning, and to Lorraine new terrors.

She had got hold of herself by dinner. And the meal went smoothly. André was especially gallant—as if to make up for his shortness with her this morning. Gradually Lorraine's mood changed and she forgot about the Strangler of Bordeaux.

It was a hot night. As usual Lorraine sat plaiting her long hair into two braids before going to bed. Raile, whose mouth had formed a grim straight line at the amount of badinage that went on between her and the Frenchman during dinner, did not come back to the cabin. She supposed he was taking the watch or perhaps it was just too hot for him in the stuffy cabin.

It was too hot in the cabin for her also. She turned and tossed, perspiring, on the bunk. Then she got up and roved to the porthole. There was a light fog that made the calm sea seem mysterious, and the moon and stars were obscured. It was as if a damp blanket of white had closed down softly upon the ship and its passengers and they were drifting on a voyage to nowhere, toward a port that they would never reach.

Tossing back her long damp braids, Lorraine threw the bedsheet around her like a shawl, for she slept in her chemise, and moving on soft bare feet, went out.

The deck was silent. There was only the slight creaking of the ship and an occasional rustle of the drooping shrouds overhead. She padded about restlessly, trying to cool herself. Up ahead she could dimly see Raile in the prow looking out over the empty ocean. It was so dark and misty that she indentified him really only by the broad set of his shoulders and his height.

She stood there trying to cool her hot face, looking in his direction and wondering if she should go and speak to him. She took a step forward, intending to do just that, when she felt a sudden rush of air like a dark wind coming at her. Something flapped against her. She whirled as her hair was seized, one of her plaits caught and pulled. A cry broke from her lips as something damp and heavy slapped against her face, and from the prow a dim figure came running.

Raile was by her side in a moment and had seized her by the shoulders.

"What is it?" he demanded sharply. "Why did you cry out?"

"Something came at me out of the dark!" she chattered. "It seized me by the hair!"

"Could this be what seized you?" he asked. He was holding her damp russet skirt hung out to dry. Beside the skirt swung her russet bodice. She could only glimpse it, because it seemed to be mainly behind her. "One of your plaits seems to be caught in the hooks of this bodice," he told her. "Hold still while I free you."

Her laundry! She had washed her tavern garb—which she sometimes still wore—late this afternoon, hung it out to dry, and forgotten it! A sudden gust of wind must have whipped the skirt past her. And as she recoiled from that, she must have collided with the bodice, whose hooks had caught in her long plaits.

"I thought someone had caught me by the hair," she gasped, shuddering. "And after hearing about

LaGarrotte today . . ." Her voice trailed off. She was still shaking.

"Who was fool enough to tell you about La Garrotte?" Raile growled, setting her free at last from the clutching hooks.

"Nobody—I mean I overhead Derry Cork telling Jakob Helst about his victims."

Raile snorted. "Derry knew you were listening, I'll be bound!"

Lorraine gave him a wild look. Her face was pale in the darkness.

"Come, I'll take you back to the cabin," he said more kindly, for he could see how truly frightened she was.

The lamp swinging overhead seemed very friendly after the misty darkness outside. The cabin was washed in its golden light and the tall man who looked down at her seemed a citadel of strength.

"You need have no fear of La Garrotte," Raile told her, frowning. "They hanged him while we were in Bordeaux."

Lorraine stared at him. "French justice cannot be so fast!" she protested. "I heard Derry Cork say they were searching for the Strangler just before you left Bordeaux."

"And found him." Raile nodded matter-of-factly. "The mob was not to be appeased, for he had strangled two"—he had almost said "waterfront whores" but he amended that to "fancy women"—"that very night. The Strangler was caught bending over the dead body of one of his victims. The mob dragged him away and hanged him from the yardarm of one of the ships in the harbor. It was the last sight we saw as we pulled away."

"I see." She moistened her lips. "Derry didn't talk about that."

"Lorraine." Raile ran a hand through his dark hair. "I've told you that Derry Cork—"

"Is just a small boy at heart," she finished for him. "I know." She sighed.

His lips twisted into a half-grin, for he had been about to use those very words, but he was still worried about her.

"Derry likes to tell ghoulish stories," he explained.

"He is full of them, and if he thinks they frighten you, he will tell many more in your hearing."

Lorraine felt rather foolish—but that feeling she had felt outside had been real and was the stuff of pure terror. When her hair had been seized, all she could think of was: *The Strangler—he has been on board all the time! He has got me!* She determined to give Derry Cork a very wide berth.

"This will be a long voyage," Raile told her soberly. "And oft times the men will have little to do. If you are wise, you will not show yourself to be gullible or they will make your life unbearable."

Gullible! Lorraine turned away, feeling rebuffed.

She soon found herself distracted by an entirely new problem, for as Raile turned to go back out on deck, he flung over his shoulder, "You'll have a respite from ship living soon, lass, for we're in Bermudan waters. Tomorrow—or next day at the latest—we'll drop anchor in St. George's harbor."

"What?" cried Lorraine.

"You'll like Bermuda," he told her.

"But we *can't* stop there!" she wailed.

This caused him to turn around and consider her in wonder. "Can't?" he repeated. "Indeed we can do naught else. We're headed for the Indies and we need to stop in Bermuda to provision and take on fresh water."

Lorraine gave him a wild look.

"But . . . but I've been telling everyone that when we reach land we'll be married. They'll all expect us *to be married* in Bermuda!"

Raile considered her calmly. "Are you saying you wish to make it true?"

"No, of course not!" Lorraine blushed furiously. "I'm just saying that everyone will *expect*—"

Raile's voice was bitter.

"Be damned to what they expect!" he said shortly. "Tell them anything you please."

He stalked out, leaving Lorraine's mind in a ferment.

CHAPTER 14

St. George, Bermuda
Summer

IT WAS WITH foreboding that Lorraine, peering forward from the prow of the *Likely Lass*, watched the peaks of that great submarine mountain known as the Bermuda Islands rear up before her out of the deeps of the Atlantic. Westward across the warm blue waters of the Gulf Stream lay the American coastline. North and east lay the volcanic Azores, and beyond them, Europe. To the south, past the sluggish reedy whirlpool of the Sargasso Sea, was the land of adventure: the Caribbean sailed by golden galleons; the Spanish Main with its sweating mines and its treasures; the Indies, a sugar world of rum and romance.

But Lorraine, her mind in turmoil, could think only of the humiliation that lay in store for her here when the men of the *Lass* discovered that she was not to marry their captain after all.

They had stood out to sea last night, waiting for dawn before braving the shark-toothed barrier reefs that guarded the hundreds of tiny isles and islets that made up the circlet chain men called the Bermudas. With daylight they had negotiated that guardian ring of dangerous coral reefs that marked the graveyard of so many tall ships, and sunlight found them sailing down the Narrows. Above them brooded the thick walls and battlements of Fort St. Catherine. Past Paget

Island and Smith's Island they sped in brilliant blue-sky weather to reach at last the sparkling waters of St. George's harbor.

A sudden buzz of excitement swept the ship at sight of the scattering of vessels anchored there, and Lorraine, who was standing at the rail beside the ship's doctor and had noted that he too came suddenly alert, turned to him nervously.

"What is it, André? What do you see that I don't?"

"Warship," he muttered, and she followed his gaze to a large frigate that lay at anchor near the town.

"Does that mean we won't be going ashore?" wondered Lorraine hopefully.

Beside her, the Frenchman snorted. "A prudent captain might avoid it, but that wild Scot yonder? He'd take us ashore through a brace of warships!"

If he had meant it unflatteringly, to daunt Lorraine and make her doubt Raile's judgment at taking this risk, it went wide of the mark, for Lorraine felt a little thrill of apprehension and of pride as they sailed boldly on, casting anchor as casually as might any merchant vessel carrying cheese and cloth and in need of fresh water and supplies.

Now the longboat was being lowered. That meant they were about to disembark. Lorraine's nerves were drawn so taut that she jumped when the Frenchman again addressed her.

"You are nervous today, *mademoiselle*," he commented. "Bride's nerves perhaps?" he teased.

"No, of course not," she defended, feeling her face grow hot under his amused inspection.

"But I thought you were to be married as soon as we reached land?"

Lorraine turned, at bay—and suddenly in that moment she had decided on her story.

"Captain Cameron is displeased about it, of course," she said, stiffly formal. "But I have decided that I will not marry him until we reach my guardian in . . . in Barbados." She choked slightly over the words.

"Guardian?" The Frenchman blinked. "This is the first I have heard of any guardian, *mademoiselle*."

"Oh, did I not mention him?" Lorraine feigned

surprise. "Raile is taking me to him in Barbados—I thought you knew. My guardian would be very hurt if he were not to be present at my wedding."

"I can well imagine," murmured her companion, but one of his eyebrows was cocked at her sardonically. "So we are not to have a wedding in Bermuda after all? I am disappointed, *mademoiselle!*"

"That is unfortunate," said Lorraine with asperity. "But I think you will have to let me be the judge of where and when I am to be married, André!"

He held up his hands, laughing, as if to ward her off.

"Ah, less heat, *mademoiselle!* Anyone would think you were in no hurry to be married at all!"

Fortunately Lorraine did not have to answer that, for she was just then hurried away to the longboat, where she sat beside her silent captain. The impudent ship's doctor had managed to secure the seat behind her, and now, as they were being rowed ashore, he leaned forward to keep up his banter.

"Do you know Bermuda well, Raile?" Lorraine hoped by ignoring him to quench the exuberant Frenchman, who was breathing almost in her ear.

"Not so well as Helst does," was the reply. "He was shipwrecked here once and stayed for several months, I believe."

"He insists there are no rivers or streams here and that the wells all yield salt water," put in the ship's doctor.

"Really, André?" Lorraine wished he would not lean over her. "What do they drink then?"

She had half-expected him to say "Wine," but he surprised her.

"Rainwater, according to Helst. All caught in catchments and stored in great cisterns. The cisterns are kept clean by putting a busy goldfish inside," he added with distaste.

"Poor little thing!" Lorraine's heart went out to that small trapped creature; she was thinking how truly dreadful it would be to spend one's life in a dark cistern. "They should at least put *two* goldfish inside to keep each other company!"

L'Estraille was laughing now. "Mademoiselle Lorraine, you are French at heart. Indeed it is true—the world should travel in pairs!"

Lorraine turned her head to study a square-rigged two-masted merchantman which the big warship had heretofore hidden from her view. Lorraine gazed upon it in dismay. She had no need to read the name *Mayapple* painted on that sturdy hull—she had seen that ship too many times before in Providence harbor!

She clutched Raile's arm. "That ship—she's the *Mayapple*. Her captain's name is Bridey—he's a friend of Oddsbud's, he was at the White Horse Tavern the night before you came!"

A pair of cool gray eyes swung toward her. "Indeed?" said Raile softly. "Perhaps I will run across Captain Bridey in the town."

"Oh, don't—" she began, but her words ended in a gasp as a longboat shot out from between the *Mayapple* and the warship, heading for shore. "That's Captain Bridey—the gray-haired man in the bow." She was staring at a heavyset fellow with a shock of unkempt gray hair above a weathered face and square-cut grizzled beard. "And"—her voice sank to a whisper—"*he knows me by sight!*"

The pressure of Raile's hand on her arm silenced her but she noted that he swung his broad shoulders about to shield her from the grizzled captain's view. In panic, Lorraine pretended to find something wrong with her shoe and bent double, adjusting it as the *Mayapple*'s longboat paced them over the blue water to shore.

No one else had noticed this exchange between the captain and his lady, for there was a raucous conversation going on around them among men eager to set foot on land, but behind them, silenced at last and with eyes sparkling with curiosity, André L'Estraille was taking it all in.

When they landed in St. George's Town, Lorraine found a wall of not one but two solid masculine bodies between herself and the just-landing crew of the *Mayapple*, some of whom were craning their necks for a better view of the blonde in the blue dress.

Raile shot a glance at them, saw that they were headed down Water Street toward the taverns.

"Lorraine," he said abruptly, offering her his arm, "I'm going to show you the sights of St. George!"

Lorraine's look of wild protest went unheeded.

The Frenchman chuckled and promptly attached himself to them, swinging along on Lorraine's other side. Raile did not seem to mind. Lorraine had the sinking feeling that he welcomed having L'Estraille along, should a fight develop.

For Lorraine knew that she had been living in a fool's paradise. Somehow the unfamiliar carefree life on shipboard, sailing over endless smooth waters in the company of adventurous men, had given her a sense of security, of breaking her ties with the past. She had managed to forget that she was a runaway bondservant and had thought of herself as just another girl with her future in doubt.

Now, as they turned toward King's Square, with its stocks and pillory, it was all brought sharply back to her and the real world came into focus once again.

From the stocks a woebegone drunken face stared up at her. Nearby, bent over with her head and hands sticking out of the wooden pillory, a thin middle-aged woman with wispy hair glared at them as they passed.

Lorraine was relieved when they left the stocks and pillory behind and paused to look at the handsome State House built more than half a century before with turtle-oil-and-lime mortar.

"Helst tells me the Bermudians have borrowed a marriage custom from the Dutch of New York," remarked L'Estraille as they turned down York Street toward the massive pile of St. Peter's Church. "The bridegroom has a gold-leaf wedding cake, but in the top of the bride's cake is stuck a cedar sapling which she must then plant. How it grows will determine the future of the marriage." He grinned at Lorraine. "Have you selected a suitable sapling, *mademoiselle?*"

Lorraine gave him a tormented look. At the moment, marriage was the farthest thing from her mind!

"André is teasing me," she told Raile with a sigh. "Because I have told him how we must wait until we reach Barbados for our wedding, so my guardian can attend."

"A pity to wait," murmured the Frenchman, gazing up at the square tower of St. Peter's. "Such a romantic setting. . . ." He gave them both an innocent look. "I have spent some time on Barbados. What did you say your guardian's name was, *mademoiselle?*"

Lorraine's heart thumped. She felt for a moment ringed by enemies—first that ship from Rhode Island and now André.

"I didn't say," she choked, but Raile cut in swiftly.

"His name is Ambrose Lyle, L'Estraille." He gave the Frenchman a steady look over Lorraine's head. "Is he perchance of your acquaintance?"

"No, somehow I seem to have missed him," said the Frenchman airily.

"I wonder how you managed that." There was a steely note in Raile's voice. "He is sixty years old, a bachelor, a saddler by trade—all in Bridgetown know him."

Lorraine's blue eyes shone with beleaguered gratitude as she looked up at her tall captain. "I will make it a point to introduce you, André," she flung over her shoulder.

"Perhaps we should go inside the church and pray for our sins," murmured the Frenchman half-humorously. He was peering inside at St. Peter's three-decked pulpit. She ignored the comment.

Under blue skies, quaint St. George's Town with its twisting alleys and colorfully named streets—One Gun Alley, King's Parade, Featherbed Lane—went by Lorraine in an unhappy blur as she waited tensely for Captain Bridey or one of his crew who might know her by sight to loom up suddenly from around the next corner and confront her.

After a time Raile said, "Now we'll find us an inn," and they made their way back to the jostling crowds that roamed up and down Water Street, for two more ships had come into harbor and the street was teeming with action. Lorraine, swishing along in her elegant blue gown and trying to hold her blonde head high, was made aware that she was now in a fisherman's world, a land of deep-water sailors, of browned muscular men who stared at her admiringly as she passed—and sometimes winked at her despite the sobering clank of swords and clomp of boots of the two tall men who flanked her.

Just ahead a large woman in faded homespun was coming toward them carrying a brace of squawking chickens upside down. The crowd eddied to let her through and Raile quickly pulled Lorraine aside to avoid bumping into her.

As she did so, they both looked up and saw a thick plume of smoke rising from the green hills above the houses. The wind was carrying it toward the town.

"What is all that smoke up there?" Lorraine asked uneasily.

"Alas, mistress, those are fires deliberately set in the cedar forests above us," said a voice behind her.

Lorraine turned to see a soberly clad wisp of a fellow, bespectacled and as thin as any skeleton, both skinny arms grasping a muslin sack from which peeked out two leather-bound volumes. " 'Tis thought by burning the forests to destroy the plague of rats that has come upon us," he explained. "But in my view it is a shocking waste to see great cedars—some of them fifteen feet around the trunk—consumed by the blaze!"

"I should think so," agreed Raile, his gaze straying to the stacks of squared cedar logs, some of them enormous, piled up for shipment on the nearby beach. "Many a stout ship could be made of them."

They had paused momentarily for this conversation and would have moved on but for a sudden shout. Lorraine stiffened as a whip cracked and an audible groan reached them.

A moment later they saw the cause. A cart was being driven by, parting the crowd, and tied behind that cart, bent over and stripped to the waist, a sandy-haired young fellow was struggling to keep his footing as a heavy whip descended with agonizing regularity upon his naked back. A small crowd surged behind, some laughing in derision, others crying out encouragement to the beat of the whip.

"So they've caught Jeb," the wispy fellow muttered on a drawn-out sigh.

"Caught him?" Lorraine swung about indignantly. "What on earth has he done to deserve such cruel treatment?"

The wispy fellow regarded her owlishly. "Cruel it may be, mistress—and Jeb Smith would agree with you—but yon groaning lad is a runaway bondservant. He'll be whipped out of town as a reminder not to wander away again."

A runaway bondservant! And this was his punishment. . . . A shiver went through her and both Raile and André were quick to note it.

The cart and its followers had gone by, heading toward King's Square, and now a carriage dashed past them, almost overturning as it reeled onto Queen Street. It was driven by a black driver whose eyes were so wide that the whites of them seemed to be his most prominent feature. He was beating a pair of lathered horses and in the back a angry-looking older man in burgundy velvet was holding on to a screaming young girl to keep her from leaping out of the carriage. But in the moment that the carriage came abreast of them, the girl spotted the wispy fellow.

"Charles!" she called in a voice of wild appeal. "Don't let him do this!"

Beside Lorraine, Charles seemed to shrink still further. He watched the carriage disappear with hunted eyes.

"Who is she?" gasped Lorraine.

"She is Trinity Pomeroy," she was told bitterly. "I am her tutor at Cedarwood. Though what she thinks I can do—"

"But that man clutching her?" interrupted Lorraine.

"Her father, John Pomeroy of Cedarwood Plantation, and he cares naught for—" He seemed to collect himself. "He is also my employer. Young Trinity had the bad taste to run away with her father's clerk—Jeb Smith, the lad you just saw being whipped at the tail of the cart—who is bound by his articles for three more years. After her lover recovers from his beating he'll no doubt find another year or two added to his period of indenture, while Mistress Trinity will be sent overseas to England to get her married—and quickly—to someone her father can approve of." His Adam's apple worked and there was the glitter of tears in his eyes.

Lorraine's gaze followed the disappearing cart where the beautiful red-haired girl with the tearstained face had been struggling with her father.

"It should not be allowed!" she cried, quivering. "All this interference with lovers—it is not right!"

"I'm sure Trinity would agree with you but it's John Pomeroy who will have the ordering of the matter," was the bitter rejoinder.

The crowd had been eddying about them, passing on both sides, and of a sudden someone jostled against the wispy fellow's birdlike chest. The slight impact caused him to lose his hold on the linen bag he carried. It fell to the street and out of it spilled not just the two books at the top but silk stockings, a woman's green satin slipper, and a froth of lace on what looked to be feminine underthings.

He fell to his knees, clawing them back into the bag. "I'm not a thief," he panted, red-faced and defiant. "These things are—"

Lorraine had bent swiftly down to help him collect the items. "You were helping Trinity escape, weren't you?"

His face, which had been suffused with color, lost it instantly and turned a dirty gray. "Mistress," he whispered hoarsely, "if you spread that word about, I'll be dismissed—*and where will she be then?*"

"No one will hear of it from me," Lorraine promised him warmly. They both scrambled up. "We're in need of an inn, sir. Can you recommend one?"

"You're standing before one of the best." He waved his arm toward an open door over which hung a painted wooden sign announcing this to be the "Gull and Tortoise."

Raile peered casually inside. "No, I think not." He shook his head regretfully. "Too noisy for my lass here."

His lass stole an involuntary glance through the

doorway. There in profile was Captain Bridey's familiar weathered face. She jumped back with alacrity.

"Aye, 'tis noisy," agreed their mentor. Charles thought a moment. "There's a place around the corner on Duke of York Street. They've applied for a license as an ordinary, and when it comes through they'll be called the Crown and Garter, but until then, there's no sign and they take guests on the quiet to avoid the tax collector." He winked at them. "I warn you, though—they lock up early."

"We'd be obliged if you'd take us there." Raile smiled enigmatically. Lorraine wondered if he had heard their low-voiced conversation when the bag fell to the street, decided he hadn't.

The man led them down Old Maid's Lane. On the way introductions were made. They learned that he was Charles Hubbard, impecunious son of an English country vicar. He had been lured to the Bermudas by a shining offer to tutor a young genius in a stately home. "Poor Trinity's no good at sums," he sighed. "And she gets her geography all backwards!"

There was a catch in his voice when he said that, and Lorraine thought stabbingly: *He's in love with her. Poor Charles Hubbard cares for Trinity so much he was even willing to help her run away with another man—and now he's got to take her things back to Cedarwood and watch her weep for him. . . .*

"And the stately home?" she asked quickly.

Hubbard grimaced. "A plain enough house—far up." He jerked his head toward the hills behind the town, where heavy smoke was rising.

They had reached the Crown and Garter, a name Lorraine thought mightily overblown for such a humble low wooden building with its palmetto thatched roof. The landlord offered Hubbard a bottle of wine "for bringing me custom" and Hubbard offered to share it with them. Raile excused himself on the grounds he had much to do and must be about it, but L'Estraille said, "I'll share a glass with you, Hubbard." His glance strayed to Lorraine, hoping she'd join them.

But the landlord was already bustling Lorraine upstairs. She found herself on the second floor in a front room whose wooden shutters stood open. One window looked down upon the street below; the other had a view of the next building, where two workmen were busy lime-washing the walls. The only furnishings of the low-ceilinged room were a small wooden table, a couple of straight-backed chairs, and a large double bed—all rudely crafted from the island cedar.

It had been an exhausting morning. Once the landlord had gone, Lorraine threw herself facedown upon the bed. Safe at last!

The thought relaxed her. Without meaning to, she drifted off to sleep while downstairs André L'Estraille and Charles Hubbard tossed off a second glass of wine.

When Hubbard took his leave, the Frenchman decided to go looking for Helst. But first . . . He cast a thoughtful look at the stairway. It was very silent upstairs on this sleepy afternoon.

The landlord was not about. L'Estraille tiptoed up the stairs, stood outside the door. *Her* door. It *must* be her door, it was the only door that was closed and he could see that the other rooms were unoccupied. He lifted his knuckles to knock, changed his mind, and tried the door. It opened silently, for the landlord had oiled it only yesterday and its iron hinges made no sound.

Before L'Estraille was a pretty picture. A girl in a blue dress with her blonde hair cascading over an unbleached muslin coverlet. Her skirts had ridden up as she moved restlessly, so that one silken leg lay exposed in a billow of chemise ruffles and shimmering blue-gray satin petticoat.

He caught his breath at the sight.

It would have been second nature for L'Estraille to close the door softly behind him and tiptoe to the bed, to make his presence known by pressing his lips firmly upon the curving half-parted lips of the sleeping girl, to begin his wooing where he hoped it would eventually lead—her bed.

He stood there for a long time and a look of enormous longing spread over his jaded countenance. She was so lovely—and so trusting. She had not even locked her door. Anything could happen to her!

"Mademoiselle Lorraine!" He heard himself bark the words, to his own astonishment. "I find your door unlatched!"

Lorraine started up, confused.

"Oh . . . André," she said. "I . . . I must have forgotten to latch it. Thank you for reminding me."

She was moving toward him with that walk of hers, so feminine, so enticing. His hard face softened. When she reached him, he leaned over and spoke in a roguish whisper. "You should ask me to remain here to guard your virtue," he declared. "For I'm a man of many talents. Did I ever tell you that I could remove your chemise—entire—in the night without ever waking you?"

Lorraine laughed. "Then I shall assuredly latch my door, André," she told him composedly. "And I need no one to guard my virtue!" Her voice held a tinge of haughtiness and she held the door a bit wider that he might depart.

The Frenchman drew back, bowing, and allowed her to close the door to his face, heard her latch it.

In the hallway he stood irresolute, his face a mirror of amazement as he stared at the closed door. Why, his behavior was . . . it was maudlin! Here they had been alone at last—really alone—and he made no effort to touch her! He could not understand himself.

As he went down the stairs he heard a roll of distant thunder—even the gods were growling at such mortifying behavior.

"Helst, I am twice a fool, but I must have her," he confided moodily to his friend an hour later in a waterfront tavern. "The *demoiselle* has taken a hold on me here"—he made a dramatic gesture toward his heart—"such a hold that even I do not understand."

Helst favored him with a jaundiced look. "Find another woman," was his advice. "That's the way to erase another man's wife from your mind!"

"She is not his wife yet, Helst!"

"No, but she soon will be."

"Perhaps not." In the last glow of the setting sun

the Frenchman's amber eyes had turned metallic; they seemed to reflect the golden light like a cat's. "Perhaps not. If only I could find a way to *shine* in her eyes. . . ." He drummed his fingers on the table and his expression was dangerous. "I mean to have her, Helst."

Helst lifted his tankard in derision.

"I will say a few words over you after the captain kills you," he promised cheerfully.

CHAPTER 15

RAILE WAS LATE to supper, which was served in their candlelit bedchamber by Mistress Pym, the landlord's plump middle-aged wife. The meal consisted of fish chowder and shark pie, washed down by the local cedarberry wine. The evening's calm was disrupted by vivid lightning flashes, every one of which brought forth muffled shrieks from across the hall, where two maiden ladies were staying.

"You'd think they'd never seen a storm!" muttered Mistress Pym as she nearly dropped a platter at their cries.

"You should have gotten us two rooms," Lorraine sighed after the woman had left. "Mistress Pym knows we're not married and she disapproves. Did you notice how careful she was to ask us no questions?"

"The Crown and Garter has no license yet," Raile told her cynically. "Mistress Pym will look the other way until it does."

Lorraine flushed. "You still should have taken two rooms, Raile!"

"Impossible. We got the last one. Those two ships that arrived just after us have overcrowded the town's accommodations. Of course I could have let you share a bed across the hall with those two maiden ladies."

Lorraine gave him a haunted look. The two ladies would have asked endless questions, she had no doubt.

And she was a girl whose past did not bear prying into.

"All in all," he added sardonically, "I felt you would prefer the same arrangement we had on shipboard—you in the bed, me by the door. I am sorry you have had a dull afternoon, locked away in your room."

"André came by to remind me to latch my door," she blurted out before she thought.

"So you whiled away the time with him?" Raile's voice was casual but his throat felt tight.

"No, he just told me to latch my door and left."

"He did not mention it when I ran across him."

"No, he wouldn't." She laughed. "I suppose he thought you would be angry with me. He must be curious about the odd way we behaved this morning! Didn't he ask you why?"

Raile gave her a thoughtful look. "No he did not." He fished in his pocket. "Here. I have brought you something." He produced a small packet which he tossed upon the bed. "Hairpins."

Lorraine pounced upon the hairpins with joy. Tomorrow she would rid herself of that tiresome scarf and arrange her hair fashionably. She looked up at him with shining eyes. "Oh, Raile, I do thank you!" She leapt up and began to comb her long fair hair vigorously, preparatory to plaiting it for bed.

Raile gazed upon her for a moment in a kind of masculine wonder. Lorraine had been very near discovery today. And he might not have been able to prevent her being taken if Captain Bridey had seen her and raised a hue and cry, yet she had asked him nothing about Bridey—she was entirely absorbed by *hairpins!* Shaking his head, he arranged his long body on the floor by the door.

Lorraine blew out the candle and threw the shutters wide before she got into bed. The night air rushing in was cool and damp and had the feeling of rain in it, though not a drop had fallen. A cold white moon shone down upon this island that the Spaniards called the "Isle of Devils," for many a proud galleon had been wrecked upon its jagged reefs. St. George's Town seemed very peaceful tonight, though there was still a racket coming from the waterfront.

In a tavern on that waterfront André L'Estraille was pounding the table in a passion. "*Mon Dieu,* I tell you I *must* know, Helst!"

"You'll wish you hadn't inquired," Helst warned owlishly.

A brilliant flash of lightning lit up the tavern windows and threw the Frenchman's intent face into hard relief. The words seemed wrung from him. "Dammit, Helst, I *will* know if he sleeps with her!"

His last words were drowned in a crash of thunder, and with that crash a man in a torn shirt sprang through the open door of the tavern. From his soot-blackened face his eyes looked wild. "The lightning has set new fires in the cedars," he panted. "They're burning out of control and threatening Cedarwood Plantation. If Cedarwood goes, the other outlying plantations will go too. There's a call out for men to help fight the blaze." He collapsed onto a long bench amid the sudden clamor of voices and drained the contents of a pewter tankard an excited tavern wench had thrust into his hands. "There's more," he cried hoarsely. "That pair of lovers from Cedarwood are off again and John Pomeroy is offering a reward for anyone who can find his daughter. It's thought they're hiding in the cedars and don't know yet that they're trapped. Men are needed for the search."

There was a general surge toward the door. L'Estraille and Helst—neither of them particularly civic-minded, but never lacking in gallantry—had sat unmoved during the first part, but at the suggestion of a female in distress, and better yet, a reward, they came to their feet as one. Helst seized the bottle from their table and they joined in the general exodus.

Once outside on Water Street, L'Estraille came to a halt. Suddenly he laughed and clapped Helst on the back.

"Helst, we've a duty to inform our captain of this crisis—and I'll have the answer to my riddle at the same time!"

Down Old Maid's Lane and around the corner onto

Duke of York Street they went. There L'Estraille gingerly tried the door of the future Crown and Garter—and found it locked. In the fitful flashes of lightning that lit the empty street he spotted and pounced upon the wooden ladder workmen had left standing against a nearby wall. Over Helst's muffled protests, he set it with stealth beneath Lorraine's window.

"Set that bottle down, Helst. Are you going to steady this ladder or not?" he hissed.

"I will—but it may be my last act on earth," was Helst's gloomy response.

Slightly wavering—for indeed he would not have attempted anything so rash had he been entirely sober—André L'Estraille softly ascended the ladder until he reached the open window, then waited, leaning upon the sill.

He had not long to wait. Another jagged bolt of lightning struck the hills and illuminated the room almost as bright as day. Before him beneath the un-bleached coverlet lay Lorraine, asleep. And Raile's long body, trouser-clad, lay across the door.

The Frenchman drew a deep triumphant breath. She did *not* sleep with him. Ah, his *demoiselle* was a virgin!

He would have gone back down the ladder but that the horizontal figure by the door had suddenly become vertical and had leapt forward to grab him by the throat. L'Estraille could feel the ladder shake as Helst groaned.

"Captain . . . Captain!" gasped L'Estraille. He was clawing desperately to get strong choking fingers from his throat and still keep his footing on the ladder. "I came . . . to tell you . . . that the fire . . . has spread!"

The big hands relaxed. "So it's you, L'Estraille," Raile growled. "Why didn't you come knocking on the door like a civilized man instead of creeping up to the window like a thief? I might have killed you!"

"There's a call out for men." L'Estraille was stroking his throat. He sounded aggrieved. "They've locked up for the night here. I couldn't rouse the inn!"

As if in corroboration, the church bells began clanging.

"They're aroused now," said Raile grimly. "Fire's spread, you say?"

Lorraine had just waked up to the sound of the bells. Her bewildered "What's André doing here?" was cut into by the Frenchman's reply to Raile.

". . . out of control and menacing the plantations. Also they're searching for that runaway pair we saw today. They're thought to be hiding out in the cedars and don't know their danger." He made an expansive if ironic gesture. "Will you not take this way down, Captain Cameron? It's faster."

"Yes, but you two go on. Do what you can. I'll round up some of the lads and join you later." Raile was pulling on his shirt as he spoke.

"Take me with you," cried Lorraine. She sprang from her bed and began to scramble frantically into her petticoat.

"No. Too dangerous." Her captain was already out the window as he spoke.

"But you'll need help!"

Raile paused in his descent down the ladder. "Stay here," he commanded sternly. "I'll not risk your being recognized."

He would not risk it! Half-dressed and indignant at being left behind, Lorraine ran to the window. Above the clanging of the church bells she heard a voice calling urgently, "Captain Cameron!" She peered into the darkness and a lightning flash illuminated the scarecrowlike figure of Charles Hubbard, his long arms flapping as he ran.

She called out to him to ask if Trinity had been found, but her voice was lost in the clangor of the bells. Another lightning flash showed Raile and Charles Hubbard marching away together.

Lorraine came away from the window with a sigh. She had a good reason for going downstairs; she must remove that ladder from her window.

She finished dressing—in her blue gown, for she had not brought her other from the ship—and went downstairs to find the wood-paneled common room in an uproar. The two maiden ladies from across the hall, both clad in dressing gowns, were wringing their hands and crying out that if the wind changed, the town would go. The other guests—male passengers who had come in on the ships—clapped their hats on their heads and stalked out through the front door.

Lorraine went out and moved the ladder away from her window. When she returned, she found the landlady locked in dispute with her husband.

"I tell you, Pym, I *must* go!" she was crying out distractedly. "She's my little sister and she's up there at Cedarwood about to have a baby!"

"When your father drove her out of the house, he meant her to stay out!" snarled Pym. "And now you want to bring her into ours! He'll cut you off without a farthing if you interfere. Let John Pomeroy look after her—she's *his* housekeeper. Aye, and the baby will be his too!"

"How dare you say it?" Mistress Pym drew back her arm and slapped his face. " 'Tis her dead husband's—just a trifle overdue, that's all!"

"Vixen!" Pym looked ready to explode. "I'll not stay here and listen to you!"

"You will!" she shouted. *"It's my house!"*

"Then rot in it!" he bellowed, and charged through the door into the street.

Nearby the two maiden ladies continued to moan.

"I've a cart," stated Mistress Pym, looking around her defiantly. "But I'll need help hitching it up and, later, getting my sister into it, for I'm bringing her back here to have her baby, no matter what anyone says about it!"

And she was *right!* Lorraine's blue eyes flashed.

"I know how to hitch up a cart. And I'll go with you too!" she offered recklessly. For who would recognize her in the darkness and confusion out there?

"God be praised!" Mistress Pym seized Lorraine's arm. "Come, the cart's this way."

Moments later an excited Lorraine, her blue scarf wrapped turbanlike around her head, found herself driving a strange cart through the night down Duke of York Street. Around her now the town had waked up. Candles were being hastily lit in the town houses whose

gable ends faced the street medieval style. Lanterns
flitted past. Shouting, calling out to each other over
the incessant pealing of the bells, the citizenry of St.
George's Town was pouring out, on horseback and on
foot, toward the low forested hills from which dense
columns of smoke rose in ominous silhouette against
each lightning flash.

Finally, despite the darkness and confusion they
reached the outskirts of the town. The sky, between
lightning flashes, was heavily overcast and obscured
the stars. With the town behind them, the lanterns of
the searchers looked like giant golden fireflies dotting
the dark upward slopes.

"Which way now?" cried Lorraine.

"Straight ahead." Mistress Pym waved her own lantern. "I'll tell you when to turn." And although she
clutched the side of the cart every time the cart lurched,
she gave good directions.

"I don't want you to think bad things of my sister.
Pym had no call to say what he did. 'Twas my father
forced Hattie to marry Warren—frail lad that he was.
Papa said she smiled too often at the widower John
Pomeroy and he'd have no harlot living under *his*
roof—watch out there, the road narrows around that
big stump! So he forced poor Hattie to marry Warren.
I'm not saying Hattie should've done it . . ."

"Perhaps she wanted to break free of her infatua-
tion," suggested Lorraine softly.

"That was it," agreed Mistress Pym with satisfaction. "To break free. . . . Only Warren took sick and
died and Hattie was a widow then and not even Papa
could keep her from smiling at John Pomeroy. One
thing led to another—watch out for that rock there!"

Lorraine managed to miss the rock. "So she became
his . . . housekeeper."

In the lurching darkness Mistress Pym gave her
driver a grateful look. "Hattie loves him too much,"
she said darkly. "She was always telling me she was
sorry for him—*sorry!*" She sniffed. "Tied to the memory of a dead woman and trying to bring up his daughter in her image!"

"You mean Trinity?"

"Look out for those ruts!"

Lorraine managed to hang on to the reins and right the cart. Mistress Pym was talking again.

"She told me his first wife was an aristocrat—which *he* wasn't. He was forever trying to live up to her high-and-mighty ways when she was alive, and after she died it was even worse. He insisted Trinity had to be as elegant as her mother!"

"It must have been a strain," commented Lorraine dryly. "No wonder Trinity ran away!" She winced at the thought of Trinity and her lover hiding in some secluded copse, thinking they were safe, while the fire ringed them.

The air was filled now with the tang of acrid smoke that made Lorraine's eyes smart, and the distant cries of the searchers seemed to have moved closer.

"Oh, God, the wind has changed!" moaned Mistress Pym as a swirl of smoke obscured their vision. "Poor Hattie—Cedarwood could be cut off!"

Although they could not yet see the actual flames, the sky ahead was lit by a dull red glow and the unpleasant thought came to Lorraine that not only Cedarwood but also she and Mistress Pym could be cut off by the fire.

In the lantern light two figures had appeared, leaping out in front of the cart.

"Who's there?" called out Mistress Pym sharply.

"Why, it's André!" cried Lorraine in relief, reining up. "And Helst! What's happening?"

"The wind has changed and it's sweeping the fire this way," André told her. "They're abandoning the search, letting the outlying plantations go—they mean to save the town instead. Turn back!"

"Oh, poor Harriet!" screamed Mistress Pym, collapsing into a moaning heap in the cart.

"Her sister's trapped at Cedarwood," explained Lorraine, distressed.

The road was suddenly filled with men—L'Estraille and Helst had been just the vanguard. Behind the retreating searchers came the ominous hissing roar of the fire. And over the brow of the hill rose licking tongues of orange flames advancing across a long front.

In the confusion as Lorraine tried to get the cart turned around in close quarters, lanterns were lifted about her so that for a few moments she was bathed in gold. The faces of the men encircling Lorraine were illuminated too, and suddenly one of those faces seemed to spring out at her. Her hands froze on the reins as she saw startled recognition leap into his eyes.

Lorraine's breath seemed to leave her body. Her worst fears had come to pass. The man who stood spraddle-legged in the road was Captain Bridey.

CHAPTER 16

"MISTRESS LONDON!" RUMBLED that familiar voice. "What are *you* doing here?" He looked about him in bewilderment.

Lorraine got control of herself. "I'm with another master, Captian Bridey."

Beneath bushy gray brows, Bridey's hard eyes were focused intently on her flushed face. "I can't believe it—Oddsbud swore he'd never sell your articles of indenture to anyone." His voice was heavy with accusation.

The heat of the fire had reached them, and the horse was beginning to panic, but Lorraine felt as if a chill wind had passed over her. Her hands were cold on the reins and her head swimming, when of a sudden she heard André L'Estraille speak up.

"Ah, but he did sell them. To Captain Cameron—and for such a price that Oddsbud can retire from—"

"From tavernkeeping," Lorraine cut in desperately. "This is André L'Estraille, Captain Bridey. Indeed he was present in the White Horse Tavern when my papers were signed over."

The Frenchman had been about to say "retire from all endeavor," which was pleasantly vague, but he looked with approval upon Lorraine for her quick uptake.

"Aye, in the White Horse Tavern," he agreed pleasantly. "Our captain fancies her," he added with a broad wink at Bridey.

Bridey scowled and turned away with a grunt.

Curious glances were directed at the bound girl in the elaborate blue gown who had been sold to a captain who "fancied" her. Hot with embarrassment, Lorraine wished for a wild moment that the smoke would close over her head. Fortunately, at that moment there was a horrendous flash of lightning and an accompanying crash of thunder that seemed to rock the earth. The heavens opened and water cascaded down in solid sheets. Lorraine felt the cart beneath her shimmy with the force of the downpour.

"The Lord be praised!" Mistress Pym had struggled to her feet and was standing up in the cart, holding up her clasped hands to heaven while the rain battered her and poured down her joyful countenance.

"Sit down or you'll fall out!" Lorraine pulled her back down.

"The fires will be drowned out, now that it's raining. We can go on!" shouted Mistress Pym. "Cedarwood is over there—to your right. The fire can't have reached it yet or we'd have seen it—and now it won't."

"Out of the way!" cried Lorraine. "We're coming through!"

The men surrounding the cart stumbled aside. Horse and cart floundered on.

The way to Cedarwood was short, but to Lorraine, humiliated, frightened, gasping at each new onslaught of rain, and nearly blinded by the curtainlike downpour as she followed Mistress Pym's shouted directions, it seemed interminable.

Though John Pomeroy's "plantation house" was large, it was certainly no mansion. It was a rude half-timbered cottage much like the other medieval-style houses Lorraine had seen in the town, and rain was creating a veritable waterfall off its palmetto-thatched roof.

There was no need to pound on the door. It flew open at their approach and a scared-looking servant girl grasped Mistress Pym's arm. "Oh, do come quick," she pleaded. "Hattie's pains have started and the midwife didn't come. I'm the only one here!"

"Yes, yes. You go take care of the horse, Marnie," directed Mistress Pym. "Get him under cover." As Marnie left, a woman's scream reached them from some distant part of the house. Mistress Pym let her drenched cloak fall to the floor and sprang forward. "Stay here," she called back to Lorraine. "I'll see to Hattie and find us some dry clothes."

Lorraine, standing in soaked shoes, was dripping a puddle on the floor. She unwound the drenched blue scarf from around her head and looked around as she shook out her wet hair. If this house had ever known a woman's touch, she decided, it must have been long ago. The main hall had no furniture at all save for two stiff upright chairs and a gateleg table.

Mistress Pym bustled back shortly. "It's good we got here, the baby's coming soon."

As if to underscore that, another scream rent the air.

Mistress Pym led Lorraine through the dining room, which was cozy and bright, lit by tapers in brass candlesticks. Its furnishings were handsome against walls painted a soft blue. Enshrined above the fireplace was a portrait of a woman whose resemblance to Trinity, the red-haired girl she had seen earlier, was the first thing Lorraine noticed.

"That's Trinity's mother." Mistress Pym paused to glare at the portrait. "She died bearing Trinity and that was the trouble." She sighed. "Pomeroy loved her too much. He keeps all the things she brought from England in this room and he broods on that picture of her at dinner every night."

"Until your sister . . . ?" asked Lorraine hesitantly.

"Even now," was the mournful reply. "And poor Hattie, caring for him so much!"

Lorraine's heart went out to Hattie, whom they found lying on a tumbled bed in a small room at the back of the house. She had thick soft brown hair and when her face relaxed after being contorted with pain, Lorraine could see how kind it was and the honesty that shone from her hazel eyes.

Lorraine, swept along by circumstance, found herself swiftly attired in a clean homespun bodice and kirtle and apron. Her own sodden clothing, she hung dripping over chairs in the kitchen. Protesting that she knew nothing about such things, she found herself assisting Mistress Pym in the delivery of Hattie's child. She was soon fetching and carrying, wiping Hattie's forehead with a damp cloth—and all to the accompaniment of the rain on the roof, pouring down in torrents.

On her treks to the kitchen, where Marnie was kneading dough and making hot broth on Mistress Pym's orders, Lorraine learned more about John Pomeroy's runaway daughter.

"Poor Trinity." Marnie plunged floury hands into the dough. "She loved Jeb so, but her father said he wasn't good enough for her. Jeb swore he'd been pressed aboard a vessel in Portsmouth and then sold as an indentured servant to cover up the crime. He insisted he had a wealthy sister in Somerset and was going to inherit a tidy sum from his grandfather there—but nobody believed him."

Lorraine picked up the hot water she'd been sent to bring. "Couldn't Jeb have written to his people?" she wondered. "And bought himself free?"

Marnie shrugged. "Jeb was a sporting man, he was, and he'd never learned to write."

Sighing for the lovers, Lorraine turned away with the bucket of hot water. At that moment, a long drawn-out riveting scream came from the back of the house.

"Lor'!" cried Marnie.

Lorraine hurried back through the dining room to find Mistress Pym, beaming, holding up a tiny red-faced bundle that emitted little mewing sounds.

"Why, he's crying to be fed already!" her landlady exulted. She thrust the baby into the outstretched arms of the exhausted woman on the bed, who gazed proudly upon her son.

"He looks like John!" Hattie cried happily.

Lorraine found it hard to believe that little screwed-up face resembled anyone at all, but Hattie's remark brought instant agreement from Mistress Pym.

"The living image!" she echoed breathlessly.

Marnie, still somewhat floury, arrived with hot broth for all, then retreated to the kitchen while Mistress Pym and Lorraine tidied up the room. They whisked away the sheets and remade the bed, plumped the pillows, and settled Hattie comfortably with the babe on her breast. It was a far different scene from the tumbled agony they had first come upon in that room.

Leaving the mother and her sister alone to croon over the baby, Lorraine went in search of her clothes, which she hoped would be dry by now.

They were gone.

"Captain Cameron took them," Marnie informed her importantly. "He come by with Mr. Hubbard looking for bandages to bind up one of his men that got hurt in the fire. He said your clothes were ruined and he'd rip them up for bandages too and they went away with them."

Her beautiful blue dress! Her petticoat! Her chemise!

Lorraine fled back the way she had come.

"Oh, Mistress Pym, what am I going to do?" She burst in upon the two women. "All my clothes have been torn up for bandages!"

"You can take what you need of my daughter's," came a tired voice from behind her. "For Trinity will not be needing them ever again."

Lorraine whirled to see a man standing behind her in a drenched burgundy velvet coat and muddy boots. He looked years older than when she had last seen him wrestling with Trinity in the carriage.

"Oh, John—no!" That sincere cry of grief came from the woman on the bed. "Surely there's hope!"

He shook his head. "Charles Hubbard saw them slipping away into the deep ravine to the north of us. He and Captain Cameron have been searching, but the fire surrounded that ravine first and it's burned to a cinder. I must face it, Hattie. I've lost a daughter through my blundering."

"Come see your son, John," she whispered.

He came and stood over her, peering down at the baby now suckling at her breast. "I'm going to marry you, Hattie," he said, breathing hard. "As soon as the banns can be cried. The baby's mine, I'll swear to that. 'Tis true I've lost a daughter—and I'll put up a stone to her—but you've given me a son to take her place. And he'll grow up strong, Hattie, and make us proud."

The glory that broke over Hattie's face was a wonder to see. Lorraine turned away from that sight with her eyes misty.

Mistress Pym nudged her. "Come, we'll find you some proper clothes." She led Lorraine to a handsome bedroom and opened the big cedar wardrobe. "Here, you might like this one." She held out a lovely gown of coral pink linen over a peach-pink sarcenet petticoat. "Trinity was a mite taller than you, but if you turn over the petticoat band and hitch up the overskirt into panniers—"

"I know how," said Lorraine. "But I need a chemise."

"La, she had plenty of those!" Mistress Pym rummaged in a trunk and produced one. It was dazzlingly sheer and trimmed with expensive point lace. "I'll wager her shoes will fit you too."

Lorraine took the things in silence. First, Jocko the Wolf's pall; now, a dead girl's finery. She had the eerie feeling that nothing would ever be truly her own.

"Do you think Jeb Smith's story was true—about having rich relatives in England?" she asked soberly.

"La, who knows? Poor things."

Outside, the rain drummed a funeral dirge.

"You might as well take the gloves too." Mistress Pym held out a pair of peach kid gloves that matched the slippers. And when Lorraine hesitated: "Trinity won't be wearing them and they're too small for Hattie."

Lorraine pinned up her fair hair with Trinity's hairpins and cleverly worked in a shining ribbon of coral satin. The effect was too festive, so she wrapped a scarf around her hair. But even so, as she turned about critically before the mirror, a shimmering vision of peach and pink greeted her sober view.

"*Lor*'!" gasped Marnie, who entered at that mo-

TO LOVE A ROGUE 199

ment. Her mouth was agape. "I'll grant you Trinity was pretty, but *she* never looked like *that!*"

Lorraine's smile was a bit wan but Mistress Pym looked as pleased as if Lorraine were her own daughter. "Where is John Pomeroy?" she asked. Lorraine hoped she wouldn't run into him.

"He's sitting on Hattie's bed and he's promising her the moon. Charles Hubbard is back and he'll take you both back to town in the canopied cart—to keep the rain off you. He'll send your horse and cart down later. And Hattie asked that you please not let him see you in his daughter's clothes—it would hurt him too much."

"I'll be careful," promised Lorraine with a catch in her voice. Kindly Hattie, who had endured so much. From a full heart, Lorraine wished her well.

Charles Hubbard's thin shoulders drooped as he led the women to the canopied cart a servant brought around. He helped them into the back in silence, draped a light coverlet around them to keep them from being splattered when they hit ruts that were still rivulets even though the rain had slackened.

Lorraine did not try to talk to him as they made their way back to St. George's Town. Even Mistress Pym's ebullient spirits were dimmed in the presence of such misery as was evinced by the hunched-up figure of their driver.

When they reached the inn, Hubbard handed over the reins to a servant who dashed out and helped them alight. He appeared about to speak to Lorraine, but Mistress Pym pulled her away with an impatient "Get inside quick or your dress will be ruined!"

In the doorway Lorraine turned to look back and saw Hubbard square his shoulders and walk away rather jauntily into the rain. That jauntiness jarred her—Trinity was barely dead and he was able to forget her already! She turned to observe Mistress Pym's reunion with her irate husband.

"They're going to be married!" that lady cried joyfully. "Now Hattie can make up with Father. Isn't that wonderful, Pym?"

Forgotten for the moment, Lorraine trudged upstairs, still heartsick at what had happened to the runaway lovers. Fatigue washed over her in waves. Her room was empty and she stripped down to her chemise and crawled gratefully into the big square bed.

It was after sunset when she waked to find Raile smiling down at her. From the eaves she could hear water dripping, but the rain had stopped and stars shone cold and white in the black patch of sky she could see through her window.

Raile was in an excellent mood. "Your wild escapade as a midwife has netted us one reward," he told her. "L'Estraille tells me he completely convinced Captain Bridey that Oddsbud had sold me your articles. So since Bridey will be none the wiser until he returns to Rhode Island, you may come out of hiding and dine out with me tonight."

Lorraine glared up at him. "How *could* you tear up my clothes for bandages? The house was full of linens!"

A glint came into his gray eyes. "You disobeyed me," he said silkily. "I told you to wait for me here. When I chanced upon your clothes in Cedarwood's kitchen, I realized you had not. Anyway, you look to have fared rather well." He eyed the coral-pink gown and peach sarcenet petticoat flung over a chair.

"No thanks to you!" she flashed. "Didn't you realize those were the only clothes I'd brought with me? Did you expect me to come back to town naked?"

"Oh, hardly that," he said easily. "I'd have turned up eventually with something—an old shirt, patched trousers . . ."

He was teasing her! She glared at him. "Go away." She waved him to the door. "I want to dress."

"Hurry," he counseled, sticking his head back into the room. "We're dining on Hoppin' John and cedarberry wine at the best hostelry the town affords."

It was hard to resist the impulse to throw a slipper at him. Even so, she hurriedly pulled on her clothes, telling herself the eagerness she felt was entirely due to hunger.

True to his promise, they dined that night in the

low-ceilinged common room of the Gull and Tortoise—dined upon fish chowder and Hoppin' John—that popular Bermuda dish made of rice, peas, and salt pork—and cassava pie. Lorraine created a sensation as she entered the smoky room where at that late hour mainly seafaring men sat about drinking from pewter tankards and smoking long clay pipes. All eyes turned toward the girl in a low cut gown which made a reckless display of the smooth pale skin of her bosom and the silvery sheen of the tops of her firm young breasts. Across the room at a long table surrounded by men from his ship, Lorraine saw Captain Bridey staring at her. She remembered how often he had ordered her to "Bring more ale and be quick about it!" at the Light Horse, and the thought made her give an extra swish to her silken skirts as she returned him a cool look.

They had just settled down at the oaken table when L'Estraille and Helst came in and joined them. Raile was in an expansive mood and did not seem to mind.

"Always you find wonderful clothes, *mademoiselle*," commented André in wonder as he took his seat. "*Mon Dieu*, it is a talent!"

Lorraine tried not to remember whose dress it was. She smiled at André. "I want to thank you," she said softly. "For rising to my defense when Captain Bridey turned up last night."

"I would always rise to your defense," he told her, and there was a richness in his tone that made her color deepen. "Although I will admit that on the way back to town it was difficult to fend off questions from Bridey's crew."

Raile's dark head swung toward him. "I thought you told me you entirely convinced Bridey," he said in a low voice. "Yet all at his table are viewing us with suspicion."

"I did convince him." L'Estraille shrugged airily. "I told him I witnessed the sale—I even told him you were bound for Virginia, so he's not like to follow you. You have nothing to worry about."

Raile's eyes narrowed. "Why did you choose Virginia?"

"Why not Virginia?" countered L'Estraille. "Mac-

Tavish says the *Lass* does not frequent Virginia ports—and 'tis a long way from Barbados.''

"Aye, it's that," Raile muttered.

There was an undercurrent that made Lorraine lean forward.

"Raile rescued me from a terrible situation in Rhode Island," she said impulsively.

A melancholy look played over the Frenchman's handsome features.

"I wish I could have been the one to rescue you," he murmured. Lorraine felt a sudden catch in her heart. André had teased her aboard ship, he had pursued her unmercifully, but he had unhesitatingly sprung forward to save her, not knowing what he might be getting into.

Raile did not notice them, but looked across the room at Captain Bridey and his group. He drummed his fingers. "We'll sail tomorrow night," he decided abruptly. "We've taken on fresh water and our provisioning is completed. I had thought to stay over mainly to give Lorraine a chance to walk free on strange shores." He looked regretful and Lorraine felt her anger at him melting away.

"Perhaps she will walk between us—as she did upon arrival," challenged L'Estraille.

Helst rolled his eyes, fearing a clash. Fortunately the food arrived just then and they were all hungry enough to attack it at once.

"I had hoped to explore the island with you," Raile sighed as Lorraine ate her pudding. "I've heard a great deal about the famous Cathedral Rocks of Sandys and the caverns around Harrington Sound, where I'm told there is a fairyland of stone icicles and winding underground waterways, cool as ice."

"Stay till the end of the week," suggested L'Estraille draining his tankard. "We'll all go!"

"Couldn't we stay, Raile?" asked Lorraine longingly. She had never seen either caverns or cathedrals.

"If we stay too long, the whole crew may defect," Raile said moodily—but he was looking across the room at Captain Bridey, who sat chewing on his lip and glaring at their party.

"Why?" demanded Lorraine. "Is there such a demand for seamen here?"

"Always. A few years back the Bermudians took over the Turks Islands and now they engage in a triangular trade."

"I've heard men at the Light Horse speak of the triangular trade, but I never knew what they meant."

"Each spring Bermudian ships sail to the Indies," explained Raile. "They carry cargoes of cabbages, onions, building stone—this porous coral limestone can be cut with a saw—and whale oil. On the way they leave men at the Turks to rake the salt pans, and after that—"

"But I heard Mistress Pym say the ships bound for the Turks Islands had already left," objected Lorraine.

"Not all," cut in Helst. He was studying two of their French crewmen who had just come in escorted by a Bermudian captain.

"After that," said Raile, "they trade in the Indies for sugar and rum, then trade *that* in the American colonies for Indian corn. In October they pick up their men on the Turks along with the salt, in another triangular voyage. But they're always in need of seamen, and we well might lose our entire French crew—as for example . . ." He nodded toward the two French crewmen the Bermudian captain had in tow. "We've lost three men already, I'm told. *They* sailed on the *Swallow* this morning bound for Bristol—but I've managed to replace them with Bermudians disgruntled with their shares on the last triangular voyage. How long I could keep on doing that, I don't know."

L'Estraille had been listening politely, watching the pair of them with narrowed eyes. He seemed puzzled by this conversation. Helst, whose gaze was on *him*, could imagine what the Frenchman would say later about it. "In France," he would tell the Dutchman, "our dashing captain would be telling his lady about perfumed flowers and sparkling beaches and shady glades among the high cedars—but *this* fellow tells her about salt and onions and she listens to him as if every word he utters is of the utmost importance!"

"They are in love," Helst would explain. And L'Estraille would give him a baffled look. . . .

Now, over his cedarberry wine in the common room of the Gull and Tortoise, Helst sighed. He liked the Frenchman, but if it came to a mutiny, he would side with the captain. And it well might come to that, he mused, with such a fiery wench aboard. They would be lucky to reach the Indies without blood being shed over her.

Helst tossed off his wine and they finished their dinner amicably. Helst and L'Estraille seemed about to embark upon some serious drinking and Lorraine wondered restively if it was not time to go, when suddenly Raile leaned toward her.

"Steady," he murmured. "Be quiet and let me handle this."

She turned to see that Captain Bridey and his group had left their table. But they were not moving toward the door—instead, they were headed in a body in their direction.

Bridey came up to Raile and stopped, legs spread wide apart, rolling slightly on his heels, his thumbs thrust into his belt. Beneath his shock of gray hair his eyes were bloodshot and there was a sneer on his lips that not even his grizzled mustache could hide. His first words drained the color from Lorraine's face.

"The wench lied," he said heavily. "I've been told by my men that the Frenchie said earlier that he'd never set foot on the American coast. So 'tis plain to see that he never witnessed the sale of any articles in Rhode Island!"

" 'Tis plain to see that you're meddling in what's none of your affair," ground out Raile.

Bridey's grizzled jaw was outthrust. "Oddsbud's not only a friend of mine, but he bought a part of the venture of this voyage, and so if I find stolen property of his along the way, 'tis my intention to bring it back to him."

"Are ye saying that I've *not* bought her articles?" asked Raile silkily. There was a dangerous look in his gray eyes.

"I'm saying that tomorrow the law here will call on

you and ask you to display them," growled Captain
Bridey.

"Be damned to you!" Raile was on his feet, his hand
on his sword. "I'll see you in hell first!"

The men around Bridey tensed. Helst and L'Estraille
were edging to their feet. In another moment a fight
would break out and the men of the *Lass* were
outnumbered three to one.

At that moment a wild figure burst through the
open door of the Gull and Tortoise. The whites of his
eyes were the most conspicuous feature of his weathered face and his sandy hair—hacked off seaman
fashion—seemed almost to be standing on end.

"Somebody get the constable!" he shouted hoarsely.
"There's a woman lying dead in the alley out here! I
think it's Dr. Hale's wife! She's been murdered!"

His words brought Lorraine and everybody else to
their feet. As one, the patrons of the Gull and Tortoise surged toward the door, sweeping Captain Bridey
and his men along with them in the general exodus to
the alley.

"I'll see you tomorrow, Cameron," Bridey turned
his head to call to Raile as he was shoved along.

"Depend upon it!" rasped Raile. "And depend upon
seeing this as well!" He drew his sword and brandished the naked blade. In the crowd Captain Bridey
ducked his head and made haste to be among those
pouring out the door. The Rhode Island captain, who
was no swordsman, had no stomach for a fight with
that firebrand. Let the law handle him!

The room was nearly clear now. Raile turned to the
Dutchman. "Take Mistress Lorraine aboard the *Lass*,
Helst—as speedily as you can."

"I'll be glad to take her," volunteered L'Estraille
eagerly.

"No, you speak the best French. Move up and down
the street collecting the men. We've little time if we're
to make the tide."

"But what of you?" cried Lorraine, pulling back
from Helst's urging arm. "Where will you be?"

"I'll be strutting about, being seen by all—as a

symbol that nothing's amiss," was her captain's laconic reply.

"But suppose—"

"Suppose nothing," he said quietly, and there was a reassuring light in the gray eyes that looked down at her. "We'll clear Bermudian waters before the dawn breaks. Who'll search for us on a trumped-up charge made by a captain who—I'll make sure everyone understands—has a grudge against me?"

IV:

THE GIFT OF
THE SEA

CHAPTER 17

The Storm-Lashed Seas

THE FLIGHT FROM St. George had an eerie quality for Lorraine. It was like a nightmare—dreamed twice. In silence she and Helst glided across the water toward the waiting *Lass*. In silence she was hoisted aboard. Shortly after that the men came, in a longboat. And after what seemed an interminable time to Lorraine, Raile arrived, rowing out to the ship with hardly a plash of the oars to mark his passage.

Without lights they drifted out of the harbor, skimming the dark waters to negotiate the dangerous reefs.

Lorraine had retired to their cabin. It was still dark when Raile joined her.

"I promised you that dawn would find you beyond Bridey's reach—and so it will," he said.

Lorraine looked up, a little dazzled at the sight of him standing there inside the cabin, tall and dark and resolute in the glow of the ship's lantern. He looked rather splendid, she thought wistfully. And ruthless too—a man born to prevail.

"I never doubted it," she said simply. Nor had she. Indeed as she had waited at the ship's rail, twisting her hands together and willing him to return safe, she had had time to think about how he had defended her with reckless disregard for his own life. She blushed to think that she had chided him about using her dress for bandages. "You have saved me again," she said softly.

A slow smile lit up his hard features. "Did you think I would let such as Bridey take you from me, lass?"

She made a little fluttering gesture, and looked down at her dress. "If only poor Trinity and her lover could have been as lucky. . . ." Her voice was wistful.

He spoke deliberately, divesting himself of sword and coat as he did. "I did not tear up your blue dress for bandages after all."

She drew in her breath and involuntarily cast a look around her. "You didn't? Then where is it?"

He gave her a droll look. "I gave it away—to a lady. And before you strike me, Lorraine, let me say that the lady, wearing your blue dress and with her red hair concealed by your blue scarf, rode through the rain alongside me yestermorn in the company of a man swathed in bandages. All the town will tell you that you and I and my wounded crew member struck out in the *Lass*'s longboat—but none, I daresay, will have noticed that, oddly enough, we did not approach the *Lass* but instead made for the *Swallow*, which was just then putting to sea—destination Bristol."

Lorraine's eyes widened. "*Trinity?*" she breathed.

"You're very quick," he said, pulling off his boots. "And Jeb was swathed in bandages so as to be rendered unrecognizable. So"—he was shrugging out of his shirt—"they're safely on their way."

Lorraine threw her arms around his neck with a whoop. "Oh, Raile, that's wonderful!" She drew away in quick embarrassment, for the sudden assault of her young female body against his naked chest had brought a hot light to her captain's eyes.

"And so," he drawled, throwing his shirt aside, "if Jeb Smith hasn't lied about his prospects, he and Trinity should have a good life ahead of them in England."

"Oh, he hasn't, I'm sure of it!" cried Lorraine. "If Charles Hubbard thought him suitable for Trinity, I'd trust him!"

You'd trust L'Estraille as well, thought Raile dryly, but he did not voice the comment.

"But . . . their passage money!" She looked worried.

"Already paid. The *Swallow* was where they were headed when they were caught that day."

"Paid by whom?"

"By Charles Hubbard. All his savings went into the voyage. He indentured himself to John Pomeroy for three years to raise the rest—telling Pomeroy a trumped-up story about his mother back in England needing money."

Lorraine stared at Raile, round-eyed. Charles, that scrawny scarecrow with the kind heart, had sold himself into bondage to send his only love away from him—forever. And he had walked away looking *jaunty!* Her eyes filled at the memory.

"Oh, Raile," she said softly. "Why didn't you tell me?"

"Because that expressive face of yours mirrors your thoughts. And Hubbard and I wanted you to have just the right amount of indignation to be plausible while we supplied the gloom. It was Hubbard's plan. He had hidden the pair in a ruined cistern. He came into town to find me, hoping I could get them aboard the *Swallow* before she sailed."

"And you did!"

"Yes, I did."

Lorraine hadn't known she could love a man as much as she loved Raile at that moment.

"What will become of Charles Hubbard now?" she asked anxiously

"Why, he'll keep Pomeroy's books for him as Jeb Smith did, and he'll tutor Hattie and her newborn in the ways of the gentry, as befits the new mistress of Cedarwood!" His gray eyes danced and Lorraine choked off a sputter of laughter.

"Hubbard begs you to keep forever silent about this, Lorraine. If it becomes known, it would mean the whipping post for him and pursuit and capture for the lovers."

"None will hear it from me," she promised. "Oh, Raile . . . it was wonderful of you." Her voice was tremulous, her face upturned, blue-gray eyes luminous, soft lips parted.

Captain Cameron was quick to note these things—and quick to take advantage of them.

"Lorraine . . ." he murmured, and took her in his

arms. She went into his arms as if it were the natural, indeed the *only* thing to do. The sudden impact of her soft body against his hard one sent a tingling shock through her and she trembled against him.

Gently his strong hands caressed her. He stroked her long shining hair as his lips roved over her face and throat—and every inch of skin he touched felt alive and warmed by the pressure of his masculinity.

He began unhooking her bodice and she did not care. A kind of wild madness swept over Lorraine, enveloping her in its warmth, its sweetness. She had been wrong about Philip—he had never been the man for her. Raile was her man, her dreamed-of mate, and now she knew it with a blazing certainty.

Her very flesh tingled with desire for him. She met his ardor kiss for kiss, touch for flaming touch. Somewhere in this scorching madness their clothes had left them, and in dawn's pale light they swayed to the bunk and sank upon it blissfully.

Her body was cushioned beneath his straining one. He entered her purposefully, sure of his reception. She moaned beneath him, matching his strong rhythm with her own. Their bodies, their very souls seemed to flow together, to become one, inseparable.

There in the purity of the pale dawn they took each other as the first man and the first woman might have taken each other—in wonder and delight and with a kind of reverence never to be forgotten. Raile was the perfect lover, thoughtful, ardent, fierce, yet leisurely, driving her on to a zenith of passion before seeking his own satisfaction.

Dawn's pink light had turned to gold before the magic burst for them in a shower of stars and together they zoomed to heights undreamed-of, and floated down in a sea of sighs to the quivering lovely afterglow of passion spent.

They gazed upon each other silently, needing no words.

Raile smiled down upon her naked form and bent to press a kiss upon each shell-pink nipple. Then he burrowed with his lips in the rising and falling area between her breasts and his dark hair spilled over upon the pearly pallor of her skin.

She reached up to touch his hair. It was like gleaming heavy silk. All of her being felt aglow with tenderness for him. And when at last he took her again, took her with yearning, as if he could never get enough of her, it was a woman as pliant as a willow who moved against him, glad to be in his arms, content to find fulfillment in his warm embrace.

When, later, Raile slept soundly beside her, Lorraine's eyes were wet with unshed tears. Tears of happiness, that in her muddled life she had found someone at last. Someone good, kind, wonderful, caring. . . .

The age-old murmur of the sea blended with Raile's steady breathing. The lean ship creaked companionably. And it seemed to Lorraine, as a veil of sleep fell softly over her, that the love she had found was a gift of the sea.

She woke luxuriously to find the sun streaming through the bank of stern windows. Feeling as if she had been enjoying lovely dreams, she let her eyelids drift closed again—and then she remembered. She had spent last night in Raile's arms.

She reached out a lazy arm to caress him—and found he was not there. Her eyes snapped open then and she saw him, clad only in his trousers, leaning upon the sill of one of the stern windows, looking out.

She stretched and sighed. "Good morning," she volunteered.

"Good morning." He did not turn.

She gave his broad muscular back a questioning look.

"Are you coming back to bed?" she asked hopefully.

"No, I am not coming back to bed." He spoke still gazing out of the window. His voice was stern, self-accusing. "I am a blackguard indeed," he muttered. "No better than the rest—and deserving less."

Lorraine blinked. And waited. The answer was soon forthcoming.

"I have lured you to my bed," he said heavily.

Lorraine laughed.

Her laughter seemed to goad him. He swung about and it was a haggard face that greeted her.

"You are young, you know nothing of life. I used your joy over learning that Jeb and Trinity were safe. *That* is what brought you to my bed. And I knew it!"

But I *wanted* to come to your bed! her heart protested.

"I promised to transport you safe to the Indies."

"And that you will do," she said, puzzled.

"To the Indies—but not unsullied. I stand before you shamed."

"Why?" she demanded, and his next words splashed the cold truth upon her.

"Because, as I told you from the first, I am not a marrying man."

Lorraine's heart flinched—and then she thought about that. After all, she asked herself sturdily, what could marriage offer that would outshine such joyous wonders as she had known last night? Her pride flared up.

"So you are not a marrying man? I believe that I am not a marrying woman."

He stared at her, thunderstruck. "*All* women are marrying women." He stated it flatly. "There *is* no other kind."

"Ah, but there is. I myself am such a one." With a saucy gesture she threw back the coverlet and in doing so revealed the full beauty of her naked breasts. He caught his breath at sight of them. "What is it that makes you think I would marry you?' she challenged. "Have I seemed so eager to wed?"

He groaned. "No, of course not. But—"

"Well, then?" She stood naked on her slender feet and stretched luxuriously. Her long blonde hair rippled down over her white gleaming shoulders and cascaded down her smooth back to brush the soft roundness of her pale buttocks. She turned toward Raile with a mocking look, for somehow seeing him so upset—and for such a reason!—made her feel perversely confident, buoyant, in control. "Indeed I think I would prefer being a mistress to being a wife."

He looked shocked. "Nonsense," he said roughly.

Her smile was mocking but her blue-gray gaze was

very level. "I will be your mistress until we reach land," she told him softly. "But after that I will make you no promises."

Her wicked smile followed him as he left, looking decidedly ruffled.

While she was dressing, he came back to stand studying her. She greeted him with total unconcern, but made sure that she took a long time pulling on her stockings so that her shapely legs remained temptingly in his vision. After all, he *deserved* to be tormented for practically telling her to her face that she was a hot wench, but one he had no wish to marry! It would have been more satisfying, she told herself, to have had him offer for her—and be able to turn him down!

She continued punishing him. By pulling the neckline of her pink dress down until it was disconcertingly low. By adopting a slight sidle in her walk as she breezed past him in search of her shoes, which had somehow got kicked across the room. By combing her long fair hair out in a cloud and letting it carelessly brush against his face as he walked by.

He seemed undecided about how to treat her. By the time they had finished breakfast, he waxed expansive.

"You will not find me ungenerous," he suggested tentatively.

Lorraine brushed that remark aside. "I would not sell myself for gold," she told him coldly.

"I only meant—"

"I know what you meant." Her head lifted and defiant pride looked out of her blue-gray eyes. "As long as I find your company pleasurable, I will stay with you, Raile. And no longer."

A slight frown creased his brow. "I see. You are giving me notice that you will then seek other arms?"

"I did not say that," she said impatiently. "And anyway, why should we think about it now?"

"Why indeed?" A mask seemed to slip over his face. But she could see that she had upset him.

The wench had spirit, he told himself uneasily. Perhaps more spirit than he was prepared to handle. He had expected—indeed been steeled for—an emotional scene when he informed her that he was not a marrying man: tears, accusations, sulks. But to be blandly regarded as a light love, to be worn or tossed away like a favorite ball gown, was unsettling.

It was bravado on her part, of course, he told himself, but—perhaps not!

He wondered suddenly if she was considering L'Estraille as a replacement for him, and his strong hands clenched. By God, if that Frenchman . . . !

"What is the matter?" Lorraine interrupted his turbulent thoughts. "You look as if you are about to murder someone!"

"I must see to ship matters," he said abruptly, and left.

Later they strolled companionably about the deck. André L'Estraille, seeing Lorraine leaning slightly against her captain and smiling up into his dark face, turned a haggard countenance to Helst.

"It has happened, Helst," he said hoarsely. "They are sleeping together at last."

"It was to be expected," growled Helst. "The wonder is that it has not happened before this! Look at her, L'Estraille!"

"I am looking," groaned L'Estraille.

Helst's gaze was rapt. "Indeed how could any man share a room with *that*"—he nodded across the deck toward Lorraine's glowing countenance and lissome figure in her shimmering pink gown—"and *not* sleep with her? You should put her out of your mind, L'Estraille, and wish them both long life and happiness!"

"Put her out of my mind?" growled L'Estraille. "Ah, that I can't do, Helst. She was made for me, and by all the gods, I'll have her yet!"

Helst sighed and watched his friend hurry away. André went down to visit the four men who were in sick bay, suffering either from food poisoning got in the lowest of Bermuda's waterfront dives or from cuts and gashes received in fights that broke out over St. George's waterfront whores.

But before he went, the Frenchman had given Lorraine such a look of anguished yearning that she was touched by it. André had guessed the way things now were between herself and Raile—he had not had to be told. And André was so plainly in love with her—he deserved some word from her own lips.

So when Raile left her side to confer with MacTavish, Lorraine seized her chance and hurried after the ship's doctor.

It was dark down below, the only light a swinging lantern that did not light up the mysterious dark corners of what seemed a gaping hole. Lorraine had not been in this part of the ship before. At some distance she could see the two men who had been made ill from bad food, and a little nearer, one of the two who had been injured in a fight, lying despondent, swathed in bandages. After the brilliance of the sunlit deck, it took Lorraine a moment to accustom her eyes to the dimness and find the doctor.

He was bent over, attending his fourth patient, Gautier, the big hairy mute. Lorraine had noticed Gautier before up on deck. His huge hands, always clenching and unclenching, his unchanging expression and hulking walk—indeed the impression he gave of sheer brute force surging mindlessly forward—had always frightened her. Now at close quarters she took an involuntary step back away from him, and as she did so, the ship's doctor looked up, astonished to see her there.

"André," she said impulsively. "I had to speak to you. To tell you how it is with Raile and me."

L'Estraille put down the bandages he was holding and seized her by the arm, moving her away to one of the darker corners, where they could have more privacy. The big mute's hungry eyes followed her.

"There is no need to tell me how things are between you," André said bitterly. " 'Tis plain you have accepted his offer—and not mine." He was still holding on to her arm.

"André, you have been kindness itself." There was grief in Lorraine's voice that she should have hurt him so. "It is just that . . . that . . ."

"That you have chosen him," he finished for her. She was so close, so maddeningly close. The touch of her seared him and his bitterness spilled over. "Ah, Lorraine, Lorraine, did you not know how that would turn the knife in my heart? Is there no chance for me?" His grip tightened and impetuously he caught her to him. "Let me prove to you that I am the better lover—let me spend my life making love to you!" His lips burned down upon her own.

Lorraine was unprepared for the suddenness of his onslaught. She had thought only to let him hear from her own lips in private that she loved the captain. As she felt herself tipping backward and caught at his coat to keep from falling, she heard a stern voice ring out.

"L'Estraille!" Raile's voice pierced the dimness, and Raile's strong hand snatched her suddenly from the Frenchman's arms and spun her about to face him. "What is the meaning of this, Lorraine? Did you think I would not notice that you had followed L'Estraille belowdeck?"

Her face was flushed. "I only wished to speak to André alone, to tell him—"

"Yes, and she has every right to speak to me!" interrupted L'Estraille hotly. "You have snatched an innocent girl from her native shores, Captain Cameron, a *jeune fille!* You have kept her closed up and not allowed her to see the world!"

"*Your* world, I suppose, L'Estraille?" drawled Raile.

"A world she might well prefer to yours!"

"Apparently she prefers it already." Raile gave Lorraine a bleak look. "She followed you here."

"No!" choked Lorraine. "Raile, you don't understand!"

"I understand well enough. Mistress London, will you be good enough to accompany me topside?"

"So that you can fill her head with lies?" That heady contact with Lorraine's fresh young female body had made the ship's doctor ignore all caution. Now he thrust Lorraine aside and stepped between them.

"Stand aside, L'Estraille," his captain warned. "I'll overlook that last remark because this voyage needs a doctor."

The Frenchman was breathing hard. "By God, you shall not have her!" he cried, almost on a sob.

Raile reached out a strong hand and gave the Frenchman's chest a solid shove that sent him stagger-

ing back against the wooden wall. He rose with a
snarl—and with a naked blade in his hand.

Catlike, Raile responded. His own blade was out,
and he had pushed Lorraine behind him. "If it's a
fight you want, L'Estraille, you shall have it," he told
the Frenchman evenly. "But it will be on deck in the
light of day and Mistress Lorraine shall be a spectator
along with the crew."

"No, that it will not," panted L'Estraille, his brassy
gold eyes gone bloodshot with fury. "It will be here
and now where your officers cannot interfere."

"As you like." Raile parried the Frenchman's sudden thrust, on legs that seemed to be steel springs in
themselves. He was out of range of that flashing blade
even as Lorraine shrank back into the shadows.

The Frenchman laughed. "You cannot escape me
by these tactics," he mocked, crouching and swaying
from side to side, his long blade snaking out and
catching the light.

"I do not seek to escape you," was the level response. "I only ask that you allow Mistress Lorraine
to leave us so that she may not be hurt."

"She will receive no hurt from me," mocked the
Frenchman. "Is it yourself you doubt?"

"André," cried Lorraine. "Do not mock him! It is
your life you chance! Lay down your sword!"

"Yes, listen to her, L'Estraille." Raile's voice was
heavy with irony. "She gives you sound advice."

"Ha!" Maddened that he should be thought the
lesser man by Lorraine, L'Estraille lunged forward
recklessly—but he had miscalculated the motion of the
ship. It sent him ever so slightly to the right of his
target and with that opening Raile stepped in and sent
his own blade neatly through the doctor's sword arm.

Swearing, the ship's doctor dropped his sword and
clutched his arm. Raile picked up L'Estraille's sword
and sheathed his own. With his other hand he grabbed
Lorraine's wrist and dragged her protesting to the
deck.

There he encountered Helst and tossed the Frenchman's sword to him. "Take charge of L'Estraille's
sword, Helst—he'll not be needing it for the rest of the

voyage. And go below and see what you can do for him. He was ministering to the sick and wounded and now has joined them."

Helst caught the sword and stared openmouthed at the sight of the captain dragging his flushed-faced lady along the deck. L'Estraille's mad passion for Lorraine had caught up with him, Helst realized. He hurried below to find the Frenchman cursing and binding up his own wound—somewhat awkwardly, since he had to use his left hand.

"You have brought this on yourself, L'Estraille," Helst told his friend severely. "You are lucky the captain did not clap you in irons."

"Oh, go to the devil," L'Estraille groaned. His throbbing arm did not hurt him nearly so much as the memory of those warm—even though protesting—lips that had been so briefly his, or the thought that he had not cut such a fine figure in the lady's eyes. "You do not know what it is to be in love, Helst—unswervingly in love, past all repenting!"

"I know what it is to be a fool," sighed Helst. "You have just shown me!"

"Topside, Raile had dragged Lorraine to his cabin, closed the door with his foot, and spun her about.

"Is this the way you keep your bargain?" he demanded harshly. "I understood you to say you would not seek other arms until we reached land."

"Raile," Lorraine protested, "you do not understand. André is in love with me."

"Oh, that's plain enough!"

"I have hurt him by"—she swallowed—"by *preferring* you, can't you see that?"

"And so you followed him belowdecks and took him in your arms to soothe the pain?"

"I did nothing of the sort!" Her impatience flared. "He misunderstood me is all."

"Well at least *I* do not misunderstand you." Raile's voice struck her like a slap. "You are a light wench. Did you think I would not see you slipping away to follow L'Estraille below? I do not invite such easy women to my bed."

Lorraine drew herself up. "And you need not join me in this bunk!" she cried in a voice that shook.

"I do not intend to," was the savage response. "You can sleep on the floor or on the deck for all I care, but from this night on I will occupy my own bunk!"

In silent rage she watched him go.

Dinner that night was not well-attended. The ship's doctor was "indisposed" and rumors of the cause of his indisposition flew about. The captain's lady sent word via Johnny Sears that she was not hungry and would not be joining them. And the captain himself spent the time stalking the deck and studying the sky.

Inside the cabin Lorraine was pacing about, hot with indignation. How dare Raile think those things of her? Could he not see that she had only been . . . What had she only been? Certainly André L'Estraille's admiration was ardent and intense, certainly she found him attractive, but she would never have betrayed Raile—how could he think it?

First, she latched the cabin door—let him kick it in!—then she unlatched it, all too eager to give him a piece of her mind. Why did he not come back? It was growing late and the long swells the ship rode were dulling her senses, making her sleepy.

Raile did not return to the cabin. She did not know where he slept—or if he slept.

By morning the strong wind that had sprung up in the night was bearing them rapidly south. Lorraine skulked in the cabin, not caring to have her confrontation with Raile on deck where others could observe them. He was wrong, wrong! But . . . how could she make him see it?

Plainly the evidence was against her. She ate her breakfast and then her lunch alone in the cabin.

By late afternoon, she could stand it no longer and went out at last upon the deck. Raile stood some distance away conversing with MacTavish. As Lorraine approached them, MacTavish bowed and gave her a civil greeting. Raile appeared not to see her and continued talking earnestly, managing adroitly to turn his back to her. MacTavish looked distressed but Lorraine was furious at being ignored.

"I wonder if you could tell me of André's condition, Mr. MacTavish?" she interrupted them sweetly. "He is suffering from a wound given him by our captain in a fit of jealousy."

A sudden quiver went through the broad back that had been presented to her. Raile wheeled around, and although his dark face was impassive, there were little sparks flashing in his cold gray eyes.

"Our ship's doctor is resting nicely. Helst attends him."

"Perhaps I should see him myself," she caroled.

For a moment she thought he would spring at her—and indeed in that reckless moment she would have welcomed it to break his insulting indifference. Then his iron control returned. "You will return to your cabin, mistress," he instructed her. "And make no more trouble aboard this ship."

Several sailors had stopped to stare.

"You have no authority over me, Raile Cameron," she heard herself say perversely. "I am not one of your crew that you may order me about!"

Raile took a threatening step toward her. "If you defy me, you will find that I have nothing against putting a woman in irons."

MacTavish rolled his eyes toward heaven, but Lorraine, well aware that she had gone too far, could not resist a parting shot as she turned to return to her cabin. "To think," she said icily, "that I had believed you to be a gentleman!"

"Well, now you know that I am not!" Raile's hard voice followed her. "But I am captain here and you will damn well obey me!" He turned to MacTavish as her skirts swished away from him. "What am I to do with the lass, Tav?" He was shaking his head.

"Take her to Barbados," growled MacTavish. "And set her ashore."

"Aye," said Raile morosely. "To Barbados."

Feeling mutinous, Lorraine went down to dinner unescorted. Conversation among the ship's officers stopped abruptly at sight of her. André was absent, but Raile arrived shortly and made her a brief but civil bow. All eyes were on them. Lorraine felt embarrassed.

Conversation at dinner centered mainly upon their last port of call, Bermuda, and Lorraine was treated to all the grisly details of the two women who had been found murdered there. "With their own hair," Derry Cork declared, shaking his big head. "Same as in Bordeaux. Can't understand it."

Suddenly Lorraine was reminded of all those times she had felt eyes watching her on deck and she jumped when one of the English officers at her elbow asked her if she would like more wine.

"No, thank you," she said weakly and, as soon as she could, excused herself.

As she made her way back across the deck to her cabin, she looked about her fearfully, but the watched feeling she had known before did not return. There was no watcher in the shadows now.

She wondered if Raile would join her tonight. He had not spoken two words to her at dinner. Rebelliously she climbed into the bunk. If he did not want her there, he would just have to put her out by force! He would not find her submissively stretched out upon the floor just because he had ordered her to sleep there!

But Raile did not join her. She guessed he was drinking with his ship's officers, exchanging stories, talking of . . . What did men talk of? Women, more than likely. And money. Perhaps they were gambling. She wished she could join them but guessed she would not be welcome. On the way to Bermuda Helst had taught her to play cards and she had enjoyed it—she was even learning to wager, vast mythical sums which no one ever expected to be called upon to pay.

It was after midnight when the squall struck.

Lorraine was pitched from her bed by the sudden violent blow of the wind which shook the *Lass* through all her timbers. Then, as Lorraine struggled to her feet, the lean ship seemed to charge before the wind. Lorraine, gasping, held on to anything she could find and watched the chairs slide across the floor to collide with the table.

Outside it was worse. Spray from the tall waves burst over the deck and the heavy canvas was being hauled down with difficulty. Some of it never made it. With a wrench that could be heard throughout the ship, the sailcloth ripped, tore free, and collapsed upon the deck amid a tangle of cordage. Men swarmed over it, half-drowned by the wind-driven spray.

They had been driving steadily south with favorable winds, skirting the Bahamas to their right, intending to slip through the Mona Passage into the Caribbean Sea and thence to Barbados. But now the wind had tricked them and was driving them steadily westward. Though they struggled to hold a southerly course they were being swept irresistibly along the northern coast of Hispaniola—west toward Cuba.

Lorraine, crouched in her bunk and holding on for dear life, looked up as the door burst open and Raile came in along with a sheet of rain. He was drenched to the skin. Water poured off him and when he shook his head to toss back his dark hair, the air was filled with a shower of droplets.

He seemed to have forgotten their differences. "We are being swept west by this gale," he told her. "With luck we'll ease through the Windward Passage."

"And where is that?" she asked fearfully.

"Between Cuba and Hispaniola," he told her tersely. "Stay inside, you could be blown from the deck. Johnny Sears will bring you anything you need."

Feeling helpless, she watched him depart.

All night the men of the *Likely Lass* fought their way down the Windward Passage, straining to keep their light craft from being wrecked upon the eastern tip of Cuba. By morning they had made it and the Bahía de Guantánamo lay somewhere to starboard through flying mists of spray.

But their wild passage had brought them something else. The parts of another ship—perhaps broken free from her Cuban moorings and smashed by the heavy seas—broke over the deck, knocked one man senseless, and fouled the rudder. It was impossible to fix the rudder in the gale, and they were driven forward, at the mercy of wind and current, pursued by screaming winds down the length of the Greater Antilles, with the coast of Cuba somewhere beyond their vision streaming by to the north of them.

All day the heavy gale hounded them through the water, and evening brought no respite from the howling winds and wild seas. In her cabin Lorraine could hear the protesting timbers creak and shudder under the battering of the wind. Raile came in on occasion, but not to sleep. He gulped down soup or coffee and made his way out through sheets of rain onto the deck again, leaving Lorraine to shudder at the violent force of nature unleashed.

The next afternoon the winds finally abated and even then there were squally gusts that struck the ship solid shuddering blows.

"Where do you think we are?" Lorraine asked Raile when at last, weary, he came back to the cabin and threw himself down upon the floor.

"God knows," he said. "We're still being driven west."

And fell asleep.

With those disquieting words echoing in her brain, Lorraine leapt up. "You're tired," she said solicitously. "Wouldn't you like to sleep in your bunk? I could . . ." Her words trailed off. Exhausted by his long battle with the sea, Raile did not even stir.

She sat on the edge of the bunk wondering if she should do something. There seemed to be nothing to do. Eventually she climbed back into the bunk and, with Raile's long body lying prone before the door, she had her first good night's sleep since their quarrel.

CHAPTER 18

The City of the Dawn
The Coast of Yucatan, Mexico

LORRAINE AWOKE TO find calmer waters, sunlight, and Raile gone. Outside on deck she could hear his voice giving orders. She dressed quickly in her old clothes, for her brief glimpses of the deck during the storm had shown her a sodden shambles of cordage and canvas and shattered timbers.

Around her, when she reached the deck, the clouds had blown away, the sky was clear and blue, and the ketch was wallowing in heavy surf, being driven ashore by the still-turbulent waters.

And it was a strange shore indeed that confronted them when the crew of the *Likely Lass* cast hasty anchor lest their damaged craft pile up on the rocks.

Lorraine stood by the rail with the others and stared up in awe at the sight that confronted them. Sheer limestone bluffs, forty feet high, some of them severely undercut by the ocean, rose before them. To left and right they could see the heavy surf breaking over strips of white beach, all fringed by what looked like an impenetrable dark green forest that stretched away endlessly.

And atop those cliffs rose a city of stone, a fortress city surrounded by a thoroughly defensible wall twelve feet high that extended outward for some twenty-two hundred feet. It did not look like any town that Lorraine had ever seen or even imagined. Rising—almost as if it had grown out of the solid rock—was a massive three-story building, terraced and strange, the apparent command post looking out to sea.

In the little knot of officers Lorraine had joined at the rail, someone expelled a long slow breath. "*Mon Dieu!*" The words were uttered with feeling.

Lorraine turned to see that André L'Estraille had joined the group. His right arm was in a sling.

But it was Raile, leaning upon the ship's rail, who spoke.

"We are in luck," he said softly. "I think I know this place. A couple of years ago I picked up a ship-wrecked Spanish friar. He told me about it. This place is called Zama, City of the Dawn—perhaps because it faces east and catches the first rays of the morning sun. That building up there"—he nodded toward the frowning stone fortress above them—"is the Castillo, a temple to ancient gods long gone."

"Yes, but where are the people?" muttered MacTavish. "A city so large should have dozens of laddies and lassies swarming down that cliff to greet us—for good or ill."

"It is a place of devils," muttered Derry Cork.

Lorraine flashed the big Irishman a nervous look, for she too felt the old stones seemed—even shining in the clean-washed morning sunlight after the storm—to be somehow fraught with menace.

"The friar told me this was the first city the Spanish visited on the coast of Mexico," Raile told MacTavish soberly. "The Indians here—as in all of Yucatán—were presented as slaves along with the land by royal grant to various conquistadors around Valladolid, which lies some distance to the northwest. If I am right, this is an empty city."

An empty city. . . .

So far Raile had not acknowledged Lorraine's presence.

"We will go ashore," He said abruptly. "Tav, you'll come along, and Helst. L'Estraille, you stay on board with the sick and wounded."

He went on, rattling off orders. Lorraine watched

the French crewmen go over the side into the boat. She saw Gautier, the big mute L'Estraille had been attending when she had ventured below, climb in with surprising agility for a wounded man. So the doctor had managed to heal some of them, even during the storm.

Plainly they were going to leave her behind—and suddenly she did not want to be left behind. "Do I accompany you to shore? Or do you wish me to stay and attend the doctor's wound?"

Raile turned to look at her then. His eyes glinted at her tone, but something in his face softened as he looked down at her. Lorraine had been—like the *Lass* herself—a gallant voyager, brave and uncomplaining, breasting every wave. She deserved her shore leave. He did not think there would be much danger.

"You may accompany us ashore, Lorraine," he said.

Lorraine was surprised. She had expected to be locked in her cabin to keep her away from the ship's doctor. She gave Raile a smile of thanks, but he chose not to look at her, and her heart hardened against him. With suppressed excitement, she got into the longboat.

The shore party from the *Likely Lass* was silent and uneasy as with long strokes of the oars they approached the alien shore, the longboat tossing in the still-wild surf. With guns at the ready and swords eased in their scabbards, the men approached the desolate fortress. They found their way in through one of the five narrow entrances that gave access to the city through a mighty wall, which rose twelve feet high and was nine feet thick.

"Even that did not keep out Corté's and his five hundred followers," muttered MacTavish, shaking his head.

"With cannon mounted on these cliffs, I could hold off a fleet," was Derry Cork's comment.

"Quiet," muttered Raile, for they were about to enter what appeared to be the main thoroughfare.

Glancing nervously about them, they explored an empty city that, Lorraine thought, looking about her, must once have rung with children's laughter and market bargaining and all the normal sounds of everyday living.

"It is as I thought—deserted," Raile remarked with satisfaction. He had been carrying his sword warily unsheathed and now he stuck it back in its scabbard.

They reached the top terrace of the sprawling gray Castillo, having made their way up the broad central stairway of that monumental structure. Before them two heavy serpent pillars supported a portico that fronted two small vaulted halls. The silence was oppressive.

"The friar was right, this does seem to be a temple," Raile mused. "And this must be the main sanctuary." For before them, centrally located in three rectangular niches in the frieze molding, was a statue of a winged god, crowned and plunging downward.

"A falling angel," whispered Lorraine, impressed.

"I doubt they had angels. But some sort of deity certainly. The friar said no one knew what god this was, but he described him well enough."

Lorraine was glad to leave the vaulted dimness and return to the bright glare of the terrace that overlooked the sea.

"Are we safe here?" she asked, looking around her uncertainly.

Raile shrugged. "This is a pirate coast. The Spanish consider it unhealthy, so they have moved inland to places like Valladolid. If we are lucky we can make our repairs before we are discovered by either pirates or Spaniards. We'll go inland in two parties: one to find suitable materials to repair the ship, the other to forage for whatever food the land has to offer. We will be back, I hope, before dark."

"You won't leave me here alone?" Lorraine asked, alarmed.

"Helst will stay with you," said Raile tersely. "Should any problem arise, he can signal the ship and someone will come ashore to pick you up."

Lorraine glanced out to sea, where the battered *Lass* glimmered in the sun. It was not a bad place to spend an afternoon, she told herself, with an interesting fellow like Helst to keep her company.

The exploring parties were quickly chosen and marched away, Raile leading one, and MacTavish, who had been warned not to venture too far inland lest he come upon the Spanish *vecinos* of Valladolid, leading the other group.

Helst was curious about the town. Lorraine accompanied him as he exclaimed over everything, wondering aloud why the people had fled, why they had not fought for such a citadel.

Peering at the frescoes, the painted stucco, Lorraine could find no answer. The pictures and bas-reliefs seemed to depict a strange primitive people with flattened foreheads and cross-eyed gods.

"It's a strange place. The walls of the buildings seem to flare upward," observed Lorraine. "Of course, perhaps they did that to highlight all that carving?" She waved an arm upward at the sculptured relief.

The Dutchman considered—then he grinned. "No, 'tis to let the rainwater drain down without damaging those corners." He pointed to the painted stucco molding.

Lorraine sighed. Plainly Helst was not a romantic. It would have been nicer to believe that the shadowy builders of this ancient city had built with only beauty in mind.

"But they did choose a good defensive site," granted Helst, looking around him appraisingly.

The sun's rays were dazzling. Lorraine was aware that her damp chemise was sticking to her in the heat. They had been walking a long time, prowling the deserted avenues, puzzling over the strange stone structures. A pair of seabirds dipped suddenly overhead, and Lorraine, attracted by the whir of wings, looked up. She was momentarily blinded by the sun's brightness.

But not before she saw a slight figure dart behind a nearby building. She had caught only a brief glimpse before the sun blinded her, but her impression was of a barefoot young girl in strange dress, a girl with long black braided hair.

"Helst!" She clutched his arm. "I saw someone— over there!"

Helst sprinted forward, dragging out his pistol.

"Oh, don't use that!" Lorraine was panting, trying to stay beside him in the wretched heat. "It was a young girl, I think."

After a while they gave up the search, and Helst found them a shaded place to sit between two buildings.

"You must have imagined it," he told her. "The sun plays strange tricks on the eyes."

"Yes, it must have been that," she sighed, sinking down upon the stones and leaning against the shaded wall.

But in her heart she *knew*. She *had* seen a young girl. Running. It was not quite an empty city. Perhaps others, like themselves, sought refuge here from time to time. Perhaps the girl was trysting with a lover here and had run away at sight of them. . . .

Helst was determined to entertain Lorraine. He told her about the girls of Holland: of fair-haired Greta, who had led him on and then married someone else and gone to Leyden to live. Of Katje, who had drowned in the canal. Of beautiful Annjanette, who lived in a handsome house and looked right past him even though he had shown his admiration by journeying upriver to bring her a whole boatload of flowers from the tulip lands. And he told her of dainty Maargret with her clubfoot and her soft eyes, who had grown up next door—Maargret, the girl his mother had always wanted him to marry.

Lorraine, who had been watching a small bright green lizard dart in and out of the crevice of the sunny wall across the way, thought he had best stick with Maargret and said so.

Helst smiled at her. "It was because I could not decide that I sailed on this voyage," he confided. "When I return to Amsterdam, I must make up my mind."

He rose, stretched, told her he would be back presently, and strolled away.

Lorraine leaned back and closed her eyes against the fierce afternoon heat.

Suddenly she snapped awake and realized she was alone. Something had wakened her—some loud noise? She had been deep in sleep and could not remember. Now it was quiet, but she looked about her uneasily.

The shadows had lengthened appreciably. It was growing late. Helst should be back by now. What could he have found of such interest that he would be gone so long?

She rose, shook out her russet skirts, and set out to find him.

She came out upon the central avenue and looked about her. Empty, from end to end. But some prickly feeling kept her from calling out "Helst!"

She kept on walking, turned a corner, prowled farther.

That was when she saw the boot.

It stuck out from the far end of the next building, and she approached it with a thumping heart.

It was Helst. The side of his head was bloody—he looked dead. Beside him lay the pistol he had dropped. And nearby, like a broken doll, sprawled the body of the Indian girl—her neck broken. She looked so young and defenseless lying there. Lorraine sensed that Helst had died protecting her.

Poor Helst. He would never be returning to anyone now—not to his lost Greta or cold Annjanette or dainty Maargret. Helst had found the Indian girl—and someone else had found them both.

The frozen horror that had held Lorraine spellbound, looking down in disbelief at the tragic scene, was dissipating now and a tingling awareness of her own danger took its place.

For whoever had done this was not dead.

Her head swung around and she studied the nearby walls, but the silent stones gave her no answer. She turned about, headed back the way she had come— but that took her into a broader avenue of strange flared stone buildings. She looked up and down it . . . nothing there.

In sudden panic, she realized she could be seen from many directions now, for her bright hair was catching the long rays of the sun. Which meant she would be conspicuous to watching eyes. . . .

Out beyond these stone walls lay the cliffs and the sea lapping the rocks. And the *Lass*.

Suddenly she knew what she must do. She picked

up Helst's gun and fired it. It made a deafening roar and she dropped it. But they would hear it on the *Lass* and send a boat. She must find some high place to show them where she was.

The Castillo lay ahead and it was tall. Fear lent wings to her feet as she fled toward it and scrambled up the wide stone steps toward the sanctuary with its serpent pillars high above. Halfway up, her shoe struck a pebble, sending it clattering down. At another time she might have looked down and noted that the pebble was a jade earplug once used by the Mayans who had lived in this place, but now she paused and her head went up to listen. Did she hear a footstep somewhere in that maze of deserted buildings behind her? Or did she . . . only imagine it?

Around her all was silence.

More carefully now she ran upward. She had reached the terrace. She could see the nine-foot-thick city wall—and she could see the sea. The world looked so beautiful here, so tranquilly blue, it was hard to believe she might have a deadly pursuer. Below her the ocean beat against the old limestone cliffs, sending up plumes of spray. Before her the sea was a vast blue glitter.

And down below, the *Likely Lass* rode saucily at anchor. Lorraine could see that a boat had been put out, and now someone in that boat saw her and stood up to wave. Lorraine waved back frantically.

Help was on the way—she had only to wait.

And then she heard it.

A footstep, soft but real.

A small stone rattled down the wide steps. Lorraine's frightened gaze was riveted on the corner of the sanctuary around which death could come, but she could see nothing.

Was the foot that had dislodged that stone a dark and sandaled one? And did those sandals bear a powerful native of this place, long dispossessed and mad for vengeance?

She backed along the terrace. Below was a sheer drop to the edge of a forty-foot cliff, and the only way out was the way she had come.

A head and shoulders appeared around the corner

of the sanctuary—and then a body. Lorraine nearly fainted. Then relief flooded over her when she saw it was the big French mute, Gautier, coming toward her. The scouting parties must be back.

"Oh, thank God!" she cried. "Gautier, I know you can't speak, but listen to me. Helst has been killed, he's lying down there between the buildings. The scouting parties must be warned!"

He kept walking toward her. His face betrayed no emotion, and Lorraine was not sure he had understood her.

"Helst is dead," she repeated carefully.

She had expected Gautier to bob his head to show that he understood, but instead, his lips opened and a perfectly good, if somewhat hollow-sounding, English voice answered her.

"I know," said the mute. And then, still in that hollow-sounding voice, but almost dreamily, "You have beautiful hair." He seized it even as he spoke.

Unable to twist away, Lorraine tried to scream, but the sound was choked off by brutal hands that seemed intent on crushing her windpipe.

They had hanged the wrong man in Bordeaux. The glittering eyes upon her were English, not French— but their owner was La Garrotte. La Garrotte, who strangled women with their own long hair.

"Don't try to scream and I'll let you breathe," her captor muttered. "Be a sensible girl and plait your hair. That's the way I like it best—plaited."

Lorraine's world stopped whirling and came to a dizzy stop.

She was aware that she was close to the edge, aware too that perhaps in a surprise move she could hurl herself over. But the will to live was strong in Lorraine, and although being crushed against the sharp rocks below might be preferable to death by strangulation, she kept telling herself she would wait a few more heartbeats. Perhaps she could distract the madman until help arrived.

"Who are you?" she asked from between stiff lips, even as her fingers moved mechanically to fashion her hair into two long plaits.

"Does it matter?"

She tried another tack. "Those women you killed, they were French. Perhaps you had something against them. But I'm not French, I'm—"

"Before I went to Bordeaux I lived in England," he told her almost absently. "They called me The Strangler in London town." His avid gaze was still fixed on her long fair hair. "I've been watching you on the ship . . . waiting my chance."

And so he had. She remembered that eerie feeling of being watched on the *Lass*. Now she knew that he was the one who had watched her from the shrouds above, scrambling up the ratlines. She could not control a shiver.

"But *why?*" she pressed, desperate to keep him talking and letting her fingers slow almost to a stop, for she sensed he would not kill her until she had finished plaiting her hair. "Why me? Why any of us?"

"Why?" His gaze roved momentarily to her pale face, studying him so raptly. "Because I saw a woman once—tied to a cart and whipped through the countryside. A tree fell and a branch caught in her hair—the cart kept going and her hair strangled her." His voice had a hollow rumble in it now. "I saw it—it was beautiful. So now I make it happen."

Mad! She had reached the end—her plaits were completed.

At that moment over Gautier's shoulder she saw a black-haired youth stealing up behind Gautier on sandaled feet. He was clothed in a costume as odd as the Indian girl's and he carried a spear. His black eyes burned with a fierce light.

If she could only distract Gautier a moment more!

"I am the Captain's woman!" she screamed in Gautier's face—for even then the wiry youth was drawing back his spear arm. "*He will avenge me!*"

What might have been a laugh rumbled out of Gautier's throat, as his big hands closed on her long braids.

Her world seemed to explode.

The spear caught Gautier in the side and spun him around. His hands left Lorraine's braids with a jerk that nearly snapped her neck—but the convulsive motion of his great body as the spear penetrated sent her spinning to the edge of the stone terrace. Below her yawned death, and she feared that her frantic clutching hands would not be enough to slow her momentum and keep her from sliding over the edge to oblivion.

She fell forward with a choked scream and felt her legs going over the edge, hands scrabbling at the stone.

Above her Gautier's big body was performing an agonized dance of death as he teetered on the edge of the stone terrace clawing at the spear. Lorraine did not see him but the men in the boat below watched in awe as that powerful body writhed above them, his pain so fierce he did not realize he was but a breath away from hell. With a last convulsive gasp Gautier wrested the bloody spear from his side and toppled, headfirst, from the gray-stone fortress. His gigantic form described a long arc that brought a howl of horror from those in the boat below as they watched him plummet downward, strike the cliff's rough edge, and bounce horribly down its forty-foot rise to the rocky surf below.

Immersed in terror, entirely occupied in trying to maintain her desperate slipping grasp on the smooth stones as she dangled helpless over the terrace edge, Lorraine saw none of this, heard none of it. She was not even aware of the clatter of booted feet. She did not see Raile come skittering across the terrace. Even his sharp cry of "Lorraine—hang on!" barely penetrated her paralyzed brain. It seemed to her a miracle when his strong hand seized her wrist and dragged her back to safety.

"Lorraine." His voice was choked as he embraced her.

"Gautier was . . . La Garrotte." The words sobbed in her throat. "*It was Gautier who murdered all those women!*"

"So I guessed."

Lorraine looked up. "How? How did you guess?"

"We stumbled over Renaud's body. Tav and his party joined us about then and Tav said Gautier had been retching, so he had detailed Renaud to stay with him. It all came together for me then—the stranglings in Bermuda, the same pattern as those in Bordeaux. I feared Gautier had gone for you."

"And you came back." She collapsed against him.

"Yes, I came back," he said gently. "Did you think I would not?"

But Lorraine was overcome by the narrowness of her recent escape. She shuddered in his arms.

He caressed her, murmuring soothingly. The words she had been shouting as he came up the stone steps three at a time still warmed him. "*I am the Captain's woman!*" Whatever happened, he would never forget that she had said that.

The others surrounded them now. Lorraine looked up. "What happened to the Indian boy?" she asked.

"What Indian boy?" came a chorus of voices.

"The one who threw the spear. I think he was avenging the Indian girl Gautier killed when he killed Helst."

"Helst is not dead," reported MacTavish, coming up just then. "He is badly wounded but he is still alive. He may live if we can get him back to the *Lass* to the doctor."

"See to it, Tav," said Raile over his shoulder. At that moment he had eyes only for the beautiful girl who a moment before had been so frighteningly near death herself.

"Aye." MacTavish took a long hard look at the lovers and shook his head. The laddie was mad with love, but she was a spirited lassie, strong-willed, independent.

The laddie would have his work cut out for him.

CHAPTER 19

THAT NIGHT BENEATH the cold white stars, the coast of Yucatán was bathed in moonlit splendor. Lying naked in the warm night on the white sands, Lorraine and Raile were wrapped in each other's arms in wildest passion. The storms that had rent them asunder had been washed away, gone like the raging winds. The white surf that lapped gently at their toes murmured an endless love song.

Raile embraced his woman fiercely, his heart blazing with the triumph of that wild admission on the brink of death: *I am the Captain's woman!* She was his, she loved him—had she not shouted it out for all to hear?

Lorraine had forgotten even that she had said it. She had loved Raile all along, any fool could have seen it! So she reasoned as she fitted her pliant form the more tightly to his strong body and they moved together in silent joy to a rhythm old as the sea itself.

Side by side they lay panting in the warm light, looking up at the brilliant stars. They were safe, she knew, because they were hidden from the sentries Raile had posted by the towering cliffs. Their private world was complete and perfect.

But not lasting. Tomorrow they must face the future.

Beside her, Raile's dark face turned toward her in the starlight and he reached out to run a possessive hand down her bare arm. It came to rest lightly on her smooth stomach, where he tweaked the silky hairs of that gentle triangle at the base of her hips. When he spoke, his voice was resonant with love.

"I had not been sure of you, lass—not until today."

Had it taken a brush with death to convince him? Lorraine laughed shakily and clasped her arms behind her head. The gesture imprisoned part of her long hair and threw into high relief her white breasts, pearly in the starlight. Still aglow with the fierce rapture of his love, she let her own hand drag lingeringly over his hard thighs, felt the muscles tighten at her touch.

"How did you become a gunrunner, Raile?" she asked softly.

He shrugged. "I suppose you could say I fell into it. One day I ran across some guns at a good price and remembered where they could be useful, so I bought them and sailed off to sell them for a tidy profit."

"Then you've always run guns?" she asked wistfully.

"Why, no." He seemed startled at the suggestion. "I run anything I can—spices, French wines, contraband lace. I'm for free trade, lass, and against the excise tax." He rose on an elbow, the better to view her magnificent body, pale against the sand. "These guns I carry now are French flintlocks. They were outlawed in France by ordinance of Louis XIV. Yet they're good guns. I stumbled upon a large cache held by a widow in Bordeaux who was afraid to keep them once her husband was dead, and she made me a good price. I thought of the colonies, where guns are always needed against marauding Indians, and so"—he shrugged again—"I went to Rhode Island."

"It was a mistake," she told him somberly. "You met me and I've ruined all your plans. If you hadn't met me, you'd have found Moffatt's group and sold your guns and been away to England or somewhere. Instead, you've piled up your ship on some heathen beach and you may never reach the Indies!"

"I'll reach the Indies," he said confidently, pressing a warm kiss on one tingling nipple.

Despite the thrill that went through her at his touch,

Lorraine's mood did not change. She had cost him so much!

"Perhaps." Her voice was somber. "But I've brought you so much grief—you may yet decide you've made a mistake."

He lifted his head and his gaze was steady. "It was no mistake, lass. The best day of my life was the day I found you."

Lorraine felt a catch in her throat. Sincerity rang in Raile's voice when he said it.

"I want you to stay with me, lass. Always."

She pulled his face down to hers, for there were tears shining in her eyes and she did not want him to see them, not now, not yet, while their love was still so new. "I will," she choked. And in her heart she made a silent vow: *I will stay with you as long as love holds true, and that will be forever.*

In silent communion, heart to heart, soul to soul, they made love again—and it was wonderful. There on that empty stretch of beach they were joined in a joy so fierce and true and cleansing that they both knew it must be everlasting.

And after that Lorraine pulled on her chemise and slept—for the crew would be stirring at first light and the captain's lady must not be seen rising like a sea nymph naked from the foam!

Now that the resources of the land had been scouted out, the real work of repairing the ship went on. Pieces of wood, precut in place, were dragged to beachside. Saws and adzes and hammers pounded and shaped and fit the *Lass* back to seaworthiness. Lorraine helped with the mending of sail until Raile saw the blisters on her hands and decided the work was too rough for her and forbade her to touch them.

"The mosquitoes out there in the bush are terrible," he told her one day. "I have ordered the men to clear out well before dusk lest they be eaten alive."

Lorraine glanced at the dark tree line. She was glad she did not have to go in there! At least here the sea breezes blew the mosquitoes away from the shore.

"Raile," she asked, "has he ever come back—the Indian boy who cast the spear at Gautier?"

"Never," he said. "But we left food out for him just as you asked. And some trade goods that he could barter or sell to make his escape from this coast if he chose."

Lorraine's face clouded. "I am sorry he did not come back, for he saved my life and I would have liked to thank him."

"He was probably not thinking of your life," pointed out Raile sensibly. "He was more likely avenging the Indian girl's death."

"Perhaps he has not taken the food and trade goods because we left it on the terrace of the Castillo—and to him it may be a temple and not a fortress. He may have thought it was an offering to the gods."

"Very well, we will leave it atop the wall at a place where it can be seen for a long way."

But the Indian lad did not return, and Lorraine would forever wonder what had happened to him.

They were finally caulking the ship. The rudder had been repaired, the sails were back in place, and the damaged mast—while not replaced, for they could not find timbers long and strong enough among the scrubby trees hereabout—had been tightly lashed and would hold "if we get not too hard a blow," according to MacTavish. They were near to casting off and Lorraine felt a wistful wrench to be leaving the place where Raile had told her *I want you with me . . . always*. The words sang in her heart.

Everyone was making final preparations to cast off, when the first man came down with fever. By the time they had pulled up the anchor, five of the crew were shaking with chills or burning up with fever.

"This voyage is cursed," muttered Derry Cork.

André L'Estraille, upon whose shoulders as ship's doctor the burden fell, looked inclined to echo him. "The sooner we clear these shores, the better!"

"Why?" wondered Lorraine. "What is the cause, do you think?"

"Poisonous emanations from the soil is all we know about it," he said, giving her the accepted medical wisdom of the day. "From such areas one must flee."

"Well, we are fleeing," sighed Helst, coming up just then. "And short-handed, too, with so many ill!"

"Can you handle this outbreak, L'Estraille?" asked Raile.

The doctor stiffened—he was still at odds with his captain. "Certainly!" he snapped. "These are mild attacks—they occur every other day."

But Lorraine anxiously noticed how hot Raile's skin was.

On their fourth day out, Lorraine returned from a walk on the deck to find Raile lurching about the cabin with his teeth chattering. She urged his shivering form into the bunk and wrapped him in blankets. "I will call André," she cried.

"It is nothing," Raile told her. "I will get over it. Do not alarm the ship."

In a few minutes he was burning up with fever.

Lorraine burst out on deck and ran into MacTavish. "Where is the doctor?" she cried. "Raile has come down with chills and fever—oh, there he is. André!" She beckoned as she saw the Frenchman come up on deck.

But when the ship's doctor started to enter the captain's cabin, MacTavish's brawny body blocked his way. "Keep away from him," he warned. "I'll have no barber surgeon attending my captain. You tried to kill him once!"

"Don't be a fool, MacTavish!" L'Estraille would have shouldered past him. "I'm a doctor—let me pass!"

The big Scot's expression was dangerous. He drew his sword. It looked very wicked gleaming in the sun. "If you do not care to have this blade between your shoulders, laddie," he suggested, "you will depart. *Now.*"

L'Estraille threw up his hands. "I have others to care for," he muttered, and strode away despite Lorraine's frantic pleas.

And so she found herself caring for Raile. It was difficult to know what to do. Sometimes he shivered so violently she was afraid he would fall out of the bunk. The blankets, the hot stones at his feet, were not enough. In desperation she stripped off all her clothes and climbed in beside him, pressing her warm flesh against his shivering body and wrapping them both with blankets. But then, of a sudden, he would be burning with fever again, gasping, throwing off the blankets, tossing, crying out for water. Distracted, she cared for him—bathing his hot face, holding water to his lips for him to drink.

"Vile," he kept saying thickly. "Vile." And then he would fall back into a stupor.

Lorraine thought he was commenting on the water. " 'Tis the best we've got," she told him unhappily. "You must drink it, no matter how it tastes—to bring the fever down."

He sat up suddenly, his eyes wild. "She can't have!" he shouted. And then, in a mumbling tone, "I'll kill him . . . kill . . ." He sank back, exhausted.

She realized then that he was delirious and that his oft-moaned "vile" was only a part of that delirium. One night, as she crossed to the other side of the room to get the can of water the cabin boy had left just inside the door—for Johnny Sears was deathly afraid of any kind of illness, every member of his family having succumbed to fevers of one kind or another, and he stubbornly refused to go near any of the sufferers—her footsteps were arrested by Raile's murmured "Lorraine, Lorraine," uttered in a plaintive tone. She turned, smiling sadly at him, and then realized with a shock that he was not saying "Lorraine." He was saying softly "Laurie Ann, Laurie Ann," and then he said intensely, "Marry me—I promise I will quit the sea after this voyage!"

Lorraine almost dropped the can of water she was pouring into a basin. She went to stand over him, looking down uncertainly. He was muttering incoherently now.

But as time went on, his incessant half-coherent calls for "Laurie Ann" grated on her nerves. Who was this Laurie Ann anyway?

At dawn she trudged outside to find MacTavish and beg him again to let the doctor see Raile. MacTavish remained adamant.

"You are going to try to sail the *Lass* all the way to

Barbados with a captain who may be dying?" she challenged. "*And not help him?*"

"I will sail the *Lass* to Jamaica," MacTavish told her grimly. "There are plenty of doctors in Port Royal—good ones too."

"There are pirates in those waters who will take your guns," she reminded him, hoping to make him change his mind.

"Bedevil the guns!" exploded the burly Scot. "I'll not have my laddie butchered by any scheming French barber surgeon!"

Tav's affection for Raile ran deep, she knew—but his streak of stubbornness ran even deeper. Exhausted by her long hours of struggle in the cabin, Lorraine sagged against a ratline for support.

"Tav," she said, using Raile's name for him, "you've known Raile for a long time, haven't you?"

"Since he was a wee laddie living over a stable and his father in the great house not willing to claim him," was the morose answer.

Lorraine's eyes widened. So Raile was illegitimate?

"But his mother?" she protested. "Couldn't she . . .?"

"His mother had come to the house as a servant and she bore Raile there in the master's bedroom. But when the master of the house married, he sent her away. Oh, the man came to visit her from time to time in the little cottage where he settled her, and she bore him a second son there. But when she died, her two little lads were left homeless and penniless. Raile was the best of the two, but too young to be apprenticed— the other one wasn't worth powder and shot! But the grand lady in the big house wouldn't allow either of them under her roof and she could always bend Raile's father to her views. So they both ended up in the stables. I used to seethe with rage at the way the poor little laddie was treated. They were always flogging him for something his little brother, Rory, had done. I would have taken him away with me to serve as cabin boy but I couldna take care of them both and Raile refused to be separated from his brother—he said with no one to protect Rory, 'twould be the finish of him if he left."

Lorraine's heart went out to that younger Raile, beaten, abused, yet sturdily standing up for his weaker brother. Her eyes smarted.

"Did his father never claim him?" she asked wistfully.

"Not ever!" MacTavish's voice was savage. "His own sons, mind you, wearing rags and living in his own stables eating scraps—when by rights they should have been wearing velvet and lace and dining in the great hall on pheasant!"

Lorraine had never heard such an outburst from MacTavish. His face was thunderous.

"What happened?" she asked. "How did he get away?"

"His father died and *she* turned him out." MacTavish sat and smoldered for a while. The sky above them was a clear unaltered blue, reflecting no storms of the flesh or problems of those born on the wrong side of the blanket. "That was when I took him to sea," he added moodily. "I was a first mate then on the *Heather.*"

"And his brother?"

"Rory? He went to work on a farm. He'd no liking for the sea."

"But why didn't Raile become a first mate on a merchantman like you? How did he get into smuggling?"

MacTavish looked surprised. "The *Heather* was a smuggling vessel herself, lassie. 'Twas how I first met the lad, when I was taking contraband lace into the countryside to sell to his father!"

So Raile had become a smuggler because that was the only opportunity that had reached out to him! "So it was you who taught him his trade, Tav?"

The big Scot looked proud. "Aye, lassie."

Lorraine took a deep breath and plunged. "Did you know Laurie Ann?"

"Laurie Ann MacLaud?" He spat. "Aye, I knew her. And a bad piece of goods she was!"

"You say she was bad? What was she like, Tav?"

He shot her a long hard look. "Slim, red-gold hair, eyes that laughed up at you."

And a mouth made for kissing, no doubt! Was she

always to be plagued by beautiful redheads? Lorraine wondered. First Lavinia, now Laurie Ann!

"That's how she *looked*, Tav, but what was she *like?*"

"Wild and reckless—with a restless foot." He studied Lorraine from beneath bushy brows. "Like you," he sighed, "she was too beautiful for anyone's good!"

Coming from anyone else that would have been a compliment—coming from Tav it was not.

"Is this . . . is this Laurie Ann's picture?" Lorraine asked hesitantly. She pulled out the gold locket from where it was tucked into her bodice and opened it.

MacTavish did not even need to glance inside. He recognized the locket from its case. "Aye. The laddie bought that for her. 'Twas to be a gift for her when he returned from sea—the locket to frame the picture she'd given him of herself."

So much for Raile's insistence that he did not know the girl in the locket.

Lorraine sighed and dropped the gold locket back down the neck of her bodice. She would pry that picture out when she got back inside, and dispose of it!

"Raile said he asked her to marry him."

"Aye, and was accepted," was his dry rejoinder.

"Why didn't she marry him, Tav?"

"Because she was a faithless jade!" said MacTavish savagely. "She dinna like the sea so she sent my laddie away with the promise that it would be his last voyage— and he came back to Scotland to find she'd married while he was gone and had journeyed to America on her father's dowry!"

"Did Raile follow her?" Lorraine asked, almost fearfully.

"To Virginia?" MacTavish snorted. "He did not! He had too much sense!"

"Where is she now, Tav?"

"Still living on the Curles of the James River, I suppose—though like as not she's run away with someone else by now!" He gave Lorraine a fierce look. "She broke my laddie's heart and it's been slow a-mending. I'd not like to see it broken again!"

"Nor would I, Tav." Lorraine sighed—and decided on one last try. "It's not his heart, but his body that I'm worried about now. Oh, Tav, won't you let Dr. L'Estraille see him? Raile is like to die if you don't!"

The big Scotsman slid his long leg from the rail and reared up to his full height. "My laddie is not like to die!" he thundered. "He's lived through sword thrusts and knife wounds and twice being shot! I'll have no French barber surgeon finish him off!"

Lorraine sighed and went back past the stolid guard to her sickroom duties. Plainly Raile was not to have medical aid. She tried to force some hot broth into him but he was shivering so violently that both spoon and bowl crashed to the floor. Lorraine sobbed as she retrieved them.

Sometimes he shook so violently she had to fight to keep him in the bunk at all; at other times his skin seemed to scorch her palm and she poured water down his parched throat.

He will die, she thought in terror, watching him. *He will never reach Jamaica. He will die here aboard the* Lass *with no one to help him.* And for a bleak moment she hated MacTavish, even though she knew that the stubborn Scot loved Raile like a son.

Toward noon she went out to reason with MacTavish again—and found him occupied with other business. A fat-bellied merchant ship flying the English flag was wallowing in the blue waters nearby and an interesting conversation was going on between the first mate and the ship's doctor.

"I tell you they'll not risk sending you a doctor once they know this is a fever ship," insisted L'Estraille.

"They'll send us a doctor if they have him," was the big Scot's heavy response.

Lorraine stayed to watch—breathlessly. If only MacTavish could pull it off! He had hailed the ship and gotten a response. Now his big voice was booming out across the water once more:

"Have you a doctor aboard? Our captain has fallen and been injured and we've no doctor aboard to tend him."

"That's your opinion," muttered L'Estraille savagely.

"Be quiet, André!" pleaded Lorraine.

The French doctor subsided, muttering.

But a short time later a boat was put over the side and was rowed over the quiet waters toward the *Likely Lass*.

"Oh, thank God!" cried Lorraine. Her knees felt weak.

MacTavish whirled on her. "Say naught till I get this doctor to the cabin," he warned her. "Nor you, Frenchman."

Lorraine fled back to Raile.

"A doctor is coming," she told him excitedly. But he did not seem to hear. He was talking again, incoherently, turning and tossing. "Vile . . . vile . . ." was all she could understand. And then, more clearly, "Sea chest . . . friar."

Light seemed to burst over Lorraine. Raile was not saying "vile"—he was saying "vial"! The Spanish friar must have given him a vial and it was in his sea chest! She began rummaging through both sea chests, tossing everything about. At last she found a large vial and ran to show it to him.

"Did the Spanish friar give you this?" she demanded excitedly.

"Yes." He was coherent for once. He reached for the vial but fell back, shivering violently. "It is . . . extracted from . . . cinchona bark."

At that moment MacTavish entered with the doctor. He proved to be a spry, amiable little man with twinkling blue eyes and ginger hair, who bounded along lightly despite his ample waistline. At sight of Raile, now shivering uncontrollably in the bunk, he stopped short and his demeanor changed. "Ah." He sucked in his breath. "So this is a fever ship?"

"Aye," said MacTavish grimly. "And our captain is in grave need of your services."

Lorraine waved the vial. "This is extract of cinchona bark," she told the newcomer eagerly. "Given to Raile by a Spanish friar."

The doctor brightened. "Quinine?" he said eagerly. "You have quinine? Ah, then there is hope!" He proceeded to dose the patient and leave instructions. "Are there more such?" he inquired.

"No more serious cases now," said MacTavish, taking charge of the vial. Lorraine guessed he would defend it against all comers. "Will you not share a glass of wine with me?"

"Ah, that I will," sparkled the little doctor. "I am too old for these jaunts across the water!"

He sat down at the table and was joined by Lorraine and MacTavish. He was a talkative man and over two glasses of wine he told them that his ship was the *Heron* out of Philadelphia on her way to Port Royal, Jamaica. On her way down, she had touched at Yorktown and all Virginia was in revolt. Some planter named Bacon, angered by Indian incursions on the Curles of the James River, was leading the colonists against the Indians in defiance of the governor. Everything there was in an uproar and it was said that if the rebels were not murdered by the Indians, they would surely be hanged by the governor.

MacTavish cast an uneasy look at Raile, who was resting quietly now in his bunk. Lorraine was not sure he even heard.

By that night the fever had broken, and Raile looked fairly normal. "Lorraine, send Tav to me," he said in a weak voice.

Lorraine went to get MacTavish and remained on deck, glad to breathe other air than that of the sickroom. MacTavish came out of the cabin with eyes snapping and Lorraine hurried back to see what had occasioned his wrath. She found Raile peacefully asleep and forbore to wake him.

The next morning when she went out on deck, André L'Estraille came up to her saying, "MacTavish has gone mad. We are sailing in the wrong direction."

Lorraine saw that the morning sun had indeed reversed direction since yesterday. It was coming up over her right shoulder when it should have been over her left.

"Did you ask him why we have changed course?" she demanded.

The Frenchman shrugged. "He is in such a mood this morning that none dare approach him."

"I will ask Raile!" She spun on her heel and returned to the cabin, where she found Raile awake and putting on his clothes.

"It is too soon for that," she protested. "You are still weak."

" 'Tis time I got my sea legs again."

"We have changed course," she told him. "No one knows why."

"I know why. I ordered it."

"Why, where are we going?"

"To Virginia. There's an insurrection going on—we will sell our guns there."

So he *had* heard what the doctor from the *Heron* said last night!

"I thought you were not listening," she said in an altered voice.

"I was thinking what to do," he told her. "I called for Tav once I had decided."

Word spread quickly of their new destination. Derry Cork was enthusiastically for it; so were Helst and most of the others. The ship's doctor, however, had other ideas.

"Captain Cameron." He confronted Raile formally. "We cannot sail to Virginia. You seem to have forgotten that I told Captain Bridey in Bermuda that we were bound for Virginia. Mademoiselle Lorraine may well find that she has a welcoming party to take her back to Rhode Island!"

"That's right," cried Lorraine, who had forgotten the Frenchman's lighthearted lie on her behalf.

"Nevertheless it is our only alternative," said Raile. "Our ship needs better than temporary repairs—and we can get those repairs in Jamestown. The *Lass* is in no condition to sail across the Caribbean in this season of storms."

"You were not of that opinion when we left Mexico!" challenged L'Estraille.

"That was before I knew of the insurrection i n Virginia. We will be able to make ready disposal of our guns up the James—the planters have money."

He was not to be moved.

"I will take care of you, lass," Raile assured Lorraine in a quiet voice.

She gave him a bitter look. She had suddenly decided they were not going north to sell guns or because of temporary repairs that might not hold—they were going north to save a woman named Laurie Ann MacLaud, a woman who had betrayed him but a woman he still loved.

She flung away and went to stand clutching the rail, looking out at the whitecaps frosting the blue sea.

André joined her. "What do you think of this change of course, *ma petite?*" he muttered.

"I think it is despicable!" she cried, and ran sobbing back to the cabin, leaving him to stare after her.

That night she told Raile in a tight voice that he was "not well enough" and must sleep alone in the bunk—she would sleep on the floor.

"Nonsense," he said roughly. "We will sleep together. There is room for two in the bunk!" When her chin came up stubbornly, he gave her a keen look. "It is because we have changed course, is it not?"

"Yes!" She met this gaze squarely.

He ran a hand through his dark hair. "Lorraine, I know you feel I am putting you at risk, but I *must* go to Virginia. It is not something I can avoid."

She was trembling in fury that he would admit it. And to her! "I do not need your explanations!" she cried. "I do not care *why* you sail to Virginia. But from now on you will sleep alone!"

He opened his mouth—and closed it again. "As you wish," he muttered. "You may have the bunk. I will take the floor."

"It is not necessary!"

"It is. *You* nursed me through my fever, *you* found the vial for the doctor."

Oh, yes, I have been very useful! she thought bitterly. *And convenient. Someone to warm your bed! And now we have set sail to rescue your lost love!*

She flounced to the bed, giving him an indignant look as she passed—and decided that she would flirt with André L'Estraille the whole way!

DARK OF
THE MOON

CHAPTER 20

The Carolina Coast
September 1675

UNDER FULL SAIL, with the aid of dangerously piled on canvas, fair weather, and the warm blue current of the Gulf Stream to help them, the *Lass*'s voyage through the Yucatán Channel, past the Dry Tortugas, and up the Straits of Florida was dazzlingly swift. But as far as Raile and Lorraine were concerned, it was a bumpy voyage.

Once Raile had recovered from his fever, Lorraine kept her distance from him. He wondered why she was still so upset when he had promised to protect her. He never once guessed that what he had babbled in his delirium, and not the fact that sailing to Virginia would put her in some danger, was the cause of her anger. He thought perhaps her mood was justified, but it irritated him that she spent so much time with Helst and the French doctor, who were still teaching her to gamble.

The three card players would crouch on deck in the sunshine, gaily making tremendous wagers—all with the understanding that real money would never be used. They won and lost ten, twenty, even seventy thousand pounds on a hand of cards—although André L'Estraille sometimes slyly suggested that they play "for a garter or a stocking—and the winner must of course remove it from the loser!" It amused the doctor that he could so easily make Lorraine blush.

Lorraine was a good pupil. She was learning fast and she had developed a taste for their lighthearted brand of gambling.

Raile was inclined to find it objectionable.

"What will you do with your newfound skill?" he asked her one day.

"Why, I will make my living with it, of course—once I am on shore!" she told him airily.

Raile looked amazed and shook his head, but he did not mention her gaming again.

Their steady progress northward was checked off the Carolina coast by an urgent need of fresh water. They cast anchor in the landlocked harbor at Albemarle Point on the west bank of the Ashley River where the little community of Charles Towne had been founded as the first permanent English settlement in Carolina five years before. So impatient was Captain Cameron in his flight north that, to the discomfiture of his crew, he decreed that the *Lass* would pause only long enough to refill her water casks and would depart on the evening tide.

Lorraine accompanied Raile ashore—a sulky Lorraine with her blue-gray eyes snapping angrily at the speed with which Raile had kept the *Lass* skimming the waves. She had completely convinced herself at this point that the reason for such haste was to rescue his old flame Laurie Ann.

While the others roamed about the little settlement, Raile and Lorraine repaired to the common room of a small rough-hewn inn that overlooked the Ashley River. The innkeeper, a stout friendly fellow, joined them at their table, bringing with him a bottle of indifferent wine. And as it was being poured, Raile asked, "What news of the troubles in Virginia?"

Lorraine looked up penetratingly.

While the innkeeper chewed on his lip, the saucy voice of the serving wench answered Raile. She chuckled and her big breasts strained against her homespun bodice as she looked sideways at him.

"Things are bad as can be," she averred. "Governor Berkeley's a wicked old man who's married himself a wench half his age—and what cares he if the whole

Virginia Colony gets itself scalped so long as he has his fun? Right, Quincy?"

"Poll," snapped Quincy, the innkeeper, in a quelling voice. "Try to remember that though she's young, Lady Frances is the widow of our revered Governor Culpeper of Carolina."

Poll sniffed. "Frances Culpeper's a—"

Quincy's embarrassed cough covered up Poll's opinion of Lady Frances. With a deprecating smile he explained, "Poll's acquainted with half the sailors who come this way. So she hears all the news."

"And what *is* the news from Virginia?" Raile's eyes narrowed as he sipped his wine.

"There's a war going on between the governor's clique and the settlers. A young hothead named Bacon's leading the settlers."

"Bacon . . ." mused Raile. "I've heard that name before."

"Ah, ye'll have heard of Colonel Nathaniel Bacon— this young one's his nephew and heir. His name is Nathaniel too!"

" 'Tis said his wife's father back in England disinherited her for marrying young Bacon," put in the irrepressible Poll, who, having poured the wine, was now lingering to gossip.

"Because he was poor?" Lorraine asked.

"Because he was wild!" said Poll with a leer.

"The young man's rich," sighed her employer. "Young Bacon came to Virginia two years ago with a vast sum of money and bought two large plantations—one near the Falls and the other one, where he makes his home, in the Curles."

"In the Curles?" Raile asked. His eyes had grown alert.

"Aye, those large loops and hooks the James River makes at that point. 'Tis said his plantation house is a fine one—though not nearly so fine as Green Spring, the governor's plantation."

The innkeeper was about to add that Governor Berkeley had conflicting interests since he was trading with Indians as well as being a partner in the proprietorship of Carolina—but prudence asserted itself. Poll was listening and she talked too much. "Poll," he said impatiently, "there's a gentleman over there in the corner who's banging his tankard on the table to get your attention. Go see what he wants."

Poll went off reluctantly and Quincy, companionably sipping wine with Raile and Lorraine, detailed a tangled series of confrontations and counterconfrontations—between the governor and the settlers, between the settlers and the Indians.

An uneasy peace had reigned since the terrible Indian massacres of 1622 and 1644 had nearly wiped out the white settlements in Virginia. But of late Indian incursions had been increasingly frequent, especially along Virginia's wild western frontier. There the beleaguered settlers were clamoring for war against them. Under the pretense of keeping the peace, Governor Berkeley forbade all trade with the Indians—except his own, of course, and that of his cronies, who promptly enriched themselves by monopolizing the rich Indian fur trade.

But the situation had worsened. Fleeing from their enemies the Senecas, the fierce Susquehannocks had fled south from the head of the Chesapeake, raiding at will, and joined forces with the Piscataway in Maryland. Maryland had sent a thousand men to besiege their encampment but had failed to dislodge them. When Maryland had asked Virginia for help, troops had arrived under the command of Colonel John Washington. The hasty Colonel John had ordered six of the Indian chiefs killed. Both Virginia and Maryland promptly offered reparations but the furious Susquehannocks refused. Instead, in retaliation they swept across the Potomac and all the way down to the upper James, killing "ten for one" to compensate. Having killed sixty settlers, they then demanded reparations as the price of peace or they would kill "to the last man." They were refused by the enraged colonists, some of whom had bought their land once, twice, or even three times from different groups of claimant Indians who wandered by, and were determined not to, in effect, "buy" it once again from the Susquehannocks.

The Indians then made good their threat by murdering three hundred more of the scattered settlers.

An experienced soldier was sought to fight the Indians—and found in the Cavalier campaigner Sir Henry Chicheley, who was commissioned to recruit a large force. But no sooner was Sir Henry ready to march then Governor Berkeley, exercising the almost sovereign rights granted to him and his clique by Charles II, canceled his commission and ordered a disgusted Chicheley to disband his troops.

By now the whole countryside was in an uproar. In place of action, Berkeley ordered more forts built. This struck new despair into the hearts of the settlers, for they could not fall back on those forts already built for protection. That line of forts, which Berkeley had previously taxed Virginians so heavily to build across the northern and western frontiers, had been shoddily constructed by the cronies to whom he had awarded fat contracts and had proved almost useless in holding back the rampaging savages.

The distraught settlers, driven from their homes by continuous guerrilla warfare, mourning the loss of friends and loved ones, and believing that their own families would be the next to die, now sought a leader—and found one in fiery young Cambridge graduate Nathaniel Bacon. A force of several hundred planters and frontiersmen, armed and ready to fight, descended upon him one soft spring afternoon at his plantation of Curles' Neck on the north side of the James to plead for his leadership. The reckless twenty-eight-year-old Bacon, enraged by the Indians' recent murder of one of his overseers, was quick to accept command. Gifted with eloquence, and an impassioned advocate of individual rights, the charming young planter was transformed overnight into a mesmerizing leader that men would follow anywhere.

Raile's brow furrowed at this amazing recital. "You mean Governor Berkeley provided *no troops at all* in such a crisis?" he demanded incredulously.

Quincy cocked a cynical eye at him. "And risk losing his own profitable deals with the Indians? As Poll would say, Lady Frances wouldn't like that! They have a palatial home in Green Spring. Indian troubles won't touch them there."

"And where do matters stand now?"

"The settlers proclaimed young Bacon a general. Then the governor declared him a rebel, and sent three hundred mounted men to the Falls of the James to capture him."

"Berkeley sent his forces against the settlers and not against the Indians?" Raile asked, shaking his head.

"Yes. But Bacon was gone when they reached the Falls. He had already ridden south with sixty men and subdued the Indians there. When his forces found themselves short of provisions and losing men, Bacon returned to discover the Susquehannocks had built a fort on an island in the Roanoke River. After a two-day battle, Bacon's forces won a decisive victory and broke the power of the fierce Susquehannocks. And what was his reward?" Quincy snorted. "The governor paid a call at Curles' Neck plantation to tell Elizabeth Bacon he was going to hang her husband as soon as he was caught!"

"And was he?"

"I don't know. That was the last word we had of matters in Virginia."

As she listened to all this, Lorraine could not help but sympathize with the beleaguered colonists. She remembered what it had been like in squabbling Rhode Island, where the colonists were always afraid the Indians might rise in the night and murder them all.

"Did you have a fair voyage up from the south?" the innkeeper asked.

"Aye, the *Lass* gave us no trouble," said Raile. Another lass had, however. Still puzzled by her cold behavior, Raile cast a thoughtful look at Lorraine.

As soon as the water casks were filled in Charles Towne, they returned to the *Lass* and cast off.

"What would you have done if you had been told the insurrection in Virginia was over and the planters had won?" Lorraine asked him.

"I would have repaired the mast in Charles Towne and set sail for Barbados," he said crisply.

Lorraine was surprised. She had expected him to

say, "I would have proceeded to Jamestown to have the ship properly repaired," but he had not. Was he trying to tell her that it was really the sale of the guns and not the lure of a lost love that was sending him in such haste to Virginia? Her attitude toward him softened.

"I wonder how things are now in Virginia," she murmured.

"They won't have improved," predicted Raile grimly.

He couldn't have been more right. Since the last tidings had reached the innkeeper in Carolina and while the *Lass* was making her way northward to the Virginia Capes, much had happened.

Governor Berkeley had called for an election of burgesses—the first in fourteen years—while Bacon was away. Henrico County had promptly elected Bacon and his lieutenant Captain Crews to represent them in the house.

Nathaniel Bacon, knowing his reception in the capital at Jamestown might be less than warm, had set out in a sloop with forty of his supporters, but he was soon captured by a heavily gunned vessel sent by the governor. Bacon was forced to read on bended knee a prepared confession of guilt to the governor's charges there in the State House. Loudly and publicly before the assembled burgesses, Berkeley forgave him—but by now Bacon knew the governor's temper. Fearing rearrest, he took advantage of a moonless night to slip from Jamestown Island to the mainland and ride hard for his plantation at Curles' Neck. There he assembled several hundred armed men and marched on Jamestown.

On the green between the river's precipitous bank and the State House, a wild scene took place. Bacon's men occupied both the fort, to prevent resistance, and the ferry, to prevent escape. With his fusiliers stationed in double lines commanding the State House, Bacon announced that he had come to be officially commissioned to go against the Indians.

At that point Governor Berkeley burst out of the State House, in a rage that his thirty men and four cannon were insufficient against Bacon's superior force.

Tearing open his coat to reveal his chest in its white ruffled shirt, the governor cried out dramatically for them to shoot him. While the act might have been tempting to Bacon's followers, they resisted it. Watching all this were the burgesses, peering down excitedly from the upstairs windows of the State House, where they were in session. Bacon's fusiliers suddenly aimed their flintlock muskets at those windows, and at the metallic click of the cocked fusils, the lawmakers promptly buckled to force, screaming down that Bacon should have his commission. The Assembly declared war on the Indians; the governor signed a commission naming General Bacon commander in chief and authorized him to recruit a thousand men. "Bacon's laws" were promptly passed—statutes which provided that all adult white male freedmen and not just landowners would be eligible to vote, that removed the councilors' exemption from taxation and restricted them from holding multiple offices, and a number of other changes the settlers had long clamored for as well.

The uneasy peace did not last long.

When eight more settlers were tortured and roasted alive by the Indians just forty miles away in an area Bacon had not yet cleared of marauders, the wild young leader recruited a force of thirteen hundred men to move against them—only to learn that the governor was raising troops of his own to move against *him*. Enraged by this treachery, Bacon swooped east toward Jamestown. Berkeley fled to sanctuary on the untroubled Eastern Shore, where the Chesapeake Bay would lie between him and the angry settlers.

But the governor swore he would be back.

Bacon knew how to handle that. He captured several ships and soon his little fleet patrolled the Chesapeake, holding the fuming governor at bay. Then Bacon set off at the head of his men through tangled brush into the treacherous bogs and mosquito-riden mists of the Dragon Swamp in pursuit of the now-fleeing Indians. He returned victorious but with a diminished force of only a hundred and fifty men, for many had chosen to return to their homes once the Indians were dispatched.

Bad news greeted the young rebel leader when he reached Henrico County. While he was gone, the wily old governor had returned from Accomack and by trickery captured Bacon's little fleet. Berkeley now occupied Jamestown with heavy cannon and a thousand men. The governor's methods of recruitment were extravagant: he promised his new recruits exemption from taxes for twenty-one years, spoils including estates of the rebels, and freedom for any of the rebels' indentured servants willing to join him.

Bacon was tired, and in a passionate reaction to Berkeley's constant treachery and unremitting hatred, he did not pause to gather more men, but instead whirled about and marched on Jamestown with the men he had. It was a move that Berkeley had not contemplated. So swiftly did the young rebel leader descend upon the capital that he caught Governor Berkeley unaware and had him bottled up inside the town.

At that point, the *Likely Lass* was making her way north. All the way, Raile had made no move to touch Lorraine, as if he were waiting for her anger to wane. The fever had left him thinner, exhausted, and he had been sleeping long hours every day to build up his strength.

"I do not know what we will find in Jamestown," he told her soberly. "But MacTavish will remain aboard the *Lass* while we are there. You would be safer aboard as well."

Stay aboard and miss learning whether he had come to sell the guns or to seek out Laurie Ann MacLaud? Never, she thought.

"I prefer to go ashore," she insisted.

"Very well." His tone was flat. "Either way, Lorraine—it is your decision."

As it turned out, their arrival in Jamestown was barely noticed. They had passed Cape Hatteras under full sail, gone around Norfolk, and into the mouth of the James. But when they reached Jamestown on September 13, they were astonished to find the town was under siege.

A tense atmosphere prevailed when Raile and Lorraine went ashore in the town where a roguish thirteen-

year-old Pocahontas had once turned cartwheels naked through the streets to the amusement of onlookers.
There was no such frivolity today. The town, which
straggled for a mile or so along the riverfront, some of
its row houses more suited to medieval Europe, was
filled with people.

Virginia's total population was said to be only forty
thousand but it seemed to Lorraine that they must all
have converged upon the capital that day. Armed men
jostled about—many of them raw recruits being barked
at by a handful of harassed officers. A cheer went up
as the governor, surrounded by a small coterie of
officers, rode by splendidly garbed. For a moment his
eyes rested appreciatively on Lorraine—she did not
like the look of him.

She could see Raile assessing him through narrowed
eyes.

They moved on through the crowd, Raile taking
note of the palisade the governor's men had flung
across the isthmus, and the heavy guns that commanded it.

"The governor does not like being bottled up,"
observed a voice nearby. "He swears he will have not
only Bacon hanged but all his followers as well."

"He will decimate these woods," was another settler's quiet reply. "For all the frontier now follows
Bacon."

Having overheard some of the discussion about them,
Lorraine turned to Raile in bewilderment.

"If the governor does not like being bottled up, why
doesn't he break out? If he has a thousand men and
Bacon but a hundred and fifty?"

Raile peered out into the distance. "I think I see the
reason," he said. "Observe." And Lorraine followed
his gesture.

In the distance another fortification was going up.
Men were busily working, swarming about, building a
strong earthen breastwork across the sandy isthmus, a
narrow neck of land that joined the peninsula with the
mainland. There was an earthen barricade there from
which Lorraine could see flutters of white cloth.

She peered at them, straining to see.

For a bewildered moment she thought the rebels were waving flags of truce—and then she realized that those white flutters were aprons.

"Why . . . why, those are women!" she cried indignantly.

"Aye," said a grim voice at her elbow. "Those women—wives of the governor's supporters—were captured by that villain Nathaniel Bacon. His force is small and he knows we would defeat him if he advanced upon us. So he has sent out bands and seized our women. He has made them conspicuous in aprons and is forcing them to walk back and forth as a living shield while he constructs his breastworks—for he knows that without them our heavy guns would promptly destroy him."

"An ingenious plan," commented Raile with raised eyebrows. "One that I confess would not have occurred to me. But if Bacon has no heavy guns of his own, what will it avail him?"

"He is said to be bringing up guns of his own."

Lorraine stared at those flutters of white in fascination. It was too far away to see any of them clearly, but she thought how furious those women must be, forced to aid the rebels against their own husbands! She wondered for a wild moment if Lady Frances, the governor's wife, was among them.

No shots were fired.

Lorraine would have been stunned to learn that one of the women who walked that barricade, tossing her white apron in the September sunshine and saucily impersonating one of the reluctant loyalist captives—each of whom glared at her every time their paths happened to cross—was Laurie Ann MacLaud.

Laurie Ann, a big handsome girl, was cut out to be a pioneer woman, and a pioneer woman she was. The very woods spoke to her and she was as fearless in the desolate back country as any frontiersman.

Now her wide blue eyes were flashing with merriment as she watched the captive ladies file past her atop the well-trodden earthworks. Laurie Ann, who had a big laugh and a tigerish smile, was enjoying herself as she observed the sullen women making the long trek back and forth.

"Why don't you take that cap off your hair and let the men of Jamestown see your face so they'll know you're not one of us?" snapped a plump perspiring lady in calico.

Laurie Ann laughed. She had been keeping her face somewhat averted from the town lest indeed that happen—although at this distance it was doubtful if even the keenest-sighted would recognize her. "But suppose it was *your* husband that recognized me, Mistress Council Member's Wife?" she drawled in her Scots burr. "He might take a shot at *you* just so's he could have *me!*"

The council member's wife gasped and turned pale, but she moved on, prodded by a tall woman in lace-trimmed indigo linen behind her.

"We shouldn't have to walk this barricade with you!" she flung out at Laurie Ann as she passed. "You're not one of us!"

"No, praise be, I'm not! And I'll wager your husbands are watching us over their barricade right now, laying bets on who the red-haired beauty is—and wishing themselves married to *me,* not *you!*" She burst into outrageous laughter again.

But her lightly flung remark had made several of the unwilling marchers wince, for Laurie Ann was indeed a blazing beauty—the sunlight turned her red-gold hair to flame and gilded the toasty tan her outdoor life on the frontier had given her. Clad in coarse homespun, strong and vivid, she was very different from the handsomely gowned swaying ladies with their artfully curled hair, their pale, carefully shielded complexions. Different and somehow challenging.

"Come on, ladies, step lively!" sang out Laurie Ann. "Show the gentlemen down there in Jamestown that you're still able to walk even if you're not much use in bed!"

As her clarion voice taunted the wealthy wives, there was a general bridling and grinding of teeth.

"I don't have to endure this!" cried one of them. "Who's going to shoot us down if we leave this barricade? Certainly not our own husbands down there in Jamestown! And I doubt me if these rebels will do it either, even if they did drag us here and order us to march!"

The line of aproned marchers wavered. Bacon's rebel forces were on the brink of a petticoat rebellion—although the men hard at work finishing the hastily flung-up earthworks didn't know it yet.

But Laurie Ann's voice rang out in warning:

"Your own husbands might not shoot you—unless they're tired of having you in their beds. And Bacon's men might not—*but I will if you don't keep marching!*"

From beneath her apron she pulled out a large pistol and brandished it. "And if you think I don't know how to shoot this thing, you're wrong! I've had to deal with Indians out for my blood—twice!"

A murmur of fright went through the aproned throng. "Do move along there, Hortense," a plump woman remarked nervously. "That dreadful Scotswoman would welcome any excuse to shoot us!"

"You're right!" Laurie Ann laughed boisterously again. "You're a bunch of coldhearted witches to think it's all right for you to sleep safe between scented sheets whilst we on the frontier fall into bed never knowing if we'll get through the night without being scalped! So keep walking, ladies," she added blithely. "Why do you think I'm here? To prove to Bacon's men that a woman can be as good a shot as any man! Of course, I won't have to do that unless you get out of line or try to run away!"

Somewhat subdued, the marching women continued, with murmured grumblings and black looks cast at Laurie Ann, who tossed her homespun skirts merrily as she strolled with her pistol concealed beneath her apron amidst the line of reluctant marchers.

CHAPTER 21

The Siege of Jamestown, September 1675

IN THE CAPITAL there were no accommodations to be had, as Lorraine and Raile quickly learned, even though the town seemed to be bursting with inns and ordinaries strung out along the river. All were filled to overflowing, "worse than in the Publick Days," when court was in session, they were informed. Jamestown's population was almost entirely male and Lorraine—female and a beauty—was the object of much interest. Heads turned wherever she went.

"There will be a battle when that breastwork is completed," Raile told her. "And it looks to me to be receiving its finishing touches now. I had better take you back to the ship."

"I will not go!" she flared. "These two gentlemen, Mr. Harley and Mr. Green, who have been showing us about"—indeed more than two had been clamoring to show the beauty whatever sights there were, but Harley and Green had won out—"have just told me of an inn that serves excellent food."

Raile inclined his head graciously. "Very well. We will sup there. Perhaps the gentlemen who recommended it will be our dinner guests?"

After a swift acceptance, Harley nudged Green. "The captain means to fill the wench with wine and carry her off, safe from harm," he muttered under his breath.

"Safe from *us*, y'mean," was Green's cheerful whispered reply.

Lorraine was not supposed to overhear their comments, but she did, and she vowed to be sparing of how much wine she drank. If they were lucky enough to find a bed, she would cling to that bed like a leech and refuse all efforts to dislodge her. She planned to stay right here in town until Raile had made his "arrangements"—whatever they might be!

They dined that evening with their newfound friends, Harley and Green, in the smoky common room of one of the many inns. Long boards had been spread the length of the room to accommodate the crush and at these crowded tables everyone sat. It was very noisy, merry with song and the clinking of tankards of Governor Berkeley's new recruits. All were agreed that the governor would swoop down upon Bacon "and destroy him, as soon as the ladies are taken away from the barricade!"

"I see that the governor has kept his ships handy should he have reason to flee," murmured Raile cynically. "I wonder if these young bucks would be celebrating with quite this much enthusiasm if they had noticed that."

"With five or six times the men, he has overwhelming odds," was Lorraine's comment. " 'Tis obvious he expects to win tomorrow's battle."

"If battle be joined." Raile's eyes narrowed as he glanced about him. "I doubt me these lads will have much stomach for real fighting."

Helst and Derry Cork came through the door just then and Lorraine waved a greeting. "I wonder why André did not come ashore," she mused. "It's so unlike him, don't you think, to stay and skulk aboard ship?"

"I am not as conversant with L'Estraille's likes and dislikes as you are," was Raile's answer. Then he turned to the elderly gentleman in a plum coat who sat on his other side, and engaged him in conversation about the chances of victory on the morrow.

Thus snubbed, Lorraine turned her attention to Harley and Green, who introduced her to a rakish gentleman in tawny who had been covertly admiring her. She so charmed him that within a few minutes he had offered her his accomodations—"a mere cubbyhole upstairs, mind you, but large enough to squeeze in both yourself and your husband."

Lorraine let the "husband" pass. "But what of yourself?" she demanded. "Where will you sleep?"

"I will impose upon a friend of mine," he drawled, signaling the harassed serving maid to refill Lorraine's wineglass. "If perchance one might see you on the morrow? Perhaps I could beg of you a token for good luck in the coming battle?"

Lorraine promptly gave him her kerchief. Handling it as if it were precious, he placed it inside his coat.

Raile turned in time to see that and be amused. "You have made a conquest, I see," he muttered. "Faith, it takes you no time!"

"This gentleman is Oliver Carr of Gloucester," Lorraine told him in an outraged voice. "He has taken pity on us in our plight and has kindly offered us his room for the night. You should thank him!"

"I do indeed thank him." Raile leaned around Lorraine to extend his hand. "Your servant, Carr. Raile Cameron here. I was hoping my lassie would not have to sleep in a doorway this night!"

His lassie gave him a baleful look.

When dinner was over, Oliver Carr said, "I'll take you to my inn just down the street and get you settled, else we may find the innkeeper has locked the door!"

"I would think that tonight he might not lock the door at all," murmured Lorraine. "Considering what the morrow may bring!"

"They keep early hours," Carr warned them. "I fear they may not be up."

He was wrong. They were not only up, but the lady of the house was packing. "I care not what you say," she was telling her husband in a strident tone as she panted down the stairs under a load of hatboxes. "I will not stay here with ball and shot whistling about my ears! They say there will be a battle tomorrow and I am off to the Eastern Shore at first light to stay with my cousins!"

"Even if these rebels overrun us, they will not steal your hats, Mollie," her husband remonstrated mildly. "Indeed they are more like to be after the plate."

"I'm taking that too!" she cried. "I warned you—oh, I warned you, Horace!" She turned to Oliver Carr for confirmation. "Did I not tell you when that comet lit the heavens for a week, that it was a sign? And again when that enormous flight of pigeons darkened our skies?"

"Aye," sighed Carr. "And again when those swarms of big flies rose right out of the earth and ate the trees bare." He stole a humorous look at Lorraine.

"I said it was a sign, and look what has happened! Troops marching, guns mounted! We are on the brink of something here in Jamestown, mark my words! And I'm packing my things and leaving. At first light!"

She wagged a threatening finger at her husband and bustled off again upstairs. Carr explained the situation to the landlord, then escorted Raile and Lorraine upstairs to show them their room.

When Carr had finally left them, Lorraine sat down on the bed and crossed her legs. "If you have any idea that you are going to take me back to the ship, Raile," she warned him, "I promise you now that I shall resist!"

He stood in the center of the room studying her. Then, "I have no intention of dissuading you," he drawled. "But I do intend to sleep in that bed."

Lorraine bridled.

Raile gave her an amused look and began to undress. "I realize that you are still angry that I have exposed you to danger by bringing you here," he tossed over his shoulder as he hung his coat over a chair and pulled off his flowing white shirt. "But I think you might reconsider."

"Why?" Lorraine asked in a hard voice. She was looking at his back as she spoke. It was by far the handsomest back that she had ever seen. The muscles rippled under fine tanned skin. *He has a mighty wingspread*, she thought dreamily, *and the way his lean body tapers to his narrow waist and buttocks . . .*

She dragged her mind back to her "anger." "Why should I reconsider?"

He turned to face her, clad only in his trousers, and he was even handsomer from the front than from the back. His broad chest, smooth, muscular, and sprinkled lightly with fine dark hair, was made for a girl to lay her face against—and sigh. . . .

"Because no one is taking any notice of you save that you're a beauty dressed as gentry," he said lightly. "There's a war going on in case you haven't noticed. Anyway, I expect to be here very briefly—just long enough to sell these muskets. Then we will be away, Lorraine!"

He had said the magic words! The rebel army was but a gunshot away, the rebel leader at its head. *He had not come to see Laurie Ann MacLaud after all—he really was here to sell his guns!*

A kind of glow came over Lorraine. It made all her body warm. She rose and stretched her arms over her head languidly.

"We *do* both need a good night's sleep," she said virtuously.

Raile laughed. "But perhaps we need something else first."

Lorraine was already slipping out of her dress and she felt her face and shoulders grow even warmer at his remark. They glowed pink when she was down to her thin chemise. Raile stretched out on the bed and watched her undress. She took her time about it, teasing him, making a great show of removing each slipper, each garter, propping a foot on the four-poster and slowly, carefully sliding down her stocking—after all, silk was expensive: she must not damage them.

"Come to bed," Raile suggested huskily. "You have teased me long enough."

She had been looking down at her leg; now her lashes fluttered and she looked up to see that he had divested himself of his trousers and lay sprawled in manly comfort upon the coverlet. She blushed.

At that moment he leaned over and blew out the candle. Cold moonlight filtered down through the small paned window and silvered the pair of them—a little wary, evenly matched. For even though the specter of Laurie Ann MacLaud had been removed, it had still been a long time . . .

And then all at once Lorraine was snuggling delightfully into Raile's arms, feeling his long body move like heavy silk against her own. She sighed blissfully. It had been so long, so long . . .

"Why do I love you so much, I wonder?" she murmured blissfully.

"Because you're young and lack judgment," he told her promptly, sliding an arm beneath her bare back and scooping her toward him. "If you were older and wiser, you'd be looking over those rich dandies who surround the governor and forget the likes of me!"

"I find it very pleasant to lack judgment in this case," she told him dreamily, and moved her legs to accommodate his long body the better.

He needed no further invitation. Slowly, with many kisses and caresses, Raile enfolded her, and the Virginia night was filled with magic. Lorraine's deep heartfelt sigh went right through him and he cradled her more tenderly than ever before. She was a wonder, he thought, this wild, fascinating, reckless girl who had come to him as a waif and developed into a magnificent woman under his tutelage. He was proud of himself to have found her; he was proud of her for being what she was.

Together they strained and shivered and gasped at the fierce beauty of their joining, together rose to splendor, together drifted down complete.

Lorraine went to sleep that night with her head blissfully pillowed on Raile's shoulder, certain she had no rival.

She awoke to the sound of guns. She sat straight up in bed.

"Raile!"

He was gone. She tumbled out of bed and into her clothes. Downstairs she ran into the innkeeper, who told her that Raile had been off "at first light." The thought panicked her. Surely Raile had not left her to—

Her thought was never to be completed. Raile himself was coming through the inn door.

He had come back for her. She felt weak with relief. "What is happening?" she asked.

"Governor Berkeley's troops have surged toward the rebels," he told her briefly. "They are attacking the breastwork."

"What happened to the women who were walking the barricade?"

"Oh, they're long gone." He shrugged. "They were brought in only to keep the governor's forces from attacking until the rebels were ready behind their own ramparts. He's a shrewd fighter, is Bacon, I'll give him that."

The battle was short. Incredibly, it seemed to Lorraine, the governor's newly recruited forces dissolved before the first volley of the invaders. Soon the troops were noisily falling back into the town.

Lorraine watched from the window as some horsemen charged by, shouting to each other.

"Some of Governor Berkeley's officers," Raile explained.

Lorraine turned to him in bewilderment. "But there were so many of them. How could they—"

"Lose? Berkeley may have been out for blood but his new recruits weren't so eager—they were just hungry for the rewards he promised them."

"Where will they go?" asked Lorraine, thinking of Carr, to whom she had given her kerchief for good luck.

"Back to the Eastern Shore, I suppose, where I'm told there are no Indian attacks and therefore more complacency about keeping things as they are."

"But if their countrymen are being butchered . . ." began Lorraine indignantly.

Raile cocked an eye at her. "Most men look out for themselves first, you will find. Sentiment is strongest on the frontier where men have seen their wives and children killed—it weakens the farther you get from the battle. Although two of the ringleaders, Lawrence and Drummond, live here in Jamestown, and I'm told that theirs are the best houses here. We must have seen them yesterday."

"I suppose now we will be going back to the ship?"

He shook his head. "I gave orders early this morning for Tav to take the *Lass* out to sea lest the governor's men try to seize her. Derry Cork and most of the officers are already aboard. She'll be gone at least a week, maybe longer. But that should not discomfit us. We are still ensconced in Carr's room. Perhaps he will let us stay on."

"I wonder how he fared."

"Oh, he looked spry enough when he rode by in the crush. He waved at you. Did you not see him?"

Lorraine was ashamed to admit that she had not.

Raile had anticipated this rout, and she looked at him with new respect.

They dined that night with Oliver Carr, who insisted they keep his room "for as long as you care to."

"We accept your kind offer!" said Lorraine instantly.

Carr was crushed by their defeat. He kept brooding about it all through dinner. "Our lads broke and ran," he kept saying sadly. "*Ran!*"

"They were green troops facing seasoned Indian fighters," Raile pointed out. "How many of your lads had ever fired a musket in anger?"

Carr was silenced but he was still despondent.

"What will the governor do now?" asked Lorraine. "Try again?"

"Oh, I doubt me he'll do that," sighed Carr. "He is disgusted with his forces. There's talk he will retire again to the Eastern Shore. It shames me that it should be so." He pulled out her kerchief. "I will return this to you—I have not done it honor this day."

"You are not to blame!" flashed Lorraine. "You couldn't help it if the men around you turned and ran!" She pressed the kerchief back into his hand.

Her voice had risen high enough that it could be heard by nearby diners. Lorraine was the recipient of several black looks.

"Not so much heat," Raile cautioned her. "You are attracting attention."

Reminded that in her case attracting attention could be disastrous, Lorraine subsided.

They had not long to wait to learn the governor's decision. He was going back to Accomack, and the entire population of the town, together with all their goods, was going with him. It was September 14, and he had given the inhabitants five days to pack up.

"Mollie should not have left all this to me," wailed the landlord of their inn, awash in a sea of packing.

"She could not know it would come to this," pointed out Lorraine reasonably.

"Aye, but with all her signs and portents, she should have foreseen that we'd be uprooted and moved out!" was his gloomy rejoinder.

Lorraine forbore reminding him that his wife had sensibly removed not only her treasured hats and petticoats, but their valuable plate as well.

It was strange to see the entire city loading up, emptying out their houses, piling up great carts that lumbered ceaselessly through the streets. It made Lorraine vaguely uneasy to think that she and Raile would soon be left in a deserted town with the rebel forces only a gunshot away.

Aside from that unnerving thought, Lorraine found those five days when the city packed up to leave were five of the happiest days she had ever known. Her days were spent strolling with Raile through an emptying city where guns were leveled at guns across the isthmus, dining among the diminishing crowds of loyalists, spending long luxurious nights with him in their borrowed room at the inn.

A paradise, she knew, that could not last.

But the days flew by and suddenly it was the eighteenth. By now only a hardy few of the loyalists remained in Jamestown and even that small contingent—their landlord among them—would be sailing, together with their goods, down the James and across the Chesapeake on the following day. Across the earthen barricades, with big guns now to support them, Bacon's troops had made no move to stop the evacuees. Perhaps Bacon welcomed a withdrawal without bloodshed, Lorraine thought.

She was walking with Raile down the empty street toward their inn when that thought crossed her mind. Even she and Raile, she supposed, would be leaving tomorrow, for how could they explain their desire to stay and wait for Bacon to come in and occupy the town without proclaiming themselves on the rebel side? She was sure that although Raile had not spoken of it, the *Likely Lass* would arrive tomorrow and swoop them away.

As they walked, they ate bread and cheese they had purchased because all the taverns were closed and shuttered. Even their inn was empty of guests.

"But not for long," was Raile's comment as they went through the inn's open door and made their way through the silent common room and up the wooden stairway. "Soon the town will be filled with Bacon's men."

Even their room had been dismantled—like all the rooms save the innkeeper's apartment, which would be cleared out tomorrow when the innkeeper, who was spending the night aboard ship, returned for the rest. It was strange to see that the chairs were gone, the small table, the pillows and sheets from the bed, even the big unwieldly four-poster. Only the lumpy mattress remained as being unworthy to move. Lorraine sank down upon it gratefully.

"At least we can sleep here tonight," she said.

"We will have to," sighed Raile. "Unless we choose to march under a white flag up to the barricades. And that might require a deal of explaining, for after all, it is not our battle. Why should we appear to be surrendering?"

Once again she and Raile were staying in a deserted city—only this time the city was not the seat of an ancient and exotic people, this time it was the capital of colonial Virginia.

In the quiet empty town, with the moon aglow above them, they spent another shining night on the old lumpy mattress—loving, touching, certain the magic would last forever.

Lorraine—whose eyes seemed to her to have just closed—roused suddenly. She saw to her bewilderment that even though it was barely dawn, Raile was up and dressed and standing at the window.

"Don't tell me you've been out already!" she protested, sitting up.

He turned to her, smiling. "Just checking on the rebels," he said. "But they're still quiet behind their barricade. 'Tis plain Bacon means to let Jamestown's population go quietly."

"Will Bacon pursue the governor, do you think?"

"In what?" was his rejoinder. "The governor has the ships. Bacon commands the land, but Berkeley commands the sea."

"What will Bacon do now?"

"That is the problem he faces, all right."

"What would *you* do?" she challenged him.

Striding toward the bed as he spoke, he reached down and drew her to him. "I would take an hour off and clasp my lass in my arms. And while away the time because life is fleeting for a soldier."

"Oh, Raile!" She was laughing as she struggled. "Stop it! I asked you what *you* would do. Is your heart not with the rebels?"

He grinned down at her. "My heart is always with the rebels, Lorraine. It is one of my great failings." His voice softened, grew deeper. "Still, I would embrace my love—thus. And bear her to the mattress—thus."

Lorraine had stopped arguing. She made no remonstrance when he undressed and joined her on the lumpy mattress. Making love, after all, was a splendid way to while away the day!

But the afterglow had barely faded before Raile was up and into his clothes again. He astonished Lorraine by handing her a purse. "I've arranged with the innkeeper," he told her. "He'll take you with him to Accomack, where his wife will care for you until I come for you."

"But what about you?" she demanded in bewilderment.

"I am journeying upriver. A loyalist deserter is even now waiting for me."

"But Tav will come for us here," she protested. "He won't know what to do when he doesn't find us."

"I'm leaving Johnny Sears, my cabin boy, behind to give the word to Tav. He's hiding in an empty tavern on a pallet behind some barrels right now. He can melt into the crowd when Bacon's men come in—and come in they will tomorrow."

He was serious, he was actually going to ship her off to Accomack along with the innkeeper's furniture! Lorraine tossed back her tousled blond hair and regarded Raile in consternation.

"But *why* must you go?" she demanded. She threw her legs over the edge of the mattress and made it to her feet. "Why can't you negotiate the armament sale here?" she demanded in exasperation. She pulled on her chemise as she spoke, ignoring the wistful look he was giving her. "After all, Bacon is just over that barricade with all his men."

He hesitated, unwilling to tell her the real reason that was driving him upriver—only Tav knew that, and Tav strongly disapproved. The truth might send Lorraine blundering after him. Or once back aboard ship she might be surprised into blurting it out. And in case things did not work out here—and in any rebellion there was a good chance they might not—going upriver, when he could so easily negotiate with Bacon here, might make the men aboard the *Lass* distrustful of his leadership—something a commander could ill afford. So instead he told her a half-truth.

"Not all," he corrected her. "The man I want to see is upriver. I have made inquiries through my deserter friend, and the man I want was with Bacon when he rode into the Dragon Swamp, but he did not join the march on Jamestown. Some think he may be hurt—at any rate he has been detained. He will tell me who is to be trusted—and who is not."

Lorraine's eyes glinted dangerously. Raile was lying to her! She would make him tell her to her face that his true reason for going upriver was to find Laurie Ann!

"The whole thing is ridiculous," she said contemptuously, giving her petticoat a jerk as she fastened it. "The rebels have won. How can you sell them guns *now?*"

He looked at her curiously. "Guns will be needed more than ever now, Lorraine."

"It is *over!*" she cried in an impassioned voice. "The capital is deserted, the governor has fled."

"It is not over," Raile corrected her wearily. "You forget, the governor has fled before. And returned before. He will be back—and perhaps this time he will be backed not by green recruits but by redcoats sent by the king to quell this rebellion. These colonists have the fight of their lives before them and I tell you *they will need more guns.*"

"At least you could take me with you," she said sulkily.

His face hardened. "That I will not. The main body of Indians may have been defeated, but there will still be roving bands eager to take a white woman's scalp."

She hated him for sounding so *reasonable.* "You will need buckskins and moccasins if you are going upriver."

"Perhaps I will find some," was his crisp reply. And then, because he wanted her to understand the situation here: "Lorraine, I have had more experience of war than you. And this one has come to a ticklish impasse. The settlers have been with Bacon thus far—success breeds success. But now Bacon finds himself between the devil and the deep. He holds the capital, true, but Berkeley has the ships—and the heavy guns. If Bacon dares to leave, Berkeley will take Jamestown back again. His 'hearts of gold,' as he calls his men, could find themselves on the run. This war could last a long time."

Still angry, Lorraine turned her back to him and pulled on her dress. "Go then!"

Raile stared at her rigid back for a moment. Then he turned on his heel and departed.

Lorraine paced the floor, wondering what she should do. Last night she had been so certain of him, but now that certainty had dissolved like Berkeley's forces at that first volley from the rebels.

She strolled disconsolately down into the town, where a few men were still at work busily dragging heavy cabinets and cupboards out of the houses. Afterward she walked along the waterfront looking at the ships. There were only three left in the harbor and one was about to depart.

The innkeeper bustled by her, stopping to point out

the ship that would take them downriver and across the Chesapeake. As he hurried on, beckoning to a wagoner with a team of draft horses, he called back, "My wife will make you comfortable in Accomack, you've nothing to worry about!"

Lorraine nodded unhappily—and suddenly her resolve hardened. She wanted to stay and *she would stay!* And as soon as the rebels opened up a road out of town, she would find a boat and pursue Raile up the James. She would find out for herself how matters stood between him and Laurie Ann MacLaud! But . . . she must be crafty about it.

Waiting there on the waterfront, she bided her time. The landlord came back, shouting at the wagoner not to let that cupboard slide, it was his wife's pride and joy. A moment later he spotted Lorraine.

"Come on, come on," he said testily. "Into the boat! The ship is about to up anchor, we must be aboard!"

"Yes, of course," agreed Lorraine meekly—and then in sudden excitement, "Oh, I forgot my gold locket. I had stuffed it under the mattress—I must go back for it. Don't wait for me, I'll take the next ship."

The landlord frowned at her. His wife would have his hide if he didn't personally accompany this cupboard to Accomack!

"Very well," he sighed. "But hurry back. After my ship leaves, there'll be only one ship left. You mustn't miss the last one!"

"Oh, I won't," promised Lorraine with a glint in her eyes.

She picked up her skirts and fled down the deserted street to the inn. Once there, she went to her room and closed the door. In the confusion no one would notice that she was not on the last ship to leave. They would take note of it in Accomack, but then it would be too late.

CHAPTER 22

THE NEXT DAY Bacon's victorious forces swept in and occupied the city.

From the second-floor window of her empty room, Lorraine watched with some trepidation the rebel troops pouring into town. Most of them were hardy buckskinned men from the foothills of the western reaches—that wild frontier of split-rail fences and notched log cabins. Men who walked lightly on their Indian moccasins, wore leather belts as bandoliers slung easily over their shoulders, and carried long guns, mainly flintlock muskets, with an ease that told the world they were used to carrying them—and used to firing them with deadly accuracy.

Such were Bacon's seasoned troops, which had formed the nucleus of those who had stayed with their leader through the last battle of the swamps and returned triumphant to storm the capital and take it, though outnumbered almost seven to one. They were men to reckon with! Lorraine, impressed by their almost bloodless victory and their determination, could not resist clapping her hands as they went by. Some of those weathered faces looked up and grinned.

Her fresh young beauty, her enthusiasm, easily won the sympathy of the rebel forces.

Astride a gray horse, the wealthy Scot, William Drummond, who had been Carolina's first governor and was now one of the powers behind Bacon, solemnly rode into the town. Beside him, richly garbed and looking every inch the brilliant Oxford scholar and man of parts, rode that other ringleader of the rebellion, the wealthy widower Richard Lawrence. Governor Berkeley had called him, cynically, "the thoughtful Mr. Lawrence," believing him to be the main schemer behind Bacon. Both men had handsome homes in Jamestown, and both had fled those homes when Berkeley and his troops swooped down and occupied the town. Both had been described bitterly and at length to Lorraine by the loyalists with whom she had dined. They were returning now to claim the homes they had been forced to desert in such haste.

Next, on a sleek black stallion, Nathaniel Bacon himself rode by. Lorraine recognized Bacon not only because he had been described to her, but because he was obviously in command, rising in his stirrups with jingling spurs to give orders. She saw that he was a slender black-haired man of medium height who rode with the easy grace of an English country gentleman born to the saddle. Here was no unlettered frontiersman but a polished aristocrat who had made the Grand Tour of Europe and who was said to be the forty-ninth member of his family to study law at prestigious Gray's Inn in London. He looked bone tired but he waved his wide-brimmed hat in jaunty salute. When he looked up and saw Lorraine leaning out of the window—conspicuous in her pink silk dress and with her pale hair shimmering—he flashed her a smile and made her a courtly bow from horseback. She blew him a kiss and the troops cheered.

Lorraine turned from the window flushed with pleasure. She thought of the heavy-browed governor with his prominent nose and puffy eyes and large jowls. Bacon was different. Young and carefree, with a reckless air. A man she could admire.

Now that she was alone in this world of men sweeping by, she was uncertain what to do. But elsewhere in the town the reckless young rebel leader had come to his own decision.

He put Jamestown to the torch.

Lorraine was still standing undecided in her room, puzzling over what to do next, when she heard a voice calling from the street. She went to the window and looked out.

A detachment of rebels marched by shouting, "Out, out, everybody! General Bacon's given orders to set the town alight!"

The governor, it seemed, had known what he was doing when he had packed up the inhabitants and sailed away.

Lorraine came downstairs and went out on the street into pandemonium. A general air of merriment reigned, with cheering and hats tossed into the air as if it were a celebration.

When she asked one of the passersby why all the excitement, he told her that both Lawrence and Drummond, whose houses had been looted during the governor's occupation, were off to set their homes afire.

Lorraine gave him a look of disbelief. Through the loyalists with whom she had been consorting, she had learned quite a bit about both those gentlemen. Richard Lawrence, Oxford graduate and enigma, setting fire to his own fine house? Or William Drummond, solid Scot and former governor—what would his wife and four children say about that?

"They wouldn't!" she said, repelled.

But she followed along with the crowd, and sure enough, both Lawrence and Drummond solemnly put the torch to their own handsome homes. She was told that Bacon himself had fired the old red brick church and the State House. The public warehouse, the storehouse, all the taverns, inns, and private homes were set ablaze. Soon everyone was driven back by a wall of orange flames as raging fires consumed the city.

Nothing was spared.

"It seems such a waste," mourned Lorraine.

"Waste it may be, but now this city will no longer give sanctuary to our madman of a governor," said a grim voice nearby.

"Nor will it shelter Bacon," she countered.

His only answer was a shrug as he turned away.

By nightfall the capital of a colony whose dominion

reached from the Atlantic to the Mississippi lay in ruins, a smoldering heap of ashes and charred timbers that flared up sporadically, sending showers of sparks and occasional bright tongues of flame shooting into the smoky night air.

Lorraine was standing on the steep riverbank looking at the ruins. Behind her she heard a twig snap and she turned instinctively, looking down toward the dark waters which rippled with a reflected red glow from the smoldering embers. In the near-darkness she made out a man's form. In buckskins. He was seated upon the ground with his back leaning against a tree, a darker silhouette against the shining dark surface of the river. It was his sudden rising that had alerted her. He came to his feet in a single lithe movement as a boat approached. At that moment a shower of sparks from the not-yet-dead fires of Jamestown cascaded through the air and the man's profile came briefly into view.

Lorraine's heart contracted—it was Raile!

She was about to speak, to call out to him, but as the boat touched the shore she saw that there was a woman in it. A woman with wide skirts and hair like flame. Could her hair really be that fierce glowing red-gold or was it just the fire's leaping light that made it so? As Lorraine watched, the woman brought the boat up to the bank, the man reached down and pulled it higher. The woman stood up in the boat, tossed aside her oar, and leapt lightly out upon the bank. The buckskinned man staggered backward for a moment under the impact of her body careening against his. But his arms went around her and he clasped her to him. The fiery sparks had subsided but even in the near-darkness Lorraine could see that they were embracing joyously, swaying there upon the riverbank.

The same glowing red-gold hair she had seen in the locket . . . Lorraine had not the slightest doubt that the woman was Laurie Ann MacLaud—Laurie Ann, who had run away, and now was running back, by the look of the way she had hurled herself into Raile's arms. Laurie Ann, who did not like the sea. . . .

Raile must somehow have sent for Laurie Ann earlier. At least he had taken her advice and changed into buckskins for the upriver journey. Lorraine guessed Laurie Ann would take Raile to the man he wanted to see about selling the guns. If there really was any such man!

A feeling of outrage overwhelmed Lorraine. She wanted to rush down the dark bank to that embracing pair and pull them apart and pummel Raile with her fists. She wanted to shriek and call him names and take back the love she had so trustingly given him.

She wanted to die.

Her world seemed to rock and she reeled against a tree trunk, hanging on to it for support. She closed her eyes until her dizziness left her, and as it did, she knew that most of all she wanted revenge. . . .

When she looked around, the two figures were gone. In the distance on the dark shining face of the river she could see their boat, two dark figures, one rowing. She wondered bleakly if Raile would tell Laurie Ann about her. No, of course he wouldn't, she would be just another unimportant incident in a crowded life, a girl who had happened to be at hand when the captain wanted to play. How had he said it? *I lured you to my bed.* And it was true. Oh, God, it was true!

Hot tears scalded Lorraine's eyes and she moved away from the river. She was learning what it was like to love a rogue, she told herself bitterly—but there was no consolation in the thought, only anguish. Unaware of her surroundings, she had wandered blindly out into the road.

Around her the air was full of men's shouts and horses' neighing and the stamping of hooves. Bacon's rebels were leaving the capital. Instinctively Lorraine dodged a pair of horsemen who thundered by. But as she stumbled aside from that encounter, another horseman came suddenly out of the dark. He loomed above her and as he pulled on the reins, his horse reared up on its hind legs like a dark specter against the angry red glow of the burning city.

To Lorraine, after all that had happened to her today, that sudden great body leaping above her was like a vision of hell. She screamed and jumped aside, only to lose her footing and fall heavily to the ground.

In a moment the rider dismounted and stood bending over her. "Are you hurt?"

In the darkness she could not see his face.

"I . . . I don't think so," she said shakily.

"God's teeth, woman, what are you doing here? Someone bring a lantern!" And as his order was promptly obeyed and golden light poured over Lorraine's face, he drew in his breath. "You are the woman in the window—you blew me a kiss today!"

The dark figure bending solicitously over Lorraine was the rebel leader Nathaniel Bacon.

"What are you doing here?" he repeated. "I was told that the governor had evacuated all of his people."

"I am not one of his people," gasped Lorraine. "And I evaded the order!"

Did she read approbation on that dark face bending so close?

"So? And what is your business here, my lady?"

"None. I arrived by ship only last week and had intended to go to . . . to Yorktown." Her voice trembled a little over that lie. "But the town was under siege and I could not get there."

"And in Yorktown, what awaits you?"

"A ship, I hope." Lorraine could barely keep the bitterness out of her voice. "I was on my way to Barbados to join my guardian," she added glibly. "But my ship suffered damage in a storm and let me off here while it proceeded to Charles Towne for what may be lengthy repairs."

Bacon nodded thoughtfully and rose, standing above her, a slight figure but seeming tall in this light.

"Then you have really nowhere to go?"

"Not now that you have burned the inn where I had accommodations," sighed Lorraine.

"Well, we cannot leave you here."

Lorraine was conscious suddenly of the startled face of the cabin boy, Johnny Sears, anxiously peering at her in the lantern's yellow glow.

"No, I suppose not." She looked around her hopelessly at the dark, the noise, the smoke, the confusion, the charred ruins of the capital.

"Do you ride?" Bacon helped her to stand but the ground was uneven and she stumbled against him. "You have hurt your ankle?" he asked sharply.

"No, I just lost my footing again. And no, I'm sorry, I don't know how to ride," she added, a bit embarrassed.

"No matter." He swung her up on his horse and got into the saddle behind her. "You will travel with me."

"But I am here with my little brother—there he is!"

"Someone take the lad up. He will accompany us."

Lorraine saw Johnny Sears, looking exuberant, swooped up by a long arm that reached out of the darkness.

The general's horse reared again, but her cavalier kept a firm hand on the reins and brought him down without more than slightly disarranging Lorraine's skirts in the process. He raised his arm and one of his officers barked an order which was repeated military style, echoing down the line. Then they were off at a gallop, flying through the night.

"Where are we going?" gasped Lorraine.

"To Green Spring," he told her cheerfully. "Where a lady may be entertained in some style."

If anything could have taken Lorraine's mind from her own problems, that remark was designed to do it.

"But isn't that Governor Berkeley's . . . ?" Her words trailed off.

"Just so." Bacon's voice hardened. "Berkeley has bled this colony white long enough. Tonight we will take back some of our own. Don't worry. We will be there in time for a late supper—'tis less than three miles away."

Lorraine felt the night air rushing by, cooling her hot face, felt a strong yet gentle arm about her as she leaned back against the handsome coat front of the aristocratic rebel leader. She suppressed a sigh of pleasure. Most astonishing of all—she was off to palatial Green Spring, the finest mansion in all Virginia.

Bacon talked to her as they rode, and she guessed that he had missed female companionship on his long and hard forays into the swamps and forests. There was a wistful note in his voice as he told her of his riverfront home on the James, and something of his life in England. She gathered he considered himself a bad penny but a dauntless one—and hadn't his life proved that? His resonant voice warmed as he spoke of his men.

The stars shone down, the wind ruffled her silken skirts, she could feel the gold buttons of his wine-red coat cutting slightly into her back, but she did not care. She was off on a great adventure. The arms that held her so firmly before him in the saddle were very real—and strong. The leather-clad thighs her legs brushed against through her thin skirts were real and sinewy. And the steady pounding of hooves galloping behind them was the sound of a band of strong, determined men who would fly in the face of the king himself if need be.

Lorraine knew she would never forget that wild ride through the night with the rebel leader and his men.

And yet all the way she was fighting off remembering another wild ride through the night with other strong arms holding her, Narragansett Bay their objective. . . .

CHAPTER 23

Green Spring, The Virginia Colony

THE GREAT MANSION of Green Spring was lit up as if it were being prepared for a ball. The door swung open at Bacon's approach to reveal a massive hall, the candles of its branched chandeliers glowing on its wide expanse and broad stairway.

For all his fatigue, Bacon leapt lightly down from his horse and lifted Lorraine to the ground beside him. She walked beside him into the governor's magnificent mansion, marveling at what she saw. Governor Berkeley had had no thought of losing the battle, no thought that his great estate would be occupied by the "enemy," and Lady Frances, who had departed in haste with her servants, had taken almost nothing with her.

They would be back, the governor had sworn darkly, to claim it all, and heads would roll if anything were disturbed.

Servants stood about in the entrance hall, and though clad in the governor's livery, seemed prepared to take orders. Lorraine wondered aloud how Bacon had managed that. He explained that he had sent a small band to secure the place and arrange for a staff whilst he was building the breastworks.

"While those women in white aprons were marching up and down across the barricade?" she shot at him.

"Even so," he laughed. His dark face was very boyish despite his fatigue, she thought. A beguiling

290

face. She decided that despite all this turmoil, his wife was very lucky.

"This lady will be quartered in Lady Frances' bedchamber," he told one of the servants. He turned to Lorraine. "I do not know your name."

"Lorraine London," she said.

"From London itself?" he asked politely.

Lorraine decided it was best not to say she had come from Rhode Island. "No, mine is an old Cornish family," she told him. If worse came to worst, she could always fall back on all the things her mother had told her about Cornwall!

Bacon gave her a keen look. "Well, Mistress London." He was stripping off his leather gauntlet gloves as he spoke. "Your little brother will dine with the men, but as the only lady present, perhaps you will do my officers and myself the honor of presiding at our supper table? Show Mistress London up to her bedchamber that she may refresh herself. Supper will be in an hour."

He bowed and Lorraine left him to follow the servant up the broad handsome stairway. Behind her the hall was full of the jingle of spurs from booted men who were pouring in through the big front door.

The elegance of Lady Frances' bedchamber startled Lorraine. The delicate furniture, the fine damasks, the French gilt mirrors, the scented linens. Lorraine sat down at the elaborate dressing table and stared at her own face in the mirror.

I cannot believe I am really here, she told herself. *It is all a dream.*

That feeling of unreality persisted when after combing her hair into a fashionable coiffure with Lady Frances' silver repoussé comb, and with her head held high, Lorraine trailed down the broad stairway into the male gathering below. Bacon stepped forward to offer her his arm and lead her into the great dining room. A long table had been spread with snowy damask, branched chandeliers sparkled with what seemed a thousand candles, and atop the table silver candelabra were alight as well. All of that golden light sparkled on the massive silver plate and tall salts, and reflected over and over in the many ornate mirrors that encircled the wall sconces.

"If you will be good enough to occupy Lady Frances' chair at this end of the table, I will take the other." Bacon smiled at her.

"And she fits it a deal better than Lady Frances," rumbled one of the men behind her.

There was general laughter and Lorraine found herself seated where the governor's lady was wont to dine, being served by servants attired in the governor's livery.

They dined on the best the governor's storehouses and smokehouses had to offer. A steer had been butchered, so there were not only paper-thin slices of the cured hams for which Virginia was famous but also savory roast beef which had been turning on the spit in the big kitchen.

Lorraine was seated between two men who had been called "architects of the rebellion." On her right was the learned Richard Lawrence, who was rumored to have a black mistress, although she was nowhere in evidence. On Lorraine's left sat the sturdy Scotsman and former colonial governor William Drummond. His face was rather strained and set and she guessed it had been a wrench for him to set his handsome house on fire. He spoke to her quietly of his wife and four children, who had been sent to safety. The mysterious Mr. Lawrence, rather pensive, discussed more esoteric subjects. These two men, she learned, along with Giles Bland and Captain James Crews (who had been captured by the governor's forces in a naval engagement), were the leading lights of the rebellion and Bacon's chief lieutenants.

She looked down the table where their smiling, darkly handsome leader was raising his glass in a toast to her.

But as the meal progressed, the conversation grew increasingly serious. What was to be done about the governor? His ships? His men? Could they get their word through to the king before he did? A pity they had not been able to return him to his monarch in irons as he so richly deserved!

Supper over, Lorraine could see that Drummond

and Lawrence were eager to get on with discussing pressing matters. They kept hunching forward, trying to hear what Bacon was saying at the other end of the long table.

Her mother had told her that after dinner ladies in polite society withdrew to the "withdrawing room," while the gentlemen settled down to discussion and serious drinking.

Tactfully, Lorraine excused herself, for tonight she was a surrogate "governor's lady," was she not?

And despite the seriousness of their discussions, there was not an eye that did no follow the beauty out.

Under other circumstances, Lorraine, confronted so recently by proof of Raile's unfaithfulness, might have wept the night away. But the exhausting day, the wild ride through the night, the heavy meal, the tension of knowing herself to be an impostor who might be found out at any time, all conspired to produce a blessed numbness—and to give her a good night's sleep.

Morning brought a diffident knock on her door and a servant's voice inquiring if she would honor Mr. Bacon with her presence at breakfast.

Lorraine dressed quickly and ran downstairs to the big dining room. She found the rebel leader breakfasting with Drummond and the mysterious Lawrence. They seemed to be arguing a literary point—about a play called *The Lost Lady* written some years before by Governor Berkeley. They rose at her entrance and would have seated her with ceremony at the far end of the table had she not insisted she preferred their company to the splendor of playing hostess.

They laughed at that, and Lorraine settled down to an excellent Southern breakfast. The storehouses of Green Spring, it seemed, were equal to anything.

"I am off to Curles' Neck today," Bacon informed her, "to see my wife, and perhaps to bring her back with me to Green Spring."

"I should like to meet her." Lorraine sounded sincere but her heart sank. *A woman would not be satisfied with a cursory question or two; she would ferret out the truth about her!* "But it has been a very long time since I have seen my guardian, and I am eager to find out what ships will soon be leaving from Yorktown."

There was a sudden silence in the room. It was broken by Bacon's resonant voice.

"You are welcome to stay here as long as you like, of course. In my haste last night I forgot to inquire of your luggage."

"All burned," Lorraine said quickly.

His dark brows drew together. "My troops had orders not to—"

She was getting his men into trouble! "I had hidden my things in the inn," she interrupted hastily, "lest they be carried away by mistake in the general removal that was going on all around me. The innkeeper understood that I wanted to stay and allowed me to hide my trunk and boxes in his cellar, where your troops would doubtless not have thought to look, considering that the rest of the building was vacant."

That satisfied Bacon but she could see that it did not quite satisfy Drummond. Even Lawrence leaned forward, considering her with more interest.

"A misfortune," Bacon murmured, taking his last bite. He sat back, brushing his lips delicately with a white damask napkin, his gaze upon Lorraine. She was suddenly afraid of being left alone with Drummond and Lawrence.

She ate quickly and excused herself. She was hurrying from the dining room when Bacon rose. "If you will excuse me, gentlemen, I am off to the Curles. Mistress London, if I could have a word with you before I leave?"

Lorraine waited for him nervously in the wide hall.

"Perhaps we could stroll upon the lawn for a moment?" he suggested, offering her his arm.

Together they strolled across the green terraced lawns and into the elaborate formal gardens with their artful geometric patterns of clipped boxwood surrounding handsome flowerbeds. In some of those beds late-blooming roses still stood and Lorraine plucked a white one, heavy with scent. As she bent over it enjoying its fragrance, she wondered why the rebel leader had brought her out here away from the others. She cast a look back at the handsome house and thought what it would be like to live there and stroll of evenings through the soft lavender dusk. To live here . . . with Raile—she fought back the thought.

'Your little brother tells us his name is Johnny Sears," the man beside her said abruptly.

Lorraine was instantly on her guard. "I should have told you he is my half-brother."

"Ah, yes . . . half-brother," he murmured. "He says he is from Bristol. Yet you told me yours was an old Cornish family." The keen eyes looking down were steady upon her.

"And so it is," she told him gaily, brandishing the rose. "But when my mother died and my father married again, he removed to Bristol. I did not get on with my stepmother so I stayed in Cornwall. Johnny is my father's son by his second wife."

"And his education seems to be very different too," he commented, studying the trees.

"Yes, well, that is because . . ." Lorraine began breathlessly, and stopped. They had been questioning Johnny Sears, and who knew what he might have told them?

Bacon had come to a halt. His expression told her he had not believed a word she said.

"Johnny is not my brother," she admitted frankly. "But . . . he had nowhere to go and I had to get him out of Jamestown."

"A city I had destroyed?"

"Yes."

"And the rest?"

"Only true in part. My mother was indeed of an old Cornish family. All the rest was false."

He sighed and the motion made the gold buttons on his wine-red coat flash brighter in the sun. "I do not know what you are running away from, Mistress London, and from the set of your jaw I think you are of no mind to tell me, but you heard much discussion last night that we would prefer not to reach the governor's ears."

He thought her a spy! Her eyes widened in fear.

"I am new to Virginia but I am not an admirer of

the governor. I have heard evil things of him!" she protested.

"What things?" he asked sharply.

"That he will not protect the settlers from the Indians because it would harm his own trading interests— and in this he is egged on by a rapacious wife who will stop at nothing. That he leaves the planters and their families to fend for themselves, instead of sending troops to protect them against marauding Indians. Indeed, that he sends out troops to attack the planters if they try to protect themselves. I'll warrant you he'd take a different tack if Green Spring were threatened!"

"I'll warrant you he would," murmured Bacon. He was regarding her thoughtfully. "I see that by your own words you are not of Berkeley's persuasion," he said at last. "Have you anything else against the governor?"

"Yes, I have seen him as he rode by, and I liked neither his face nor his overbearing manner. And most particularly I did not like the way he looked at me—as if I were a sweetmeat!"

Her indignation was so real that the young man with her threw back his dark head and laughed.

"Mistress London," he said, wiping eyes that still twinkled with mirth, "in all else I may condemn him, but in that last he is scarcely to be blamed."

He began walking again, a graceful figure in his wide-topped boots and jingling spurs. Taking her arm, he led her back to the house.

But for all his amusement, she thought uneasily, *he could still lock me away or possibly hand me over to the others . . . since he is still not sure that I was not sent by Berkeley as a spy!*

They had reached the drive and he stopped, turned squarely to face her. Lorraine drew a deep breath and lifted her chin. He was, she knew, a man of swift decisions and almost simultaneous action—and he was looking at her ruefully.

"Mistress London," he said, "I am noted for my rashness. So before wiser heads can counsel me, I am going to let you go. By the way, where *is* your luggage?"

"Aboard a ship I wish never to set foot on again!" said Lorraine in a trembling voice.

"Ah," he said. "Perhaps that explains it. You will forgive me, but I anticipated this contretemps last night after we had supped together."

"Why? Was I so poor at playing the 'governor's lady' then?" asked Lorraine, crestfallen.

"No, let us say you were rather too perfect—as if you had been schooled for the role. You had come out of nowhere and yet you were so instantly one with us." His expression hardened. "I have come to mistrust perfection."

There was a slightly dazed look in Lorraine's eyes. She had seemed to this born-to-the-purple aristocrat to be *a perfect governor's lady!* Surely he was jesting! But that kindly expression told her he was not.

"Since you have told me you do not ride—and that, I confess, was one of the things that set me to thinking, for it is rare to find a lady who does not ride—I have arranged a carriage for you. I can see that it is coming round now, and my horse as well. The carriage will transport you to the York and a river barge that will deliver you downstream to Yorktown."

He was offering her escape! She looked up into that darkly handsome countenance that once again looked so tired.

And he felt something for her too—he did not have to tell her. It was there between them, unspoken. *If I were free . . .*

He had taken her hand to help her into the carriage that was even now drawing up with Johnny Sears sitting in lordly fashion in the back. He held her hand a moment too long. His voice was caressing.

"Lawrence believes you may have been sent by Berkeley. Drummond is coming round to his opinion. You had better leave quickly." His smile flashed. "I would not like to have to call them out!"

Lorraine paused but a moment. "I do not know if I heard anything last night that I should not," she told him earnestly. "But whatever I heard is safe with me, I promise you." He was hurrying her into the carriage, eager to get her gone, away from danger.

"Now I know why your men are so eager to follow you," she added softly.

"Put that on my epitaph!" he laughed, and sprang lightly to the saddle of the big black horse the groom had brought.

As the carriage wheels began to roll down the drive, Lorraine leaned out and blew him a saucy kiss. "May you win all of Virginia and hold it forever!"

He waved a gloved hand to her. Then he wheeled his mount and galloped away toward the Curles of the James—and his Elizabeth.

Chivalry rode with him. . . .

He was every inch a cavalier, Lorraine thought mistily, watching him go. He *should* win Virginia—how he would grace the office of governor! In another time, another place, she could have loved this man with all her heart. She dashed a tear from her eye.

"Why are you crying?" It was Johnny Sears's curious voice.

"Because I fear for him," sighed Lorraine. For one splendid evening she had played at being a governor's lady, and Bacon at the other end of the long table had been her governor—a situation to foment wild dreams. She pressed the cool petals of the rose against her hot cheek. It was all she had taken away from Green Spring—and its petals were already blowing away on the breeze. She would not see Bacon again, she knew.

She tried to shake off her gloomy mood. She told herself the life at palatial Green Spring was not meant for such as her, but found herself hard to convince.

"Is it not a beautiful day, Johnny?" she forced herself to say. "You and I are bound for Yorktown!"

"The Captain won't find us there," he muttered darkly.

Lorraine was in no mood to bother with him. "If you object, I will put you out along the road," she told him fiercely. "And you can find your own way back to Jamestown! Do you think he will look for us in a burned-over city?"

Johnny sat back, chastened. Lorraine looked up alertly at the driver's stolid back to be sure he had not heard.

But Johnny's mention of the captain had brought back memories of Raile and the *Lass*. She was suddenly homesick for the ship where she had enjoyed being with . . . Helst and L'Estraille. She would put Raile out of her mind! But L'Estraille at least had loved her. She missed L'Estraille.

"I wonder why André did not come ashore with us," she murmured.

"Oh, I can tell you that," said Johnny brightly. "He was afraid. The law is after him. He married some Huguenot girl in Bordeaux whose family took her away to America when they learned he was already married to two other women. That's why he came aboard as ship's doctor. The Huguenot girl's somewhere in Virginia and he's afraid to come ashore because he might run across her and be clapped in jail for bigamy."

André married? To *three* women!

"It can't be true," she said slowly.

"It is," Johnny assured her complacently. "I guess you're the only person on the ship that didn't know about it."

Lorraine sat back with her lips compressed, seething with indignation. Her cheeks grew hot and her eyes snapped as she remembered how the attractive Frenchman had professed undying love and begged her to marry him!

The journey to Yorktown took longer than she had expected. They had to spend the night in the tiny village of Williamsburg and the next day were taken to the banks of the York, where they clambered into a canopied river barge going downriver to Yorktown.

During the last two days, lurching over bumpy roads in an open carriage, Lorraine had had time to think. That night spent at palatial Green Spring had given her something: perspective. The scalding pain of Raile's deception still burned bright, but there was something else too. She had misjudged herself, misjudged what she wanted in life.

She looked out at the wide river, glowing rose in the dusk of evening, flowing so smoothly down to the sea.

Her own life was like white-water rapids, always turbulent, never smooth.

What was there about her, she asked herself, that made men burn so hot—and then blow so cold? Was it the wild look of her? Perhaps. Her unfortunate circumstances? Most certainly—no one wanted to wed a ragamuffin who might at any time be yanked away by the law to a life of servitude!

And *wed* she wanted to be, she realized sadly. She wanted a lifetime of sharing—with one man. She sighed to herself. The Green Flash was what she wanted—a signal that this would be the one love beside which all others paled. She had thought to find that love with Philip, and then again with Raile—oh, especially with Raile. Perhaps she would be one of those women who would never find it, she thought sorrowfully.

But now she knew the truth about herself.

She wanted to love a man who would cherish her above all other women. Forever.

And most especially she did *not* want to love a rogue.

Not ever, ever again.

CHAPTER 24

Yorktown, Colonial Virginia

LORRAINE HAD HER first surprise when she reached the Swan, the inn in Yorktown that had been recommended to her. The Swan was a sturdy white frame structure, gambrel-roofed, with broad-based sloping brick chimneys that rose like giant slanted stairsteps at either end. Like the rest of the town's buildings, the Swan was situated on the bluffs overlooking the wide shining expanse of the York River, where a medley of merchant ships lay at anchor in the busy port.

In the common room, a little birdlike man in a bottle-green coat of conservative cut stood supervising the lifting of two boxes by a harassed lad in a greasy apron. The boy protested that he couldn't carry any more boxes down to the ship, that he was needed back in the kitchen!

The little man had his back to Lorraine, and she scarcely noticed him, for the innkeeper, a sober-looking middle-aged man in homespun, with white hair and very pink cheeks, came bustling in in response to the bell that had clanged as she and Johnny entered.

"Do you have two rooms to let?" she asked him hopefully. "This is Johnny Sears and I am—"

"Lorraine London!" cried the little man in the bottle-green coat, who had turned about when the bell clanged. "I cannot believe it is you—at last!"

Lorraine stared at him in bewilderment. "Do I know you, sir?"

"No, you do not—set those boxes over there in the corner, lad, that's right, at the far end of that table. Your father pointed you out to me one day in Providence. You were delivering a package for your mother at the time, I believe."

In Providence! Lorraine felt she should turn and flee! But his next words took a reassuring tone.

"You have . . . er . . . filled out since then, but you've an arresting face and I'd still know you anywhere. Landlord, bring us some cider, if you please— Mistress London and I have much to talk about. Is that lad with you a blood relation?"

Lorraine gave him a dazed look. "No."

He turned to the aproned boy who had just set down the boxes. "Take this lad away to the kitchen with you and give him some cider. My talk with Mistress London is private."

A bewildered Johnny Sears was hustled away to the kitchen and an equally bewildered Lorraine was led by the little man—who tugged at her sleeve—to the far end of the empty room. There he set a small leather chest that had been tucked under his arm down upon the long trestle table and beamed at her. The landlord brought two tankards of cider, stopped to study Lorraine with great interest for a moment, and left them.

The little man edged closer. "I did not want anyone to hear what I am about to say," he told her in a confidential tone. "Mistress London, I have been searching for you for a long time. My name is Nicholls."

Lorraine continued to regard him blankly.

"Benjamin Nicholls," he said softly. "Your father entrusted me with—"

He did not have to say another word. Lorraine caught her breath, and Nicholls, seeing that she now knew who he was, chuckled. He was the man her father had long ago entrusted with the wild venture of sending ginseng to China that nearly broke her mother's heart!

A great stillness seemed to fill the room.

"You have sold the ginseng?" Lorraine guessed, raising her tankard of cider to her lips.

Nicholls bobbed his head merrily. "And for a price

that will stagger you." He leaned forward and whispered, "A hundred thousand pounds."

Lorraine choked on her cider. "But . . . but that is a fortune!"

He nodded solemnly. "When I got back to Rhode Island and learned that your parents were dead, I felt it was my duty to find you. I have been chasing you ever since Captain Bridey came back from Bermuda with word that he had seen you there and that you were on your way to Virginia. Mistress London, I am told that you are your father's sole heir."

"That is true but—"

"The money is in gold on the *Matilda*. I'm about to sail on her to Barbados. Even the *Matilda*'s captain does not know that he is carrying such a great sum. But"—he looked around him doubtfully—"I would not advise you to invest so much here in Virginia. The colony is in upheaval, there is talk of confiscation when this rebellion is ended. As a newcomer to these shores, it would be easy for you to find the wrong friends and lose everything."

I have already found the wrong friends, thought Lorraine bitterly.

"What, then, would you advise, Mr. Nicholls?" she asked, troubled, for such matters were new to her.

"Allow me to suggest that you invest it where there is profit to be made, in one of the islands. In Barbados new fortunes are being made all the time. As I said, I am on my way there myself. My ship leaves tomorrow."

Barbados . . . a new life, a fresh start. She saw herself suddenly transformed into a lady, seated in her own carriage, waving a ruffled parasol in the sunlight, driving past an enormous house—her own.

"Mr. Nicholls . . ." She studied the man before her. Shrewd, certainly. And honest enough to come half around the world to deliver gold that would have made him rich had he been scoundrel enough to keep it. "Would *you* be my agent? Would you select a suitable plantation for me in Barbados—something on the sea with a handsome house? And take over the management of my affairs until I can get there?"

"Until you can get there?" His eyebrows elevated.

She drummed her fingers upon the table. She would like to straighten out her affairs, especially buy back her articles from Oddsbud, before starting her new life. "Are you familiar with my reasons for leaving Rhode Island?"

"A lovers' quarrel," he said promptly. "And we have had a deal of a time finding you! I was told your father had left you with the Oddsbuds. What a terrible thing to find them both dead and the Light Horse Tavern burned to the ground." He shook his head.

Lorraine started. A variety of emotions surged through her. The Oddsbuds were both dead and if the Light Horse Tavern had burned to the ground, then her articles of indenture must have been consumed by the flames along with it. She was free! She could hardly take that in at first, and then it washed over her. She could go anywhere she pleased. She was free!

Suddenly, she realized that Nicholls had said "we." "Who came with you?"

"Young Dedwinton, of course."

"Philip?" she said incredulously.

"Who else but a betrothed would go on such a quest?" he asked in jocular fashion.

She looked wildly around her. "Then where is he?"

"Out seeking you. It seemed reasonable to assume that you had not had time to get settled in the interior, that you would still be living near the coast. Whilst I have been making inquiries, sending word as far as the Falls of the James, he is off to the Eastern Shore to see if you could possibly be there, for we have been informed that in this rebellion that is going on, the governor himself is repairing there with the entire population of Jamestown." He patted her hand in commiseration. "Young Dedwinton will be back in a day or two—he has been gone this past fortnight."

Philip—*here!* And seeking *her!* Lorraine seemed to have entered into a mad world where nothing made sense.

And then it came to her that she was now an heiress, and Philip, opportunist that he was, was seeking her out not for love but for her newfound wealth!

All the resentment she had felt toward him welled

up in her again. How she would like to bring him down a peg or two!

Her eyes narrowed as she studied Nicholls. "How do you know Philip will be back so soon?"

"Well, he can be back no later than three days hence, for that is when the *Lizard,* which brought us here, sails back to Rhode Island. He has booked passage aboard her."

"Does Philip know of my good fortune?"

"Yes, but not the extent of it," laughed Nicholls. "I told him only that I was bringing you a thousand pounds. As for the rest, I thought you might prefer to tell him yourself."

A thousand pounds. . . . It was a great sum, but perhaps that was not Philip's reason for pursuing her. That thought suddenly put a new light on things.

She frowned. "Mr. Nicholls, had Philip already arranged for passage south before you arrived in Rhode Island?"

"No, we made arrangements together—after he told me where Captain Bridey said you were to be found."

So Philip had not planned to set out alone—or perhaps he had not had time to do it before Nicholls arrived. She checked her desire to question Nicholls further, for he had dragged out his large gold watch and was glancing down at it uneasily.

Lorraine's plan came to her all at once. "I will follow you to Barbados on the first available ship," she told him rapidly. "Leave with me only enough money for passage and a small amount over." She looked perplexed. "I have no good place to secrete it. Could we leave it with the innkeeper here?"

"I think so. Higgins is well-spoken of in the town and seems to be an honest man. One who does not overcharge!" he added with a twinkle.

"And, Mr. Nicholls . . ." She felt suddenly shy. "I have been very poor all my life and yet such wealth as this will permit me to move with the gentry. In Barbados will you keep silent about my background? Say only that I am a wealthy heiress about whom you know nothing but whose affairs you were chosen by London solicitors to manage?"

Nicholls' eyes twinkled again. A voyager to China and back, he was used to rags-to-riches stories—and sometimes riches-to-rags as well! "You can count on me," he promised. "Indeed"—he hesitated to say this, but Philip had not made a very good impression on him on the voyage down—"I gave young Dedwinton the figure of a thousand pounds because I thought it possible you might want to keep the extent of your fortune from him. Permanently."

"Why?" she challenged.

He looked uncomfortable. "His ideas of business did not sound promising," he confessed. "He was eager to venture upon tangled Rhode Island land deals that I thought unsound. But of course, as your husband he would be entitled to the management of your affairs." He was smiling at her now. "*If* he were apprised of their extent."

"Philip is not in charge of my affairs *yet*." Lorraine was looking at him with a level gaze. "In the meantime, I would have my plantation purchased in my own name. Indeed"—she cocked her head at him—"I would test Philip. Would you do me a great favor, Mr. Nicholls? Write a short note to Philip, explaining to him that, as my husband, from now on he will be responsible for my debts?"

"But every man knows that!" he protested.

"Even those made prior to marriage."

His shrewd eyes lit up with understanding; his whole face took on a gleeful look. "You are planning to make him think you have already squandered the thousand pounds?"

"Just so." Lorraine nodded.

"Well, that will bring him out," he agreed, "and make him show his true colors, whatever they are. I will do it at once, at the same time I give your passage money to the landlord for safekeeping. Mistress London, I feel I am going to enjoy being your agent!"

The deed was soon done. Higgins, the landlord, had taken her money in a small wooden box sealed with red sealing wax and stamped with Nicholls' signet ring. Then he carried it off to put it in a safe place.

Nicholls left the next day. The *Matilda* had sailed

away downriver on the first leg of her journey to Barbados.

Lorraine was glad she had not sailed with him. She would have her revenge! Her eyes glinted dangerously. Oh, she could hardly wait until the morrow to get her claws on Philip!

But the next day came and Philip did not.

After breakfast she walked along the bluffs in the bright weather. Below her, riding at anchor somewhere among the other ships, would be Philip's, the one that had brought him, and one he would be returning on tomorrow night. She inquired of a man who walked by with a rolling gait which ship was the *Lizard* and he pointed out a small square-rigged two-masted merchant ship.

"That be her," he said. "Named for Lizard Point at the south tip of England, she was."

Lorraine stood and contemplated the ship for a long time. Once she would have been thrilled at the thought of Philip Dedwinton following her anywhere. Now . . .

Now she turned with a shrug and took a stroll through the town. Fall was in the air. The breeze from the sea had freshened and sharpened. Soon the leaves would be changing color and falling, floating in showers of scarlet and gold down past the enormous brick chimneys of the white clapboard houses. A few of the town's houses were of brick but most were of clapboard, some a story and a half tall, though usually only one room deep. They were straggled along atop the bluffs, and white picket fences surrounded their inviting gardens of fruit trees and roses and box.

A pleasant town, such a town as she had thought she might someday live in with Raile—and bear his children, and give meaning and beauty to his life. With the thought, her nagging heartache at his having left her returned.

She walked soberly back to the inn and took lunch in her room. By midafternoon she began to regret that she had not sailed with Nicholls on the *Matilda*, away from everything that would remind her of the tall Scot. Yesterday she had been blinded by a wild desire to get back at Philip, but now she saw things in a clearer light.

By evening she even regretted the pact she had made with Johnny Sears when he had told her in amazement, "The landlord says you're an heiress!"

"Yes, a thousand pounds from a venture of my father's," was her answer. And then she asked him to do her a favor, in return for which she would give him money to attend tomorrow night's cockfight, as well as enough "to make a wager if he cared to." She knew that next to his adoration of his captain, Johnny's main interest lay in cockfights.

Johnny quickly agreed.

Lorraine passed an uneasy night in her room, dreaming brokenly of Raile, and by morning she had decided what she would do. To the devil with Philip! A ship from Bristol lay in the harbor. It was picking up cargo now and next week would leave for Jamaica. She would be on that ship. From Jamiaca she could easily procure passage to Barbados.

Having made up her mind, she felt better. It was late when she sauntered down the stairs, rustling in her pink silks. After breakfast, she went to the Jamaica-bound ship to make her arrangements with the captain. She promised to bring her passage money when she boarded, and strolled back through the town. On the way she wandered into a little shop and considered buying a warm woolen cloak, for the air was unseasonably nippy.

" 'Tis a good value, Mistress . . . ?"

"London. I'm sure it is. . . ." Lorraine passed a hand over the soft dark blue fabric lovingly.

"Cotswold wool," the proprietor told her hopefully.

Lorraine sighed. She loved pretty clothes. "But 'tis made for cold weather and I'm off to Jamaica next week."

She left the shopkeeper shaking his head over the folly of females who would waste a shopkeeper's valuable time looking at winter cloaks when they well knew they were off to warmer climes!

Lorraine returned and lounged about her room all afternoon, soaking in a hot bath, taking a long nap.

Finally she decided that she would dine in the common room, and dressed quickly, for the hour was late.

Lifting her pink skirts, she hurried down the stairs. She came to a sudden halt at the bottom of the stairs. For there, looking every inch as handsome and as possessive as he had in Rhode Island, was Philip Dedwinton, his brown head thrown back, his brown eyes smiling down at her.

"Lorraine!" He moved toward her and caught her impetuously by the shoulders. Holding her back from him for a moment, he devoured her with his eyes and then crushed her to his breast.

Lorraine was unprepared for the warmth of his greeting. She gasped and tried to pull away, for she could feel her treacherous heart begin to race. Philip had always exerted a powerful tug on her heartstrings, and seeing him just when he had dropped from her thoughts completely had dredged up old memories.

"I have searched the length and breadth of Accomack for you!" he cried. "And now I return and the landlord tells me you have been here the better part of a fortnight!"

The landlord had done his part—he had told the lie Lorraine had requested. But now she did not want that lie told. She wanted to tell Philip the truth—and send him away.

"No, Philip, I—" she began.

Thinking that her "no" meant for him to unhand her, he did so instantly. "Come," he told her happily, his voice overriding her protests. "I have arranged for a private dinner for us—we will have time to talk. The ship departs tomorrow morning at dawn." And with the words he led her back upstairs into the inn's tiny private dining room.

The room held a table already spread with a white linen cloth and set for two. As Lorraine sat down, there was a patter of feet on the stairs and a smiling serving wench, with her apron tucked up proudly to reveal a red petticoat, hurried in carrying a savory platter of roast waterfoul garnished with scallops and oysters.

Philip was silent until the meal was served and the door closed, but his brown eyes never left her face.

He leaned over and took her hand.

"Lorraine, I have treated you very badly," he said huskily.

"You did indeed," she agreed.

He looked a little daunted but persevered. "I came back to the Light Horse Tavern the next morning looking for you, to beg your forgiveness—as now I do."

"Very well, I forgive you, Philip," she said crisply, but she drew her hand away. "Shall we have our supper? Your ship will not wait, you know." Her voice was even.

"I see that you have not forgiven me in your heart." He sounded aggrieved.

"Did you expect it?" she challenged.

"Perhaps not," he said sadly. "But I hoped. I have never ceased thinking of you, Lorraine. Your face has always been before me."

"Except when Lavinia Todd's was there," she corrected him in a brittle voice.

He looked hurt. "How can you say that?"

"Oh, very easily." She shrugged. "I had meant to say quite a lot to you, Philip, but now I find it doesn't matter." Her eyes narrowed. "Nicholls told you of my inheritance, I take it?"

"Yes, but I hope you do not think that is why I have come all this way to find you!" He sounded so righteously indignant that Lorraine decided to play the game out as she had originally planned. She laid down her fork and leaned back, suddenly enjoying herself.

"Indeed I did think it," she said energetically. "When I discovered you did not set out to search for me until you knew I had come into a thousand pounds!"

"That's not true! I *did* search for you. All we knew was that you had run away on horseback with a stranger. I searched everywhere! It was not till Captain Bridey came back from Bermuda that we knew where you had gone."

"And as soon as Mr. Nicholls arrived, the two of you dashed right off to find me."

"Yes." Sukily.

With a shrug, Lorraine began to eat her dinner

again. "Did the landlord tell you my new profession? I am a gambler now."

"He said you had offered to play him double or nothing for the price of your lodgings on a single cut of the cards," Philip mumbled.

She laughed. The landlord was playing his part. "How did the Light Horse Tavern catch fire?" she asked. "Mistress Oddsbud was careless with fire, I know. Oddsbud was forever scolding her about it, but—"

Philip's jaw dropped. "You mean you did not know? There is little left in Rhode Island. The Indians have well nigh burned everything in sight."

"Then that was how . . . ?" gasped Lorraine.

"Yes. The Light Horse Tavern was burned and so were many other good buildings. King Philip's War has been raging since you left, Lorraine. You are lucky not to have been there. The Oddsbuds had no chance at all! The main attack was on a Sunday when everyone was going home from church. The savages butchered many of us. The MacAldies were killed, all but Andy, and the Paines, every one, and Mary Wickham and the Jarvises and Matthew Stokes and the Rawson children and more others than I can count. So far Providence has been spared, but most of New England is in flames. The war still goes on."

Lorraine shuddered. "And your family, Philip?" She was almost afraid to inquire.

"All gone." His face had gone somber.

"I'm sorry," she whispered.

He seemed not to hear her. "And our house burned to the ground, all our outbuildings and grain destroyed, the livestock run off and slaughtered. *I* was saved only because I had gone out to study the site for the stone-ender I had meant to build for you."

Lorraine gave him a sharp look. There had been a false note in his voice when he said that. It brought a turning world back into focus. Philip's home had been destroyed, he needed money to build a new one, to buy new livestock, grain. A thousand pounds would more than do it—it would give him money to speculate in land as well. . . .

A knock on the door interrupted them. Higgins, the landlord, hurried in.

"I did forget to give you this note that Mr. Nicholls left for you," Higgins told Philip, handing him a folded parchment.

Lorraine met Higgins' gaze with amusement as he left.

Philip opened the note, read it—and frowning, re-read it. "What is this?" he asked slowly. "Why is Nicholls warning me that I could be responsible for debts you made before . . . ?" His voice sharpened. "What does he mean by it, Lorraine?"

"I do not know what he may have written, Philip, but pay no attention to it. I have told you that gaming is now my profession, and of course such a life does have its ups and downs."

"You told me, but I did not believe you." His voice had harshened and he crumpled the note. "Speak plainly, if you please! Are you trying to tell me that you have gambled away your inheritance in the space of a fortnight? For if you are, I will not believe it!"

"I do not know why you are so upset." Lorraine regarded him with big innocent eyes. "My debts do not concern you, Philip."

"Everything about you concerns me," he grated. "I have a mind to throttle the truth out of you!"

At that moment Johnny Sears opened the door and stuck his head in, right on cue. "That up-country planter is downstairs asking where you are," he whispered. "Says you owe him fifty pounds."

"Oh, bother!" Lorraine laid down her spoon. "Can't you get rid of him? Tell him I have gone to Accomack. I have paid all the rest!"

"I will try." Johnny closed the door—and went on unconcernedly to his cockfight. He had done what she asked.

But Philip was pale. "Can it be true that you have really manged to gamble away your inheritance?"

"And a trifle more, as you have just heard," Lorraine told him in a bored voice. "But it is a temporary setback, I assure you. The gaming life has its ups and downs. Why, the very planter they are trying to get rid of downstairs—I won three hundred pounds from him before he broke me!" She managed to put real excitement into her voice, remembering those lighthearted games on the deck of the *Likely Lass* for mythical thousands.

"Then it *is* gone!" He rose and flung down his napkin. There was real heartfelt grief in his voice.

"Yes, it is gone, Philip." Lorraine rose to face him. "And that changes everything between us, *does it not?*"

He came around the table and stood over her, breathing hard. His expression was anguished but she was unprepared for his next move.

"It changes only one thing," he murmured. "I cannot marry you now."

And with the words his right fist shot up and caught her squarely on the left jaw. The impact would have sent her spinning across the room except he reached out and caught her, breaking her fall as she crumpled. Her pink silk figure—so slight, after all—collapsed unconscious against him. As he stood looking down at her, myriad emotions played over his handsome face.

But he knew he must be quick. He would have to chance the angry planter demanding his fifty pounds, have to hope that the lad who had warned Lorraine of his presence had got rid of him somehow. But the innkeeper—and who knew how many others in the common room—would never let him leave with the girl unless . . .

Inspiration seized him. He always carried a flask of brandy with him. He took it out and poured some of the liquid over Lorraine's face and hair, wiped away the excess with a handkerchief. He hesitated, then poured some more down the pale cleft between her breasts so that it would saturate the top of her chemise. Satisfied, he took his limp and reeking burden in his arms, being careful to see that her left jaw, reddened and swelling where he had struck her, was hidden against his chest.

Thus burdened, he trotted downstairs.

"I'm off to my ship lest she sail without me," he told the landlord breezily.

"But what's this?" Higgins cried, stepping forward in alarm.

"She's a secret drinker. 'Tis why we quarreled," whispered Philip—and indeed the landlord could smell for himself the brandy that drenched her. "But 'tis her only fault!" Philip added merrily. "I believe I paid you for her lodgings and our supper before we went upstairs?"

"Aye, but wait," cried the innkeeper, remembering the small sealed box left in his charge. "I'll just—"

At that moment there was a loud crash from the kitchen, followed by a medley of shrieks. The door burst open and a frightened face appeared.

"Meg and Cook are fighting again! Meg tripped over the dog and spilled boiling soup over Cook's arm and Cook says she done it on purpose—best come quick!"

With a curse, Higgins sprang forward and plunged toward the kitchen. By the time he returned, Philip was gone.

CHAPTER 25

The *Lizard*

LORRAINE WOKE WITH a throbbing pain in her jaw and saw nothing she recognized about her. Somewhere overhead in the dimness a ship's lamp swung, and beneath her was the lumpiest pallet it had ever been her misfortune to sleep on.

Confused, she looked about her. For a moment she thought she was back on the *Likely Lass,* somewhere belowdeck. Then she saw that there were half a dozen women in the cabin, getting dressed.

"Where . . . am I?" she managed painfully, for her jaw hurt.

The nearest woman, massively built and struggling into a green sarcenet dress, said harshly, "We don't talk to the likes of you, coming aboard dead drunk!"

"What?" cried Lorraine. "I did no such thing! What ship is this?"

"Ignore her, Polly," sniffed a thin woman in brown taffeta, and they moved away from her.

Lorraine sat up. She saw that she was still fully dressed.

"You're aboard the *Lizard,*" said a calm voice from a dim corner across the room. "Bound for Rhode Island."

Philip! She remembered then that he had struck her. He must have carried her away with him! Indignation surged through her.

"I have been abducted!" she gasped.

There was a ripple of laughter from two of the ladies nearby. They made a point of turning their backs when Lorraine struggled to her feet and scrambled up to the deck. Above her, white sails billowed. To her dismay, there was no land in sight.

"Where is the captain?" she cried, looking wildly about her. "He must put me ashore immediately!"

Her arrival on deck in such disheveled state, hair wild, jaw swelling, clothes rumpled, still reeking of brandy, created a stir. Passengers collected around her.

"I tell you I have been abducted!"

Philip appeared from nowhere, shouldering his way between two male passengers who looked distressed. He seized Lorraine by the wrist.

"What have you been telling these people?"

"I have been telling them the truth," gasped Lorraine, trying vainly to extricate herself from his grasp. "That you took me away from Yorktown last night against my will!"

A short stocky bearded man had come up behind Philip. He laid a heavy hand on Philip's shoulder. "Here, what is this commotion?" he asked roughly.

Philip shook the hand off and turned about, perforce dragging Lorraine with him. "Captain, this matter is between me and my bondservant," he snarled.

"I am not his bondservant!" Lorraine appealed to the captain, whom she felt had an honest face. "He's lying!"

"When you brought her aboard last night, you told me she was your betrothed, the wench you had come south seeking, and that she had gotten drunk celebrating your arrival. Now you tell me she is your bondservant. Which story is true?"

"Both!" exploded Philip.

"Neither!" screamed Lorraine.

Philip flung Lorraine from him with such force that she was catapulted against the chest of a passing passenger. The big man caught her breathless form and set her upon her feet, looking indignant that a young girl should be so roughly treated.

"Here, I will prove it to you!" Philip fished inside his coat. "I have here her articles, duly signed over to me by one Oddsbud." He thrust the folded parchment at the captain.

With deliberation the captain read the paper and looked up at Philip. "This appears to be in order," he sighed.

"It cannot be!" Lorraine leaped forward to snatch at the paper. "Oddsbud said he would never sell me!"

It was the wrong thing to have said. It made clear that she was bound to *someone*. The buzzing voices around her stilled suddenly. Her remark brought a hard smile to Philip's face.

"But he did—after you ran away," he told her. "And I came searching for you."

That put a different complexion on everything. Lorraine fell back. "I can buy back my articles, I can pay in gold for the remaining time of my indenture!"

The captain frowned and pulled at his beard. It was customary for a betrothed to pay in money for the remaining time of a woman's indenture so that he could marry her—but this situation seemed a bit different.

"Do you have this gold?" he asked her.

"No, but I can get it!"

"She lies," said Philip flatly. " 'Tis true she came into an inheritance whilst she was hiding from me, but she has spent it all—and more. Indeed she has run up debts and was trying to escape her creditors when I found her. She should count herself lucky to escape debtors' prison."

"The poor child had to live, and food and lodgings cost money," cried a female voice that Lorraine recognized as belonging to the woman who had volunteered the information earlier that she was aboard the *Lizard* bound for Rhode Island.

Philip swung about to address the voice. "They were gaming debts." He sneered. "She has already squandered a fortune."

"It is not true!" cried Lorraine distractedly. "I made it all up to get back at him. He had done me a hurt in Rhode Island—"

She was never to finish her sentence. Philip's hand lashed across her face. "Lying wench!" he growled. "I'll take a whip to you!"

"There will be no flogging of women aboard my ship," thundered the heavy voice of the captain. "Mistress London—is that your name? For it is the name on your articles."

"Yes," whispered Lorraine, clutching at the nearest arm to steady herself.

"You will be treated as any other passenger on board. You will sleep with the women belowdeck, and when you are on deck you will be treated with respect and propriety." He turned to Philip, concealed rage in his voice. "I think you may be practicing some ugly game upon this girl, and I would have you know that if I discover what it is I will haul you before the authorities when we reach Providence."

Philip stood white-faced and undecided for a minute. Then he bit back the angry words that sprang to his lips, turned on his heel, and stomped away.

The passengers seemed to melt back from Lorraine. Only the captain remained, chewing his lip as he considered her. "Is it true you have gold to pay this man off?" he asked sternly.

Lorraine nodded hopelessly. "I had saved passage money for Barbados out of my inheritance," she said sadly. "It is true that I ran away from Rhode Island because of . . . of something bad that happened there, but I was told that Oddsbud was dead, and since he had no living relatives, I had assumed that I was free. Then yesterday Philip turned up and seized me and carried me off."

"Where is this gold?"

"It is being held for me in Yorktown. Oh, could you not turn the ship around and sail back and let me get it? It is twice enough for my passage on your ship!"

"No, I cannot do that," he said thoughtfully.

"But this man is carrying me away for years of servitude!" she cried. "And you heard what he said about a whip!"

The captain continued chewing his lip. "What is this man to you?" he shot at her.

"Once he was everything," admitted Lorraine. "But now he is nothing."

The captain had no mind to become involved in lovers' quarrels.

"He came south to marry me to secure my inheritance," she explained anxiously. "But I tricked him into believing that it was gone—and that is when he struck me down and carried me onto your ship."

"You arrived reeking of brandy," he reminded her grimly. "He said you had been celebrating your reunion."

"Another lie! He must have poured it on me while I lay unconscious."

"It will have to be sorted out in Rhode Island," he declared. "Meantime you will be well-treated on board my ship."

The female passengers did not share his opinion. They had already "sorted it out." To a woman, they drew away from her. Even the one who had spoken up for her. Lorraine heard the woman's sister whisper, "Leave her alone, Susie, we don't want to know *that* sort!"

Miserable at being treated like a leper in the women's quarters, Lorraine sought the deck on every possible occasion. But even that did not give her much companionship. The married men aboard, who slept in separate men's quarters belowdeck, had been instructed by their wives to avoid the "loose-living" bound girl in their midst. Of the three bachelor passengers, one had a melancholy air, coughed a great deal, and kept to himself. The other two were each separately threatened by Philip, who offered to "break their bones" if they trifled with Lorraine.

The voyage north was maddeningly slow. The *Lizard* had no fore and aft sails at all, no spritsail below her bowsprit, and was an indifferent sailer. Ordinarily passengers were kept below in bad weather, but the captain made an exception for Lorraine. Her woebegone face touched his heart and she was allowed to while away the time on deck in fair weather or foul.

Philip did not like that.

It rained their first two days out of Yorktown, but on

the third day the weather cleared and the other passengers were allowed on deck. Philip came up with the others—and found Lorraine already there, looking beautiful in the sunlight. When she saw him, she promptly turned her back—and one of the passengers tittered.

Philip, seizing Lorraine's arm, swung her around to face him. "You are my bondsevant," he rasped. "How dare you turn your back on me?"

"I will always turn my back on you," declared Lorraine bitterly. She was struggling to break his grasp. "For I cannot bear the sight of your face!"

Infuriated by the remark, which had been overheard by several of the passengers, Philip raised a hand to strike her.

The captain, who was watching them from the bow, strode over and promised Philip in a bellow heard throughout the ship that Philip would travel to Rhode Island in irons if the blow fell.

"You have bewitched him, Lorraine," panted Philip, leaning down over her fiercely after the captain had gone. "As you bewitch all men."

Lorraine looked up at him with flashing eyes. "If I am a witch, then you are a devil! I will find the money to pay for my indenture if only you will let me go!"

"And we both know how you'd 'find' it—by selling your favors to any who offered!"

Paling at that insult, Lorraine drew back her arm to strike him, but he seized her wrist before she could and bent it downward so that she was hard put not to cry out.

"If you call for the captain now, it will be the worse for you later," he warned. I am your master, Lorraine. Accept it!" His brown eyes gleamed down upon her with a kind of demonic triumph that made her shrink inwardly. At that moment she wondered how she could ever have loved him.

"Well, you are not my master on *this* ship!" With a wrench that hurt her wrist, she managed to free herself from his grasp. *"And maybe never!"* she flung back tauntingly as she moved swiftly away. She could see Philip's shoulder muscles hunch under his tan satin coat and stayed away from him, prudently hovering in the captain's vicinity all afternoon.

"I would like to help you, mistress," the captain told her bluntly. "But if the papers are not a forgery, if Dedwinton actually bought your articles, there is nothing I can do."

"Even if they are not genuine, I could not prove it," said Lorraine with a bitter glance back at Philip. "For Philip tells me the Indians killed Oddsbud."

"Then you must either placate him or"—he gave her a wintry smile—"find someone to buy you from him."

I found such a man once, she thought sadly. *Raile Cameron.* And just thinking of him caused her to fall further into a brooding mood.

The full splendor of the New England fall was all around them as they sailed into Narragansett Bay. On either side the trees in their autumn colors made a brave display of crimson and scarlet and russet and lemon and gold. Rhode Island looked to be the promised land.

It was not. Suddenly, before the horrified passengers on board the *Lizard* stretched a leveled skyline broken only by charred beams and burned chimneys.

"The Indians have burned Providence!" screamed one of the women passengers on a high keening note.

"Aye," muttered the captain soberly into the hubbub. "I suppose it was bound to happen, with so many other towns already overrun." He sighed.

Philip stood clutching the ship's rail, staring at the town in enraged disbelief. *"Damn them!"* he cried with a sob in his voice, and Lorraine followed his gaze.

The distillery that belonged to Lavinia Todd's father had been leveled.

For all that she was stunned by the magnitude of the devastation, Lorraine could not restrain herself from giving Philip a mocking look.

"Lavinia will not have such a large dowry to give you after all," she could not resist saying.

From the rail Philip whirled. His rage and frustration had now found a target.

"If you can't keep a civil tongue in your head, I'll truss you up like a chicken—yes, and gag you too!"

Lorraine's arrival in Providence harbor was made doubly ignominious because Philip had a heated discussion with the captain in full hearing of the passengers over whether or not to tie her up. Lorraine stood rooted to the deck, red with embarrassment, while they discussed it.

"I will not land a woman from my ship in bonds," insisted the captain.

"But she will try to escape!" protested Philip.

The captain's short laugh had a snarl to it. "That is your concern, not mine!"

So Lorraine made the shore with Philip's left hand clamped tightly over her arm while his right hand held a heavy length of rope. Once ashore, Philip—with a dark look back at the ship he had just quitted—set himself to tying her wrists together.

There were a number of people standing on the wharf to witness Lorraine's degradation—but not much else had been left standing. Around them Providence was a scene of utter desolation. The buildings Lorraine remembered lay in charred ruins. Warehouses, mills, distilleries, tanneries, cooperages, inns, taverns, private dwellings—all had been destroyed. Here and there chimneys of stone that had not split and fallen to the fire's rage remained standing—mute evidence that here had once been a human habitation. Some sites were being cleared and on others there was evidence of rebuilding having begun, but to Lorraine's shocked gaze, the Providence she had known was gone.

Around them on the wharf—amid the moans of those who, like Lorraine and Philip, had not seen the town since the Indians had ravaged it—there were excited questions.

The war, which had begun in June and swept through Massachusetts and Connecticut as well, had flashed into neutral Rhode Island again as the Indian fighters—always avoiding direct contact with colonial troops—raced from settlement to settlement making lightning-fast strikes and leaving death and smoking ruins everywhere behind them. Rhode Island had raised no troops.

After all, Rhode Islanders had *bought* their land from the Indians, it was explained, and who could expect this? And Governor Roger Williams, a longtime friend of the Indians, who had learned their language, had used his best persuasion. But eloquence had not saved Providence and Governor Williams' own house was burned to the ground along with the rest of the town.

Standing near Lorraine on the wharf, a gentleman from Warwick was informed that he would find the same desolation in Warwick as he now saw in Providence. The Indians had raided all along the bay. Wickford fortunately had been evacuated, but Smith's trading post had been burned, Warwick too—although it was nearly deserted at the time. Then Providence, garrisoned by only about thirty men and no match for the superior forces that overran it, had fallen victim to the flames.

Once Philip had attached the length of rope securely to Lorraine's already bound wrists, he was prudent enough not to be too rough with her, for that might bring immediate repercussions from men on the dock who moved restively and looked uneasily at one another to see a young woman tied up.

"What is her crime?" muttered one.

Lorraine heard that. "The crime of wishing to be free!" she cried, and pulled backward violently from Philip's clutches.

The lurch had put her off balance. Calmly Philip let go of the rope and let her fall.

Lorraine landed on her back with a sob. But—made awkward by her bound wrists—before she could scramble up, Philip was there, relentlessly reattaching the rope to her wrists.

"Up and walk!" he ordered grimly. "For if you fall, I will not hesitate to drag you."

He left the wharf and set off along Towne Street, pulling Lorraine along behind him on the makeshift leash.

Lorraine met the astonished and disapproving gaze of those they met along the way. She was preoccupied **enough with trying not to fall, for they were leaving** the charred remains of Providence behind them, and Philip strode along at such a great pace that Lorraine was hard put to keep up with him.

"Where are we going?" she gasped, casting a look about her. "Surely you do not intend to *walk* all the way to your family's farm?"

"It is my farm now," he flung over his shoulder in a hard voice, "but there is nothing left there. I had *hoped* to rebuild."

With my thousand pounds! she thought. *Oh, how he must have counted on that!* She stumbled as he gave the rope a vicious jerk that almost sent her headlong.

After that she fell silent, half-running, trying not to trip over her skirts on the uneven ground. Around her there were fewer remains of burned chimneys and sad trampled garden plots, and the glory of the trees took over in bursts of scarlet and gold. She did not ask their destination again but suddenly it came to her where they were headed.

They were going to Lavinia Todd's house.

Lorraine stared ahead of her with a set face as the house came into view. Lavinia had always had luck, she thought bitterly. With all Rhode Island a charred ruin, *her* home had been spared. The Indians had somehow missed it.

The handsome "stone-ender" was set among stately maples, leaves flashing gold against the dark trunks and the vivid blue of the autumn sky. She saw the familiar steep gable at the front and the huge stone-pilastered chimney which had so awed those here about. Although she had never attended any of the many parties held there, Lorraine had been told about the grandeur of Todd House often enough.

Eleazer Todd's splendid mansion. . . .

The front door swung open at their approach and Lavinia Todd herself, wearing a ruffled white cambric apron over her violet lutestring gown, cried ecstatically, "Philip, you're back!" Rushing toward him, she threw herself into his arms with such force that he staggered a step backward.

Although he did not release his grip on the rope,

Philip's arms enfolded Lavinia. He held her for a long time, his brown head bent over her bronze one.

"How I have missed you!" he murmured on a long drawn sigh.

Lorraine, standing with one hand resting on her hip, cocked a skeptical eye at them both.

A few moments later she was being dragged on her crude halter behind Philip into the house she had so often wistfully wished to enter. Luxurious paneled walls with beaded and beveled edges gave the house its interior tone, and the furnishings, most of them locally made of cedar or rock maple, were well-crafted. Hand-braided rugs adorned the random-width floor planking. To Lorraine's surprise, no one was about to witness her meeting with Lavinia.

Lavinia, who apparently had missed seeing Lorraine in her excitement over Philip's unexpected arrival, now stepped back.

"What is this, Philip?" She frowned. "Why is *she* here?"

The sight of her old enemy had restored Lorraine's flagging spirits.

"Behold," she mocked. "Philip adores me so much that he pursues me to the ends of the earth! And ties me to him with rope lest I get away!"

Lavinia paled and took a step backward. She did not look as well as when Lorraine had last seen her. Her wonderful thick hair had lost some of its luster, her face had a sallow look. Only her bronze eyes burned as brightly as ever.

Philip turned upon Lorraine savagely. "You will keep a civil tongue in your head or you will feel the lash," he warned her. "Lavinia and I are to be married next month."

"But what are you doing with her? Why did you bring her here?" demanded Lavinia.

Lorraine answered before Philip could form a reply. "Philip was so enamored of me that he bought my articles of indenture from Oddsbud," she drawled. "He sailed south to—"

Her words were cut off as Philip gave the rope a violent jerk that flung her full length on the floor at

Lavinia's feet. His foot menaced her. "We'll have no more lies from you," he growled.

He turned to Lavinia. "Oddsbud owed me money, Lavinia—a gambling debt." After all, he reasoned, from the grave Oddsbud could not refute it! "He was short of coin, so he signed over Lorraine's articles of indenture to me as security until he could raise the money. When the Indians killed him, I was left with the articles. Lorraine had run away, she was my property—I had no choice but to pursue her."

"But you could have sold her articles once you found her!" protested Lavinia in an anguished voice. "The house is full of people, Philip—neighbors who have lost their homes, as many as it will hold! Everyone is out now, poking among the ashes, trying to see what can best be done, but what will they think when they return and find you here with this . . . this woman? You did not have to bring her *here*, Philip! Oh, why did you do it?"

Lorraine thought it would be interesting to hear Philip's explanation and looked up expectantly.

"Lavinia," he pleaded, seizing her hand, "my family home is in ruins, I have naught left but the bare land. Your dowry will build us a house, true, but what else had I to give you? It was my thought that this would be my wedding gift to you—a serving wench who would be above the bumbling country girls, one who could serve you as a lady's maid, for 'twas always my wish that we should live in style!"

How glib he is! marveled Lorraine.

Lavinia's eyes on Philip took on a melting look—but hardened again as they fell on Lorraine.

"I may wish to sell her," she told him in a dissatisfied voice.

"In time," was his lazy answer. "Meanwhile you can teach her humility. With a whip, if it pleases you."

Lorraine closed her eyes.

CHAPTER 26

*Todd House, Near Providence, Rhode Island
October*

LORRAINE'S FIRST LESSON in humility came just after her arrival. While she was still on the floor, some of Eleazer Todd's guests could be heard coming toward the house and Lavinia in sudden panic said to Philip: "We'll have to get rid of Lorraine until we know what to do with her."

Lorraine was jerked to her feet and summarily dragged to a small dark cubbyhole in the attic. She remained locked in and left there without food or water for hours.

By the time she had gotten her wrists free from the ropes—and in her desperation she had even attacked them with her teeth—Lorraine had decided what to do. She was being foully treated and she would pay them back!

Through the cracks in the floorboard she could hear noises downstairs. They must be having supper, she decided, and pangs of hunger assailed her. But no food was brought to her. Still she bided her time. Eventually the dark hole in the attic assumed a deeper darkness and the house settled down for the night.

Finally, Lorraine made her move. She took a deep breath and began to scream—terrible, bloodcurdling screams that shook the rafters and resounded throughout the house. She punctuated her shrieks with loud wails of "Help me! I'm locked in the attic!"

Downstairs, people who had gone to bed feeling safe from Indian attack, sprang up and stumbled around in the darkness, groping for muskets.

"They've got her, someone's got her!" screamed a voice in the darkness, followed by cries of "Indians! Indians!" Others took up the howl. Pandemonium reigned before candles could be lit and the source of the noise located.

Eleazer Todd himself unlocked the door. Philip, who figured out what was going on, tried to make it to the closet first. Hurrying upstairs, he bumped into stout Mistress Plemmons, who wrapped her big arms about him in terror and refused to let go. As Philip fought to free himself, Lavinia came up carrying a candle and hissed at him, "You've let Father reach the attic first?"

"What is this noise? Who are you?" cried Eleazer Todd, bursting in upon Lorraine. "Why . . . why, it's Mistress London! What are you doing here? And what ails you to scream out in the night like this?"

Lorraine, struggling up from the floor, had stopped in mid-shriek. "Your daughter and Philip Dedwinton dragged me up here, sir, and locked me in. Without food or water or even a blanket." She shivered. "They left me bound, but I got loose." She indicated the heavy lengths of rope on the floor.

"Left you bound . . . !" Eleazer's scandalized expression told her he could hardly believe what she was saying.

Behind him Lavinia panted, "I can explain, Father. Philip brought this bound girl to me as a wedding gift. He said I should teach her humility."

"With a whip," said Lorraine wryly.

Eleazer Todd was an upright man. He was proud of his stature in the community and all too aware of his goggle-eyed guests who had swarmed into the attic after Lavinia. They were all staring at Lorraine London—whom most of them knew by sight—standing in a closet exhibiting the red weals on her wrists where the ropes had bitten into her soft flesh.

Todd turned to his daughter. "I would not have

thought it of you, Lavinia," he growled. "To leave a young woman to spend the night tied up in a cold attic!"

"It is none too cold." Lavinia tossed her head.

"Silence!" roared Eleazer, shocked to the core. "Come downstairs, Mistress London. We will find a place for you."

"There is no room," objected Lavinia, pouting.

"I can take the girl in with me," interposed a kindly voice. "There is room in my corner for another pallet."

"There are six of you in that small room already, Mistress Bowman," protested Lavinia.

"We can manage." Through the crowd Lorraine saw a square matronly figure in a voluminous dressing gown beckon to her with her pewter candle holder. "Eleazer, do you think you could find us another pallet?"

"There are no more pallets!" Lavinia was almost crying with rage.

"A blanket would do nicely," said Lorraine quietly. "Anything is better than being locked in to sleep on bare boards."

Eleazer winced and shoved his daughter aside. "Take the girl with you, by all means, Mistress Bowman. I cannot believe that such a thing could happen in my house," he said, shaking his head.

"No matter, Eleazer," said Mistress Bowman cheerfully. "You have set things to rights. Come along with me," she told Lorraine, who followed her past a trembling Lavinia and a seething Philip, past numerous curious eyes, to a small back room.

"This is my corner." She indicated the far side of the small room littered with pallets. "For 'tis farthest from Mistress Laite, who snores loudest," she confided with a chuckle. "You gave us quite a turn . . . ah, what is your name, dear?"

"Lorraine," supplied Lorraine. She liked the older woman at once. There was a motherly air about her. "Thank you for befriending me," she said, and added wearily, "But I fear Lavinia will find some way to take a whip to me tomorrow."

"Oh, I doubt that," said Mistress Bowman tranquilly. "Eleazer Todd—he's my second cousin on my mother's side—is a good person. I can't always say the same for his daughter."

A moment later his daughter appeared in the doorway and threw a blanket at Lorraine.

Lorraine caught it and made a mock curtsy.

"You'd do well not to antagonize Lavinia," advised Mistress Bowman, who had watched that little display. "She is noted for her high temper."

"I antagonize Lavinia just by living," said Lorraine bitterly. "She is jealous of me because of Philip."

That night, after the others were asleep, Lorraine told much of her story in whispers to the older woman. She did not mention the extent of her fortune beyond the thousand pounds, however, nor her affair with Raile other than to say that Captain Cameron had transported her to Virginia.

"Eleazer will not make Lavinia free you, for your articles are valuable, but he will see that you are not injured on his premises," Mistress Bowman told her.

On his premises . . . But what would be her lot when Philip and Lavinia had their *own* premises?

"Do not give up hope. Perhaps someone will be found to buy your articles."

Mistress Bowman had meant to cheer her, but in the darkness Lorraine shuddered. "Lavinia would sell me to the devil if she could," she muttered.

"Pish tush!" said Mistress Bowman comfortably. "Eleazer would never allow it."

"If only I could get to Barbados," mourned Lorraine.

"Barbados . . ." murmured Mistress Bowman. "I am told it is a land of eternal summer, of flowers and winged fish that fly through the air for great distances. Imagine, no cold Rhode Island winters!" She shivered as if in anticipation of the winter snows to come and then came back in practical fashion to the matter at hand. "You are not to worry." She patted Lorraine's hand. "There will be ships leaving for Barbados in a few weeks, and we can send a letter on one of them. Meantime things will work out."

But the next morning proved that things weren't working out and probably never would.

After a plain breakfast, which she ate on a wooden table in the kitchen while being stared at by the Todds' two housemaids, Lorraine was summoned out "to help with the wash."

There Lavinia confronted her—a confident Lavinia, for there was no one about. The guests—even kindly Mistress Bowman—had poured out of the house early on this clear bright day to see to their own affairs. Lavinia's mother was in bed with one of her constant migraines, her father had ridden away, and she was in complete control of her world.

"How did you get that dress?" she demanded of Lorraine, scowling at the fashionable pink silk gown that the blonde beauty wore.

"It belonged to a dead girl," replied Lorraine. "Her father gave it to me in gratitude for helping to deliver his second wife's baby. In Bermuda."

Lavinia's face mirrored her disbelief. "Do not mock me," she said sharply. "Captain Bridey has told all the world that when he discovered you in Bermuda you were some sea captain's doxy!"

"Then believe Captain Bridey!" was Lorraine's short answer.

"Take it off," ordered Lavinia.

Lorraine cast an outraged glance at a grinning teenage boy who was stirring the boiling washwater with a broomstick.

"I will not!"

"Tess, Marthe, remove her dress," snapped Lavina, turning to the two housemaids who were carrying out large stacks of linens to be plopped into the boiling washtubs. "If the wench resists, tear it from her back. And her chemise too, for I am sure it is crawling with vermin and will have to be boiled."

"It is not!" protested Lorraine, struggling in the hefty Marthe's strong grip. "You can see it is perfectly fine!" But there was no escaping Marthe's big hands, and despite the tussle, her dress was already unhooked and half off.

"Hold still or Marthe'll rip it," advised Tess, plummeting her load of laundry into the hot water and turning to help Marthe.

"Oh, it doesn't matter if you rip it," said Lavinia in a bored voice. " 'Tis an unsuitable costume for a serving wench. I intend to have it washed and then cut the fabric into trimming for the new draperies in my bedchamber."

A sob of rage escaped Lorraine as the pink silk gown came away from her body with a loud rip. "My chemise is perfectly clean," she panted. "For shame that you would strip me naked in public merely because you believe I am your rival for Philip!"

The boy stirring the washwater sniggered. Marthe and Tess rolled their eyes at each other. It was too much for Lavinia.

"Rival for Philip?" She surged forward and would have struck Lorraine across the face but that out of the corner of her eye she had seen Philip come around the corner of the house. "Rival?" she scoffed, shaking her curls. "I have no rivals!"

Lorraine, suddenly conscious of the fact that she was almost naked in her sheer chemise, saw Philip staring at her with hot possessive eyes. Swiftly she turned her side to him, revealing as she did against the blaze of sunshine the silhouette of a perfectly molded bustline and delicately sculptured buttocks.

Philip's preoccupation with Lorraine's body did not go unremarked by Lavinia. She turned on him in fury. "How dare you come here when you can see—"

"Why? Is washday sacred?" he demanded, lifting his brows. His intent gaze never left Lorraine's dainty form, so artfully revealed in the strong light.

"You can see this wench is exposing herself to you!" rasped Lavinia.

"Oh, is that what she's doing?" Philip grinned at Lorraine.

Enraged, Lavinia ran up to him and slapped his face. He turned and caught her wrists.

"Are we to quarrel over some serving wench?" he growled. "I came to tell you that your father is on his way here. He may take a whip to you if he finds her like this."

Panic overtook Lavinia. She whirled about and began pawing through the dirty laundry.

"I won't wear somebody else's filthy clothes!" shouted Lorraine.

"You'll wear what you're told!" Lavinia screamed.

The commotion brought Eleazer Todd striding around the house. He stopped stock-still at what he saw, and his jaw dropped.

"What madness is this?" he demanded.

Lorraine tried to cover her breasts with her hands as he approached.

"I had her change her dress because of the vermin she may have brought from the ship," cried Lavinia desperately.

"Out there? In the open?" he thundered. "With your betrothed and a half-fledged youth looking on? She will work in the house henceforth—and you will not have charge of her. I will ask my cousin, Mistress Bowman, to supervise her."

"She should be helping Marthe in the kitchen!" wailed Lavinia.

"Go to your room," roared her father. "Or I will have *you* helping Marthe in the kitchen! You are making a scandal of us. What has happened to the girl's dress?" he asked, looking around him.

"Lavinia plans to cut it up to decorate her room," said Lorraine in a clear voice.

Eleazer turned to his daughter, appalled. "It will be washed and returned to her!" he thundered. "Meantime, Tess, find the wench something decent to wear. Take her with you and be quick about it!"

Lavinia fled, sobbing. Philip shrugged and turned away. Tess, thinking she had better move fast if she knew what was good for her, grabbed Lorraine's hand and ran with her to the house. And washday continued as always, with Marthe stolidly carrying out dirty clothes and linens and the "half-fledged lad" energetically stirring the caldron and grinning over the tale he would have to tell his friends later.

Lorraine soon found herself clad in a coarse scratchy gray kirtle and bodice until her dress could be washed and ironed. She hoped Lavinia would not egg on Tess, who did the ironing, to scorch it.

Under the supervision of kindly Mistress Bowman,

Lorraine was put to work at the less arduous duties of making beds, setting the table, and mending. She might have found her existence at Todd House bearable had it not been for Philip.

He pursued her relentlessly, whenever Lavinia wasn't looking. He confronted her in dark hallways to push against her struggling form, he jostled her in doorways and surreptitiously pinched her buttocks or breasts, he caught her on empty stairways and ran an impudent hand up her thighs while she kicked at him helplessly.

"Come spring, my house will be started," he told her lazily one day as he cornered her in a narrow upstairs passage and blocked her way with his arm. "Come fall, it will be finished."

"Philip, let me pass," said Lorraine impatiently. "Mistress Bowman is waiting for me to bring her these pillowcases."

He made no move to let her through, but instead reached out and tweaked the nipple of her right breast— savoring the feel of it through the thin silk, for, unsuitable though it might be, Lorraine was again wearing her pink silk dress. She jumped back angrily.

"Why are you here at all?" she demanded. "Connecticut is waging counterattacks against the Indians. Your whole family was murdered by them, yet you have made no move to strike back! Why are you content to let others fight your battles? Why don't you join the Connecticut men instead of staying on here in this overcrowded house and pestering me?"

He seemed not to hear her. His smile was sensuous. "You have a body made for pleasure, Lorraine. . . ."

"I cannot respect you!" she flashed. "And neither would Lavinia if she were not so besotted. At least *she* has some pride!"

Her words did not move him. It was as if he considered her too far beneath him for her opinions to matter. Oh, how she hated his lordly ways!

His smile had deepened. Lorraine did not like that smile. There was something *devouring* in it. "Before the winter we will move into my house, the three of us. Lavinia will be pregnant by then—Eleazer is hot for a grandson. And you and I"—he reached out for her again but she eluded him—"will play." He was breathing harder now. *"Think on our nights together, Lorraine."*

Lorraine stared at him. She did not want to think about it. Too clearly she envisioned what her life would be like if Philip ever got his house finished. She would be up before dawn slaving away till after dark. Then through the night hours being stalked and over-powered by Philip. Lavinia was no fool. She would surmise what was going on. Lavinia would break in on them, find them locked in a desperate embrace, and Lavinia would take a whip to her. And by then *she* would be pregnant too. . . .

There was no hope for her.

"Let me pass, Philip," she said in a hard voice. "Or I will scream to Eleazer Todd that you are trying to rape me!"

"Eleazer is not here," he taunted.

"He is!" she snapped. "I heard his voice on my way upstairs."

Philip stepped aside with alacrity. "I can afford to wait!" he called after her.

Mistress Bowman had heard that interchange from a doorway nearby. She drew Lorraine aside, bade her put down the pillowcases.

"I think you are right about your situation here," she said in an altered voice. "Your only alternative is to be sold."

"Philip would resist selling me," said Lorraine with a sigh. "He has other plans for me."

"So I heard," was the older woman's grim rejoin-der. She thought for a while. "Is it true that this man in Barbados holds gold in your behalf?"

"Better than a thousand pounds," confirmed Lorraine.

"I had been thinking that we would send a message to Barbados, but now I am not sure that it is prudent to wait. . . ." Mistress Bowman drummed her fingers. "The *Dolphin* is in Providence harbor bound for Bar-bados," she told Lorraine. "My nephew John is her captain. He engages in the 'triangle trade.'"

Lorraine nodded soberly. She knew what the trian-gle trade was. West Indian molasses was shipped to

New England, where distilleries made it into rum; the rum was then run to Africa to trade for slaves, who were then sold into the West Indies to work in the sugarcane fields to make more molasses—a vicious circle. And Providence ships made the New England–West Indies run.

"My nephew cannot risk assisting a bondservant to elude her master," said Mistress Bowman slowly. "But perhaps . . . yes, I think we might do it."

"But if I am found missing, will you not be charged?" asked Lorraine anxiously, for she had come to love this compassionate woman who had lost not only her husband but also her two sons in the Indian raids.

"No, I am too quick for that," chuckled Mistress Bowman. "Indeed"—her calm gaze met Lorraine's—"I think Eleazer would breathe a sigh of relief to be rid of you. He fears Lavinia will publicly disgrace him."

Lorraine felt a surge of hope.

"I will speak to my nephew," said Mistress Bowman with decision.

Together they devised a desperate scheme.

CHAPTER 27

Narragansett Bay

IF THE CREW of the *Dolphin* noticed that their captain seemed unusually worried as one of a dozen new barrels was taken aboard just before they sailed, they did not mention it to each other. Not even his "Ho, there, that's no way to hoist a barrel! Gently now!" caused remark, for he followed it immediately with an explanation. "That barrel contains dishes and other goods that are being sent to a lady in Bermuda. Careful you don't break anything!"

The barrel was set down gingerly and, like the others, lashed to the deck, for there was no room in the hold.

"Did ye know, Cap'n, this one has a hole in the top?" asked one of the men who had just set the barrel down with great care. "The rain'll get in."

"We'll see to it later. Over here now! Waste no time, lads, we want to clear the harbor, there's a fair wind and it's blowing in the right direction!"

Later Captain Bowman chose his deck watch with exceeding care. The sailor he named was a burly man and, like most of the seamen of his day, Duncan was superstitious. He believed in signs and portents; he would go to his grave believing he should beware of witches and demons. Captain Bowman was aware of these failings and hoped to exploit them if necessary. Duncan also had the strength of two men and was surprisingly agile up in the yards above them. For this night's work, however, Duncan was blessed with an even greater virtue—he was slow-witted.

It was a moonless night. The captain thanked God for that as he strolled about the deck. "Look sharp out to starboard," he had shouted to Duncan. "'For I thought I glimpsed a ship running without lights—and that could mean a pirate vessel stalking these waters."

While Duncan was peering out across the dark ocean, the captain, praying Duncan would not turn around, furtively pried loose the top of the "barrel containing dishes" and with a finger to his lips beckoned to Lorraine.

She was so stiff from her cramped position in the barrel that she could hardly move, and he had to help her out of it. After all, it had been many hours since she had run into the woods while Mistress Bowman distracted Lavinia. In the woods she had been met with a cart containing empty barrels. Lorraine had made her trip through the ruins of Providence inside one of those barrels, which had then been hoisted aboard the *Dolphin*. Several hours had passed since their sailing, and every muscle protested as she was helped over the barrel's side.

The captain beckoned silently toward the open door of his cabin and Lorraine nodded. It had all been discussed. She was to creep alone across the deck whilst Captain Bowman distracted the deck watch. Cursing herself for not having remembered to take off her shoes, she was tiptoeing across the deck lest the tap-tap of her heels give her away, when the deck watch suddenly turned and looked full at her.

Duncan's eyes bulged at the sight of a wraithlike figure with long fair hair streaming over a dark cloak.

"Gor!" He sucked in his breath.

But Captain Bowman was equal to the occasion. "Out there, a sail!" he bawled, leaping forward so that his body was between Lorraine and the deck watch. "Look, you fool! D'you not see it?"

Duncan turned around to stare at the empty sea, and in a trice the captain was beside him, striking the rail with his fist in mock disappointment. " 'Tis gone!" He turned to Duncan. "Did you see nothing?"

"I saw . . . a lady!" Duncan turned to point. "There!"

The captain turned. To his relief, the deck was empty, his cabin door closed. "Bah, we've no time for visions, Duncan! I meant on the water, man!"

Thus admonished, Duncan sighed. "No, not on the water." His eyes must be playing tricks on him, he decided.

"Well, keep at it, lad. For 'tis a night that bears watching. That's twice I thought I saw a ship out there." He clapped Duncan encouragingly on the shoulder and walked back to his cabin.

"That sailor saw me, Captain Bowman!"

"Naught to fear, he thinks he saw a vision." Captain Bowman was as matter-of-fact as his aunt, indeed he looked much like her. They had the same steady blue eyes and square build, but while her hair was gray, his still retained its sandy hue. "We've one more shoal to get over. After that it will be up to you. Meantime, you can sleep in that corner, where you can pull blankets up over you if someone should burst in. And when the cabin boy knocks to bring food—I will tell him I'm hungry so there'll be enough of it—you can hide in yon sea chest with the top open and I'll pile my shirts in on top of you to make it look merely untidy. There's some food left on the table. Eat it and rest on my bunk until I get back." He gave her the same calm smile she had seen on Mistress Bowman's pleasant face. "Be of good heart, Mistress London. We'll get you to Barbados yet!"

Lorraine ate quickly and climbed gratefully into the captain's bunk. She fell immediately to sleep.

She awoke to his shaking her and the sound of a knock.

"Into the chest with you, Mistress London," he muttered. "That's the cabin boy knocking."

Lorraine went into the chest thinking: *How like his aunt he is! He never once woke me, just let me me stay there in his bunk all night! And how like another captain . . .*

But she must not think of that now.

The cabin boy reported to the cook later that the captain was in good appetite. He had eaten four eggs for breakfast!

It was a dangerous situation, that could not last. Calm and even-natured though he was, Captain Bowman breathed a sigh of relief when they reached Bermuda, where they would take on fresh water for the long journey to Barbados.

Before they sailed into St. George's harbor, back into the barrel went Lorraine—and even that took some doing, but it was accomplished just before dawn under cover of a fog bank.

"Don't worry, mistress, I'll get you ashore as soon as possible," was Captain Bowman's last whispered reassurance as he fitted the barrel's top back down.

After that it was another bumpy journey, over the side, into the boat. And then once more she was traveling through town by barrel—only this time the town was St. George and her destination was the Crown and Garter on Duke of York Street. She felt the barrel thumped down in what she guessed was the common room, heard Captain Bowman's rumbling, "Mistress Pym? I've a barrel of goods for you from Rhode Island, which I promised a lady I'd deliver to you personally." And Mistress Pym's excited, "Whatever can it be? Oh, do help me open it. Pym, come and see!"

Captain Bowman's impressive figure protected the barrel as he said, "I was told the contents were personal and should be opened by you alone in some private place."

"Very well. Have your man bring the barrel back to my bedchamber, do! How exciting!"

And Lorraine felt herself once again carried along and thumped down none too gently.

When the lid was tugged off finally, Lorraine came up like a jack-in-the-box. Mistress Pym staggered backward in shock with a slight scream.

"Oh, please don't scream, 'tis only me!" cried Lorraine, leaning out of the barrel. "Oh, Mistress Pym, you must help me," she entreated, "or I'll be living in this barrel all the way to Barbados!" And her whole story came pouring out.

Mistress Pym listened intently and then entered into

their plans with the boundless enthusiasm of the true conspirator. Captain Bowman had hoped only for Lorraine to be allowed to hide there at the Crown and Garter during their short stay in Bermuda, but Mistress Pym had a better idea. She pointed out that a ship from Bristol, the *Magpie,* had been wrecked off Sandys less than a fortnight ago. Only a handful of survivors had made it through the wild surf to shore, and among them had been several young women who had since departed. Why not have Lorraine claim to be a survivor of the *Magpie* disaster? It would explain her lack of luggage when she went back aboard the *Dolphin,* her need to get quickly to her "guardian" in Barbados.

Soon Lorraine found herself eating fish chowder and Hoppin' John and shark pie washed down by cedarberry wine. She enjoyed listening to gossipy Mistress Pym detailing the remarkable "progress" in education her sister was making under Charles Hubbard's excellent tutelage. Hubbard seemed quite content, Mistress Pym said, now that things had settled down at Cedarwood. It was sad that Trinity was dead, but maybe it was for the best.

Lorraine forbore to tell her good friend that Trinity was very much alive and probably at that moment enjoying married life in England with Jeb!

When Lorraine reembarked on the *Dolphin* it was not in a barrel but like the other passengers—via longboat. It was far more comfortable and there was only one rough spot to be got over,—Duncan, the sailor who had seen her fleetingly the night Captain Bowman had first gotten her out of the barrel.

When Lorraine came aboard in the sunshine, Duncan was on deck. He stared at her openmouthed, and took a step backward.

"Let me handle this," murmured Captain Bowman, and went over to Duncan, who was standing transfixed.

"I seen her before," Duncan gasped, pointing a shaky finger at Lorraine. "She's the one I seen that first night out of Providence! You remember, Cap'n, I told you I seen a lady crossing the deck—looking just like her!"

Captain Bowman peered into Duncan's face, hoping he conveyed an impression of awe. "You've had a visitation, Duncan." He managed to sound impressed. "For this lady was shipwrecked off Sandys the very night you thought you saw her!" Heartily he clapped Duncan on the shoulder. "You have The Sight, lad! 'Tis a gift to be proud of!"

Duncan, round-eyed, would later embroider on the tale. He had the Sight, he would stoutly maintain in waterfront taverns and inns. On board the *Dolphin* one dark night he'd had a vision. He'd seen a woman float out of nowhere—from the air she must have come, for she was all ashimmer and her pale hair had given off a strange light. She had floated two feet above the deck planking and then swirled upward into the rigging and vanished! And that same night the *Magpie* had been ground up by the reefs off Bermuda with that very woman aboard her! That story was to buy Duncan many a free drink in ports around the world.

But now, aboard the *Dolphin*, Captain Bowman turned with a deprecating cough to Mistress Hurst, the ship's only other female passenger.

"Duncan is a good lad," he said, noting that the seaman was now out of earshot. "A little slow, unfortunately. Imagines he sees things. Best to humor him."

Mistress Hurst nodded conspiratorially. She turned alertly to Lorraine. "Did the captain say you'd been shipwrecked?" she asked.

Lorraine glibly recited a tragic story of shipwreck that she had rehearsed with Mistress Pym. Mistress Hurst, a widow from Boston, still in her weeds, on her way to join her wealthy brother's family in Bridgetown, listened intently as Lorraine explained how a storm had driven the *Magpie* off course and the ship had broken up on a sawtooth reef off Bermuda.

"Oh, you poor thing!" cried Mistress Hurst, thrilled.

She kept repeating "Poor thing, poor thing!" as Lorraine explained that her parents had died in Cornwall and her guardian had removed to Barbados. She had been en route to New York to visit a school friend when the storm had blown the *Magpie* off course, but now had to sail straight to Barbados instead, to inspect her new plantation.

"And I shall arrive in Barbados to see my guardian with no clothes, all my luggage gone—"

"That you will not! You may borrow what you like of mine to wear! Oh, poor thing, poor thing!"

So the "shipwrecked heiress," as Mistress Hurst called Lorraine importantly to the other passengers—for none but the wealthy could afford to dash across oceans to visit school friends or casually have plantations bought for them! enjoyed as much attention and gallantry on board the *Dolphin* as she had suffered ostracism on board the *Lizard*. The bachelor Captain Bowman went back to eating light, and no one remarked it. Like the rest, he paid gallant court to the "shipwrecked heiress"—as was expected of him.

Philip was beside himself with anger when he was told Lorraine could not be found. He turned on Lavinia, backing her against the kitchen wall. "You have got rid of her, admit it!" he cried." 'Tis your insane jealousy! By God, I will shake the truth out of you! What have you done with her? What?"

Philip seized Lavinia by the shoulders and shook her so violently that her hairpins came loose. Lavinia, thus unjustly attacked, spit like a cat and tried vainly to claw at her lover's face. "I have not done *anything* with Lorraine!" she screamed. "Although I should have! You were always after her!"

Philip flung her against the wall so hard she bounced away from it. He stood glaring down at her, breathing hard. Lavinia burst into tears.

There were several witnesses to this demonstration, among them Mistress Bowman, who spoke up.

"Lorraine may have tried to go overland to Connecticut," she sighed. "I warned her not to attempt it."

Philip sneered, "More likely she'll to Providence to try to wheedle some ship captain into taking her aboard."

"A search of the town should find her then," remarked Mistress Bowman, content in the knowledge that the *Dolphin* had already sailed. "But Lorraine confided in me that she would go to Connecticut to escape Philip. That was the day he cornered her in the hall and pressed his unwanted attentions upon her."

Philip reddened to the hairline. "I did no such thing!"

Mistress Bowman regarded him calmly. "Lorraine was bringing linens to me that day. I was witness to the whole encounter."

"You are a slanderous old woman eavesdropping around corners!" Philip's jaw thrust out threateningly. "After Lavinia and I are married, you will not be welcome in our home."

Mistress Bowman shrugged. "I am grieved," she said shortly.

"There will be no marriage!" shrieked Lavinia, stamping her foot. "Our bethrothal is at an end!" And she threw the new betrothal ring Philip had given her in his face.

Meanwhile, in Virginia, much had happened.

Raile had not lied to Lorraine that last morning in Jamestown. He had found his experienced boatman and gone upriver just as he had said he would do, but he had missed his man again. As he began his journey back downriver, he saw coming toward him a boat carrying the very man he was looking for, accompanied by a woman whose red-gold hair flamed in the sunlight.

"Ho, there, Rory!" Raile called.

The pair in the other boat stopped rowing at sight of him and stared in amazement.

Moments later both boats were beached on the shore of the James and all three had disembarked. The brothers shook hands.

"How are you, lad?" asked Raile heartily. "Laurie Ann." He acknowledged her presence for the first time. "Has this young brother of mine been treating you well?"

Laurie Ann was a little ruffled by the indifference of

his tone. "Well enough," she said shortly. "Save that he leaves me alone too much!"

"She didn't like my going off with Bacon to the Dragon Swamp," Rory laughed. "I figured she'd be getting restless in the cabin, so as soon as we won, I hurried back. But on the way home I met someone who told me Laurie had left me again, so I went down to Jamestown to rejoin Bacon. That was where Laurie Ann found me. I decided it was best to take her back upriver before she could stray too far!"

"Aye, she always had a wandering foot. Now, if you'll excuse us, lass, I want a word with my brother."

Leaving Laurie looking affronted, Raile took Rory aside to discuss the guns. "Can Bacon's group pay for them, do you think?"

Rory stroked his chin thoughtfully and looked out toward the tree on the opposite bank. Although there were many dissimilarities between them, the brothers' profiles were strikingly alike. It was not surprising that Lorraine had mistaken Rory for Raile in darkness lit only by the flickering light of Jamestown's dying fires that night on the riverbank.

"I would think so. Both Lawrence and Drummond are wealthy men—and Bacon too, of course, but he's a spender, probably deep in debt." Rory looked at Raile curiously. "You said you were in Jamestown when Bacon rode in. Why'd you not ask him?"

"In my experience," was the dry response, "I've found that men in desperate need of guns will take them without paying for them. I had no reason to believe Bacon to be any different."

"Oh, but he is," said Rory carelessly. He's an idealist—like you used to be." He grinned. "Laurie Ann used to complain of it all the time!"

Raile remembered Laurie Ann's complaints: he was too easy on people, he did not drive a hard-enough bargain!

"Bacon's fighting for the good of the colony—and for justice and all that."

"And you weren't, little brother?" Raile asked.

"I was fighting to drive the Indians out, not for

some high moral purpose. They burned out two families who lived near me—scalped them all, even the toddlers. Who could tell? Laurie Ann might be next."

"You are content here, Rory?" It was an important question and Raile watched his brother's face intently for the answer. After all, Raile had been more like a father than a brother to Rory for such a long time.

"Well enough." Rory shrugged. "I've got a good piece of land and I'll expand my cabin to two rooms in the spring—if the Indians don't burn it over my head first!"

"And Laurie Ann?"

"She gets restless sometimes and wanders off, but then, she always did."

"Yes, she always did," echoed Raile soberly. "The governor will take reprisals if Bacon loses," he told his brother.

Rory shrugged. "So then Laurie and I will go deeper into the woods and build a new cabin. She won't mind—she likes change. Perhaps we'll go south this time, somewhere down into Carolina."

Raile was cheered. The little brother he had worried about for so long was going to be all right. It seemed he might even be able to steady Laurie Ann, who had always been a handful. He got back to the business at hand. "To your mind, should I contact Lawrence? Or Drummond?"

"Neither. Go directly to Bacon."

"Will you come with me?"

"No. I'm tired of the war. I want to stay home with Laurie for a while." He grinned. "Why don't *you* join up?"

Raile laughed. "Why? I'm neither frontiersmen nor Virginian!"

"Bacon's very persuasive."

"Well, I'm away downriver, then, to sell my guns in Jamestown."

"It's not there."

"What?"

"Burned to the ground. Bacon's gone to Green Spring, a couple of miles away."

Raile frowned. "I left someone in Jamestown. A woman."

Laurie Ann, tired of being left alone, had sidled up in time to hear Raile, and her expression went blank from shock. *Both* the Cameron brothers had always belonged to *her,* and Raile's showing up in Virginia had seemed to her to confirm that ownership.

"You didn't tell us that, Raile," she said with an undertone of resentment.

Raile's thoughts just then were on Lorraine. "I made arrangements for her to evacuate with the loyalists," he said in a worried voice.

"Then she's safe in Accomack by now!" Rory assured him.

"Unless maybe she's like me and doesn't always stay where you put her!" suggested Laurie Ann with an edgy laugh.

There was always that. Raile felt himself breaking out in a cold sweat. She was a reckless lass, was Lorraine. And she *didn't* always stay where you put her.

"Well, if she did stay and Bacon's lads found her, she'll be all right," declared Rory staunchly.

Raile wished he could be sure.

"Unless of course Bacon thought she'd been left there by the governor to spy out what he was going to do next," drawled Laurie Ann.

Raile turned to stare at her. There was malice in the wide beautiful eyes he once had drowned in.

Anything he had ever felt for Laurie Ann perished at that moment.

"I'm away to look for her," he said abruptly. "Good luck to you, Rory. And"—he gave the woman who had once been his lover a steady look—"to you too, Laurie Ann."

Raile paddled off downriver, heading for Accomack, where the governor's forces had taken the inhabitants of Jamestown. When he stopped to eat at an inn frequented by rebels in Williamsburg, Raile overheard one of Bacon's men talking about the "pretty spy Bacon had found in Jamestown."

Cold with dread, Raile eased into the conversation.

The fellow's description of the blonde beauty in the pink dress left no doubt in his mind that the "pretty spy" was Lorraine. The fellow said he didn't know what had happened to her after Bacon took her to Green Spring, but that Drummond and Lawrence would know how to deal with her kind!

Terror drove Raile as he hired a horse and thundered to Green Spring. If Bacon's forces had done aught to harm Lorraine . . . !

At Green Spring he learned from Bacon that Lorraine had gone on to Yorktown. At Green Spring too, negotiating with the debonair rebel leader, he sold the guns. The arms were needed, for there was word that a force from northern Virginia headed by the half-Indian Giles Brent was on the way and Bacon was eager to be off across the York to Gloucester County to intercept him.

On a horse he borrowed from Bacon, Raile pounded toward Yorktown. Just out of town, he ran into Johnny Sears.

"Where is Lorraine?" he cried, dismounting almost before the horse came to a sliding halt.

"I've been waiting for you," said Johnny. "I didn't know whether you'd come here or to Williamsburg. Lorraine's gone. She come into a thousand pounds from a venture of her father's."

The ginseng, thought Raile. His world went very still.

"And there was some fellow off a ship that she wanted to think she was a gambler and had lost everything even though she hadn't."

"What was the fellow's name?"

"I asked the innkeeper. He said it was Dedwingen or Dettenton or some such."

"Dedwinton," said Raile softly. *So Philip had followed her down here. The lad must love her after all. . . .*

"And they went away together," blurted Johnny. "I didn't see them go. She'd sent me out to a cockfight."

"Went where?" *But he knew, he knew. . . .*

"Sailed on the *Lizard.* Bound for Rhode Island,

Innkeeper Higgins told me." The lad looked at Raile anxiously. "I doubt I could have stopped her even if I'd been there."

"No, you couldn't have stopped her," murmured Raile. *Nobody could—not if she loved Dedwinton.* And it was obvious she did love him, and not some adventurous fool without a future whose life she had lit up like sunlight after a storm. Young Dedwinton could give her the things she wanted—and deserved: a home, children, security, a steady life day after day, year after year—all those things that *he* could never give her.

His lass had done the right thing, he told himself dully, though it did nothing to quiet the ache in his heart. *And it was a good thing he'd not been there to stand in her way. For stand in her way he would have, against Philip Dedwinton or anyone else who tried to claim her.*

"Johnny," he said, trying to keep the pain from showing in his face, "where is Tav?"

"I just got word from him. He told me to stay here. He's waiting for you. He wondered if you'd sold the guns yet."

"I have," said Raile. "Once we get them unloaded, we're for Green Spring, Johnny."

"Good," said Johnny. He brightened. "I liked it there—so did she."

She would have, his lovely valiant lass. No, not *his* lass—Philip's. He must remember that.

And so the French muskets were delivered to Bacon in Green Spring and were paid for in gold.

After which Raile got drunk as a lord and in a burst of romantic patriotism for a cause not his own, joined up with Bacon, roaring into Gloucester County with the rebels to intercept the forces led by Giles Brent.

" 'Tis the lassie," muttered a grieved MacTavish to Johnny Sears when he learned Raile was gone. "I always knew she would break his heart."

Johnny was bewildered. "Will he come back to us, do you think?"

"Aye—if he lives. We'll sail up and down the coast for a while, do a bit of coastwise trading. And wait for him. Would you like to be left in Yorktown to keep watch for him? 'Twill be a man-size job."

"Aye," agreed Johnny. And then, wistfully, "But why would he join up with General Bacon? The captain's not a Virginian—this isn't *his* war!"

"Right now any war is his war, Johnny," was MacTavish's moody response. "He's lost his lassie and my romantic laddie cares not whether he lives or dies."

VI:

BENEATH SOUTHERN STARS

CHAPTER 28

Bridgetown, Barbados
December 1675

WHILE SNOW DRIFTED deep in Rhode Island and the settlers of New England fought Indians across swamps and bogs that had turned to ice a man could walk across, the *Dolphin*'s prow cut through blue Caribbean waters. At last she nosed her way into the Careenage, the crowded inner harbor of Bridgetown, capital of the pear-shaped coral island of Barbados.

Benjamin Nicholls was inquired after—and promptly found, since he had taken a room at the town's best inn. Mistress Hurst bade Lorraine good-bye and reminded her that she was invited to sup with her at her brother's home upon the morrow.

Lorraine hurried to the inn and greeted Nicholls, who met her in the cool high-ceilinged common room of the Conch and Turtle. They sat down to a delicious lunch of green turtle soup, flying fish, and rosy-gold mangoes in a quiet corner of the spacious jalousied room. While they ate, Lorraine told Nicholls in a low voice of her adventures. He clucked sympathetically but she could see his mind was on something else, and after lunch she discovered what that something else was.

"I will take you sightseeing," he promised, escorting her out onto Broad Street, where smiling dark-skinned women walked along carrying everything from wooden bowls of fruit to heaped-up baskets of laundry on their heads. It was a sleepy town at that time of day. Palm fronds stirred gently. The tropical heat pressed down and Nicholls fanned himself with his broad-brimmed straw hat.

"You will need a straw hat too," he said. "At least until we can get you a parasol." And promptly bought her a floppy-brimmed hat from a street vendor whose white teeth flashed as he bit into the coin Nicholls gave him.

"Ah—there goes our governor, Lord Rawlings," Nicholls said, looking down the street.

Lorraine turned to see a rider on a pale gray horse just disappearing around a corner in the distance. She had a fleeting impression of height and breadth of shoulder and commanding bearing.

"He sits his horse well," she commented, for she was learning to be a judge of such things.

Nicholls chuckled. "He does other things well too, I'm told. There are interesting stories about him. 'Tis said he left London in a hurry because two titled ladies both claimed to be betrothed to him. King Charles took mercy on his plight and gave him this appointment to help get him away! He is a rakehell—not at all like the last governor, who, I'm told, was a staid family man." His eyes twinkled. "All the ladies on the island are vying for his attention."

Lorraine shrugged. "I doubt I will be seeing much of him. Come, show me this island you have been telling me about.'

"I took the liberty of buying you a carriage," Nicholls told her. "And a horse."

They were brought around. The open carriage was commodious, the horse a sleek shining chestnut. It seemed a dream to Lorraine after so much misuse to find herself stepping into her own horse-drawn carriage. After all, she had been dragged through the streets of Providence but a short time ago!

Nicholls sprang into the driver's seat. She could never quite guess his age but his nimbleness belied his weathered face and the experience that looked out of his shrewd eyes.

They drove south down the coast, passing groups of fig trees whose long "beards" hung to the ground and rooted there. Those bearded figs had given the island its name, Nicholls told her. He pointed out landmarks and where the island notables lived. He was remarkably well-informed. But he obviously had a particular destination in mind and soon the carriage was moving smoothly up a long driveway bordered by stately white hibiscus and tall majestic royal palms. Lorraine peered forward as the house came into view. Built of smooth white coral stone like many of those in Bridgetown, it was by far the handsomest dwelling she had seen on the island. The setting was magnificent, and the house was situated high upon a cliff overlooking the turquoise waters of the Caribbean.

When they reached the entrance, where, beyond a sweeping stone-floored veranda, carved doors of the hard purple wood known as logwood marked the main entrance, Nicholls reined to a stop. "Are we coming to call?" she asked in surprise.

"Yes," he said, jumping out and reaching up to help her step down.

"What a beautiful place," she commented, looking around her admiringly at the green velvet lawn that ran to the cliff edge, the big mahogany trees. "Who lives here?" she asked. "The governor?"

"No. You do." He was watching her face.

Lorraine's blonde head swung about, trying to take it all in. "Mr. Nicholls," she said slowly, "I cannot believe that all this is really mine."

"Bought in your name. I have the deed here." He patted his pocket. "I do think," he added, "that not only was it the best buy on the island, but it is the best plantation in all ways. There is a mahogany grove just down there, and orchards of lime and lemon and orange and grapefruit and avocados and pomegranates, and the sugarcane fields—"

"I'll look at them later," Lorraine laughed, snatching off her wide-brimmed straw hat and letting the sea breezes blow through her fair hair. "Just now I am reveling in this view of the ocean."

"You can view it every night from your veranda

while you drink tall cool drinks," was his comment as
he beckoned her inside.

As Lorraine walked into the cool high-ceilinged interior, her heels echoing on the stone floors, she marveled at the light. The windows were all floor-to-ceiling
casements and gave the rooms an airiness she had
never seen in a house before. The drawing room and
long dining room were on a scale that astonished her.
Certainly they dwarfed the largest rooms of Eleazer
Todd's "splendid mansion" and made even Cedarwood
in Bermuda seem small. There was a vast fireplace.
("You will seldom need it," Nicholls told her.) And
stone stables out back. Her bedroom was huge and
jutted out from the side of the house, giving it a
double exposure so that it had not only a view that
reached forever out over the ocean's endless blue but
also a view of the gardens as well. All the ceilings
were enormously tall. ("You will need tall ceilings;
this is a hot climate.")

"The house looks . . . old," she said meditatively as
they strolled through the elaborate gardens, elegant
with the waxy blooms of frangipani and overrun with
pink and scarlet hibiscus and bougainvillea.

"A dozen years—no more."

"I mean, the stonework outside where the sun does
not strike it has a mossy look, as if it has been here for
centuries."

"That is because of the porous nature of coral stone."
Nicholls explained.

"It's wonderful. But the rooms are so empty. Will I
have enough money left to furnish it?"

"As handsomely as you wish. We got it for a price!"
boasted Nicholls, who was enjoying his role of agent.
"For the owners had just inherited the family seat in
Kent and were eager to return to the arms of their
relatives! We were the only ones who could pay so
much in gold. All the other offers were in molasses,
which would have to be transported to New England
to be made into rum. But we could close the deal—
like that!" He snapped his fingers.

They strolled on, with Lorraine drinking in the sights
and smells of this tropical paradise.

"There is a second plantation I am negotiating for in your name," he told her soberly. "But your next move, I believe, should be to buy a ship. Perhaps more than one ship. We should carry our molasses to New England in our own bottoms."

"In our . . . own bottoms?" echoed Lorraine faintly. It was all moving too fast for her.

"Yes, indeed—in our own ships." Nicholls said, proud to show that he had picked up some shipper's terms. "We can then bring back New England goods to sell in the islands. Another, smaller ship would be best for the inter-island trading—that is easily arranged. Of course the real future lies in making our molasses into rum right here, cutting out New England, and shipping it to England direct—and possibly some other ports as well. You see . . ."

His voice went on, delineating shrewd plans and initiating Lorraine into the world of high finance. Nicholls was by nature an empire builder, and a fortune had been delivered into his hands for management. He meant to make the most of it. He would set this slip of a girl on a financial throne—if only she would let him.

"Mr. Nicholls," Lorraine said gently, "I realize I can learn much from you—and believe me, I will apply myself to such lessons. But for the moment" —she drew a deep breath—"let me enjoy just being here in"—she turned to him inquisitively—"what is its name?"

"The last owners never could agree on a name. They fought it out between 'Folly' and 'Seacliff' —nobody won. An older house formerly stood on this site but it too had no name."

"I shall call it 'Venture,' " she said. "For 'twas a venture that brought me this. And perhaps . . . perhaps our ships should be named 'venture' too, in a way—*Bonaventure, Island Venture, Proud Venture.* What would you think of that?"

"I think," he said softly, "that if you will give me leave to do so, I will blazon the name of Venture around the world!"

"Then you have my hand on it!" she cried.

Nicholls shook her slim hand energetically. He was afire with enthusiasm. "We will need good seafaring men," he said. "Captains who know ships. Honest ones to advise me. Because," he confessed, "I do not know what makes a fast sailer or a sound bottom—I only know capacities and prices and tonnage."

"I know just the man!" Lorraine was entering into the spirit of their venture, swept along on the wings of Nicholls' boundless enthusiasm for trade. "He captained the ship that brought me here. You could discuss it with Captain Bowman."

"Later, if you please, Mistress London. I am hoping to close the deal on the small plantation I mentioned this afternoon—it is a small place on the Atlantic side of the island but it is being offered for a good price—we wouldn't want to miss it."

"Then I will speak to Captain Bowman on your behalf," she said, thinking: *I might as well begin to understand commerce now.*

Nicholls blinked; he had not expected her to enter into the plans quite so soon. "As you wish, Mistress London—but leave it tentative, so I can shore up any problems."

"And, Mr. Nicholls—this is a very large house. There is plenty of room for you in it if you would care to move in."

As he helped her into the carriage, he looked up at her and said, "I am grateful for the offer but I prefer to be in the center of town in the thick of things. One hears of all sorts of business matters when one takes his meals in the common room of an inn!"

By the end of the week much had been accomplished:

Lorraine soon ensured her entry into Bridgetown society by inviting Mistress Hurst and her sister-in-law to Venture and tactfully asking their advice on how to furnish it. "I have fallen in love with this huge long trestle dining table," she admitted. "It is of polished mahogany and was considered too awkward and heavy to move all the way to England, so the last owners left it. I have thought of having mahogany furniture made locally. What do you think?"

"A wonderful idea!" breathed Mistress Hurst, eyeing

the table enviously. "And your stables, you will want to keep horses—everybody does. Do you ride?"

"No," admitted Lorraine. "I was forbidden to ride as a child because of a terrible accident that happened to my aunt," she improvised glibly. "But now I intend to learn."

"And your slave quarters," pursued the sister-in-law. "It is a pity the last owners sold off all their slaves. I suppose you will be in the market to replace them?"

Lorraine, who had inspected the barren stone slave quarters, shuddered. "No, I expect to use all hired labor or indentured servants," she said crisply. That was greeted with such astonishment that she felt constrained to add, "I am in the market to buy up the articles of indenture of likely persons who have some skills."

For an idea had come to her. If she could offer a bondservant a shortening of his period of indenture for superior work or innovations, would she not be the winner? Not to mention the sympathy she felt for bondservants slaving away for what must seem endless years.

"I have in mind to start a furniture business," she said. "Since there is so much good mahogany and other fine woods on this island."

"It might thrive—but it will be so costly to ship it," protested Mistress Hurst.

"I will be shipping it in my own bottoms," announced Lorraine proudly.

Soon, Lorraine had assembled a small house staff and she and Nicholls had struck up a deal with Captain Bowman. The *Dolphin* was a stout three-masted vessel, and Bowman promised to speak to the owners about buying it. If they agreed to sell, he would captain the *Bonaventure,* as it would then be called.

"And I hope the first passenger the *Bonaventure* carries to Barbados will be your aunt, Mistress Bowman," Lorraine said sincerely. "For nothing would please me so much as to have her come here to live with me as my companion and friend."

The captain smiled. "I will try to convince her," he promised.

"But be careful that the Todds or their friends do not hear of my offer," Lorraine cautioned him. "I would prefer them to think me dead."

"I understand." He wrung her hand.

Captain Bowman was true to his word. No sooner had he cast anchor in Providence harbor than he repaired to Eleazer Todd's mansion to have a word with his aunt.

He found her with her legs propped up on a sofa in the parlor nursing an ankle she had turned the day before. Despite the fact that her foot was supported by a pillow, she would have sprung up to embrace him but that he waved her back.

"Is your injury a serious one?"

" 'Tis nothing—a day's rest will cure it. How was your voyage, John?"

"Excellent. I came at once because I knew you'd want to hear about—" He stopped abruptly. "Are we alone in the house?"

"Oh, yes, everyone's gone but me."

Mistress Bowman was not quite correct in that statement. From the woods nearby Philip Dedwinton had observed Captain Bowman's arrival, and had hurried to the house, sneaking inside on his soft Indian moccasins. He was now flattened against the wall of the next room with his ear inclined toward the door. He heard Captain Bowman say, "I saw Mistress London safely to Barbados. Her guardian has purchased a handsome plantation for her there and she hopes you will join her there to live with her as her companion and friend."

"Oh, John, I'm so glad she's all right! But I couldn't be dependent upon her, you know that!"

Captain Bowman smiled upon his aunt. "I do think she's in need of a housekeeper—and she'd like nothing better than for you to take the position. Think about it. I'm off to buy the *Dolphin* for her, if it can be done. When I return, you may have decided to go. Barbados is a pleasant place to live."

"I do not have to think about it," said his aunt with energy. "I will do it."

"Good. Then you will sail with me on my next voyage."

In the other room Philip was no longer listening. The words "Barbardos" and "a handsome plantation" were scudding through his brain. Lorraine had tricked him! Nicholls had taken the money to Barbados, and there she was living on "a handsome plantation" while he, cast out by Lavinia, was staying on here at Eleazer Todd's sufferance!

He waited until Captain Bowman had left and then stole out of the house. He needed to think.

By nightfall he had decided. Lorraine had always fancied him—it was not too late to mend his fences. Besides, he could always frighten her by threatening to expose her as his bondservant! *That* should bring her to heel!

Long before Captain Bowman returned for his sister, Philip had taken passage to Barbados.

CHAPTER 29

Venture Plantation, Barbados

IN BRIDGETOWN THERE were only two topics of conversation: the fascinating black-sheep governor and the shipwrecked heiress.

Lord Rawlings was not at the moment in residence at Government House. He had sailed to nearby Martinique and lingered there from week to week. Gossip had it that he was having a wild affair with the beautiful and promiscuous wife of Martinique's French governor. The general belief was that it would end in a duel, and the sighing ladies of Bridgetown watched the harbor brightly for his return.

Of the shipwrecked heiress there was not much at the moment to report, but any word from Venture was seized on by the gossips and exaggerated. Mistress London was, they said, a most unusual woman. She made no effort to enter into the social life of the town, gave no parties, held no balls. She spent her mornings learning to ride and her afternoons, oddly enough, attending to plantation matters. Brows lifted at this last, for it was most uncommon for a woman to take so much interest in business affairs.

In truth Lorraine was very busy—and what consumed her time would have astonished Bridgetown.

Will Shelby, Lorraine's nearest neighbor, had been quick to call. Lorraine had come out onto her veranda one morning after she moved in and found him just dismounting from his horse.

362

"Mistress London!" He swept her an impetuous bow.

Lorraine looked at him quizzically. She saw a rugged-looking young gentleman in sweat-stained orange satins who looked as if he belonged more on a horse than in a drawing room. His sandy hair was unruly and tended to cascade over his eyes so that he was constantly giving his head a shake to toss it back into place and his hazel eyes held a merry gleam.

"I am Will Shelby, your neighbor at Clifftop." He jerked his head toward the winding cliffs to the south and managed to clear his vision again. "I have come to welcome you to Barbados and to take you riding." He peered at her. "You are more beautiful even than they said you were."

"I do not ride," Lorraine admitted, smiling at Will.

"Then I will teach you!"

"But at the moment I have only a carriage horse—"

"I will be back in a trice with a gentle nag from my own stables!" Before she could protest, Will had leapt back upon his horse and was thundering away down the drive.

He was back within the hour with a docile bay mare, which Lorraine timidly mounted. A little apprehensive at first, she clung to the horn of the sidesaddle, but soon found that keeping her seat was not so difficult after all.

That day was a revelation to her. Will Shelby led her down into the canefields, past his own well-run plantation, and onto the land of his neighbor farther south—a plantation that seemed not so well run. The fields were rougher, such buildings as they passed seemed to be in poor repair. Lorraine remarked on it.

"Aye," Will agreed readily. "Pinchot is no manager, stays drunk most of the time, leaves the running of the place to his overseer." He frowned suddenly. "I would not have brought you this way had I known we'd run into this!"

Shelby was looking slightly to his left, and Lorraine followed his gaze. She saw a man tied to a tree. He was stripped to the waist and sagged in his bonds. The sun beat down on his bare back, which was striped from the whip.

There was no one about.

Shelby would have wheeled his horse around, but Lorraine protested indignantly. "We cannot leave him there like that!"

Will Shelby sighed. "The man is a bondservant. His name is Maughan and he tries perpetually to escape. I don't doubt that's what brought on this whipping."

They had come up close to poor Maughan and Lorraine saw that he was a mass of bruises besides bearing the welts of the whip. A bucket of water stood nearby, and a dipper—but both were beyond Maughan's reach.

Lorraine climbed down from her horse and proffered Maughan a dipper of water. He straightened a little from his slumped position and gave her a grateful look.

"They left it that I might gaze on it and yearn for a drink," he told her.

"Why?"

"To torment me."

"No, I mean why did they punish you at all?"

"He tried to escape again," interposed Will Shelby. "Didn't you, Maughan?"

The answer was a resigned nod of a shock of brown hair. "I'm a groom by trade, mistress," Maughan told Lorraine. "I'm good with horses, but the owner of this plantation cares naught for his animals. I dared to tell him they were underfed and needed currying and he sent me out to the canefields—and there I've been ever since, working in the cane."

"I'm in need of a groom," said Lorraine. "Perhaps you would come to work for me?"

Maughan gave a short bitter laugh. "I'd like nothing better, but I'm indentured for four more years."

"I see," said Lorraine. She gave him some more water and sponged off his forehead with her kerchief.

Will Shelby looked at her anxiously as he helped her back upon her horse. "I had not meant for you to see that," he said as they rode on through the canefields. " 'Tis a bit strong for a lady's tender gaze."

She turned on him in consternation. "You mean such treatment is *usual?*"

Will moved his shoulders uneasily beneath that alarmed gaze. "Well, not at Clifftop it isn't, but many plantations, like Pinchot's, are not well run and some bondservants tend to rebel."

Lorraine shivered. "Bondservants are no better off than slaves then!"

"Worse off," he agreed readily. "Slaves are better treated." At her shocked expression, he explained. "A slave's contract is for life—his owner has a vested interest in him. But a bondservant's contract begins to run out the day you buy him—at the most he will be with you no more than three, five, or seven years, say. If the most is to be got out of him, he must be kept tractable—and at home. Usually the whip takes care of that."

"At least bondservants eventually regain their freedom!"

"Not always." His voice was sober. " 'Tis common practice in the islands to beat and starve them in the last year of their indenture until in desperation they agree to bind themselves for another term of indenture— as long as seven more years."

Lorraine almost rode into a projecting palm frond. She brushed it back just in time. These islands in the sun were strange tropical things, she realized suddenly. Here man and beast—and even plants—vied in ferocity, in thorns, in bites and stings, in human cruelty. . . .

"But such matters need not concern a lady," Will added pleasantly, and Lorraine gave him a wan look. A "lady" today—but perhaps a luckless bondservant whipped at the tail of a cart tomorrow!

"Mr. Shelby," she asked impulsively, "do you know this Pinchot very well?"

He shrugged his orange satin shoulders. "Well enough. I have lent him slaves from time to time when he could not get his cane cut for one reason or another."

She pounced on that. "Then he is in your debt? Would you do me a great favor?"

Will Shelby looked dazzled. He would do this beauty any number of favors!

"I would like to buy the articles of this man Maughan and make him my groom. Would you arrange it for me?"

"But Maughan is known to be unruly!"

"I will chance it," was her firm reply.

It was arranged that same afternoon. Pinchot was drunk and hiccuped that he would gladly rid himself of Maughan, who was a firebrand and forever making trouble.

Maughan was delivered to Venture, and Lorraine sent immediately for a doctor, who cleansed and salved the weals of the whip and prescribed better food and rest.

"You will no longer cut cane," Lorraine told Maughan when the doctor had gone. "Nor will anyone attack you. Are you well-acquainted with this island?"

He nodded, almost struck dumb by his good fortune at having found such a kind mistress.

"I mean to use all bondservants or hired labor for the furniture business in which I propose to engage, and they will need shelter. Decent cottages must be constructed to house them. As my groom, you can mix about under the pretext of looking for horseflesh for Venture. Actually, I wish you to find me good carpenters and other artisans skilled at their crafts. If they work for hire, I will pay them more than they are now getting—if they are bondservants, I will buy their articles of indenture. And I will need a house staff as well. All will be well-treated here and if they serve me well, I will increase their wages or strike off part of their period of indenture."

Maughan's eyes filled with tears. "I had thought to be starved and beaten into signing again," he muttered.

"Not ever again," vowed Lorraine grimly. "Nor will anyone else on this plantation!"

Gradually she assembled a small house staff, men to work in the fields, and skilled artisans to shape and build mahogany furniture. There was a relaxed air to working at Venture, a breezy hope for the future. The food was good and plentiful and the work congenial—

for Lorraine was not trying to stuff square pegs into round holes. They all adored her and word went round the island that there was no better place to work than Venture.

Nicholls watched Lorraine's progress with interest, but he was mostly occupied with refitting a newly bought sloop, *Island Venture*, arranging for its cargo, and scheduling its ports of call. He had also begun to draw up plans for the new sugar mill.

Will Shelby continued to pay Lorraine court. Under his tutelage she had a surer hand on the reins and soon graduated to a more spirited mount. She was trying to fill her days so that she might forget Raile, when she met the governor.

She went riding with Will Shelby every day—and hardly a day passed but they were intercepted by some interested young buck who desired to meet the new mistress of Venture. Soon some of those fellows were paying morning calls on Venture to bring Lorraine flowers and trinkets and pay her extravagant compliments, while Will chafed at the bit to get on with their ride and frowned mightily at the interlopers.

Early one morning, Lorraine decided to escape them all. She left word that she was "indisposed" and drove down into Bridgetown in her new carriage. She observed that several of the ladies coming out of the shops on Broad Street looked askance at her—doubtless for driving about herself, but she did not care. Why should she be shackled to what servants could do for her when she had a perfectly good pair of hands and feet of her own?

She visited the market and purchased some palm-leaf fans and a large green parrot in a wicker cage. The boy who lifted the cage into her carriage was jostled. The cage door, not too securely fastened, struck the side of the carriage and the frightened bird flew free to perch upon the back of the carriage, squawking and flapping its wings.

When the boy made a grab for it, the parrot promptly bit his finger. He gave a yowl and the crowd laughed uproariously.

"Quiet!" said a deep voice of authority, and the

crowd fell suddenly silent. Lorraine turned to see a tall man striding purposefully toward her, moving with the swift grace of a fencer. He stripped off his black-and-silver coat as he walked, revealing a flowing white cambric shirt trimmed in expensive point lace. Black silk trousers encased his long muscular legs. Gently he brushed the anxious boy aside and approached the parrot, which was unhappily ruffling its wings.

Suddenly the man swooped and the parrot was, clasped in a strong firm grip. Gently he eased the bird, now only making softer rasping noises, back into its wicker cage and fastened the door.

He flashed a winning smile at Lorraine. "I am good with birds."

"I can see that." Lorraine was impressed. "Indeed I was afraid I had lost this one." She extended a tentative finger toward the cage and jerked it back as the parrot's beak darted forward.

"The bird is frightened by all this noise," observed the tall man. "It will settle down when you get it home."

Lorraine looked charming in her new butter-yellow sprigged-muslin gown which a local sempstress had hastily cut for her. A dozen more gowns were being made up for her in the town at that moment. The man's glance lingered on the smooth curving lines of her low-cut bodice and the narrowness of her waist, which was accentuated by the panniers tucked up at the sides to reveal a lemon linen petticoat, and lemon kidskin shoes. His look returned to caress the smooth expanse of her white bosom and throat and lovely face framed in hair like sunlight.

Lorraine flushed a little at the overlong inspection. "I am beholden to you, sir." She would have stepped into the carriage, but instead of offering his hand to assist her, his broad-shouldered form blocked her way.

"Might one know your name?" he murmured.

"I am Lorraine London. And you are . . . ?"

"Lord Rawlings. I have the honor to be the governor of this island."

So this was the rakehell Governor of Barbados!

Back home at last! Lorraine maintained a suitable gravity but her voice held a note of irony.

"One hears much of your exploits, Lord Rawlings."

"Nothing good, I'll be bound!" He was laughing now.

Her eyes twinkled. "Much that is . . . *interesting*," she amended. "Somehow I had expected you to be a much older man."

He laughed again. "The king has promised me that this climate will age me! He and I agree that one can live three lifetimes in one—if one works diligently at it." When she again made to enter her carriage, he offered her his hand in courtly style.

"Might one hope for your presence at Government House at tea this afternoon?"

"I would be honored," said Lorraine. She was uncomfortably aware that people in the crowd were nudging each other with their elbows and shaking their heads and grinning. She wondered wildly if the governor pounced on his teatime guests and carried them away to his bedchamber—it seemed unlikely. In any event, she was eager to find out!

With the parrot in tow, she drove back to Venture, stopping on the way to inquire if any of her new gowns were ready. None were quite finished but one was nearly so. It was of sheer white cambric with a flounced skirt and narrow black velvet ribands drawn through white embroidered eyelets at the low-cut neckline and edging the wide ruffles that spilled from the full elbow-length sleeves. On impulse—even though it was only lightly basted together—she decided to take it with her. The sempstress looked doubtful and hastened to add a few stitches to the bodice "so the seams will not burst when you breathe."

Thus it was that, clad in virginal white—with just a suggestion of wickedness from the black velvet ribands that not only decorated her dress but also hung from a sparkling rosette in her hair—and wear-ing a white straw hat with a sweeping brim, Lorraine drove up to Government House. There, she sur-prised the groom by leaping lightly down from her carriage unassisted to land on dainty white leather shoes with fashionable red heels.

"I believe the governor is expecting me," she said, looking around for the other carriages. There were none.

Feeling slightly apprehensive, she followed a servant into a large stone-floored hall only a trifle more impressive than her own at Venture, and through several cool dim rooms until they came to a wide veranda looking out on green lawns and gardens bursting with colorful exotic bloom. The veranda chairs were of cane with high flying backs—Lorraine recognized them as island-made. And there was a low table inlaid with ivory that had the look of the Orient about it.

Plainly the governor lived well.

He strode in a moment later, walking vigorously as though undisturbed by the stifling heat of the afternoon. He was dramatically garbed in dull-finish black silk trimmed with silver embroidery. Lorraine was told later that he always wore black and silver. There was a burst of Mechlin from the cuffs of his flowing white cambric shirt and another burst of Mechlin at his throat, held in place by a large sapphire a shade lighter than his own dark sapphire eyes.

"Mistress London, how nice of you to come!" He swept her a courtier's bow.

"I was summoned," she said warily. "Am I to be your only guest?"

He grinned at her and sank down into the chair opposite. "I assure you, your virtue will be quite safe. I am least dangerous at this enervating time of day. 'Tis nightfall that brings out the beast in me."

"Thank you for the warning," she laughed.

The tea tray was brought in.

"Would you not prefer lemonade in this heat?" he asked. "Or could I urge on you something stronger?" When Lorraine admitted she would prefer lemonade, he said solicitously, "It would be far cooler inside, even though there is some shade out here." He indicated the palm fronds that waved above them.

"I think I prefer it out here," Lorraine decided, gazing into the cool dimness of the governor's lair.

"I see that my reputation precedes me," he sighed.

"But you have no need to fear me, Mistress London—by the way, does your name have some significance? Is it possible you were in London while I was there and I missed you?"

Lorraine found herself laughing. "No, I am not from London. Mine is an old Cornish family. From near Wyelock," she added, for although he had not spoken, he was still regarding her with polite interest.

"Ah, Wyelock," he said. "I am somewhat acquainted with Cornwall. That will be between Penzance and Helston," he said in so definite a tone that Lorraine murmured, "Between Penzance and Helston, yes."

"And overlooking St. Ives Bay," he added on what seemed a note of pride that he should have such a good memory for places.

Lorraine's mother had never told her whether her home overlooked St. Ives Bay or the open ocean, but so definite in his knowledge was the masterful governor that Lorraine quickly agreed.

He leaned back. He seemed pleased with himself and Lorraine divined that he was a man to whom it was important to shine in the eyes of the ladies.

He asked her how long she had been living on Barbados, followed that up immediately by inquiring, "Are you spoken for?"

"No," said Lorraine ruefully. "But I have suitors!"

"I thought you might," he said, regarding her narrowly. "But none of them yet has won you?"

Lorraine shook her head. "I think they are more struck by Venture than by me," she told him frankly.

"And honest as well!" he said, delighted.

"Are women then not so honest at court?" Her clear blue-gray eyes were looking into his sapphire ones.

He shrugged. "Some are not." Sensing her interest, he launched into stories of life at King Charles's court—and she asked him avidly what the ladies wore, how they spent their days.

At last she said, puzzled, "*I* think they must lead utterly useless lives!"

He burst out laughing. "It is the fashion to be useless!"

"Then I shall never be fashionable," she vowed, "for there is too much of interest to be done. Did you know that I am starting a furniture factory at Venture?"

"Anything to bring commerce and wealth to this island," he murmured. "But you're busy for one so young? You cannot be more than—"

Lorraine flushed. "I will be seventeen at the end of May."

"Born under Gemini, the sign of the Twins? And would you be then a mercurial person, one who wars with herself perhaps?"

"I am more like to war with others!" Lorraine admitted, dimpling.

"Ah, that should be left to such as I! Mine is the warrior sign—Aries the Ram!"

Their conversation went on in this light vein, then shifted again to her new venture, the furniture factory. He listened intently while she told him about it—and about her other plans.

Lorraine had seldom enjoyed an afternoon so much. She left, promising she would join the governor for supper the following night.

He saw her to her carriage, kissed her hand, and said gallantly, "You have brought spice to a world of sugar, Mistress London. I am looking forward to having you flavor my days!"

It was easy to see why women loved him, she thought, smiling as she drove away. He was obviously a rogue, but—

That thought made her remember another rogue and what it had been like to love him.

In Virginia that other "rogue" had not fared so well. Raile had crossed into Gloucester with Bacon, where the force commanded by Giles Brent had disintegrated before them. But Bacon was exhausted, and ill, he had pushed himself too far—and in Gloucester on the twenty-sixth of October, he died.

Raile was one of those who placed the young rebel leader's body in a weighted coffin and lowered it into the York River so Governor Berkeley would not be able to chop off Bacon's head and put it on a pike as he threatened.

The forces that had ridden with Bacon split into five bands and manned strategic points on the peninsula between the York and the James. Without their fiery leader and with the onset of winter they degenerated into mere plunderers, looting plantations as far as Westmoreland County in Virginia's Northern Neck, where they occupied the house of Colonel John Washington, and continued stripping or looting numerous plantations nearer by.

Raile scorned such activity and traveled up the James to bid his brother good-bye. But Rory and Laurie Ann were already gone. They had disappeared into the southern vastness and were no doubt building a cabin in some other wilderness, perhaps in North Carolina.

Raile stood by Rory's deserted cabin in freezing sleet and wondered if he would ever see them again. Perhaps not . . . the frontier life was harsh. But it had been their choice.

Snow followed the freezing sleet and he made his way back downriver between snow-whitened banks along a James that was gray and silent beneath the milk-white winter sky. Everywhere along the way he was greeted with word of new disasters. Every day rebels deserted and the governor's forces were swooping down on such of the small rebel detachments as they could catch.

Raile crossed the peninsula to the York, where he was bottled up for a while with a group at West Point; then he slipped downriver and managed to contact Johnny Sears, still waiting hopefully at Yorktown. Before a week was out he was back aboard the *Likely Lass* with the war behind him.

Raile did a bit of coastal trading after that but his heart was not in it. He had left it with a slip of a girl in the burned-out capital of Jamestown.

As if drawn to places her slender feet had trod, eventually he touched port at Yorktown. Did he do it on the faint hope that she might have regretted her bargain with Philip and come back to look for him?

He was drawn irrestibly to the Swan, where Johnny Sears told him *she* had stayed.

His own tracks were well-covered now; he was just in from North Carolina, and he could with safety ask Higgins, the innkeeper, questions about Lorraine.

Higgins, believing he was addressing Lorraine's "cousin," was not loath to talk.

"Strange, it was," he ruminated. "Her betrothed, who came down from Rhode Island to find her, engaged my private room upstairs so that they might make up their lovers' quarrel—but they didn't stay. Odd, though I'd not have thought your cousin to be the drinking kind." He shook his head.

"She isn't," said Raile, frowning.

"Yet he carried her out of here dead drunk that same night," sighed the innkeeper. "And neither of them ever wrote back for the gold she and that fellow Nicholls, who was on his way to Barbados, left with me!"

Raile's face went pale beneath its tan. Lorraine hadn't left him—she had been carried away! And God knew what Philip Dedwinton had done to her!

Raile thanked the surprised Higgins and hurried back to his ship.

"Tav," he told MacTavish when he came over the side of the *Lass,* "we're for Rhode Island. My lass didn't leave me—she was abducted!"

In a Rhode Island tavern—for taverns were among the first buildings to spring up on the destroyed Providence waterfront—Raile learned more: how Lorraine had been jerked along at the end of a halter through the town and had since disappeared.

"I'd like a word with Dedwinton." He felt his hands clench. "D'ye know where he can be found?"

"Well, he was living at Eleazer Todd's mansion— just about the only building around here that escaped the Indians' burning. And betrothed to Todd's daughter. But then he went away and came back with that blonde bound girl and then *she* disappeared and the engagement was broke off and now *he's* gone too. Some say he took ship for Barbados."

Raile looked thoughtful. And when he left the tavern it was with a springy step. It had all come together like the pieces of a Chinese puzzle.

"Tav," he told MacTavish earnestly, "Nicholls was on his way to Barbados when Dedwinton kidnapped Lorraine. She didn't go with Nicholls *because she was waiting for me to return!* Nicholls had been to Rhode Island—he knew where Dedwinton would take Lorraine. He must have sent for her and helped her escape. She's settled down to a free and happy life in Barbados and now that Dedwinton whelp has gone down there to collect her! We'll have to get there fast, Tav, lest he do my lass some harm!"

CHAPTER 30

IT WAS A fine day in Barbados. The scent of flowers at Venture plantation was almost overwhelming and the late-afternoon sun blazed down out of a cloudless azure sky.

Lorraine intended to ride out before dinner, taking the path along the heights overlooking the sea where she could enjoy the view. With this in mind she swung blithely through the carved front doors of Venture and onto the steps, where she came to an abrupt halt. She froze with shock.

There before her, strolling up the driveway in the languid sultry air, was—incredibly— Philip Dedwinton.

He looked as he always had, robust, alert, with the sun glinting on his brown hair and his body encased in clothes that were smart enough in Rhode Island but looked a bit wintry and out of place on this most fashionable island of the West Indies. A mixture of emotions went through Lorraine at the sight of him. Memories—some of them painful—came flooding back.

Philip saw her come out and he leaned forward, peering quizzically at the elegant lady in the cool blue-gray linen riding habit and the wide-brimmed hat loaded with waving azure plumes.

"Lorraine?" he asked incredulously.

"Philip." Lorraine regained control of herself and met his gaze coolly. "What brings you here?"

Philip moved forward again, staring at her in open admiration. This was not the tired angry girl that he had last seen in Rhode Island. This slim, smartly dressed creature looked sophisticated and relaxed and completely in command.

"They told me I would find you in the house at the top of the hill," he said. "Whose place is this, Lorraine?"

"You are at Venture plantation, Philip," she told him calmly. "And everything you see here belongs to me."

He sucked in his breath at that and looked around him. His bewildered gaze encompassed the handsome stone flooring, the smooth plastered walls, the deep windows to the floor. The veranda itself was large and elegant, the carved front doors stood invitingly open to reveal a handsome interior.

"You have married?" he ventured fearfully. That would indeed put a crimp in his plans!

Lorraine laughed. "No, I have not married. I said this was *mine*." She studied him, her face inscrutable. "Would you care to come inside?"

Philip responded to that with alacrity. He was as handsome as ever, she thought with a twinge. Somehow she felt he should have looked older, cruder. She led him into the cool dim interior of the wide entrance hall.

"I cannot believe it," he murmured.

"And you have seen but the house. You have not yet seen the gardens and the mahogany forest and the canefields that go with it."

His head swung around to her, eyes widening. "Then you really *are* an heiress and you did not gamble your money away?"

"Not a penny."

"I am surprised you could buy all this with a thousand pounds." He sounded subdued.

"Oh, I inherited vastly more than that, Philip. Benjamin Nicholls told you a thousand pounds because he wanted me to have the pleasure of telling you myself the extent of my fortune. I let you go on thinking it was but a thousand pounds—to test you."

"Lorraine—" he began in a strangled voice.

"Please, no apologies now, Philip. You have come a long way and you may save all that for dinner—which will be here." She pointed toward the long dining room. "It is hot and you must be desirous of a bath and a nap before dinner. Myself, I have just risen—I always take a nap during this laziest part of the day. I am told it is too hot for all save the bondservants and slaves in the sugarcane fields!" She gestured to him to follow a servant. "I will see you at dinner, Philip. Oh—and be sure to tell the girl if the bathwater is not hot enough. I have come to prefer rather cool water in this climate, but you might not agree."

She clapped her hands and a soft-eyed barefoot island girl, wearing a blue-and-gold turban on her head, came forward to lead Philip away.

"Those are my new racing colors—blue and gold," Lorraine told Philip, indicating the maid's turban. "They will also be the colors of my livery when I get around to having uniforms made. The governor helped me choose them. I have ordered a coach from England, Philip."

"A . . . a coach?" he echoed faintly. No one he knew had a coach.

"Yes, the governor has promised to send instructions to the maker of his own coach, which is black and silver. Mine of course will be blue and gold." She waved gracefully to the girl. "Take Master Philip to the green bedchamber and bring him a bath. You will be called for dinner, Philip."

Stunned, Philip followed the island girl. En route they passed the open doorway of a bedchamber so large and of such magnificence that it brought him to a halt.

"Whose bedchamber is this?" he asked—but he knew.

"That be mistress's bedchamber," said the girl in lilting English.

Philip stuck his head in to survey the broad sweep of windows looking out over the blue Caribbean, and opposite, the gardens. He took in the sheer white cambric and delicate China-blue silk hangings, the thick soft pile of the dusky blue and turquoise Chinese rug, the large polished mahogany bed with its fragile ruffled white cambric coverlet trimmed in pale blue ribands, the dressing table with its French gilt mirror, the repoussé silver mirror and comb. . . . He dragged his eyes away.

And he had given up all this—for Lavinia! The thought made him feel physically ill.

But wait, all might not yet be lost! He was hardly aware of the handsomeness of the pale green bedchamber to which the island girl had led him, so frantically was his mind working. And before he was immersed in the scented soapy water of his bath, he was in schemes of how to win Lorraine back.

He had not expected her to be so rich. His head whirled with it. But not yet married—she had said that. Oh, what a fool he had been! But, he told himself, he would remind her of their happy times together, he would find a way to brush against her with his body, she would feel the nearness of him, he would heat the wench up!

He hardly noticed whether the bathwater was cool or hot. What did it matter? He had left cold, snowy, burned-over Rhode Island for a tropical paradise and a beauty of vast wealth and undoubted power. A woman who would soon own a coach! He could hardly wait for dinner—but he was forced to. The candles had been lit and a velvet darkness had descended upon the island before the girl in the blue-and-gold turban returned to bring him to the drawing room.

Lorraine was standing with her back to Philip as he entered. She had not gone riding after all. She had walked across the green lawn to the edge of the cliff that overlooked the ocean and there she had remained for a long time. Thinking. Remembering. When she had returned to the house her face was set. She had called her overseer and had given him some instructions that made him blink in surprise.

Now as she stood waiting for her guest, she gave Philip time to take in the luxury of her surroundings, the elegance of her sheer white flounced cambric gown with the black velvet ribands that made her skin seem the more radiant, the beauty of her blonde hair dazzling in the candlelight. Finally she turned to him with a brilliant welcoming smile.

"Shall we go in to dinner, Philip?" She took his arm.

Beneath the crystal chandelier, the long table was piled high with silver and flowers. When they were seated, a huge silver bowl filled with white hibiscus blossoms faced him. He had to crane his neck to see around it.

"Lorraine, I cannot see you for all these flowers," he complained.

Lorraine clapped her hands and gave a low-voiced order. The flowers were removed to a large sideboard and Philip found himself considering his hostess across a formidable array of plate. Branched silver candelabra with candles alight vied with the tall silver salts for magnificence.

"Am I to presume that you and Lavinia are already married?" she asked. "Philip, do not put down your spoon—this conch soup is very good."

"Lorraine, let me explain about that," he said hoarsely. "Lavinia and I are not married. Lavinia—"

"Oh, do not talk about Lavinia—tell me about the others. What of Mistress Bowman? Is she well?"

"She is well enough," said Philip shortly. He leaned forward. "Lavinia and I have called it off. We were not—"

"Tell me of the war," she cut in. "How fares Rhode Island now?"

Defeated, Philip answered her questions, giving her a play-by-play account of the progress of the war. No, Rhode Island still had raised no troops, they had remained neutral. The eleven hundred men serving under Governor Josiah Winslow of Massachusetts were half from Massachusetts and half from Connecticut— but those who had crossed from Rehoboth to Wickford had been carried by Rhode Island ships. Joined by those who had moved overland, skirmishing as they went, Winslow had marched over Tower Hill inland to storm the Narragansett stronghold on an island in the Great Swamp.

"When was this?" she asked him.

"In December. The swamp had frozen to ice and the troops marched in across it."

"But you were not there, were you, Philip?" she asked softly.

He flushed, sensing the censure in her voice. "Of course not! I told you, Rhode Island remains neutral, Lorraine!"

"Of course. Neutral—and burned to the ground." She smiled benignly upon Philip, but little lights danced in her blue-gray eyes.

Philip sensed uneasily that he had been found wanting and promptly launched into a spirited description of the Great Swamp Fight where some four thousand Indians, behind formidable fortifications, had caused heavy casualties before the wooden fortress they defended was set ablaze. It had taken three assaults to subdue it. The wounded had been transported to Newport. "But the war still rages," he told her. "None can tell when it will end."

He stopped as he noticed her regarding him oddly from the head of the table. She was very beautiful there in the candlelight, very desirable.

"Lorraine," he began, almost in desperation, "Lavinia and I were not right for each other—I guess you always knew that. From the moment I saw you, I knew—but I was fighting it, as would any man! Lavinia had become so jealous of you that she broke our engagement—and believe me, I felt nothing but relief when that happened, for I had been tricked into the betrothal in the first place and knew not how to escape."

Across from him Lorraine said nothing, but continued studying him.

"Lorraine, why did you not tell me of your good fortune?" he demanded. "Didn't you know that I would have been overjoyed for you?"

Lorraine's smile was deceptively bland. "But you would have insisted that we live in Rhode Island, Philip, where Livinia would forever have plagued me!"

"No, I would not!" he protested.

"Nonsense, of course you would. Eat your stewed turtle, Philip, you will find it delicious. Can you believe I have my own turtle crawls?"

He could believe anything in this topsy-turvy world into which he had been flung, where bound girls had coaches and racing colors!

"But who takes care of all this for you?"

"Nicholls does—and I am becoming more adept at handling business matters every day. These chairs, that sideboard, Philip—they are both products of the new furniture factory I have started."

He looked dazed. He swallowed the delicious food, but did not taste it. The little tavern maid he had seduced by trick in Rhode Island was gone—and in her place a princess of commerce had risen!

"How did you find me, Philip?"

"I overheard Captain Bowman tell his aunt that you were here."

"And possessed of a fine plantation, I have no doubt?" she added ironically.

"No, he said nothing like that—only that you were safe."

Philip had been too quick to protest and Lorraine gave him a mocking look. "Ah, don't deny it, Philip," she sighed. "Still . . . you have come a long way to find me." There was a soft note in her voice that a man who attracted women could not mistake.

"I would have brought you here in style had you but asked it!" he boasted.

"Would you indeed?" she murmured, and again those little lights danced in her eyes. "You must be sparing of the wine," she cautioned him, waving the serving girl away when he would have had his glass refilled. "There will be more wine—later. I would not have your senses dulled, Philip," she added demurely.

His heart leapt. The wench was leading him on!

"And now for dessert," she said mildly. "Perhaps we should enjoy that upon the veranda on such a night as this?"

Philip rose quickly to accompany her. Magic was in the air. Above them in the velvet blackness burned the brilliant white stars of the Southern Cross. The night was filled with tropical scents, witchlike, compelling. He took a deep breath. He had been afraid that all this newfound wealth would turn her away from him, but it was plain that it had not. Lorraine had always desired him and now she was making it clear that she desired him still! She would be his again! He would slip into the warmth of those soft remembered arms and feel again the unbelievably silky texture of her skin. He would woo her, he would win her—*and then all of this would be his!* She had been tantalizing him all through dinner, displaying her remarkable beauty, her elegance, her charm—and all the trappings that in his mind made up an aristocrat. Her mother had been an aristocrat, he recalled. Ah, this new sophisticated Lorraine would grace his home and his heart far better than Lavinia ever could!

"Lorraine," he said abruptly, reaching out in masterful fashion to take possession of her hand. "I am not hungry. Let us walk—I have something to tell you."

"Good, I am not hungry either," she said, lifting her hands to clap them, so as not to touch him.

She is afraid of me, he thought. *Afraid of what her senses will do to her if I touch her!* His chest expanded.

"We will stroll around the grounds, Philip. You may take those away," she told the servant who was bringing compotes of tropical fruits in silver saucers.

Lorraine kept her hands lightly clasped before her as they walked along the garden paths. Around them palm fronds whispered sensuously and the white flowers of the hibiscus glowed like pale moons in the darker shadows.

"Isn't this a romantic setting?" she asked him.

"It is your *true* setting, Lorraine," he told her warmly.

She shrugged her white shoulders. Her filmy white flounced gown floated out behind her, ethereal in starlight. "I suppose it is."

"Lorraine," he said huskily, "all could be the same between us. We could forget the past—be married right away."

She reached up to pluck a hibiscus blossom. "*Married?* Why?"

He was startled. "Why . . . because I love you, of course. That is what brought me down here!"

"Is it?" She gave him a fleeting glance. "I wonder. . . ."

They had come out now upon the green velvet of the lawn. Around them the huge old trees were mysterious in starlight.

"Oh, Lorraine, you know it was!" He would have taken her in his arms but she eluded him.

"No, Philip," she said gently. Her voice had a wistful quality. "Did you enjoy bathing in scented water in the green bedchamber, Philip, dining on silver and crystal and snowy damask?"

"Oh, yes," he sighed. "I truly did."

"Good. I am glad you did." Her voice had gone hard and she stepped back. Her eyes were blazing. "For it is the last you will ever see of any of it! Take him!"

From the shadows of the trees emerged half a dozen men, converging on Philip. They looked very intent.

Philip backed away from them. "What . . . what is this?" he cried. "Lorraine, have you lost your senses?"

"No, Philip—but you have just lost your freedom."

He was backing away toward the cliff overlooking the dark blue expanse of the Caribbean. The men were closer now. Lorraine moved along with them.

Philip had reached the edge. His voice took on a ragged quality. "Lorraine!" It had a sound of wild appeal.

"You have a choice now, Philip." She sounded bored. "You can either hurl yourself over the cliff—it's a hundred-foot drop to the bottom—or you can let these gentlemen take you."

Philip prudently chose the latter. His hands were bound under Lorraine's direction and a rope attached to those bonds.

"Why?" he cried in bewilderment. "Why are you doing this?"

Lorraine's faint smile played on her face. Only her mocking voice betrayed that she had become a woman of silk and steel.

"I am going to teach you humility, Philip."

She beckoned to the silent men who surrounded him. "Bring him along. If he resists, drag him. If he kicks at you, cuff him. Brook no resistance."

Philip did not resist. He went along with fear-crazed

eyes and a beating heart. Would this madwoman have him thrown into the fire or into a pit with snakes? He had heard evil things of the islands!

She had the men push him into the square forbidding room that had once been the old slave quarters, empty now, and affix the rope that bound his wrists to a ring in the wall.

"You will have plenty of room here," she announced. "Much more than in a cubbyhole in an attic. After all, twenty-two people used to sleep here before I came." She indicated with her foot the long low slab that ran down the middle of the room. "Each one had only that much width to sleep on—see how lucky you are, Philip? You will have *the entire room*. And tomorrow perhaps we will let you pluck some grasses and carry them in to form a pallet. You will need your sleep, for at first light you will be roused and taken to work in the canefields. Those clothes you're wearing won't be suitable. You will be given a straw hat and a pair of coarse cotton breeches. Oh, and boots too—the cane stubble, after it is hacked down, would cut your flesh like a knife. You will work from dawn until dusk, through the heat of the day—and then come back here. This is to be your life, Philip—get used to it."

The door to his prison clanged shut and one of the men inserted a heavy iron key, then handed it to the woman Philip now knew was to be his jailer.

"Sleep well," Lorraine caroled, and he heard their footsteps retreating.

He was left alone in the cell-like quarters where only a little light filtered in through a small window to relieve the darkness. The men who had bound him were more efficient than he had been in Rhode Island—he was unable to untie his bonds. Dawn found him slumped against the stone wall below the metal ring, still helpless.

The other men got him up, offered him some coarse bread and water, threw a straw hat and hacked-off cotton trousers and boots at him, and marched him to the canefields, where he joined others who looked at his askance.

In midmorning the mistress of the manor rode up to

inspect the cane. Lorraine breezed by Philip without recognition, exchanged pleasantries with her overseer, and rode on. Philip followed her with eyes filled with dull rage.

Sunburned and exhausted, he stumbled home.

Lorraine chose to visit him that night. She talked to him through the iron bars of his window that faced toward the house.

"I fear you are not used to such strong rays of the sun," she said in a lightly pitying voice. "Tomorrow we must remember to provide you with a loose cotton shirt."

"Spare me your pity," he croaked.

She laughed. "I do not pity you, Philip. I just do not want to incapacitate a good field hand. The overseer tells me you show promise."

"The overseer be damned!"

"And spirit too," she mocked. "It seemed cruel to keep you boxed in by shrubbery as you were last night, so today I have had a great bush removed so that you may look out your window. I bid you good night."

"Go to the devil," mumbled Philip.

Tired though he was, his curiosity impelled him to look out that window when a faint light shone down through it. And he beheld a vision.

The "viewpoint" in the shrubbery had been arranged with precision. From his window Philip could see the great double casements of Lorraine's bedchamber, open now to the soft night air. The hangings blowing at her window were of sheerest white cambric, almost transparent, and there was a strong light behind it. And there, against that light behind that sheer rippling curtain, Lorraine was undressing, pausing to stretch luxuriously, throwing back her head with her long lovely hair tossing about, combing it out. Her body was presented in silhouette—but what a silhouette! The vivid detail of every lovely line of her was etched into his very soul.

Despite himself, despite his anger, despite his deep fatigue, Philip felt a wild desire to break out, to fling himself through that gossamer curtain and crash to the floor with her and ravish her.

Damn her witchery! It had him in thrall again! Oh, why had he carried her home to Lavinia? Why had he not borne her to his bed that night in Yorktown, brought her to heel! That was where he had erred, by not forcing Lorraine into submission *before* he took her aboard the *Lizard*.

Lorraine moved again behind that blowing curtain. She stretched up her arms and whirled around, making a delectable display of her lovely slim torso and legs.

Philip groaned and fell back from the window.

The next day was the same for him—work and misery.

And the next night—torment and desire.

Several times after that Lorraine rode through the canefields and each time either ignored Philip or regarded him with distaste, but never again did she speak to him before the men.

By the end of the week Lorraine had tired of her sport, and regretted that Philip had ever come to Barbados. She had the shrubbery that had been dug up moved back so that Philip was cut off from his nightly agony. But by that time word had buzzed about that the beautiful mistress of Venture had a runaway bondservant she had brought back so that she might torment him—with her body!

In made juicy gossip around Bridgetown, although no one dared to confront Lorraine with it. She was too rich, too sought-after, on too close terms with the governor. Who knew to what pinnacle the shipwrecked heiress might not rise?

Meantime, Lorraine's social life was flourishing.

The governor had asked her to dine with him several times. By now, all Bridgetown was buzzing over the governor's new "lady." Two of Lorraine's suitors took umbrage.

"He is too old for you." Reggie Dorset scowled, striking a dramatic pose against the cold fireplace in Venture's drawing room—a pose meant to show Lorraine what a fine figure he cut in his new striped waistcoat and garnet coat.

"I did not inquire his age, but I am told he is a duelist of renown," she added on a warning note.

"You see too much of him. People will talk," Reggie grumbled.

Lorraine brushed that aside, just as she brushed aside Hal Pomeroy's, "Our governor is known to be a rake—indeed no woman is safe with him."

She was gentler with Will Shelby, who warned, "You will live to regret him," and gave her a wounded look.

"What is this reputation you have?" she challenged the governor the next time they were alone—this time at Venture, where he had ridden for tea on a pleasant afternoon. "I visit Government House unescorted a few times, and everybody looks at me as if I am a fallen woman!"

"My reputation is deserved, I fear," he said wryly. "But I had not meant my vices to rub off on you." He was leaning back, regarding her with a lazy, somewhat wistful look. "Perhaps you will favor me with a game of whist? And tomorrow we might ride out together for all Bridgetown to see."

He watched her deal the cards, observed her game without comment. When they had finished, he said, "I see you take your cards seriously."

"I had once thought to make my living gaming," she admitted.

He threw back his head and laughed. "You will never cease to amaze me, Lorraine!" He rose to go. "Tomorrow then?"

"You are giving me a very bad reputation in the town," she told him humorously. "By showering all this attention on me."

His whole demeanor changed.

"Let them condemn you to my face, by God!" he said through his teeth. "And I'll spit their gizzards for them!"

"Is that how it is done in England?" she mocked him. "Those who vie for a lady's favor spit each other's gizzards?"

"Sometimes," he admitted, and moved restively. "I

will not stay longer, Mistress Lorraine—lest tongues wag undeservedly about you."

He bowed and left her to puzzle about him.

The next day they rode about the town in broad daylight, along Broad Street, up Swan Street. People turned to stare at the dazzling couple, the governor dramatic in black and silver, Lorraine in black-and-silver riding habit to match his. Her own coat cuffs were almost as wide, the froth of Mechlin at her throat and cuffs as frosty.

"I am suffocating in this tight riding habit," she said. "It makes me envy those women in their loose cotton dresses carrying baskets on their heads. Tell me, do you not sometimes envy those laborers with their wide straw hats and loose cotton breeches?"

"Sometimes," he laughed. "But on the whole I would rather rule them."

She turned to meet his sapphire gaze narrowly and for a mad instant she thought of Philip, laboring in her canefields. "Perhaps—so would I," she murmured.

They reined in their horses as a group of slaves fresh from one of the ships at the Careenage was marched to the market, clanking their chains. They were Indians. Lorraine had seen their kind often, walking on moccasins down the streets of Providence. It reminded her how relentless the Connecticut men had been in their pursuit of the marauders who had burned and murdered their way through New England. The colonists had taken hundreds of prisoners, many of whom had been sent to the West Indies to be sold as slaves. These Indians, she knew, were some of them.

The governor noted how coldly her gaze brushed over the shackled men as they shuffled past. With a sweep of his arm he indicated the Indians.

"I am surprised that with your passion for freedom, you do not immediately demand that all of these prisoners be set free."

Lorraine glanced again at the dusty line of newcomers trudging along stolidly in the heat. "Those are Narragansetts and Wampanoags," she murmured, recognizing distinctive articles of apparel from both tribes.

"Aye," he said humorously. "Like many an Englishman who fought against Cromwell, their sentences of death were commuted to a life of slavery. Connecticut and Massachusetts have sent them here to us to till the canefields. These poor savages are getting the same punishment we'd mete out to an Englishman for far lesser crimes! Still I am surprised," he added, "that you aren't rushing forward to buy them all—so you can set them free!"

Lorraine thought of kindly Mistress Bowman, whose whole family had been murdered, of the Jarvises, and Matthew Stokes, and Mary Wickham and the Rawson children and the MacAldies and oh, so many others in strictly neutral Rhode Island who had been murdered by marauding Indians—possibly by some of these very prisoners—and her young face hardened.

"They mean only terror to me," she muttered, and the man beside her sighed.

"You are a strange paradox," he said. "I wonder what has made you so?"

She gave him a bleak look. "Circumstance has made me what I am."

"But isn't that true of us all?" was his rejoinder.

"Perhaps for some more than others," was her cryptic response. "Are you through displaying me to the town?"

"Is that what I have been doing?"

"Of course it is!"

"Perhaps I have," he murmured, and turned his horse about to head back toward Venture. Halfway there he turned to her. "Lorraine, as governor of this island, it is my duty to give occasional balls and other parties—a duty I have thus far shirked. I have asked you to ride with me today that I might put the question: Will you do me the honor of becoming my official hostess?"

"I cannot live in," she quipped. And at his frown, "I cannot believe you are serious," she reproved him lightly. "I have neither the social graces nor the wit—"

"Your social graces are more than adequate," he overbore her objections. "And if someone by chance should overwhelm you with his erudition—though, I cannot offhand think who on this island would be capable of it!—your beauty will stand you in good stead. Just fix those big lustrous eyes on him and he will forget what he is saying!"

For the first time the thought flitted through Lorraine's mind: *He is paying court to me. . . .*

"You may regret having asked me when I do the wrong thing!" she warned.

"Nonsense, I will school you in anything you may lack!" He sounded impatient—not at all like a lover.

Lorraine studied him. A very complex man, she decided. One who might take his choice of the unmarried girls of this island—yet he had chosen none. And apparently he had had his choice in London—and discarded them all.

Why did he choose *her!* She was mystified. And being mystified made her restive.

She thought of Philip in the slave quarters and came to a sudden decision. That night she walked back and called to him, saw his face appear at his small barred window.

"I am tired of you," she said. "I am thinking of sending you back to Lavinia. But first you must give me back my articles of indenture."

"Never," said Philip instantly. He had toughened in the canefields, he was growing wiry and hard.

"As you wish." He could almost hear the shrug in her voice. "You will remain here forever if you like."

A week later, when she asked him again, Philip had had time to reconsider. Bitterly he watched a spider walk down the wall of his cell, briefly appearing in the striped light cast by the bars of the window. He threw his boot at it.

Came her voice from outside: "I will ask you again, Philip—but it is the last time. Next time you must come to me as a supplicant."

"I tell you I do not have your articles. I buried them in a box in Rhode Island."

"Where you can get them at your pleasure?"

"Yes, if you will allow me to leave!"

He heard her low laugh. "You would be back—but with a warrant for my arrest for abduction."

It was what he had had in mind. But he protested

instantly that it was not. "I would give you my word," he insisted.

Lorraine's voice had grown suddenly weary. "I would not believe you under oath, Philip, but I do not want you near me. So tomorrow you will be moved to my outlying plantation on the Atlantic shore of the island. Your work will be no lighter there but it may be that if you are diligent you will be given special privileges by my overseer. I bid you good night, Philip."

"Curse you for a witch!" he muttered.

Lorraine heard that and laughed.

The next morning Philip was loaded into a cart along with a number of tools and hauled to the place she had named Petit Venture. There he worked in new canefields—alongside workmen new to him. And there Philip began to voice his discontent.

"If you speak ill of the mistress to the others, I will have to isolate you," the elderly overseer warned him sternly.

"Why?" snarled Philip. "Is her reputation then so fragile?"

"No," was the sober response. "But those men believe her to be the best mistress in the world and they might do you an injury if you spoke against her."

Philip did not believe it and later spoke against her in most inflammatory terms. He was promptly knocked down by the big fellow nearest him. Looking up in dismay, he saw others were moving toward him with angry faces.

The overseer stepped in front of them. "None of that," he said. "The mistress has said that she does not want him hurt." He turned to Philip. "I warned you not to speak against her. She has given us all a chance to live again. Now I will have to isolate you. At least by night. In the daytime you should be safe enough. There is a small hut atop the cliff. The door has a stout lock on it and the window shutter a stout chain that will not permit a man to crawl in or out of it—but at least you will get the breeze from the sea there, you will not suffocate!"

Philip took this new indignity in sullen silence. But

he had not been there long before it occurred to him what he must do.

The kindly overseer had provided him with a lantern and had lent him a Bible that he might read if he chose. Philip was in no mood to read holy words. He studied the shutter. It opened on the Atlantic side, and down below was the sea. He was alone. If only he could entice some passing ship to show interest . . . perchance to send someone up to investigate the source of a swinging light?

And so every night Philip slid the lantern through the opening below the heavy slanted wooden shutter where it swung away from the solid limestone building—and swung it so that its light would flash far out to sea.

He was so in the habit of it that he even did it on a squally night when the stars were obscured and the reef below a turmoil of white water. To his credit, he was no seaman and did not know about the reef—nor had anyone thought to tell him. After all, they did not know that he was endeavoring to signal ships at sea!

Through the squall a fishing skiff, the *Flying Fish*, had lost her way and was coming home late. Her captain mistook Philip's waving lantern for the lights of Bridgetown and piled up on the reef. The ship broke in half and although by a miracle the crew made it to shore through the wild water, the *Flying Fish* was no more.

Indignant and half-drowned, the ship's captain stared up at the light. But Philip had stopped swinging it and pulled it back inside. Still, Captain Mannering had marked well where the light had been.

"What is this place?" he muttered.

"It looks to be Petit Venture," gasped one of his crew, choking on seawater as he joined his captain on the wild beach. "Bought by the shipwrecked heiress not too long ago."

"Well, she's a wrecker then!"

"Don't be daft, man. She lives on t'other side of the island!"

"If this place be hers, then 'tis her responsibility and I'll have satisfaction!"

"You'll not get it. 'Tis said she's the governor's doxy."

"I'll have it nonetheless!"

But when he reached Government House, Captain Mannering lost his nerve. He turned about and made for a waterfront tavern, where he began to drink—and to tell the story of his lost ship to anybody who would listen.

Soon ugly rumors were flying about. The shipwrecked heiress had not come by her money in the usual way— the shipwrecked heiress was a wrecker.

And now she was plying her trade in Barbados.

CHAPTER 31

THE BALL AT Government House was in full swing.
There had been a storm the day before—the very
storm that had wrecked the *Flying Fish*—but the clouds
had blown away and now the stars were out. Perfect
weather for the magnificent affair.

Standing beside the tall dramatic figure of the governor, Lorraine, looking equally dramatic in white silk
with silver slashed sleeves and a deep-cut silver embroidered bodice, was pleased to see several of Bridgetown's ladies were in a state of shock.

"Where did she get that dress? Do you think it
came from Paris?" asked one breathlessly.

"No, 'twas stitched up by the sempstress who does
my gowns. I came in as it was being fitted. I wonder
why *mine* never look like that?"

"It is a scandal, the governor displaying his doxy
like this for all to see!" exploded pretty young Mistress Phipps, who had just flounced away from the
receiving line and was now shaking out her black-lace-
trimmed magenta skirts. She had designs on the handsome governor, herself.

"Oh, do be quiet, Mollie, she'll hear you!" pleaded
her mother.

"I don't care if she does hear me," muttered Mollie
Phipps, turning on her mother. "And besides, that's
what *you* called her!"

"Yes, but not in the governor's house," moaned her mother in an agonized tone.

"*I* do not believe she is what she says she is." Mollie tossed her head. "There is a story spreading in the town that she is a wrecker and that that is why she bought that small plantation she now calls Petit Venture—to ply her trade!"

There were gasps from the little knot of women fluttering their ivory fans around Mollie.

"But Mistress London does not *live* at Petit Venture," protested Mollie's best friend, Jane, a sallow young lady in pale green sarcenet.

"She does not have to!" Mollie's voice overrode Jane's triumphantly. "She has her infamous slave residing in a hut atop the cliff. There is a captain in the town who swears a light was flashed from that clifftop last night to make him think he had reached Bridgetown and safety!"

"What happened?" came a chorus of voices.

"His ship was wrecked on the reef below!"

"And *her* people plundered it?" asked Jane, awed.

"Well . . . no," Mollie admitted uncomfortably. "It was a fishing vessel and I am told the men at Petit Venture rescued the crew from the rocks where the tide might have swept them away, and sent them on by cart to Bridgetown, where they arrived late this afternoon. But how could the man who flashed the light know what kind of ship he would snare? Why could it not have been a merchant vessel or a galleon carrying pieces of eight?"

There was a general buzz at that suggestion, for it opened up interesting possibilities.

"Mistress London claims to be from Cornwall," Mollie said darkly. "And Cornwall is noted for its cliffs and treacherous rocks *and shipwrecks!*"

"Oh, dear," moaned her perspiring and frumpy mother, who was wearing one of young Mollie's made-over ball gowns. "If you say anything at all rude to her, we will never be invited to Government House again—and you know how much you wanted to come!"

"I care for justice more!" flared Mollie, lifting her rather pointy chin into the air. "Even if it costs me!"

she added with a righteous air, and shook out her amber curls.

The story circulated in whispers around the room, all but eclipsing the news from Virginia. But Lorraine was more concerned about it.

The rebellion had been crushed. Bacon was dead, his estate confiscated along with Drummond's. Lawrence and Whaley had disappeared into the frozen swamps and were presumed dead, Drummond had been caught and forthwith hanged, as had many others. Men were living in fear in Virginia; it was said many had hidden out in the snowy forests. Three king's commissioners had been sent to Virginia. Finding Governor Berkeley adamant, they had made the mistake of appealing to Lady Frances, now back at Green Spring, to help stop the wave of hangings sweeping the colony—and Lady Frances had sought to return them in a hangman's coach!

It saddened Lorraine to hear the report, and deep in her heart it frightened her too. What had happened to Raile? She was not really her most alert self when later, in a break during the dancing, Mollie Phipps cornered her as she was leaving the dance floor.

"Mistress London, where did you live in Cornwall?" asked Mistress Phipps innocently.

"Near Wyelock. Our house was on a cliff overlooking the sea," Lorraine said, for she had become adroit at giving vague or evasive answers when questioned about her background. And to turn the conversation away from such dangerous channels: "Perhaps that is why I chose Venture—because the house stands high on a cliff overlooking the sea. I really think that the view—"

"Oh, *do* tell us what your home in Cornwall was like," interrupted Mollie's friend Jane.

"It was quite large and I suppose the exterior was rather plain—but of course I loved it. I shall hope that at Venture—"

But young Mistress Phipps and her coterie were not to be swerved. "Oh, do describe the interior of your home in Cornwall," she caroled. "And the grounds!

For none of us have ever been to Cornwall." She indicated her friends.

Thus trapped, Lorraine launched into what she remembered from descriptions of her mother's home in Cornwall. How glad she was that her mother had talked about it so often on long snowy evenings in Rhode Island!

"And your father?" pursued Mollie Phipps. "Did he take you to London? Were you presented to the king?"

They would trap her if she tried to describe London, for she had never been there and half the people in this room had. Mollie Phipps had actually spent her childhood in London.

"I have never been to London," Lorraine told them. "And I certainly was never presented at court. But you must remember that I was very small when my parents died—"

"Mistress London, are you saying that your father did not side with the king?" asked Mollie Phipps in mock horror.

"Really, Mollie!" murmured her mother, shocked.

Lorraine drew herself up. "My parents did not agree on politics," she said coldly. "It is something I never talk about."

"Indeed she has been talking herself hoarse," interposed the governor, who had come up and was listening to this interchange. "I propose that she dance with me instead, for the music is striking up!"

Mollie Phipps glowered as he led Lorraine out onto the floor.

"Bravo!" he whispered in her ear when he had the opportunity. "Your description of Cornwall was flawless. One could almost be persuaded that you had been there!"

Lorraine's heart missed a beat. She looked up into a pair of wicked laughing eyes.

"When . . . how did you know?"

He whirled her out upon the veranda before he answered.

"I realized you had never been there when you agreed that Wyelock lay between Helston and Penzance—it does not. And again when you agreed that Wyelock overlooked St. Ives Bay."

"It does not?" She sighed.

"I have traveled a bit, you see." He gazed upon her curiously. And then he asked, as if it were of no importance but merely to satisfy his curiosity. "Where *are* you from, Mistress London? For you are assuredly not from Cornwall!"

"I am from Rhode Island," she said, looking into his dark sapphire eyes with a level gaze.

"Then why not say so?" he challenged.

"I have . . . compelling reasons not to say so."

He looked mystified. "Mysteries intrigue me," he murmured humorously. "I will get to the bottom of this."

"No, pray do not!" she said sharply. "I would prefer people to think I come from Cornwall."

He shook his head—but he laughed. "In my view, you have come from heaven—a shining light to dazzle us here in Barbados!"

It was a gallant speech and it gave Lorraine hope that he would keep her secret.

"Do not tell me that your intentions are honorable?" she quipped lightly. "For I will never believe it!"

"Mistress Lorraine," he said, lifting her hand and leaning over it to brush it with his lips in courtly fashion, "my intentions toward you are *entirely* honorable!"

She gave him a sidewise look and would have said something outrageous, but Will Shelby came out onto the veranda just then. "Ah, there you are, Lorraine," he cried. "I have been looking for you everywhere to claim you for the next dance—you promised it to me, you know!"

"So I did!" Lorraine glided away from the governor and accompanied the triumphant Will out on the floor. He was an energetic dancer, making up in enthusiasm what he lacked in grace. Lorraine felt they cut a very comical figure out there on the floor with Will's wildly overdone gestures, but he was so whole-souled about it and she liked him so much that she consented to dance with him again despite the disappointed glances of a little knot of would-be partners who waited to claim her the moment Will led her from the floor.

"Oh, Mistress Lorraine," cried Will rapturously, "does this mean that you *favor* me?"

"No, it means I am grateful to you for coming over so faithfully in the mornings and teaching me to ride!" She laughed. "And I promise to save you another dance later this evening for the same reason!"

Will was a little dashed at that, but he was an exuberant young man and it did not last.

"You could do worse than young Shelby, you know," the governor told her when he again claimed her for a dance. "He will never have a courtier's graces but he has a fine sound plantation and he is most besotted!"

"Besotted or not, I prefer . . . a different kind of man. And I already have a fine sound plantation myself!"

"A different kind of man?" echoed the governor. He looked as if that were very instructive. "Pray describe the kind of man you prefer."

The dance bore her a step backward from him at that moment and she cast a measuring eye up and down his long figure.

"I do not require that a man be tall," she said, and he winced slightly. *But Raile had been tall,* she thought wistfully. "Nor yet"—she studied the elegance of his black-and-silver garb—"that he be handsomely got up." *But Raile had looked wonderful, whatever he wore!*

"Mistress Lorraine," murmured the governor whimsically, "is this in the nature of a set-down?"

"What I do require," she continued tranquilly, "is that he be a man of force and character and judgment, that he be strong and resolute, a man of quick decision and . . ."

She stopped. She was describing Raile. Except perhaps for "character"—look how he had treated her!

"Oh, don't stop!" pleaded the governor, intrigued. "Tell me, have you found such a man?"

"Twice," she said.

"Then why do we find you here alone and single?"

"One that I might have loved, had things been

different, was married. And I have just learned to-night that he is dead."

The governor stared down at her. All the room was abuzz with the news of the death of the rebel leader in Virginia.

"Could it be that you are speaking of Nathaniel Bacon?" he asked softly.

Lorraine gave him a tormented look. "He was very kind to me at Green Spring," she defended. "I was thought to be a spy for the king, but General Bacon let me go!"

"I can see why he might let you go," said the governor caressingly. He had whirled her from the dance floor into the library and now he closed the door. "So that is why you wish us to believe you are from Cornwall? You were mixed up in the rebellion in Virginia?"

"No, I was not mixed up in it. I happened to be there when they burned Jamestown, and Bacon carried me away to Green Spring. And sent me to Yorktown the next day. It was not a love affair, in case you are thinking that."

"Then the other cavalier must be the one who has broken your heart?"

Lorraine flinched. Did it really show so badly?

"The 'other cavalier,' " she said bitterly, "was an adventurer and a Scot. I was his mistress," she added defensively. He might as well know that now! "And I would have sailed to hell with him. . . ." She was looking sadly out at some distant vista. "But he preferred another woman. He . . . left me."

"What appalling bad taste!" murmured the governor, but there was sympathy in those cynical eyes. *How could any man leave her?*

To Lorraine's embarrassment, her own eyes had filled with tears. "Oh, I do not want to talk about him," she whispered huskily.

"Then this 'adventurer' who sailed away with you has been your only love?" His voice was meditative.

"Oh, no," she said in a wry uneven voice. "I spent my early years adoring a man who never intended to marry me, who followed me to Yorktown and knocked me unconscious and kidnapped me. He dragged me through Providence at the end of a rope, and helped his betrothed tie me up in an attic and suggested she teach me humility—with a whip!" He might as well know *all* about her now that confessions were the order of the day!

"Kidnapping is a serious offense," he protested. "Were you not able to bring him to heel by law?"

"The law was on his side! For he had bought my articles of indenture from an innkeeper. I was his bondservant and he said he would do what he liked with me!"

"Faith, I should like to meet this lad," murmured the governor with a dark, cold tone in his voice.

"You have," she told him in a wooden voice. "The day we rode through my canefields. His name is Philip and he arrived on my doorstep thinking to win me back now that I've come into a fortune. I remembered how badly he had treated me and I decided *to teach him humility!*"

The governor remembered riding beside Lorraine through the canefields and how she had looked back at a sulky bondservant and said, "He is receiving a lesson in humility." Astonishment broke over his countenance, and he gave a shout of laughter.

"Lorraine, you never cease to astound me!" he gasped. "You are indeed a wonder! You flit from place to place. You scorn the law and exact poetic justice!"

"I do not scorn the law! It is the law that scorns me! Philip Dedwinton would not allow me to buy back my papers with the fortune Benjamin Nicholls brought back from China for me."

"But I thought Nicholls was your guardian?"

"He is my agent who passes himself off as my guardian. My mother used to receive small sums from time to time—they were bequests, she told me, from distant relatives who had died and mentioned her in their wills. My father always got drunk at such times and usually managed to squander most of the money on 'ventures' that always came to naught. One time it was ginseng, which Nicholls would take to China and sell.

By the time Nicholls came back, my mother had died, my father had indentured me and vanished into the West."

A melancholy look passed over his face. "Distant relatives . . ." he murmured. "Lorraine, I know Cornwall well. I believe I knew your mother. Could her name have been Araminta—"

"Dunning," she supplied instantly.

"Yes," he murmured. "Araminta Dunning. . . ." He looked out past her through the windows at some other vista where the Southern Cross had been absent from the night sky.

"Did you know my mother well?" Lorraine was fascinated, hoping to hear about the young Araminta, through the eyes of one of her contemporaries.

He nodded soberly. "I remember the last time I saw her," he said in a wistful voice. "We were standing on the beach below the cliffs of Cornwall and the Green Flash suddenly flooded the sky. In that light her eyes were like emeralds. . . ."

The Green Flash! It was a good thing that he was not looking at her, for Lorraine's face was so shocked that her expression was almost comical. *Her mother had seen the Green Flash only once—and with a man upon a beach in Cornwall.* The governor was the man Araminta Dunning had loved all her life long—not the man she had married! No wonder she had chosen a time when Jonas London was away to tell Lorraine about the Green Flash! No wonder when Lorraine had repeated her mother's disjointed dying words to Jonas— "Tell him I still love him . . . The Green Flash. . ."— Jonas had listened woodenly and turned away. No wonder he had drunk so much, no wonder he had deserted her—she would have reminded him of her mother. It must have been very hard indeed to know all those years that the woman he worshipped did not love him—at least not wildly, passionately, the way she had once loved someone else. . . .

Lorraine moistened her lips. "Am I very like . . ." She tried to keep her voice from shaking, for this revelation had rocked her. "Am I very like my mother?"

He turned and faced her squarely. There was a glint

in his eyes. "No," he said quietly. "I think you are more like me."

There it was, flung down between them. The shining impossible truth. This man for whom she felt such easy camaraderie, with whom she was so much at ease, *was her father.* Her real father.

For long moments she stood stunned, staring at him.

"When did you first know I was your daughter?" she whispered.

"I think I knew it the moment I first looked into your eyes," he admitted. "They were so clear, so honest—so like Araminta's." He spoke that loved name like a caress. "And then when you told me your name—for I had followed your mother's fortunes, you see—I thought it might be. But when you told me you were from Wyelock—and then knew nothing about the countryside there, when you told me your age and your birth month—then I was certain."

"You speak my mother's name as if you loved her," she choked.

"I did," he said simply. "With all my heart."

"Then why did you not come for her?" she demanded brokenly. "She loved you all her life. *Her dying words were for you!* She said, *'Tell him I still love him . . . the Green Flash . . .'* Why didn't you come for her?"

Her eyes blazed.

"Lorraine," he said, "I left Wyelock when the man I had fought a duel with—over your mother's good name—chose to die. I was a Royalist in a land where Cromwell ruled. I had no choice but to flee the country. I was shipwrecked on the Irish coast and by the time I got back to Wyelock, your mother had disappeared and no one knew where she had gone." He sighed. "I was very bitter that she had left no word for me, and I threw myself into the king's cause with redoubled energy. When King Charles was restored to the throne, he wanted to 'give' me an heiress in marriage that I might be wealthy. But instead I married a penniless young girl from Sussex whose father had died fighting in the cause. She had no one to take care of her and she was very frail."

A new siae to him, surely. Lorraine had not quite envisioned him as a protector of the weak.

"Eventually I learned that your mother had married had gone to Rhode Island to live. I could not in honor leave Mary, nor do I think your mother would have left the man she had married, to come away with me."

Lorraine was not so certain. She remembered her mother's unhappiness with Jonas London.

"You could have written," she said reproachfully.

"I did write her letters, Lorraine, and she answered them—although she never told me about you. And all during those long years when Mary was ill, wasting away, I sent her . . . ." He hesitated.

More knowledge broke over Lorraine. "*You* are the one who sent the money!" she gasped. "Not distant relatives dying and leaving my mother little bequests!"

He sighed. "From time to time I sent her a little money, for I knew she needed it. It was the best I could do. I was not rich and I had other commitments. Mary was dying."

"So it was *your* money Jonas London used to buy the ginseng!" she marveled. "And gained me a hundred thousand pounds!"

"A handsome gift," he said softly. "From a man who loved your mother. I could not have given you so much."

"You have given me something else this night," Lorraine told him tremulously. *"A real father."*

"Yes," he said. "I wanted to get to know you first, and I am proud of you. Now, it is my intention to claim you as my lawful child."

The bastard daughter of the rakehell governor! Lorraine was caught somewhere between laughter and tears.

"You will make of us a fine scandal!" she warned mistily.

"I have weathered scandals before. Had I known of you, I would have claimed you before, but now I will proclaim to all the world that here is my long-lost daughter and I will have the records amended, damned if I won't, so that you shall be not only my child but also my heir!"

"Can you do all that?" she wondered.

His jaw had a set to it that would not be brooked.

"I *will* do it!" His voice rang. "I will do it now!" He seized her by the hand and whisked her to the door, opened it upon the ballroom where the dancers were whirling about the floor.

"Stop playing!" he thundered. And when the music had faltered to a halt and the guests had stopped dancing and were regarding him with openmouthed wonder, he indicated Lorraine with a dramatic gesture. "I would present to you my long-lost daughter— Lady Lorraine Rawlings!"

Across the room Mollie Phipps fainted.

CHAPTER 32

THE MORNING AFTER the ball, an emissary arrived at Petit Venture and demanded in the name of the governor to see the bondservant Philip Dedwinton. The overseer watched openmouthed as that emissary promptly drew a pistol and leveled it at Philip.

"My orders are, if you give me any trouble or attempt to escape, I am to shoot you," he said briefly. "Would you care to accompany me?"

Philip was in no position to appreciate the irony of that tone. He had heard the shouts, the cries of "There's a ship breaking up down on the reef!" And it had come to him suddenly how it might have happened. He had pretended sleep when they had come banging on his door—and later feigned outraged innocence.

But it was a long way to Bridgetown, riding just ahead of someone who had orders to shoot you if you made a false move. Philip's relief was mingled with fear as they drew up before Government House.

All the way there he had been rehearsing the impassioned story he would tell about how Lorraine had held him captive. If he could just enlist the governor's sympathy!

Still the other matter weighed upon him and his face reflected a lively terror when he was brought in over echoing stone floors before the governor, who sat resplendent in black and silver before a small writing desk atop a gleaming mahogany table.

The figure before him was so impressive that Philip felt his resolve melt.

"I can explain about the light!" he cried on a note of desperation.

"The light?" echoed the governor, raising an eyebrow. His face showed none of the bewilderment he felt.

"The lantern on the cliffs that wrecked the *Flying Fish.*"

"Ah, yes." The governor stifled a yawn with a fine cambric kerchief, lace-edged. "*That* light, tell me about it."

"I swung the lantern only to alert the captain of some passing ship that I was there and needed help. I never meant to wreck anyone!"

The governor's dark brows drew together. "And yet I am told that you lived along the seacoast of America—the Rhode Island Colony, I believe. How could you live there and *not* know that a lantern is a beacon by night and in time of storm?"

"I am a farmer—not a sailor. I lived inland near a river."

"But what was the urgency? Why wave this lantern?" The governor lifted a jeweled snuffbox, delicately took a pinch of snuff.

Philip leaned forward. He had the governor's ear at last! "Because I have been held a prisoner here against my will by that . . . that she devil at Venture!"

"Ah, yes, the she devil of Venture—we will get to her. But meantime there is a serious charge against you." There was no charge at all, but Philip did not know that. "You are charged with wrecking a ship, and by way of that, attempted murder."

Philip's face paled beneath its dark newfound tan. "What am I to do?" he cried.

"You might begin by telling me about the she devil. I think you may be right about her. . . ." He paused as hope lit up Philip's worried countenance. "Suppose you tell me how you came to know her, your various dealings. Since I find you in poor case, one would hope that at times you had bested her. Am I right?"

Philip felt that beneath that black silk coat with its

gleaming array of silver buttons beat a kindred heart. "Indeed I did," he boasted—and told the governor about the wager.

The governor was considering his snuffbox in a rather fixed manner. "Go on," he said softly. "Surely that was not your only dealing with this wench?"

Philip went on. The entire story surged out of him. It was a relief to tell it. He felt very aggrieved—look what Lorraine had done to him! And with so little provocation!

When he had finished, the governor sat silent. There was an expression of sadness on his face but his sadness was for the desperate little bound girl with nowhere to turn.

Philip waited hopefully for the governor to look up. But when he did, those cold sapphire eyes held a leaping fury that caused him to take a step backward and look about him for escape.

"You lured a ship to its doom—the evidence against you is plain. Men are hanged on this island for less."

Philip trembled.

"But I am inclined to be merciful since it seems you did not understand. If you do not care to swing from a gibbet, you will write what I now dictate—you can write, can't you?"

"Yes, passably," Philip mumbled. He moved toward the inkwell and parchment on another slanted little writing desk, sat down on a small ornate wooden chair, and picked up the goose-quill pen.

"*I, Philip Dedwinton,*" dictated the governor as he strode back and forth across the room, his hands clasped behind him and studying the floor, "*Do make and depose the following which I swear before God and the Governor of Barbados to be the whole truth: I alone and without the aid or knowledge of any other person did light and swing the lantern that brought the* Flying Fish *to her doom but I did it without malice and I do heartily regret my action.*"

Laboriously, for he was no hand at penmanship, Philip completed the document.

"Now sign it," said the governor kindly.

Philip affixed his signature. Delicately the governor

took the parchment from him, read it, and tossed it upon his desk.

"You have just signed your life away, Dedwinton," he said with a mirthless laugh.

Philip staggered to his feet. He had been tricked into signing a confession. He lunged toward the desk but the governor's silver-buckled black leather shoe tripped him up and sent him sprawling upon the hard stone floor. As the governor stood over him, Philip quailed. Yet when he spoke, that formidable figure's tone was almost placating.

"I would like to own this she devil of Venture," he murmured. "You tell me you hold her articles of indenture?"

"They are back in Rhode Island," said Philip eagerly, for he could see a way out of his difficulties.

A faint smile crossed the governor's chiseled features. "I will not trouble you to go and get them," he murmured. "But would you sell them to me?"

Philip hesitated, cupidity creeping into his manner. "She is very valuable," he said tentatively. "If you would let me go—"

"Ah, yes." The governor's wolfish smile flashed. "But remember there is also the matter of reparations for the *Flying Fish*. There was no loss of life, but the ship is a complete loss and you alone are responsible."

Philip swallowed. "Could you give me enough for Lorraine's articles to pay for that loss?"

"I might," sighed the governor. "Write as I direct you:

"I, Philip Dedwinton, late of Rhode Island Colony, do hereby swear before God and in the presence of the Governor of Barbados that I have lost the articles of indenture that I hold on the person of one Lorraine London, late of the same colony, and that I hereby sell all of my right and interest in those articles to Lord Rawlings, Governor of Barbados, in recompense for which the governor promises to indemnify the owner of the Flying Fish, *the loss of which I caused by illegally lighting a lantern and swinging it upon the clifftop by night.*

"I further swear that my employment at Venture was

also of my own free will, for which I was well paid, and was meant to be an object lesson to the staff of said Venture."

Philip looked up openmouthed. "But that would absolve Lorraine!" he cried, outraged.

"Just so," said the governor roughly. "Do you think a man in my position can afford to have charges brought against my female bondservant? Or perhaps you have the gold in your pocket to pay for the *Flying Fish?*"

Visions of debtors' prison loomed before Philip. Sitting irresolute at the inkwell, he crumpled. Obediently he wrote the statement and signed it. The governor took charge of the paper.

"I take it," he said thoughtfully, "that you are eager to leave Barbados and return to Rhode Island?"

Philip nodded vigorously.

"I also take it that you have no funds for passage there?"

Philip made a strangled sound in his throat.

"Then write as follows: *I, Philip Dedwinton, late of Rhode Island and now of the island of Barbados, do, in consideration of receiving ship's passage from Barbados to Rhode Island, hereby indenture myself to Lord Rawlings, presently Governor of Barbados, for a period of seven years."*

Philip's shoulders jerked. He looked up nervously.

"Never mind, I shall not hold you to it," sighed the governor. "Your ship awaits you in the harbor. Just sign it."

Philip hesitated for an agonized moment—then he signed.

"And now you will acknowledge your signature and that this is your writing." The governor struck his hands together and the door opened to let in two sober-looking gentleman in dark clothing, who bowed gravely to the governor. "This gentleman is Philip Dedwinton. He wishes to acknowledge that these are his statements and that they are the truth—and that this is his signature on each. Is that not so, Dedwinton?"

"Yes," said Philip wearily. "They are written in my own hand and they are the truth and that is my signature on each of them."

"You are both witnesses to that," said the governor.

It was quickly accomplished. The two men signed, bowed, and left them.

"There is a ship in the harbor that will take you back to Providence," the governor told Philip. "She is called the *Bonaventure* and she sails this afternoon. But I warn you that if you ever trouble Mistress Lorraine again or make trouble for any who may have helped her, I will pluck you from Rhode Island or wherever you may be and force you to serve seven years in hell." The chill of his voice was unmistakable—he meant what he said. "You will forget you ever met my daughter!"

Philip looked up at the man who loomed above him. *His daughter? That* was the source of Lorraine's newfound wealth—not some trumped-up story about ginseng! Lorraine was this man's illegitimate child!

"You have tricked me!" he gasped.

The governor's wintry smile flashed. "Yes, I have, haven't I?" he said softly. "And now you had best be gone—before I change my mind and decide to hang you instead."

Overcome by the way he had been trapped and was now being disposed of, Philip forgot the consequences. With a sob of rage, he lunged toward the governor.

The governor's eyes gleamed. He caught Philip such a blow with his hard fist that it sent him spinning across the room to crack against the wall and slither down it unconscious upon the floor.

"Poetic justice," murmured the governor, looking down at him. "I would it could have been with this." He caressed the chased-silver hilt of the dress sword he wore. "But that would have made these parchments suspect." He gathered up the parchments Philip had signed and strode to the door.

"This young man could not seem to find his way out," he said pleasantly. "He has fallen and struck his head. Send for a barrow and wheel him to the *Bonaventure*. She sails within the hour."

Well pleased with himself, Rawlings watched Philip being hauled away.

He had not been able to marry her mother, but at least he had struck a blow for his daughter!

CHAPTER 33

IT WAS LATE afternoon, approaching dark. In Government House the governor had gone up to his bedchamber to change his shirt for dinner, for he was by nature fastidious and he had managed to rip it in striking Philip. The room seemed oppressive, and impatiently he went to open the window some fool had closed.

As he reached the window, there was a ripple in the heavy draperies beside him and an arm shot out, grasping him roughly by the throat. Next, he felt a pistol thrust against his neck. The governor had lived a turbulent youth—he knew what a pistol jabbed between the ribs felt like.

"Cry out and I'll blow you to hell," said a soft deadly voice in his ear.

The governor's neck prickled. That soft voice carried conviction.

"If I might be allowed to turn?" he murmured. "We are conspicuous here in the window." He hoped that his assailant would find that argument persuasive—he was right.

The governor turned to find himself confronting a dark-haired man of about his own height, a man whose lean countenance bore as grim an expression as it had ever been his privilege to meet. The gray eyes that bored into his had, it seemed to him, a peculiarly hellish light.

"To what do I owe this intrusion?" Rawlings asked, wondering if he could reach that pistol on the table nearby before he was sent to his Maker.

His uninvited guest guessed his intention. "This way." He waved the governor away from the table toward the door.

"I see. You prefer to murder me in the hallway. May I ask why?"

"I am come to rescue my lass," that hard voice told him. "And you are my hostage to that rescue."

"And your lass is . . . ?"

"Mistress Lorraine London, late of Rhode Island."

The governor's eyes were suddenly alight. "Mistress Lorraine—of Venture," he murmured. "I know the lady. May I ask what you are rescuing her from?"

"From a sea captain who, I'm told, has let it slip in the town that he will seize her tonight for wrecking a ship on the reefs."

"The *Flying Fish* was wrecked by her captain's mistaking a swinging lantern on the cliffs for the lights of Bridgetown. The lantern, you see, swung on the clifftop of Mistress Lorraine's outlying plantation."

"Well, *she* will not swing there," said that hard voice. "For unless you wish to reach hell this night, you will walk into that hallway and order your guards down below to go out and detain Captain Mannering and instruct him that he is on no account to disturb Mistress London tonight, but that he is to repair here in the morning to be instructed by you at your pleasure."

"Certainly." The governor moved forward with alacrity and carried out his bidding. He turned to Raile. "You must be the Scot!"

Raile looked astonished.

"Oh, put away the gun," said the governor cordially. "I will take you to Venture. Lorraine told me about you."

The gun did not waver. "That was a nice try," approved Raile in a slightly altered tone. "But I am used to trickery and it will not serve. You will indeed take me to Venture. Call for your horse—and a horse for me as well."

To the surprise of his servants, the governor and a

stranger—how had he gotten into Government House, they wondered, without anyone seeing him?—rode away down the coast toward Venture.

"The question she will ask you is, why did you desert her?" said the governor as they rode along through dusk. Around them sea grapes grew right down to the water's edge and an enormous turtle was lumbering across the sand.

Raile gave his companion a strange look. "Desert Lorraine? I did not desert her! She came into a fortune and deserted *me* for a lad from Rhode Island—or so I thought till I learned he'd abducted her."

"She's had her revenge," said the governor, smiling. "When that lad followed her here, she forced him to labor in her canefields—and sleep at night locked in the old slave quarters!"

"My God!" Raile's brow elevated. "Is Dedwinton still here?" he asked. "For I'd like a word with him if he is."

There was such a leaping light in those gray eyes as he spoke that the governor chuckled.

"I'll warrant you would," he said appreciatively. "But I've already had a word with him myself—and had him carried away and shipped back to Rhode Island, a bit the worse for wear."

Raile's narrow gaze considered the older man.

"What is Lorraine to you?" he asked bluntly.

"Until last night the town considered me her suitor," was the negligent response. "Now they have been disabused."

"Then you are—"

"Her friend."

The horses were climbing as Raile thought that over. "How good a friend?"

"The best." The governor shrugged, and with that bland assertion, left Raile to wonder.

They were now riding up the long driveway.

"This is Venture," murmured the governor.

Raile looked around him at the white hibiscus that lined the drive, at the imposing house looming up ahead. "She will miss this place," he muttered.

"Possibly—but that is better than being hanged as a wrecker!"

Raile gave him a black look. "None will hang my lass!"

"No, I believe none will," said the governor, amused.

They had reached the verandah and they swung down, tossing their reins over the hitching post.

"Walk before me," instructed Raile. "You are still my hostage to her safe removal!"

"By all means," agreed the governor. "Keep the pistol out of sight—no need to frighten the servants!"

They were ushered into the handsome drawing room, dim at that time of day, and Lorraine hurried in. She was wearing a light blue silk gown that outlined her perfect torso and floated out behind her in a billow of filmy skirts.

"They told me you—" She stopped at the sight of Raile. Her face had gone a shade paler. Then she observed the pistol he carried, which had gone unnoticed by the servants. "What are you doing with that?" she asked on a rising note.

"The governor here is my hostage," Raile said briefly. "There is no time. You are coming with me."

"Listen to him," advised the governor energetically. "He is here to save you!"

"Save me from what?" cried Lorraine.

"Your alleged offenses," said the governor with becoming gravity. "It is true, Lorraine, that I have a liking for you, but you must remember that I am the law here as well." He wagged a finger at her. "I cannot condone wrecking."

Lorraine fetched him an indignant look.

"There is word in the town that you are being blamed for the wrecking of the *Flying Fish* upon the reef," Raile explained. "Captain Mannering is said to be headed in this direction with a troop of mounted men to take you to jail for it. I took the governor prisoner in the hope I might head him off."

"Indeed?" She laughed. "Then I will stand off Captain Mannering. I have men of my own!"

Admiration flashed for a moment in Raile's eyes

and was instantly extinguished in the need of the moment.

"You will stand no one off," he said flatly. "You are coming with me. I will not risk having you taken. My ship is waiting in a cove near here."

"Oh, and am I to share your cabin with Laurie Ann MacLaud?" she asked sarcastically. "And do not protest your innocence for I saw you in your buckskins embracing her on the riverbank the night of the Jamestown fire—the very night that you had left to go upriver to meet some mythical 'gentleman'!"

Raile's eyes widened. "That would have been my brother, Rory, you saw. We are very like—especially in profile. He is married to Laurie Ann. He advised me about the gun sale, but they have fled Virginia and are somewhere in the wilderness. Anyway, I returned and tracked you to Yorktown, but I was told you had come into money and had run away to Rhode Island with Philip Dedwinton!"

A great happiness spread over Lorraine's face.

"Oh, Raile, I would never have gone with him willingly—he *abducted* me."

"I know that now," he said huskily. "But I had to go all the way to Rhode Island to find it out. We'll sort all this out later. There is little time. I forced the governor to give orders to the contrary, but who knows, Captain Mannering and his men may be here at any time to take you."

"You forced . . . ?" Mirth suddenly filled her voice. "Oh, I wish I had been there to see it!" She got control of herself. "Raile, I see that you have not met"—she indicated the smiling governor with a sweep of her arm—"my father. I am Lady Lorraine Rawlings now."

Raile stuck the pistol back in his belt. "I think you have made a fool of me, sir," he said grimly.

"Rather say that I have just tested out a new son-in-law," drawled the governor. "And found him to measure up in every way. Lorraine"—he turned to his daughter—"if you do not marry this man, you are more of a fool than I think you are."

"Oh, do not worry, Father." Lorraine's rapt gaze

on Raile's face was so warm it brought a hot light leaping to his eyes. "I will marry him in a trice—if he will have me after I doubted him so! And if he will not have me in marriage, I will go with him anyway! For coming to save me even though there was no need! And for loving me!" She threw her arms around Raile and he pulled her close. "And because I want no life without him!"

"On the whole, I think marriage will suit you both better," advised the governor. "Look at all the trouble it will save! You will not have the bother of later adopting your own children—as I must do with you. It makes everything easier."

"Lass, will you have me?" Raile murmured.

"I'll have you," she promised. "I'll have you in marriage, and I'll have you in my heart—forever."

"And I will give the bride away," said the governor genially. "Faith, 'tis something I've been looking forward to!"

"That can come later," said Lorraine dreamily from the circle of Raile's arms. "I think Raile and I deserve a short cruise on the *Likely Lass* before the wedding and the crush and all those congratulations and feasts to prepare and a trousseau to be made ready. Father"—she lingered over the word—"could you not hold Venture together for me while we are gone?"

"I think I might manage that," was the indulgent answer.

"We will be back before the last banns are cried," promised Raile, gripping the governor's hand.

"I will hold you to it," said the governor. "Now, carry her away!"

Raile grinned at him. "I'll do it!"

He swept Lorraine up in his arms and carried her out onto the veranda, meaning to swing her into the saddle. But of a sudden, just as the sun sank into the western sky, there was a vivid blinding flash and the world turned green.

"The Green Flash," murmured Lorraine, remembering that when the Green Flash caught you in the arms of a man he would be the one love beside whom all others would pale. *But I do not need the Green*

Flash to tell me that, she thought. *For I would go with Raile no matter what the future holds!*

"A pair well-matched," murmured the governor, watching them ride off.

On board the *Likely Lass* that night Lorraine and Raile held their own celebration, held it in the great cabin that had known such anger and such ardor between them. MacTavish—only a little mollified when they told him of their impending wedding—took the deck watch, muttering, "Who can sleep, with a woman aboard?" The couple did not bother to eat, they rediscovered instead the delights of sharing a bunk at sea. And after that—after all the golden murmurings, the touchings that burned fiery trails across the heart, the thrill of rediscovery at each other's firm young bodies, the soaring flights of passion, the marvelous contentment, the warmth of the afterglow—after all that, they discovered they were hungry. A cold snack and warm wine were brought by a beaming Johnny Sears.

After that they lay abed and talked, and then in the wondrous way of lovers, they found passion and enchantment again . . . and again . . . until the dawn. Then, as through the stern windows of the *Likely Lass,* the sun shone on their gleaming naked bodies, they fell asleep locked in warm embrace as a promise of the love they would clasp and hold—forever.

The lad she loved on Wednesday, he's been made to rue,
The lad she loved on Thursday—at least his heart was true!
Now that it is Friday, her wild heart can rejoice,
Abrim with joy and gladness at the wisdom of her choice!

—Valerie Sherwood

AUTHOR'S NOTE

THE WHOLE SWEEP of the tempestuous 1600's, when an indentured servant such as my gallant Lorraine could rise to wealth and power, has always fascinated me, and although all of the characters and situations are of my own invention (save for obvious historical characters such as Governor Berkeley and Nathanial Bacon and well-known historical events), I have striven throughout to give real backgrounds and an authentic flavor of the times—even to using archaeological findings that confirm the settlers' way of life in colonial Virginia.

"King Philip's War," when marauding Indian raiders burned homes and settlements throughout New England, wrought such devastation on the Rhode Island countryside that I have been hard put to find actual houses still in existence today in which to set my story. I have therefore used typical houses and hostelries of the day, especially the unusual "stone-enders" which were so particularly Rhode Island's own type of early colonial architecture.

For my "Light House Tavern" I have borrowed from the name of the famous White Horse Tavern in Newport—although the tavern of my story is somewhat earlier and therefore more simply constructed.

"Todd House" is based upon Eleazer Arnold's "splendid mansion" on the Great Road in the Lower Blackstone Valley. The Mayfields' home is based on the Palmer-Northrup House on North Kingston's Post Road, the old section of which is thought to have escaped intact the burning during King Philip's War.

As to the "Green Flash" to which I refer, it has a lovely lucid scientific explanation which I will not go into here. But it is also said that there are those who see it—and those who don't. And so that strange green flash sometimes seen just as the sun goes down has been noted in several parts of the world—but only at certain spots: from a point on the coast of England and from a certain cliff in Barbados, as in my story. Being rare and uncertain, it has therefore a magic quality, which makes it the stuff of dreams. So it is natural enough for my hardheaded heroine to wonder if she will ever truly see the Green Flash.

The deserted city in Yucatán where Raile brings Lorraine is of course modern Tulum, which in Mayan means "fortress." (Zama, "city of the dawn," is a Toltec name for the site and the early Spaniards kept records on it as "Tzama.") High on its limestone cliffs overlooking the blue Caribbean, Tulum was the first city on Mexico's coast to be entered by the Spanish (Francisco Hernández de Córdoba and his men, March 1517, in pursuit of some thirty Indians wearing the sturdy cotton armor of the area, who had attacked them with lances and arrows upon their landing). Tulum, city of so many mysteries, still standing in silent grandeur today, guardian of the vastness of Quintana Roo, was the embarkation point for pilgrims journeying to the Isle of Cozumel to worship the goddess Ixchel. It was surely a charmed spot in the time when Raile and Lorraine chanced upon it—as it is today.

Bermuda, with its unique white limestone cross-shaped houses with their flaring "welcoming-arms" steps and its seafaring ways, is accurately presented—although it is an older Bermuda of which I write, one with great cedar forests still towering above the islands, when the town of St. George had narrow twisting alleys and an almost medieval look.

Although for purposes of my story I have somewhat

compressed and otherwise altered events of both King Philip's War and Bacon's Rebellion (Bacon's Rebellion actually started in 1676), I would stress that the *sequence* of events is correct in both cases.

The town where Lorraine spent the night on her way to Yorktown was of course Middle Plantation, but for clarity I have called it what it was later named—Williamsburg. So that the reader may better place the action of Bacon's Rebellion, one of Nathaniel Bacon's two handsome plantations was located in "the Curles"—in other words on one of the great loops the James River made in this area. The murder of his overseer by Indian marauders took place at Bacon's Quarter, a detached plantation some twenty miles from his home, which would now be located in downtown Richmond. Bacon's Rebellion actually began as a kind of spontaneous uprising of the colonists and frontiersmen who objected to their wholesale slaughter by the Indians (George Washington's grandfather, Colonel John Washington, had ordered six Susquehannock chieftains killed and the Indians had taken revenge tenfold, killing ten English settlers along the upper James for every chief they had lost—their rationale was expressed as follows: their chiefs were "persons of quality" and the settlers killed were "of inferior rank"—thus, ten-to-one reprisals! At this point the Indians demanded additional satisfaction for the injuries they had suffered. When it was rejected, they murdered three hundred more of the scattered planters and their families along the upper James.)

The Susquehannock were being pushed south by their northern cousins, the powerful Seneca, and their flight south endangered both Maryland and Virginia.

Governor Berkeley proved to be strikingly inadequate to meet the attacks of the marauders—even had he cared to, which apparently he did not (his own commercial interests would have suffered if he had). At age sixty-four he had married the widow of Carolina's governor, a woman half his age. Now senile and ever more manic (he raved that learning had brought heresy, thanked God that there were no free schools or printing in Virginia, and fervently hoped this condition would endure another hundred years!), he showered favors on his cronies and left the beleaguered frontier planters to fend for themselves.

Desperate, they banded together for the general defense—and found a fiery leader in handsome twenty-eight-year-old Nathaniel Bacon, a Cambridge graduate who had studied law at Gray's Inn. Bacon had come to Virginia with a young wife and a large fortune and cast in his lot with the struggling colonists. A mesmerizing leader, Bacon offered to sally forth against the Indians if but twenty men would follow him—and soon assembled a considerable force. In a way, Bacon's story is the story of that young America of long ago, for he was above all a man who would dare everything for what he felt was right. Governor Berkeley promptly declared him a rebel and the stage was set for fights and flights and the eventual burning of Jamestown.

As to the "venture" which pays off so handsomely, the story is based closely upon one which actually happened—and to a woman!

I should also like to point out that although today sending the captive Wampanoags and Narragansetts to Barbados to till the canefields as slaves seems barbaric, to the English colonists of that day it represented clemency. In England hanging was the price of rebellion—but the sentence was sometimes commuted to a life of slavery in the West Indies. This was especially true of those who fought Cromwell and those who rose against James II during the Monmouth Rebellion—after both, the canefields of the Indies were filled with toiling English slaves. One of my own ancestors is a case in point. He was one of the generals who brought Cromwell to power in England. Later he became disenchanted with the lord protector (who had assumed dictatorial powers) and rebelled against him, stating in effect that "he had brought the rogue to power and now he would bring him down!" He lost. He was sentenced to death but later transported as a political prisoner to Barbados, where he died. Slavery in the West Indies was considered neither a cruel nor an unusual punishment in the harsh 1600's.

But as to that wealthy "rum and sugar world" of tropical Barbados, I have tried to bring to the reader not only the actual terrain but also the flavor and elegance of an island that in its day "looked down" upon colonial Boston as being dowdy and unfashionable. Barbados was definitely the place for such a spirited heroine as Lorraine to get herself into trouble!

—Valerie Sherwood

WARNING

Readers are warned against using any of the cosmetics, unusual foods, or remedies referred to herein without first consulting and securing the approval of a medical doctor. These items are included only to enhance the authentic seventeenth-century atmosphere, when—although many of these potions, etc., were dangerous—they were in common usage; none of them are in any way recommended for use by anyone.

About the Author

Valerie Sherwood is the author of a dozen consecutive *New York Times* best-sellers which have sold millions of copies.